SERFS ON A FIEF

BY

GENE THOMAS KEMP

This book is a work of fiction. Places, events, and situations in this story are purely fictional. Any resemblance to actual persons, living or dead, is coincidental.

ISBN: 1-4033-7352-3 (e-book)
ISBN: 1-4033-7353-1 (Paperback)
ISBN: 1-4033-7354-X (Hardcover)

Library of Congress Control Number: 2002094389

This book is printed on acid free paper.

Printed in the United States of America
Bloomington, IN

1stBooks – rev.10/30/02

Home from school

The two young men- seated side by side in a pickup- had left their campus a little too late that afternoon. As a result, by the time they reached the first big city of Holman, the morning shift was already streaming out of several parking lots at the shoe factory, headed home for the day. Caught in the midst of the traffic, they soon found themselves halted by a red-light at a busy intersection with two cars ahead of them and, behind them, a long line- bumper to bumper. After what seemed a long wait, the light turned green. The young driver jerked the clutch and stalled the engine. Then, aggravated by the bedlam developing behind him and acting in haste to start up again, he flooded the carburetor. A tumult of horns and creative invectives followed in short order. Soon vehicles were swooping out of line, workers zooming pell-mell by him on the left and right- fists shaking, some giving him the bird instead of watching the traffic flow- glaring at him and hazarding collisions with oncoming cars. The young man's embarrassment- displayed in the flush of his cheeks- turned to complete frustration as he turned the engine over and over, quickly draining all the power from the battery- none too strong in the first place. Finally, the passenger- a big fellow burly enough to wrestle a mulish mandrill to the ground- got out and pushed the battered old Ford forward a few feet until, with a few easy slips of the clutch by the driver, the engine fired up. The boys were immediately on their way to the next town.

The big guy, still puffing a bit from his exertion, noticing they had just passed a road sign, leery of losing the route, queried uneasily, "What did that sign say? I missed it."

"Not much," came the reply from the driver, also a good-sized, muscular young man, though not of the same overall dimensions or weight as his cohort. "Just a speed sign. But, if you're wondering, I'd say we had another sixty miles to go before we get to my folks' farm. And we *are* on the right route."

"We got enough gas to get there, Eric?"

Eric glanced down at the gas gauge, suddenly aware of an oversight. "We'll have to stop somewhere pretty soon. I didn't think to look before we left. About a quarter-tank left."

"Nuts! We passed a gas station just a mile back," said Brian.

"I think there's a Rotary in the next town. Their gas is cheaper."

"Cheaper? How much cheaper?"

"Costs twenty-nine something a gallon, the last I knew."

Brian seemed impressed. "Good mileage?"

"Can't see much difference," came the reply. "I always use their gas when I can. Save two or three cents."

Somewhat later, as the truck was being gassed up, Brian wandered off to the station, relieved himself, got a couple of candy bars, and returning, commented on the countryside to Eric, evidently somewhat surprised at the hilly terrain and fast-running streams, especially the one just back of the station.

The attendant, who was making change for Eric, looked up at Brian. "I take it you never been around here...."

"No, I live in pretty flat country. Never been over here. It's pretty country. But I'll bet it's tough to make a living around here."

Eric, having counted his change, picked up the conversation, nodding his head. "Mostly lumbering and farming. A few small towns. Won't see another town the size of Holman for quite a way. Don't find many fat cats down this way, either."

The attendant having checked the oil and now paid off, the boys were soon rounding a bend in the road where a group of dairy farms were nestled in a broad valley surrounded by imposing, wooded ridges. "You know, I think I'd like it down here," mused Brian.

"Well, *I* like it. That's for sure," said Eric. I guess it's kind of primitive compared to the lake country up where you live, but it's always going to be home for me."

"I'll bet its good hunting. Looks like deer country to me."

"Yeah. We even get a lot of guys come up from the city to hunt here. Best deer country for miles and miles. They say its because of the combination of cornfields and good cover. And the deer usually have twins here, unlike those up north."

"Why's that?"

"My physiology prof said that deer are more apt to twin where they have lots of feed. So we have a lot of deer here. It doesn't want to be too wild, or there won't be enough cornfields for them to riddle. He thinks the balance is just right here..., and he hunts deer. Said he got a nice big buck last fall- not far from where I live."

"Any bear here?"

Eric shrugged. "Sometimes.... Used to be quite a few. And used to be elk, too. But that's when the Indians were here. I guess you might still see a bear now and then, but I've never seen any myself. Dad has, though. Once in awhile I see something about it in the paper..., that's all."

"Speaking of Indians, when did they leave? I take it they're gone."

"Oh, that was during the revolution- or right after it. The Sullivan expedition came up the Susquehanna during the revolution to clear them out. They pretty much cleared out and ran off to Canada or west of here. They'd been raiding the homesteaders around here so bad that Washington was getting a lot of deserters..., you know- to hell with the war. Especially when he was down at Valley Forge. The guys in the militia were sneaking off to go back home and protect their own families. And I guess shooting deserters didn't help much. George tried that. Had to catch 'em first. Not all that easy back then, what with so much wilderness."

"Guess I never heard anything about that when I was taking history," said Brian, as he offered a candy bar to his room-mate. "I knew the Indians were on the side of the English. Never really knew why. What did they have against the settlers?"

"Well, the settlers were enemies of the English king. 'Great white father' and all that to them, you know. The Iroquois hated the French. So did the English. So they were allies. Later on, when we turned against the crown, we were as bad as the French..., at least to them."

"What did they have against the French?" asked Brian.

"If I remember it right, the French- when they were still holding onto Canada- were friends with the Algonquins up north. Champlain was coming down into New York up above Albany a ways with an Algonquin war party when they ran into a tribe of Iroquois- their mortal enemies, the Mohawks- alongside the lake. So Champlain hauled out a big old blunderbuss and blew away some Mohawks more or less to demonstrate to his buddies what a blunderbuss could do. Or maybe he just wanted to amuse himself. Anyway, he sent the rest of the Mohawks a-flying without even a wahoo. They'd never run into firearms before."

"Sounds sensible enough to me," said Brian.

"The Iroquois tribes- there were five or six of them- had fought the Algonquins without success for years- they were their worst enemies. And let me tell you..., the Iroquois were smart, especially politically. So, after that deal with Champlain, they were real thick with the Dutch- who gave them firearms. That quickly turned the tables on their enemies. And later, the English governor of New York. He sure didn't have any use for the French either..., and could do quite a lot to protect them, plus buy furs from them. The Pennsylvania governor was too far away to pay much attention- down in Philly. The fur trade was a big thing, of course. A lot bigger than people today realize. All the Indian tribes were competing with each other for the buck, just like we do. That's a story in itself- had a lot to do with how Canada and United States ended up. Tribes moved around all over the continent, and so on. It all began because France and England were constantly scrapping over who would get New York for a colony. The Indians didn't realize they were being taken, no matter who they buddied up with."

Brian nodded. "I remember something about a Mohawk chief involved at the Cherry Valley slaughter, over east of here."

"Yeah. That was one smart fellow.... Raised hell with the colonists. One of the last British governors in Albany- just before the revolution- name of Johnson, was a big buddy of the Mohawks. Really liked the Indians, treated them well. Even had a son name of Joseph Brant- that's the one you're talking about- by one of their squaws, a smart one, who lived with him. The story goes that Brant was a brilliant man, especially as a raider. Johnson had raised him and got him educated over in England somewhere. I think it was at Cambridge. Later on, he ran a lot of the raids against the American colonists with some help from the Tories. Colonists ran whenever they heard he was on the way. Massacred lots of settlers. Cherry Valley, like you said- near the upper Susquehanna valley..., Wyoming Valley down river in Pennsy."

Brian was a little speechless. "How come you know all that stuff?"

"I'm not really much into history, you know, but our high-school history teacher- we had a real good one- knew quite a lot about it. After all, a lot of this stuff was local history.... We were right in the middle of it. He wanted us to know things about our own area. I remember he even told us a lot about the military strategy of the English against the colonies. That kind of perked up some ears among us boys. So, basically, the English planned to block out the coastlands themselves- Manhattan and New Jersey to the east- and use their

Indian friends to block the rest of the territory clear to Lake Erie to the west. Of course, we had no navy to get around that way. They wanted to divide the country- north from south. This was the area to focus on, early in the war."

Brian yawned and nodded, looking over at a distant hill. "Looks like a lot of chicken coops over there." Eric's eyes followed Brian's hand, pointing over to the right.

"Yeah. There's still a lot of chicken farms around here, Brian."

"I thought this was all cow country."

"Well, it is," said Eric, "but I guess a lot of the farms here were too small to really make it as a dairy alone, so they kept chickens too. Some even had pigs and sheep, just a few years ago. I think they are going away now, a little at a time."

"Wouldn't think there was much money in chickens," muttered Brian.

"Oh, I don't know," said Eric. "It had its ups and downs like anything else in the farm business. But a lot of the old fellows said that the chickens kept the farm going when the dairy business was down…."

"You mean, during the thirties?"

"Yeah. During the depression. If one thing was down, the other might be up. Even having a few pigs was a little extra insurance. Kept a lot of guys from losing their farms."

"That isn't the way they want you to do it, up at school. They say that's for losers."

"I know they do. That's for sure," said Eric. "All they want now is for farms to get bigger and bigger, and forget the diversification."

"Sounds good to me." said Brian. "That's the way you can make real money. You have to out-produce the other guys. It's the only way. Can't do that if you're spread too thin or too small. Inefficient use of capital. Especially farm machinery. Labor, too."

"Don't you think that's riskier, though?"

"Not anymore. Wait till you get into the farm economics course I'm taking. Then you'll see some stats that will pop your eyes out of your head. I mean, they show you what real efficiency can do- and you should see some of the farms they took us to."

"I guess the field trips are pretty great. A lot of guys say so, anyway." said Eric. "But I guess I've listened to my dad too much. He told me not to believe everything you hear while you're in the agriculture college."

"You sound like my foster brother did."

"By the way, Brian, has your family heard anything from him?"

"Still missing in action, Eric. Missing in action. We hope he got out of the B-25 before it went down. And his wife still thinks he'll come back home after the war."

"I sure hope so. That time I met him he really seemed like a great guy." Eric rubbed his nose briefly, then continued. "I suppose you've heard the North Koreans are brainwashing our men in their P.O.W. camps."

"I know. But they won't break him down. He's tough. Besides, I don't know if I believe everything I hear on thc news. Who says they're doing that, anyway?"

Eric grinned. "Like I don't believe everything the profs tell us, either," came the retort. "Do they get fed a lot of bull by those farmers- the 'big boys' they're going 'wow-wow-wow' about? After all, they like to pretend they're hot stuff, even if they're a mile in debt."

"Don't have to be afraid of debt," said Brian. "You get into a bank far enough and you don't have a creditor, you've got a partner. All it takes is moxy and know-how."

The Clinic

Brian, slumped in the passenger seat, where he had been dozing for twenty or thirty minutes by the time the two lads from the university arrived in the little village of Sturgis Valley, began to stir as Eric stopped in front of his brother's house.

"Pretty near dark, I see." murmured Brian, stretching and then rubbing his eyes, looking around. "We there?"

Eric shut off the engine. "Not quite. I thought you might like to stop and meet my brother, Sean, while we're going by. It's easier to catch him this time of day. And I thought you might like to see his clinic while we're here. We're only about ten miles from the farm. I promise we won't stay long. You game?"

"Sure thing. I'm game. I always thought I'd like to meet the Doc. I've heard a lot about him. And, let's see- his wife is..., Nancy?" said Brian, yawning and stretching again, as he muttered, "Boy! It seems like I could sleep a long time."

"Well, we just got over the exams. If you're like me, you didn't get much sleep for awhile. Yeah, her name is Nancy. She doesn't like her name, so we all call her Nan. Just don't call her Nanny. She hates that."

"O.K., I can go with that," Brian said, as he opened the door, got out of the truck and stood there re-orienting himself for a moment, sizing up what little of the village was visible at dusk. "Looks like a nice neat little town," he commented, "and I see there's a post office and a small bank just down the street." He peered further down the street. "And a gas station down there a little further."

"It's O.K., I guess. That's about all there is here, though, adding about forty houses. Down around the corner on the street that runs up the hill, there's a brick school-house and a grocery- it's really an old-fashioned general store."

"Don't see many of those anymore. A little hardware..., shoes, groceries, and so on?"

"You got it. I reckon stores like that will be pretty rare in a few years," said Eric. "The guy that owns this one is pretty well up in years, had it for sale; and I don't see much future there for a younger man. He's had a few bites, but no takers. He'll probably close down in a year or two. I hear he has emphysema pretty bad."

"How far will folks here have to go then, to find a store?"

"Probably thirteen miles over the hill to Damon. That's a bigger town- about four thousand over there. Maybe a tad more."

"How many here?"

"Not more than two hundred or so, I reckon. I understand they're going to ditch the schoolhouse here and ship the kids over to a new school in Damon, when it gets built. They're centralizing all over the state, wherever they can. Efficiency, they say."

"I suppose that's progress."

"That's what they say, anyway. Maybe. And maybe not. A lot of folks here think that'll just raise the cost and not do a helluva lot better job teaching the kids."

Brian accompanied Eric into the house where he met Nan. Doc was due home soon, presently returning from a maternity case. So Nan hurriedly led them out through a breezeway into the clinic, where she left them in order to get ready for a school meeting.

Eric turned to his sidekick, "Well, Brian..., let's look the doctor's clinic over while we're waiting for him. This here is the waiting room..., that we're standing in."

"Does he have much staff?" asked Brian.

"I don't know. He may have, now. He just added on this section we're in so he could do more. But I don't know how much business he's picked up since. He didn't have enough room before..., I do know that."

"Look here in the old exam room Brian," said Eric. "See, he has an X-ray now! I'll bet he's pretty proud of that. He's talked about getting one for years. He sees a lot of fracture cases, you know. He's the only doc around that uses a Stader splint."

"A Stader?"

"Yeah. As I understand, they used something like them during the war. Navy, at least. External fixation, you know. See, here- in the glass case- see those bars? You stick pins into the bones from alongside them in a V-pattern, then attach them to the bars and set them with nuts and bolts to line them up. Then you leave them in for about six weeks till its healed.

"Don't the pins hurt?" said Brian.

"I guess not. Of course, you have to use general anesthesia to put them in."

"That's what those cones are for?"

"I think so. Gas. Ether, something like that. I don't know a whole lot about it."

Eric showed Brian some more of the surgical and obstetrical instruments, the lab, with a spanking new binocular microscope equipped with oil immersion lens, the autoclave set-up, boiler and surgical drapes, the office and small library with multiple texts and journals, the treatment room, pharmacy and surgical section.

In short order Dr. Sean arrived, coming in the back door. The front of his clothes were covered with clots, still dripping blood. Seeing his brother, Sean nodded, said hello, shook hands perfunctorily with Brian, and excused himself to remove his bloody clothes and take a shower. Brian stood there without a word, in a state of shock, eyes opened wide as they followed the doctor's departure. Turning to Eric, he whispered, "Is that what happens on a maternity case?"

"Oh, yes. They can be pretty messy." said Eric nonchalantly.

A little while later, while they were back in the kitchen, Sean returned to the scene. He seemed to be in a hurry, almost annoyed that the boys were there. Once again he seemed indifferent. Finally, he apologized. While the boys were in the clinic, he had gotten a call from his answering service. He had another maternity case.

"I'm sorry, fellow, I've been running ragged all day. Dumb guy waits all day and then wants to bring the damned bitch in and get her checked over. I'll probably have to do a C-section."

"Do you need help, Sean?" said Eric. "If you do I can help."

"No I can do it alone. Damned bitch anyway! The guy can help me do the C-section if he really wants it done. It'll probably take forty minutes. I don't know why these guys always wait until the last minute and then want to rush in when my staff is gone for the night."

A few minutes later the boys were just pulling out of the driveway, heading for the farm, Dad, and Mom, when the guy with the maternity case pulled in with his bitch beagle, the one that had been trying all day.

"Boy," said Eric, "Those dystocias can sure mess your day up. Did you see all the blood my brother got on him delivering that calf?"

"Is that par for the course?" asked Brian.

"Sometimes. A vet has to dive right into the cow, you know. If he has to do an episiotomy, like they do if the calf is too big or the vulva too tight, they can really bleed, especially if the calf comes out hard. Usually he wears a rubber suit. I guess he didn't have it with him..., at least, not this time."

Barn and Herd

At the first sound of his father's stirring- headed as usual for the bathroom down the hall- Eric, in his unheated upstairs bedroom, threw off his smoldering pile of blankets and rose from his bed. According to the Westclox on his bedstand- confirmed by an endless crowing contest among a trio of roosters in the hen house as well as the brightening eastern horizon, it was now time to milk the cows. Either that or risk an altercation with the old man.

The fact that Eric was home on spring break would cut no ice with his hard-working dad, to whom less than seventy hours of steady work a week was a disgrace to mankind. In the first place, like many old time farmers, he didn't believe in vacations or whole days off, much less "personal days," never having taken any for himself except a couple of days when he was married, or when something like the "walking grippe" transformed into the "pukin', scourin' vertigo-nies." After all, the cows could not be ignored. They had to be milked and fed no matter what, and suitable labor was neither easy to find nor keep. Although the neighbors might help out, as he had done himself for a neighbor on occasion, a real man just had to be tough and get on with it. Thus it was that, without some very good excuse, all able-bodied hands- whether male or female- were to be on deck at the crack of dawn.

Two rules applied. Lay-a-beds, of course, were an abomination and not to be tolerated. Though as a rule not expected to work, house guests should at least get out of bed and look alive, if for no other reason than granting mother Rachel the courtesy of sharing, as one with the barn crew, the hearty breakfast she always prepared for them once morning milking was finished.

Second, milking was to start precisely the same time each morning and night barring an emergency by something like distant thunder and a darkening western horizon- a summer storm in the wind- with acres of good, milk-making hay windrowed, dried and heading desperately for the security of the hay loft before its ruination arrived.

Eric yawned a few times, stretched as though he meant it, and then waddled into the adjoining room where his buddy from college,

Brian Miller, was sleeping. Knowing Brian's somnolent tendency, he reached down and shook his shoulder vigorously. Since Eric hadn't barked in the necessary manner, Brian groaned, rolled over and- no more awake than a hibernating sow bear nursing her young one- proceeded to bury his head even more deeply into his pillow. Now- recognizing his error- his voice roaring as unabashedly as a drill instructor's, Eric repeated, "I'm going down to the barn and help Pop with the chores. You hear me?" Still getting little response, he chuckled and shook Brian's shoulder again, fairly thundering, "You don't have to come along, but I thought you might like to look the place over before it *burns down*!"

That worked. The big guy rolled up with a start, sat on the edge of the bed rubbing his eyes as he looked out the window in bewilderment. Finally he seemed to remember where he was. "Hell yes," he said, clearing his throat. "That'd be great. Couldn't see much of the place in the dark last night."

"No," said Eric sympathetically. Everybody was in bed except Ma. Probably I shouldn't have stopped at my brother's. Hustle along and I'll take you down to the barn. Dad's already there- the lights just went on."

Brian stood up, adjusting his twisted shorts as he continued peering out the window. "Boy, this is some lay-out! I *like* what I see.... Already! Man! Look at this place."

Some fifteen minutes later with the sun still awaiting its cue from offstage, the two young men plodded from the house to the cow stable- warmly dressed in the customary barn clothes beneath coveralls and wearing heavy shoes- greeted not only by some brilliantly helio-lighted, wispy stratus just above the eastern horizon but also a bustling vernal cacophony of chattering birds scattered in several grand old elms and maples that nature had distributed rather informally about the premises many years before. A few low-lying tufts of grass had been touched overnight by fingers of frost, while high overhead on tree branches and the gambrel roof of the dairy barn, broad patches of glistening rime bespoke a frosty haze that had lifted earlier, adding to the charm of the whole farmstead. The walls of the barn resonated with the interior lowing of stanchioned cows, bleating calves eager to be fed, and the familiar rumbling of ensilage and feed carts being pushed down the alleys in front of the cows.

Such an idyll did not last long. Milking was about to begin, and inside the barn, someone was at that moment reaching for the switch to turn on the vacuum pump for the milking machines. This pump happened to be a noisy varmint that roared like a Harley starting up. Everybody within a mile knew when Drew Auchinachie was milking- which, naturally, was before anyone else within an ear's reach of the place. Drew rather liked it that way. Had he seen Brian jumping out of his skin as he was walking past its exhaust at that exact time, he would have liked it even better.

As with most dairy farms, the immediate needs of the family's livestock were always attended before anyone would even think of sitting down to breakfast. Of course, this meant not only feeding the animals- which, incidentally, helped to settle them down- but milking the cows. Like most farms, this required a couple of hours. Using five Surge milking machines with their fairly unique design involving a surcingle acting as a sling over a cow's back, thus supporting the Surge's bail with its wide and low sealed pail under her belly, the teat cups were applied to her teats and left on for three to six- or more- minutes, pretty much depending on the production of the cow. Milk so acquired from each cow, which in Drew's time amounted to roughly ten to thirty or more pounds each end of the day (22# equals 10 quarts), was then poured into stainless steel pails, carried by hand to the milkhouse and passed through a strainer into ten gallon cans owned and obtained from their local milk plant.

Once the morning milking was completed, all such cans, whether from the morning or previous evening- the latter cans being removed from the milkhouse cooler- were rolled to the loading block outside and hoisted onto a truck, which was usually owned and driven by a neighboring farmer-for-hire, if not the producing farm itself. Once delivered to the creamery, the milk was inspected and processed by its employees, garbed in white clothes and cap, who wasted no time inspecting and preparing the milk for shipment by train to an associated plant close to its market city.

After a short wait for his emptied cans to return, washed and steam-sterilized, during which some juicy local gossip was often exchanged among the haulers and thus spread all over the county by the next day- the hauler's truck was reloaded, subsequently returning each can to its farm of origin during the forenoon so that it was ready for use during the evening milking. Accordingly, most of the consuming public received their milk fresh, pasteurized, bottled and delivered to their doorsteps within 24-36 hours of leaving the farm. And in the process, happily, the farmers could keep up with everybody else's business.

Turning to Eric as they approached the barn, Brian said, "I'll be in to help out in a minute. I just want to look around outside the barn." Eric nodded, and with that, they parted- Eric disappearing into the milkhouse.

At least in some small way, every well-aged barn is unique, having an ever-changing history of progress and failure to tell those who are interested. Newer ones, lacking such background, speak instead of aspirations- the hopeful innovations for which farmers are necessarily so famous. Brian, having acquired considerable ability to estimate when and how and why a barn was built a certain way, took a brief walk around the structure until he rejoined Eric in the stable, having satisfied himself that the original structure dated back to at least 1850, and that three more expansive sections had been added to it later. Once inside the barn with Eric, he planned to examine its supporting timbers for further details. Much can be learned about any building's age by simply observing how such timbers had been cut out of the log and then joined together.

In short order, Brian met Drew Auchinachie, Eric's and Sean's genial and studious old father, as well as Jim Holland- a wiry, energetic farmhand, the young son of Drew's cooperative neighbor, friend and small time farmer. Jim was temporarily filling in as a part-time replacement for Drew's last hired man- who was currently fleeing the local sheriff.

Seeing an opportunity to help out with the milking and yet knowing that many farmers preferred that their cows not be milked by strangers, Brian offered, instead, to carry milk out to the milkhouse for the three men who were actually parked beside the cows doing the milking. Eric, he knew, having been away at school, would appreciate a chance to talk with his dad. Likewise with Jim, who was like one of the family. They all had some catching up to do.

Brian was standing nearby, waiting for the next pail to carry, when Drew asked him if he'd noticed the cows up near the entrance as he'd walked in from the milkhouse. "We've got some nice Holstein purebreds we bought up at the Earlville sale," he said.

Brian blinked. "I was going to say no but, come to think of it, I did see a few purebreds in the line up near there. Even have their names, production record and pedigree on a placard over each of them. Look like good ones to me."

Drew replied, "Yeah. At least, I think so. We're gradually replacing the grades with purebreds. Those are Winterthurs and Dunloggins we found here and there. Got one Rag Apple, too. They're bigger cows than our grades and so we put them in roomier stalls up there where you walked in." Drew continued, fishing a little, "You like them, then?"

"Pretty nice cows, I'd say. A couple of them would do pretty well in the show ring. And they look like they can milk. I see that one of them gave 22,000."

"You noticed that then? Yes, we're pretty proud of her. Butterfat a little low..., that's the only thing. And, of course, she didn't get that 22,000 pounds here. The best one of ours ever did was 18,000, and that was in twelve months, not ten..., 305 official days, like she did. Of course, where she came from, they were milking her three times a day, instead of just twice- like us dirt farmers."

"You must've paid a pretty price for her," said Brian.

Eric interrupted, "Not Dad. He never buys anything unless its a bargain. And don't let him kid you. He puts his best cows up near the entrance by the milkhouse where the other farmers walking in can't miss them. He likes to impress folks."

"Now there, son," drawled Drew, with a mocking little hick-lilt, evidently amused. "I just cain't cotton to tha-at kind of talk." He grinned like he was hiding something from the boys. "Ah dun paid me a real fair price fur them thar animules." Then, straight-faced, he continued, "Believe it or not, they were going to cull her out. She has Bang's. Aborted a couple times in a row, dried off..., hadn't given any milk for awhile so I did get her pretty cheap. Beef price, in fact. We hope to breed her artificial to some real good bull- she'll probably catch now that she's cleaned up, according to their vets. Might get some extra-nice heifer calves out of her, if the old girl lives long enough. Hope so anyway.

"She's getting up there- nine years old. Lots of guys would ditch her just because of that, and we might have to if she doesn't breed right back. We'd like to keep her two or three years. Longer if she can pull her weight. Since she already had two abortions from the Bang's, they say any calf she has now will probably go term and, if it's a heifer, could well be an outstanding genetic foundation for a Brucellosis-free herd. That's the trick, you know. We want a good strong cow family just like her."

Eric seemed surprised. "I don't get it, Dad. What are you saying? You bought a sick cow?"

"Well, like I said, I've been told by a pretty good vet that that's one way to start a herd of cattle that are immune to Bang's disease. That's the old name, of course. Some guy named Bang discovered it. Probably your professors- and you- would call it Brucellosis. As we all know, it's contagious as hell and can wipe out a whole year's income by aborting cows- even if they don't get sick- right when they're pretty close to time to dry off. Then they usually have a long, long dry period recovering and don't make you a cent- no milk of course- before they finally carry a calf to term and freshen again."

"I see," said Eric. "guess they didn't explain all of that to us in school. Did you know that Brian?"

"Can't say as I did," came Brian's reply. He had been listening intently.

Drew went on. "Try to tell the state legislature all this though, when you ask them to give us a little help. Bunch of city guys. Hardly know their food comes from farms. 'Just go to a store, you know. What do we need farms for?' But say a little about people getting undulant fever from raw milk, then they prick their ears up a little in the statehouse. It's amazing how dumb most people are about life…, and reproduction. Don't even realize a cow won't milk unless she's had a calf, and that they need to have one about every twelve months if they're going to pay off- otherwise they start to go dry.

"Of course, if you get a cow that's aborted once or twice- like this one has- she's licked for awhile, and you may be, too. But on the other hand, a cow that's been the course twice like the one we're talking about, should have calves now that survive and are permanently immune. At least, that's what one vet said. That's why I got her…, and a few of the others up on that end of the barn."

"Are you sure they won't abort too…? I mean- their calves- when they're bred?" asked Eric, having just admitted that it was all new to him.

Drew understood. Unlike many fathers, he had always been patient with young folks- provided they weren't trying to protect some personal image as history's first genuine know-it-all. He went on, "Not likely..., so said this vet to me. When little calves get the disease, unless you are keeping them on infected milk for quite a spell, they apparently throw off the disease by the time they're of breeding age. Sort of a *natural* immunization, you might say- for a live calf from a cow testing positive for the disease."

"But," said Eric, "I understand most everybody is using a calfhood vaccine now- came out somewhere around 1944. Call Sean and have him vaccinate them around their sixth or seventh month. Why go through all this?"

"I know that, Eric. And we've started doing that, too- on our ordinary animals. But don't you see..., they were going to send this cow off to slaughter, even though she's something special- just because they wanted to eliminate the disease quick and get it over with, here and now, instead of poking around. They didn't dare keep a single cow- in a hurry-up program like their's- that tested positive and still be sure the rest of the herd was safe. By the way, did you two boys ever hear of Tarbell Farms?"

"I've heard of it at school. Don't remember what they said about it," said Eric. "Upstate New York, isn't it?"

"Sure. And I'm trying to do something like I heard Gage Tarbell did a few years back," said Drew. "Guess he ended up with the first Brucella-free herd in the country. Bottled his own milk after that..., you know- and shipped it to the big city- the only one that could sell raw milk..., certified by the state..., and he did it at a good margin. Got a premium for his milk before anyone even had a proven vaccine for calves, like we have now. Some folks in the city, you know, still prefer raw milk to pasteurized. Tastes better, they say. That may change after awhile- it wouldn't surprise me."

Eric interposed a question, "Where exactly was the Tarbell herd?"

"Oh..., I forgot.... You wouldn't know. A little hamlet called Smithville Flats. Tarbell Farms- real famous among farmers before the war. Had Guernseys, you know, not Holsteins- and a big herd, at that. Tarbell and some profs at the Cornell vet school worked together and cleaned out both tuberculosis and brucellosis..., *both* diseases, mind you- practically unheard of at the time..., right out of the herd- and, like I said- it was a big, big herd. Once clean, he kept a closed herd..., brought no outside additions into the herd, so as to *keep* it clean. Real careful about that, I hear, otherwise it wouldn't have lasted long. Of course there were a bunch of people who claimed they'd catch it back from deer. Well- far as I know, that never happened. A lot of disgrunts around, you know. Up to then, some vets were none too popular telling farmers to clean up on a disease or else lose their business some day, even though the state was behind it. Had to duck a few bullets when they came around to check their cattle. T.B. pretty well done, now they're working on Brucellosis."

Brian asked Drew, "Does that old cow you bought still react to the blood test?"

"Oh, yes, though the titer is going down. We have others in the herd like that. We have about a dozen of them we plan to move out some day. Eventually we hope to have a clean herd. Meanwhile, we have to keep a closed herd, like Tarbell did, or at least just buy cattle tested clean and unexposed to cows that *do* have Bang's disease.

"Then I take it," said Eric, "you just figured this was a way to get started with a real good blood line- without paying the usual high price."

"Now you get it, son," said his dad. "Now, let's go get a bite. I'm hungry, aren't you?"

"By the way, Dad," said Eric, who's the vet that tipped you off on all this? Must be pretty sharp. I never heard about any of this before."

"Your brother…, Eric. Your brother and my son," said Drew. "I think he's a pretty good vet. Don't you?"

The Counsels of Experience

Having finished the usual early morning chores at the barn, Jim, Eric, and Brian, trailed by Drew- whose arthritic "dairyman's" knees were troubling him- walked up the driveway and through the back door of the farmhouse into the laundry room. There, before washing up in a laundry scrub sink, they removed their footwear and coveralls, reeking heavily of organic acids usual to ensilage. The sink, of course, was one of those antiques with two side-by-side compartments, each with built in scouring-surfaces- and had been located next to a modern Bendix washing machine. While waiting his turn at the sink, Brian noticed that the room, like his bedroom of the previous night, bespoke the house's age. Figuring Drew would know if anyone did, he asked him how old the place was.

Drew was amused. It had not escaped his attention that Brian, while in the barn, had seemed to be interested in the structure of old buildings, especially those husky beams in the barn- hewn by broad-ax and joined by mortise and tenon. Seeing an opportunity, he thought he'd see how sharp the lad was. Responding to his question accordingly, he asked him, "How old do you think, Brian?"

"I don't know. Most plank houses like this one, would date back to the 1830's..., maybe earlier."

Drew, washing his hands, turned his head toward Brian and grinned. "You're pretty sharp, kid. My great-grandfather finished the main part of the house in 1832. Of course the east wing, with the two gables, was added later on..., by my grandfather..., most likely because he had eight kids. That part was frame, as I'm sure you know already. I think that was built sometime in the late 1800's."

"I've always admired these plank houses. They're sturdy as all get out," replied Brian. "Almost indestructible."

"Yeah, they sure are." replied Drew, "they never seem to go out of square like the others. This one is just as square now as it was when it was built, unlike the frame part. The only trouble we had was when we were wiring it for electricity for the first time. Took a little more ingenuity than a frame house would."

"Yeah, I know." said Brian. "Hard to run the wires through some of the walls of a plank house, especially where you run into a big beam. At least where I used to live."

"Your folks had a house like this?"

"I don't know. I never had any folks, you know. Of course…, I'm talking about the orphanage where I lived."

"You were an orphan? I didn't know that," replied Drew. "How long were you there?"

Brian started washing his hands. His answer was matter of fact, so casual that it seemed he would rather not pursue the subject. "From the time I was born until they put me in a foster home…. It was quite a long time."

Drew glanced at Brian's face and nodded his head respectfully as he handed him a towel. "I see," he said simply, this being no time for curiosity much less any need for further explanation- unless Brian, on his own, chose to do so.

The men filed into the kitchen one by one, each sitting down at the table in the center of the room at his usual place, hungering for the breakfast that awaited them. To preserve its polished hardwood floor from excessive wear and tear, and being mama Rachel's special pride, the ornate dining room just beyond the kitchen was hardly used-exclusively reserved for three or four special family occasions a year.

Rache, as she was called, her graying hair tied into a bun back of her head, convinced no one with her insistent denials she had done anything special for breakfast. But then, just because her son was back home for the first time in three months and had even brought along his fraternity brother from college, there was no reason to think she wasn't entitled to stretch the truth a bit.

Brian still didn't know exactly where he should sit, though there were still two unoccupied seats. Teasingly, she said to him, "Now, Brian, I guess you'll just have to sit here in this chair alongside me, where I can keep an eye on you. That's where we usually seat our guests. Especially now, since I expect Drew and Eric will try to hog your attention. I want a chance to talk with you, too." Brian, amused by her ingenuous hospitality, smirked and sat down.

With places set at the breakfast table and several serving dishes of hearty farm victuals now on deck, the men had the option of oatmeal, toast, buckwheat pancakes, fried eggs, pork sausage and maple syrup, the last four produced right there at the farm. Brian, without thinking, reached for the pancakes, then hastily drew back and, closing his eyes, bowed his head in conformity with the others. Though normally reticent to discuss, much less partake of religion- Brian was surprised to hear Drew give grace with such conviction and clarity that its unadorned power, though the prayer was brief, almost startled him. But the idea that there was anything real in the ritual, for him, was a fleeting thought.

He had often puzzled how any intelligent man, granted a measure of sanity, could talk to himself- which looked foolish enough- but, far worse, talk to empty air as though some unseen mystical presence, listening intently to every word, was standing close by- someone like the mythical character called the "Shadow," back in the days of early radio- minus the Shadow's hypnotic "power to cloud men's minds." Even worse, for men to do so in *public*, where everyone else could watch the complaisant idiots pay the fantasy even a pittance of obeisance. Why, pray tell, weren't they gritting their teeth, growling, and stalking off? For that matter, why did he allow such a thing himself? At the same time, he sensed in himself a strange, secret envy- almost a longing- for some such belief as Drew's, so simple and sincere. Or was Drew, despite his considerable wisdom, just another flawed fool- vacillating between poles of sanity and lunacy?

In mere seconds, with plates loaded and men's mouths stuffed- incapable of words- the inelegant sounds of mastication and deglutition, unattended by any redeeming conduct, briefly took over. Wincing imperceptibly- reacting to gluttony, thankfully, as any civilized wife and mother might where her heedless brood of barbarous males might not- Rachel struggled to think of something, anything, that could politely drown the din. Finally, it came to her. Without hesitation, she said, "I had the radio on this morning. The fire trucks were headed over to Hensen Corners about five this morning. A barn on fire."

It worked. Provided the offending person is not one who talks with a mouth filled to overflowing, it is worth remembering that conversation can stave off- though not cure- edacity. Jaws dropped. Drew lifted his eyes from his plate, staring at his wife. "Whose barn? Not Harvey's, I hope."

"They didn't say. Sounded like they were calling in another company out of Black to help out."

"That doesn't sound good. Harvey's the only one over there with that big a barn- one that might possibly require a second squad." Drew went back to eating, more quiet now, his face serious.

Even with good financial coverage, few things are more disastrous to a family farm than a fire- nor more piteous than the heart-rending cries of terrified cattle hopelessly trapped, being broiled alive by a flaming hay-loft roaring overhead. Often occurring at night with no one about, it is not often that many cattle can be saved even when taking suicidal risks as some desperate, tearful farmers have done, and *died.* For mercy's sake the animals are, if possible, shot from a safe distance through open doors, windows or the like.

Looking first at Eric, and then especially, Brian- knowing he was a relative neophyte- Drew brought up something he wanted to impress upon them "I don't know if your professors mention this, but a fire like that makes me think of something..., something I learned the hard way..., that you may need to remember about insurance..., someday..., when you have your own farm. And I hope you'll be careful about it."

"What's that?" asked Eric.

Drew thought for a moment, rubbing his nose a bit as he was cogitating. Finally, when he had their complete attention, he proceeded. "There are all kinds of insurance, and if you're not careful, you can carry so much insurance that it ruins you, especially when you're starting up as young man and don't have much liquidity. They're like a pack of vultures buzzing around a place the minute they see a new farmer in town."

Brian looked up, took a drink of coffee to help wash a slug of pancake down his gullet, and then queried, "I've wondered about that. Back at school, we already have a bunch of insurance agents prowling around in the frat houses. According to them, we need all kinds of stuff. How does a guy know if he needs insurance? In the first place, I don't have any money for something like that."

"Well," said Drew, "they're trying to sell you something while it's not so expensive. Probably life insurance. If it was me, I'd forget it..., for now. But if you're talking about later on, when you have your own place and a family, that's another matter. Certainly, fire insurance is another one you'll need then, for sure. It's bad enough to lose your barn, your herd and have to clean up the mess and rebuild. But if you have enough insurance, you can survive it- bad as it is. My granddad had a fire before he moved back here where he grew up…, and his farm survived it. But just barely. Took years to recover completely."

"I can see that one all right," said Jim, also interested, since he'd never thought about the issue. "But what else should you carry?"

"There's a general rule I've learned over the years, and I hope that both you young college boys, and you, too, Jim…, remember it. *Be sure that you insure against a misfortune that is not too likely to occur, but would ruin you if it did.* Best example I can think of is fire insurance. That will usually be a good investment for a relatively small premium. I wouldn't insure for something that's relatively likely to happen, but wouldn't be exactly disastrous, as long as you have enough cash to cover it. Or, at least good enough credit. That kind of insurance, in the long run, is apt to cost you more than it's worth, and it'll make you 'insurance poor,' as a result."

"Give me an example, Dad," said Eric.

"Easier said than done, because…, well, it depends a lot on your equity at the time, and that might change a lot over time. For instance, if you're young, and you have a nice new truck, you might want to carry 'collision,' as well as liability insurance, because you don't have the liquidity to repair your truck, say…, after a major accident, and you may already be up to your limit in debt. Especially if you've just started to farm. When you're a farmer, you can't be any too sure that the *price* you get for your milk, or whatever it is you're producing, won't…. Well, you know, the floor could drop out *overnight.* It happens all the time in this business, and you don't want to get caught when you're vulnerable like that. Besides, unlike most industries, a dairyman has a very perishable product. He's trapped…, can't hold back on selling his produce, waiting until the price goes up again, like, say, a wheat farmer might do for awhile. And, you know as well as I do that dairymen have no control over what the creamery will be paying them for their milk. They just have to sit there till the end of the month and take whatever somebody else decides to give them. Aren't many industries like that, with no clear-cut contract."

Jim hadn't been saying much till then, but he interjected, "That's what my dad says, too. Same thing. And, if the processor should go bankrupt in the meanwhile, there's no telling if you'll ever get paid. The biggest jokes, he says, are all the know-nothings who think the farmer 'charges too much' for his milk."

Drew laughed. "I sure wish I *could* set my price. I don't have anymore power over what I get paid than one of my horses has control over how many pounds of oats I feed him in the morning."

"But the city folks think we do," said Jim.

"Sure, I know," said Drew. "But thinkin' something ain't makin' it so."

"While we're talking about it, there's something I wanted to ask you, Mr. Auchinachie," said Brian.

"Sure, go ahead."

"I'm going to ag school on free tuition plus working at a few jobs…, and I don't have any relatives. How can a guy like me- no family or anything- get his own farm when he's out of school? I can't believe anybody would lend me money. I've thought of hiring out, and saving some of my pay working for someone else. But hired men don't make very much, from what I see. Seems like I'd have to work thirty years before I had enough for a down payment on a farm."

"You're probably right, Brian." said Drew. "In the first place, there's a sneaky way you can get some credit. One guy I knew years ago had a situation something like yours, so, after a few refusals for a big loan at the bank, he pleaded with them to just give him a measly $1000 for one month, because he had an investment opportunity he'd learned about from another guy…, a tip on the stock market that was so hot he had to keep it a secret. They were so curious they gave him the loan. Then he just stuck the loan in a desk drawer and paid it back with interest a week early, pretending to be real excited about how much he'd made off the investment, and giving them a cock and bull story about still keeping his source of information secret. That was the beginning, and he ended up a millionaire years later."

"Drew, why don't you tell Brian what Stanley did when he worked for us?" said Rachel. "That seemed to work pretty well."

"You tell him, Rachel. It was your idea, anyway," Drew said, as he reached for another piece of toast, adding a comment for the boys' benefit, "Rache liked Stanley real well and put the bug in my ear…, but you go ahead, Rache."

With that, Rachel explained that Stanley, a particularly skillful and dependable farmhand, had worked for them a couple of years until finally, as an incentive, the farm gave him a Christmas bonus- a good yearling heifer, which was kept on the farm with the other heifers and fed with them without incurring any cost for its care at the farm till it started milking as a two-year-old, following its first calf. At that time, her milk was weighed each day, and at the end of each month, the farm paid him for his heifer's milk, after recovering the cost of feeding her in the milk-line with the other cows.

Then Stanley was given another yearling each year at Christmastime, with the same stipulations. Finally, after nine or ten years, he owned about twenty cows and ten young stock plus having enough money in the bank to buy about fifteen more cows, which he did when he left, having started farming on his own.

Brian's face betrayed his fascination. "I have a question, Drew."

"Go ahead," said Drew.

When he left your place..., how'd he get a farm?"

"Good question. He rented a farm. In fact he rented that farm for six years, got married, had kids, and then after that he bought his own. He had almost sixty cows by then, all paid for. And they were good cows. He did real well. About all the debt he had by then was long term debt, and he could handle that. Having too much short term debt can kill you, you know. He learned to consolidate those under a long term loan from the bank."

Brian was still puzzled. "Rented a farm? I'd think that would be hard to do."

"I suppose it could be. But if your credit is good, you have a reputation as a good worker and already own your own herd, it's a cinch. Believe me, it's pretty easy to rent a farm when you already have demonstrable assets. Another thing- a place may not be ideal, but there are always a lot of old geezers like me who want to sell out to the right guy, but the right guy never seems to come along. They don't want to take a lot of risk, you know. But they want to get out so bad that they'll finance your farm..., maybe a land contract or mortgage. And there's another way you can get a farm of your own."

"A junior partner?" said Brian.

"Ah, you beat me to it," replied Drew. "I've known a few good men around here that worked as a hired man for an older man and eventually became a junior partner. Then after awhile, when the old man retired, he finished buying him out. Of course, you have to be patient and put up with the old man's funny ways of doing things for awhile. Then, there's another way that's pretty common."

Eric laughed facetiously. "I know. Marry the farmer's daughter!"

At that point, a jeep drove past the house and parked near the barn, and a man dressed in coveralls and boots got out, accompanied by a teen-age girl. "That must be Sean," said Drew. I called him last night. Said he'd be up again to look at the cow in the box stall…, down at the end of the barn- you saw her, Brian, while you were down there looking at the joists- freshened a couple of days ago."

Brian was skeptical. "I didn't know anything was wrong with her. She was eating good. What's the matter with her?" he said.

"Had a problem calving. Big bull calf, had to use a little traction…, but stuck half-way out for too long before we knew she was trying. Anyway, she hasn't gotten up since then."

"Oh," said Brian, "you've got a *downer*…. And who's the girl with Dr. Sean?"

"Oh, that's Penelope- my granddaughter, Sean's girl. She's probably coming for the day. She likes to help out up here when she's not in school…, in the barn as well as here in the house with her gramma."

"She's gramma's baby," said Rachel, parting the window curtains and looking out at Eric and Penny, smiling broadly as the girl waved to her.

The crew rose from their chairs. There was, after all, work to do, and the vet, Eric's brother, was here to see the downer. No more time for blather. Sean was expected at a social gathering of community movers and shakers in the evening, to which a number of professionals had been invited and, with a long schedule ahead of him, he needed to make time.

Mrs. Chadwick

"I'm Mrs. Chadwick," cooed the lady in red, "I don't believe we've ever met." A little unsteady on her feet, she seemed to be captivated by the doctor she had cornered at the party, towering nearly a foot and a half above her. The doctor could hardly fail to perceive her as a lush morsel, even with her diminutive stature. But, additionally, her breath and effusive manner indicated the lady was not only lush, but a bit tipsy- and just perhaps, a chronic *lush.* Weaving a bit, she took his hand as though to shake it, and then clinging to it as though she might fall if she let go, she introduced herself again. "I don't believe we've met, Doctor," she repeated. "You can just call me Madge. I'd like that- it's more..., *personal.* Mrs. Hanover pointed you out to me and said you were such a nice man and that I ought to come over here to talk to you. It's so nice you could come to the party." Her voice was naturally soft, intimate, but overly so as she gushed on, "Madge..., if you want, my dear. That's what everybody calls me. Eleanor said so many nice things about you..., and I can't tell you how pleased I am to meet you. I understand that even though you were a busy, busy man as a doctor, you cared enough about children... to have been president..., I *think* she said it was president...? of the board of education over in Sturgis Valley. I think that's wonderful. I would feel like our kids were so much *safer* if we'd had a doctor on *our* board here in Damon." She looked up at him, batting her eyes. "You don't mind if I call you Sean, do you?"

Sean's eyes twinkled in amusement as he looked down amiably on the rosy face of the plumpish but vivacious and highly attractive little woman, perhaps thirty-two, her eyes firmly fixed on his like a love-sick puppy. He doubted not that she was probably a pretty nice woman- thoroughly respectable- when she was sober. Even if he was wrong about her better nature- something that is hard to tell when a well-dressed lady is both inebriated and forward- he didn't want to embarrass the little soul by brushing her off like a tawdry little tart, even if she was acting like one.

Nor did Sean enjoy being cornered. Already, he wished he could just think of a graceful way to take his leave of her. She was making him more and more uncomfortable, suggestive, as she was, of a heifer in heat. He cast his eyes uneasily amongst the crowd around the room, in an effort to spot her husband whom he'd met a few minutes before. No doubt his presence would defuse this encounter. Unfortunately, he was nowhere to be seen. Sean tried to deflect her attention. "I think I met your husband here a few minutes ago.... Don't know a lot of the people here..., but isn't he the electrical engineer?"

It seemed to work. She backed off for the moment. "Oh, you've met him, then! I was going to have you meet him. I'd like to meet your wife, too. Where is she?"

"She couldn't come with me tonight, Madge. Usually we come to these things together, but we couldn't get our usual girl to answer the phone- she's out of town. So Nancy had to cover. I'm on call tonight, you know."

Seizing now the moment, as though the wife of the poor doctor had totally neglected him, and perhaps flattered that he'd used her nickname, Madge's voice fairly oozed, dripping with such syrupy compassion that the manly war veteran turned doctor, mighty man of the world, was growing visibly uncomfortable. "Oh, *Doctor*...! I'm so sorry...! It's wonderful that you are so dedicated to your profession. And I'd just *love* to meet your wife sometime..., you know.... It's so great to find new friends. I've heard such nice things about her, too." She looked up at Sean in wonderment, her fervid, soft brown eyes once again peering into his brain, making him wonder if she was noticing that he was squirming, or even worse, reading the imbalance between his superego and his id- which he was frantically attempting to control. Unfortunately, there was by now something about her that had his motor stirring, even against his will. How this could be was beyond him. His mind was scurrying about for a quick and decisive exit, but with finesse.

Madge didn't seem to notice his discomfort. "Sean," she said in a tone of noxious familiarity, "Do you have any children?" She moved her face closer, leaning into his, her bosom threatening to press him against the wall, her eyes piercing, studying his face like a paramour-hers for the taking.

Ye gods, he thought- where is this one going? She sure doesn't waste any time. "No. I mean..., yes. Yes, of course."

"I wish I did. John and I have tried for years, but we never had any children. How many children do you have?"

"Just one. She's sixteen."

Madge looked him over, puzzled. "You don't look old enough to…." Suddenly her face began to flush as she locked her eyes on his, turning rapidly to a full-fledged blush. Her voice now husky, a moist glint about her eyes, she reached up and tenderly straightened his tie. "Well, excuse me, Doctor, I…. Well, I guess you've just managed to stay so *young!*" she exuded, breathlessly, without missing a beat.

Sean laughed nervously, hoping to shake her off with some comic comment that, unfortunately, escaped him in the pressure of the moment. "Well, thank you, Madge." he replied flatly. "I'll tell my wife you said that the next time she tells me that I'm getting too heavy."

"Oh, Doctor, You aren't heavy at all! You are such a handsome man. She should be so proud of you, a *doctor* at that! I would be! Why, look at you!" Then she adopted a more serious tone. "Doctor, while I have you here, I'd like to ask you a rather personal question. I do hope you won't mind."

Quizzically, Sean's pursed his lips, his eyebrows raised and expecting the worst, but he could not bring himself to be unkind. "Yes?"

"I've never asked a doctor why we didn't have any children. It just seems so… personal. But somehow, I just feel like you'd be understanding. Do you do any infertility work? I've heard you do."

"Yes, as a matter if fact, Madge, I do a lot of it."

"Oooh," she cooed, whispering, her neck now turning as crimson as her features. "Do you suppose it's because my husband and I…. Well, we don't… you know… uh…."

"I suppose that could be, Madge. But, you'd better talk to somebody like Dr. Gunther. He might be able to help you." Sean, realizing he had come across a possible escape from the uncanny temptation this extraordinarily attractive and seductive, though inebriated, little woman presented- was now sensing a way out of his predicament without the threat of becoming an insufferable laughingstock regarding his manhood.

"Oh, is he a gynecologist?"

"Oh no. He's a physician. But he's a good one. He's here in Damon."

"Yes, I know," she said. "But you do a lot of that kind of work. He's just a G.P., isn't he?"

"Yes, he's a physician. But I'm a veterinary doctor, not a medical doctor."

Madge's face went blank, at first, then gradually she drew her hand up a bit toward her face in an expression of shock. "But, but, Doctor… you said you do a lot of infertility work. I don't understand."

Sean smothered a little sigh of relief as he now recognized an easy escape plainly laid out for him. "Yes, ma'am," he said as naturally as he could in the awkward heat of the moment, trying desperately to give a wide berth to the levity pounding on the door and asking for a guffaw. "Cows, Madge. Infertility work on cows. Lots of it. Every day."

Madge was speechless, instant sobriety hitting her as she realized what a fool she'd been. She drew her hand on up to her mouth, covering it as she stared at Sean with a look of betrayal. "Oh, my! Oh…, my word! You aren't kidding!" Then her face reddened in anger as she saw the bland look of relief crossing Sean's face. "Well, Mr. Sean Awkon Ahkie, or whatever it is," she huffed, "I…, I just remembered I have to find my husband. It's getting late, and we'd better go home!"

Now she had offended Sean. And he had a caustic side. "I'm sorry about that last name, but I was born with it. It sounds different from how it's spelled. The name is Auchinachie, Sean Auchinachie." He spelled it out sarcastically, then went on, "But we *poor country folks*," he drawled out, "usually pronounce it Aw- hahn- a- hee."

"What an awful name! And you're distasteful. You're not even a *real* doctor!" snapped Madge, ferociously glaring at him. She turned on her heels and flounced away, leaving Sean scratching his head in bewildered relief, wondering what he'd done to deserve this, and reminding himself to read once again the book entitled "How to Win Friends and Influence People." He must have missed something the first time. Perhaps, he thought, if he were to write a book on how to make an enemy unintentionally….

B. J. Pierce

It was not because B.J. was a good, likable guy, family man, well educated- an Ivy League graduate. Nor because everybody knew that his father had been a highly visible superintendent of a major metropolitan public school system. Certainly he did not lack for brains or bright ideas. He was, in fact, highly inventive. Yet none of these were what really set B.J. apart. Not, at least, among the farmers in Sean's area. It was simply that B.J. was not afraid of hard work.

In fact, B.J. was not the least bit afraid of work, though he seemed to be afraid *to* work. It had even been noised about that he could lie down beside it and doze all day. That may be why he was so proud of his barn. It was unique. Absolutely so. B.J.'s barn was the not only the dirtiest in the county, but would be at least runner-up state-wide and, on a national level, unquestionably achieve dishonorable mention.

For some reason or other, most all vets avoided his place. Not Sean. The only thing that seemed to bother Sean at all about B.J. was the petty fact that his statement balance seemed to grow every month- payments always enough short of the past month's services to substantially build up, given enough time. B.J. must have thought this was what was meant by the accrual method of accounting. At least, he was good at letting debts accrue. But B.J. was Sean's friend.

Nor was there much effort on B.J.'s part to catch up, despite Nancy's taking her husband aside and ringing the tocsin whenever she was making out his monthly statement. Nancy had seen this before. It was a deliberate scam used in the past by a number of Sean's more genteel and accomplished deadbeats. For them, it was not unmitigated theft. It was simply a means of getting a nice fat discount over a period of time. Sean, being an honorable man, assumed that his friends would, of course, honor any debt just as he would himself. And who were his friends? His old buddies from years past, and every farmer who was his client. He wouldn't shaft a friend so, of course, no friend would shaft him. Case closed, Nancy- B.J. was Sean's friend.

Nevertheless, there were times when B.J.'s abysmal stable conditions appalled even Sean, such as several times he'd had to treat a semi-comatose cow for milk fever while she was sprawled out, untethered, behind her tie-stall, floundering in a drop that hadn't been cleaned in days. On three occasions, there was not only solid filth, but great volumes of fetid fluid, much of it splashed all over Sean as well as B.J.- who wasn't daunted in the least by it. No wonder Sean's Jeep stunk. Of course, he eventually got himself a rubber suit. B.J. was still his friend.

B.J. had decided to build himself the latest thing on the dairyman's dream list- a milking parlor with a pipeline running directly from milking machine to a bulk-tank. Real sanitation. Closed system. No flies or problems of that kind. No more carrying pails of milk from stable to milkhouse; no more milk-cans. No more flat-bed truck to take milk to the creamery every morning. And, not having to get the milk to the plant at a certain time, a farmer could milk whenever he chose- early, late, three times a day. Of course, no longer being sure when a particular farm would be milking, this messed up vets like Sean, who had previously tried- for the sake of both himself and the farmer- to avoid milking time.

A tanker would now be picking the milk up and haul it to a bigger plant far away, much closer to its eventual marketplace. The plant would now be paying for the hauling, instead of the farmer. Wow! thought the farmer. That would sure help pay for the new installations. What an incentive! Unknown to him the processor had planned from the first, when enough farmers had complied, to nix the free transport and plunk its cost back on the farmers. Oh, Khruschev's good old carrot and stick!

There was a great deal of salesmanship on the part of creameries, health officials and manufacturers that went into the bulk tank "option." It was not, of course, called collusion. And, admittedly, it was surely the brightest thing on the horizon for a dairyman at that time. No longer milking in the same messy old stable where the cows were housed, fed and bedded down, he could now stand, proudly erect, in a modern, well-designed and sanitary parlor, milk the cows more efficiently as groups of them- coming from the holding area, eager for the grain waiting for them- moved into the parlor, were locked in, milked and discharged back to the stable- the milking crew neither being kicked, nor developing the knee and back problems that came, over time, from the old way of milking.

B.J. was proud to be one of the very first to build such a thing, and invited a good many of his compatriots to come see what he'd done. Solely for the sake of impressing them, his barn was now so immaculate that a gullible reporter for a farm journal actually published a piece about it, complete with photos of this "model" farm. When he was shown the article by B.J., beaming like a new papa, Sean, of course, found it all very amusing- discreetly holding his tongue.

Inevitably though, the adulation wore off, no more visitors showed up, and B.J. was back to his old habits. It only took about a year. The place was, once again, irredeemably, an abominable sinkhole. And once again, B.J. had a milk fever case flat out, struggling in the drop- no longer tidied up for the visitors- but this time she was upside down and completely helpless. Meanwhile, waiting for Sean's arrival, B.J. blithely went about feeding silage while keeping an untroubled eye on his semi-comatose cow, frantically struggling to avoid drowning in the slop in the drop or choking on her own bloat-induced vomitus. This notwithstanding the fact he could, alone and in a jiffy, have taken a rope and relieved her misery by pulling her out and righting her. B.J. was not afraid of work, though. Or, perhaps, rather than hogging the glory for himself, he wanted to share with the friendly doctor the exquisite joy of salvation for the poor beast, freeing her from her desperate plight, while her tail and appendages slapped each of them, whipping the foul contents of the drop into frothy waves and showers of pure, putrid sludge. The cow was saved. And B.J. was still Sean's friend.

Such a perverse sense of humor, to this very day, has not been completely extinguished among country rubes. In fact, in the face of growing farm bankruptcies, it may have become even more of a necessity for them. Humor is, after all, not only the balm that preserves sanity, but, for the dairyman, the last and best refuge from udder desperation.

Sean arrived at the farm early one cold winter morning, finding B.J. about to milk his last group of eight cows in his, by now, much dilapidated parlor- his pride and joy of a mere two years before. Much of its metalwork, like the feeders, looked like it'd been battered with a sledge hammer. Not quite as delicate or agile as the ballerinas they pretend to be, big cows like Holsteins can cause more property damage over time than a mob of acrimonious inner-city nincompoops.

Wearing hip boots as he hosed off the manure from a cow's bag while standing in the pit in a good foot of filthy water, B.J. gave Sean a cheery greeting. "The drain is plugged," he said, nonchalant as usual.

Well, that was not so bad. Drains do plug up. But when Sean went back about ten days later, it was even worse. The slop was now two feet deep and, once again, B.J. seemed unperturbed, explaining that- being as how it was winter and the ground was frozen- nobody with the necessary equipment for digging would come to help him out. The truth was that they expected to be paid and, for B.J., in particular, right up front.

All this was but a prelude to the day when Sean came to the farm to find B.J. in a real dither. The parlor was even worse. The creamery had shut him off. That is, they wouldn't take his milk. He was dumping all his milk- his income- in a water-trough and giving it to a hog-farm, just to be rid of it. The creamery's normally placid inspector had been there on his regular inspection of farm premises, saw the mess, got in a tirade and told B.J. he'd never seen such a f….g s…hole in his life, though he'd seen more than his share of them. Told him that not until he cleaned the place up and passed his next inspection would the creamery take him back. That being quite a project, B.J. had tried to get some other milk company to take his milk- sans clean-up. Nobody wanted him. In fact, some of them admitted, unwittingly, that they *weren't allowed* to send their own inspector until the first creamery passed it. So it quickly became evident that each of the companies- some five or six in the area- having been contacted by the original milk plant, had been anticipating B.J.'s call and were fully prepared to give him the brush-off. A brush-off with relish, on the inspectors' part.

Sean was on a friendly working basis with Harvey Kane, the same barn inspector that had ostracized B.J. It was Kane that assigned him the herds for his annual herd inspections. Awkward situation. In effect, then, B.J., as a farmer, and Harvey, representing the creamery, were each a client of Sean. Considering his responsibilities, Kane had never seemed to be a peremptory sort. Usually he would give a delinquent a specified number of days to comply with the city health dept. regulations, after which a farmer might be shut off until his demands were met.

On the other hand, B.J.'s livelihood would quickly be obliterated unless he could find a market for the milk he was now dumping down the pigs every day, since not even the last resort for his milk- a cheese plant, without either the higher facility standards or payments associated with Grade A bottled milk- would take it.

Sean could see that B.J. was faced with a disaster, and was, for the first time since he'd known him, worried- facing a hell of his own creation. And as much as he figured B.J. had it coming to him, there was one thing that gnawed at him: Was it right for the creameries to gang up on him? Why couldn't a different creamery send out their own inspector to B.J.'s farm? Why deny him such recourse, granted it probably wouldn't help, instead of just throwing weight around? At the time, being no uniform health requirements from city to city, and with some of the local creameries not even sending to the same cities, thus under different jurisdiction, there was a possibility of varying requirements. That being the case, it was possible that B.J. could find a market somewhere. And, after all, B.J. was still Sean's friend.

"You sure these other companies *can't* send anyone out to your farm unless Kane approves it first?"

"Absolutely," replied B.J. "They even admitted it themselves."

Sean felt his blood rising, having sensed on many occasions while at the creamery office that, despite the fact the milk plants were themselves subject to city inspection, the closer, almost day-by-day relationship between inspectors and operators of the creamery, made it only natural they would tend to support each other against a solitary farmer they considered helpless. Just another name to them. It seemed to Sean there should be a discreet separation of any corporate interest from what was actually a governmental agency. To him, it was one thing to refuse the man's milk, but another to blacklist him, denying him an alternative market- nothing less than tyranny. Knowing it would require a lawyer to determine if there was, in truth, an illegal restraint of trade, he decided to stick his neck out, despite the obvious fact B.J. was far from blameless.

"It seems to me, B.J.," he said quietly, "you might have a case if you took them to court."

"You really think so?" said B.J., brightening a bit.

"Well..., I'm no lawyer, but there's a possibility. I can't see a bunch of these inspectors and processors- who, seems to me, ought to be completely independent- teaming up together on one little guy. Can't see any justice in that, can you? I know these health departments have rules of their own- and the politicians keep their noses out of it, if they can, but I'd at least talk to an attorney. Maybe there's nothing you can do. I just don't know enough about it."

B.J. shook his head. "No, I don't, either. But what do you think the legal grounds might be?"

"Well, it might be restraint of trade- using a governmental agency to rig things up against one outfit, namely you, to favor another private outfit. The health department should be impartial, separate..., at least as I see it. At another level, it might be lack of due process- sort of like the federals do when they bully somebody.

"I had one client, a hard-headed German, who refused to pay into the social security fund when they changed the rules and made farmers belong. He ignored them for a long time. Of course, he was asking for it, but he figured he had no say in the new requirements. Then, one day, he bought a nice new tractor and paid for it in one big fat check. He never had check bounce- had thousands in his account, and never owed anybody more than a few days. Then the doggone check bounced! He thought the bank had made a mistake. When he checked with the bank, it turned out his account had been stripped. The federal agents just walked in and took it.

"Now, personally, I thought the guy was wrong in the first place. He hadn't tried to fight it legally. But I thought since there was no hearing of any kind, no notification about the withdrawal by either the bank or the I.R.S., there was a due process complaint. I hear more and more about this high-handed stuff going on- all the time. And I think it's getting worse.

"But then, B.J., I'm no lawyer..., though sometimes..., when I see a case like this, I'd like to be. The way they're teaming up.... The whole process stinks, whether your place passes or not. You don't even have the right to dispute one of their butterfat tests or bacteria counts by hiring an outside lab. If they tell you something, it's so. And there should be no reason another creamery's inspector can't give you a look, that I can think of..., except some blasted conspiracy." Sean was red-faced, eyes fiery by now. "Something's wrong with the way they're treating you. You better go see a lawyer!"

"All right, Doc. But I don't know any lawyers. Do you know who I could get?"

"Well, let me think a minute. There's Foley, and Dewey, and there's Glasser. They're all good. But let's see. Maybe the old judge, himself- if he'd take the case. He's the best lawyer in the county. I'd try him, if I were you. He's really been around."

"What's his name?"

"Clancy. Judge Clancy."

"I think I've got a better idea, Doc."

"What's that?"

"Did you read in the paper about that farmer east of here? Think it was three days ago. Morning paper."

"No, don't know as I've read a paper in a week or so, B.J...."

"Well, some hot-head over in the next county- tough guy..., drunk, I guess- got mad at his farm inspector for something..., dragged him out of his barn, lifted him up and threw him in the manure spreader." B.J. laughed heartily. "And it was full. Left him there to crawl out of the crap on his own. Of course, they put him in the jug a little later- assault and battery."

"Don't even think of it- they'd send you to the gibbet." said Sean. "Besides, you aren't big enough."

Wild Heifer

Eric pointed over to his left as he was driving down the Highfield road. "See that railroad crossing over on the left?"

"Yeah, I see it. What about it?" replied Brian.

"I just gotta tell you about something Sean told me. See down there just beyond that shed near the tracks, where the telegraph pole is?"

"Sure."

"Well, I'll have to tell you the whole story. That's where it happened."

"*What* happened, for Pete's sake?" said Brian.

"Sean was driving down this road one day with Jim when he ran into a bunch of guys trying to drive some big yearling heifers across the road from the pasture to the barnyard near that shed. The barn is gone now. But that's where it was. Sean and Jim stopped and got out to help drive them through the barnyard gate. I guess they were a little short-handed, and some of them were slipping through the ring of men- only about four of them. Anyway, they got into the circle and were gradually driving them- one by one into the barnyard- all except one heifer. She just wouldn't go. Finally, even though she was almost the last one, she wouldn't follow the other ones, like you'd expect, and she tried to force her way through the circle of men. One of the farmhands tried to stop her, but she put her head down and charged him…, threw him up in the air with her horns and broke out and ran off down the road. Got clean away."

"Hurt him?"

"Didn't think so at the time, but it turned out she did break one of his ribs. I guess he went up in the air three feet over the back of the heifer, according to Sean." said Eric, as he zipped around a cat flying across the road. "But after they shut the other heifers in the barnyard, they tried to get the wild one back up the road so they could drive her in, and they couldn't do it. Sean and Jim finally gave up and went on."

"End of story?" asked Brian.

Eric laughed. "Nope, there's more. That's not the best part of the story. Don't worry, I won't take long." He paused long enough to sneeze, wiped his nose, and continued, “The farmer called up Sean a few days later and asked him if he had something he could slip in some feed for the heifer that would knock her out.”

“I take it they couldn’t catch her?”

“No way. Tried everything. Just went wild, couldn’t get near her or she’d take right off. And I guess they didn’t want to give up.”

Brian pointed to a white building as they were approaching it. “Is that the Grange hall?”

“No, that’s the old schoolhouse where Jim lives. He bought it when he left his father’s farm.”

“Jim? Sean’s driver?” said Brian.

“Yeah, and Drew’s hired man. Yep, that’s him. School was closed when they centralized all the little school districts around here, they wanted to sell it, so Jim bought it cheap. Grange hall looks something like it, white clapboard- but it’s two storied. It’s about a mile yet before we get there…. Anyway, Sean gave the farmer some chloral to put in the bucket with the grain they were feeding her in the morning.”

“Chloral? What’s that?” said Brian.

“Chloral hydrate. You ever hear of a Mickey Finn?”

“Oh, that stuff they used to slip in a guy’s drink to knock him out?”

“Yeah. Same stuff. Sean uses it for a sedative for horses and cattle- like when he’s going to do some surgery or just needs to tame them down a little. Sometimes he puts it in a bucket with some other medicine for a horse with colic and pumps it down their stomach with a stomach tube. Works pretty good for the pain. Then they aren’t so apt to lie down and roll around and make things worse.”

“You mean…, like twisting a gut.?”

“Exactly. I’m talking about horses…, not cows. He just uses that stuff on cows to take the edge off so he can give them a local anesthetic pre-op for hardware surgery without getting kicked…, you know, open up their stomach- their rumen, technically- to reach in and remove some nails or wire from the reticulum- just ahead of the rumen. Uses it for a few other things like that, too.”

“They do that with the cow standing, I understand.”

“You’re right. I don’t know as you could do it with them down. You’d have stomach contents all over the place.”

"I wondered about that. No way you can empty that out, I suppose."

"If there is, it wouldn't be practical, I'm sure. Every vet does them while the cow is standing..., now what was I talking about...?" said Eric.

"I don't know.... Oh..., it was the railroad track..., and the heifer that knocked somebody down and broke his rib. Keep going..., I'm listening."

"Let's see..., where was I? Oh, yeah. Well, Sean gave him- the farmer, that is- more chloral quite a few times. He kept trying it in the feed, raised the dose and everything but it still didn't seem to work. Maybe a deer was eating the bait, or she didn't eat enough, or whatever. The farmer tried to nail her like that several times and never managed to catch her. Didn't even stagger her."

Brian chuckled. "You mean they never got her?"

"Right! Sean sort of forgot about the deal and a few weeks went by and he had to go to the farmer's place to see a sick cow- another cow. Happened to think of the heifer and asked the farmer if he'd ever caught her."

"Did he?"

"Said she was dead. Sean asked him if he'd shot her. Sometimes you have to do that so somebody doesn't complain about a heifer running around loose on their property..., especially a lawn. Said he hadn't shot her. Sean asked him what happened..., starve to death, freeze, or what? Farmer said no, but a neighbor had seen her on the railroad track- right where I showed you..., and a train came down the track and when the engineer tooted his whistle, the dumb thing just lifted her tail up and charged the locomotive full speed just like she'd done with the hired man."

"Yow!" said Brian. "Killed her then?"

"No, she just tossed the locomotive over her back like she had the hired man. Wrecked the whole damned train, then she kicked her heels and ran off into the woods again."

"All right. Dumb question." said Brian a bit sheepishly.

"Could be, at that." said Eric, snickering. "Anyway, the guy was standing in his backyard when it happened, then he told Sean about it and he went down. He said all there was left of the heifer was a few shreds of hide laying along the tracks in pieces."

"Say, is that the Grange hall over there?" said Brian, indicating with a flick of his hand, off to the right.

"That's the place all right," said Eric, as he eased off the throttle and turned into the parking area to the side of the building, still a bit too fast, in the process almost splashing a huge puddle over a group of farmers headed for the entranceway. "Missed, dammit. One of the guys in that gang was old man Heller- never paid my dad for a load of hay he got from us five years ago."

The Grange

Oliver H. Kelly and six others are credited with founding the "National Grange" in Washington, D.C. c. 1867, otherwise known, among other variations, as the "Patrons of Husbandry." While there were fraternal and educational motives for the movement, its driving purpose was the economic survival of farm individuals in the face of ever larger, more powerful business conglomerates- and political indifference. Under the protective wings of the Grange- and similar organizations at the time- were included all kinds of farm operations, such as poultry, beef, wool, cotton, tobacco, grains, dairy, vegetable, fruit, and others. Not all of these have every interest in common, being natural competitors in the market place and even opposed on various issues. For example, dairy farmers in general are coming to view the neighboring dairy farmer as a market competitor. Different meat commodities such as pork, beef and poultry are also fierce competitors. And the livestock man is cheered by the fall in price of western soy or corn, since he can afford to feed his livestock cheaper and increase his own margin- at the expense of the other.

Politically speaking, the natural vulnerability of farms- the very base of the country- had long been ignored. Economically, for them, it was "take it or leave it." With little power to negotiate in the face of big outfits, farmers were often snookered, forced to take whatever price they were offered wholesale for their produce- or forking over, buying without recourse, at urban-based retail prices when purchasing necessary items and services.

The latter brings with it the issue of credit. Farm operations- especially in the spring planting season- customarily require credit, but lenders' terms were more appropriate to municipal businesses than to those men of the field who were largely a bunch of marginals and paupers.

Things like that, of course, have been the fate of farm people world-wide clear back into antiquity. Governments around the world- stationed, as they are, in cities- have historically favored urban interests over those of distant serfs, peons, peasants, rubes or slaves. *Plentiful* supplies of *cheap* foodstuffs are thus their main concern. Remember the French Revolution? Why was that? Politicians, mindful of mobs, evidently figure that the squeakiest and nearest wheel better be oiled before the whole wagon collapses, crashes, and brings them "down to earth." Down to earth- where the farmer is.

The 1940's and 1950's were relatively good years for home farms. Even then, average income of a farmer hovered at half the American average, despite much longer hours and unrelenting days of work without perquisites, and despite a breadth of knowledge and skills that would baffle most urbanites. Meanwhile, to the eye of the passers-by, the farm itself was often a picture of wealth- inspiring little sympathy- despite the fact that, at least for the first farm generation or two, much of the visible property was an *illusion* of wealth, actually being on loan from a far bigger capitalist with city connections. And if it was ever sold in a time of distress, only a fraction of its real value would return.

Of course, the farm family in America *could* eat, unlike Ukrainians in the 1930's or the Irish in the years around 1846.

Over the years there were ups and downs, but the "Granger Movement" quickly reached a peak in the early 1870's, though membership quickly dropped during the years of 1875 to 1880, due to the same sort of internal dissension that has persistently denied farmers their rightful share of the national economy. It is not that farmers are oblivious to the enormous power they could have if unified. But the pride of a few seems to require their separation from the less successful masses, as though none of their own success could possibly be laid at the door of plain good fortune.

It is like a few big hogs- each figuring that if a few of the smaller hogs could disappear, he'd have more swill for himself- never seeing that the cycle, if continued indefinitely, may well finish him off, too, when big-time super-hog takes over the whole trough.

After 1880, membership in the Grange gradually recovered, so that strong cooperation among their local farm fraternities, especially in the states of Ohio, New York, Pennsylvania and the three west coast states, made them a power to contend with, thus correcting some of the same political and economic injustices suffered by individual workers at the hands of larger and larger business enterprises, resulting in labor unions.

There were, as anyone can see, similarities in the collectivism of Grangers and that of the early labor unions, though most Grangers- unlike industrial workers- had some capital. At their best, the collective efforts of Grangers and similar farm groups gained them favorable legislation regarding shipping costs charged them by railroads- or the charges levied at grain elevators- especially in the Midwest. When necessary, it enabled them to circumvent certain large businesses- even monopolies- through cooperative purchases. And, if they chose not to sell their produce directly through a co-op, its price could be negotiated elsewhere by the co-op, though their success on behalf of fruit or dairy businesses was naturally limited; all kinds of "forced" sales, even due to natural perishability- being a buyer's market- handicap sellers to some degree.

The National Grange supported the Agricultural Adjustment legislation of the 1930's, as well as some modifications legislated around 1950 in its advocacy of a commodity by commodity approach in dealing with farm problems, as well as domestic parity programs for various export crops such as wheat based on a period of relative stability in the prices and costs of production that existed in 1910-1914. But despite tons of advice and endless effort, no magic switch or throttle was ever found to turn farm production on or off, thus stabilizing notoriously vacillating commodity prices- the bane of the producer in debt. Being dependent on natural forces, farm production is like a steam engine, heating up or cooling off only over a period of time.

Bits of Controversy

Normally, neither Eric nor Brian would have been much interested in a farm extension meeting. Many students at their agriculture college considered it a little low-brow to take a major in extension work rather than in some specialized scientific field such as pomology, agronomy, poultry genetics, dairy science, or the like. Nobody, of course, wants to be considered low-brow at a university. It can be bad enough, at times, simply to be an aggie among liberal-arts brahmans who regard you as an unsophisticated hick- a disgrace, an unmentionable at an institution of higher learning, if not the very abomination of desolation.

Nevertheless, Eric had been looking forward to this day, when he planned to attend a particular farm extension meeting- one that had been arranged, as usual, to meet in the local Grange hall. One of the speakers would be a young professor from his school that would be teaching a new economics course of interest to him. Oddly enough, Eric perked Brian up enough to tag along with him- though he was notably weary of lectures- by simply dangling the word "agronomy" in front of him, mentioning that none other than the head of their agronomy department would also be speaking at the meeting.

The *Extension Service* was founded early in the twentieth century as an educational and generally supportive field service for farmers through the joint efforts of various state colleges of agriculture, local counties, and branches of the American Farm Bureau, which was founded in 1919 with an eye toward legislation favorable to farm interests, eventually becoming the largest farm organization. Of more recent vintage than the Grangers, the Farm Bureau similarly contributed much to promote cooperation and education in rural communities.

Eric still remembered the time, as a high school junior, he'd accompanied his father to this same Grange hall when, at the close of the meeting, the highly respected sixty-year-old extension agent, Ben Birchard, rose to give some concluding remarks- which would turn out to be his last words as an agent to the farm community he knew so well. After summarizing what the college professor speaking at that time had said and thanking him for his lecture to the local farmers, he had gone on to announce his retirement.

They knew they would feel his loss. He had been one of the pioneer agents- in fact, second in the whole state. There were groans all over the room, looks of consternation, and then, as he proceeded to tell anecdotes drawn from his years as a county agent, people had eased back in their seats and relaxed, with fond remembrances brought back to life from his long experience. At the conclusion, Mr. Birchard had asked if there were any questions. The last question addressed to him on that occasion had been that of Drew Auchinachie, Eric's father, as he rose and said, "Mr. Birchard, if you were to summarize what you've learned here about us farmers, what would it be?"

Eric could still see it in his mind's eye. Mr. Birchard had scratched his graying pate a moment, pursed his lips, then with a wan sort of smile on his wrinkled face he'd said, in that manly, deep and rasping voice of his, "I've loved my work with you people, and I've seen a lot of good things, and a lot of bad ones, too. I don't know any class of people more deserving than you farm folks..., more hard-working..., more caring of your families and churches..., your communities. Nor have I seen people more long-suffering..., or courageous, in spite of all kinds of tragedies and set-backs. You seem to be made of iron. But I know you're not. I've been there beside you when you have lost your homes, your farms, your cattle you've taken years to improve by breeding and culling, seen your kids show them at fairs and take ribbons out of the ring with them. Seen them grow up, and take over. Seen more leave the farm forever. Seen the old depart..., good friends all. I don't know what keeps you driving on.

"Now you probably don't want to hear this..., some of you, anyway. And I mean no offense. But I've come to the conclusion that a dairy farmer that hasn't decided to quit after a few years of farming has to be either an absolute idiot or a dedicated fool, and I know which of those two attributes it must be because I've never seen such dedication anywhere else in my life. And it has to come from nothing less than love for your work." With that, Birchard had looked down at the floor, lifted his face and spoke with solemn conviction, his words measured, coming slowly, "I honestly believe there is a reward for all of you waiting somewhere, though you may not see it here on earth. But I dread what I think I see coming for you here in the future, despite the fact it may look better for a few years, because there will be fewer and fewer of you, and many people demanding more and more from you, until even the best of you will turn away in despair."

Eric had been somewhat shocked. He'd had, like everyone else, the highest respect for Birchard and had always figured when he said something was so, you could pretty well bet on it. But, on this occasion, he'd thought the old man was having a bad day. Afterward, as they drove away together, his own dad- much to his surprise- agreed with Birchard. "No, son," he said, "he has it exactly right. It may be a hundred years yet, but I think the day will come when nobody will want to farm anymore. I have to admit to wondering, sometimes, if you ought to get into something else..., but I know you won't."

\- - - - - - - - - - - - - - -

The two young men had a little trouble finding seats in the back of that same Grange hall, about sixty others having already been seated. "Well," said Brian, as he and Eric took the last two seats together, in the next to last row, "That's great. I see Prof Brown sitting up front. I was sure hoping I'd get a chance to hear him sometime before sign-up time for his course. Glad you told me he'd be here, Eric."

Brian's voice instantly awakened Eric from his reverie of the past. "Yeah," he replied, "it's a good idea to learn all you can about a class before you sign on."

"Supposed to be the best in the agronomy department," said Brian.

Eric nodded in agreement. "I've never heard him lecture, of course- but he's one of the best, so I hear. Anyway, I want to pick the other guy's brain, if I can- that young fellow with the kinky hair sitting next to him. He's the economist. I think he'll be talking first."

"I thought, after you nearly flunked that economics course last year, you'd never want to try it again." said Brian. "You sure were mad about it."

"Well, I still think they bushwhacked me because I argued with them..., and then, of course, there was that term paper I worked so hard on. I just didn't agree with their 'get big, borrow big' philosophy, and I dared to say so. I still think it'll be the path to ruination for a lot of young farmers. Anyway, I think this fellow might be different. He went to school out in Wisconsin, where they really live and breathe the dairy industry."

"Well," said Brian," they have some pretty solid statistics at our school, too. It seems to work. I think they're just ahead of the other schools. Like they said, if you can borrow big, do it."

Eric frowned. "I know we won't agree on that. But just as sure as hell is waiting for sinners, they're suggesting, at best, a path that not everyone should take. Maybe some, but not all. That was my point. One size does not fit all, you know. I'm kind of curious if this young prof follows the same line of bull."

Brian raised his eyebrows, rolled his eyes as he turned his face away, shrugged, and simply said, "O.K. Let's talk about it later. You'll soon find out. He's getting out of his chair…, about to talk."

The first lecture went off real well. Eric was especially impressed with the young economist- a breath of fresh air for him, who was evidently much less enthralled with the credit machinery as a means of forging ahead to boundless riches. After all, as he pointed out, if prices drop off suddenly- as often happens- a big debt can kill a typical low-margin farm operation in short order. Eric noticed that while the prof from Wisconsin was speaking, Brian frequently shook his head, rubbing his nose in disagreement, but said nothing.

At the close of the second lecture, the older man, Prof. Brown, chairman of the agronomy department at the school, asked if there were any questions. At that, an up-and-coming young, progressive, sometimes cantankerous farmer named Mark Gordon raised his hand and was acknowledged. Right off, everyone that knew him suspected he had something up his sleeve- without knowing what. "You mentioned, Doctor," drolled Mark, "that birdsfoot trefoil would be ideal for some of our hill ground hereabouts, particularly where the soil is too shallow for alfalfa to root out real well."

"Yes, indeed," said the professor. "Our field trials at the university have convinced us that trefoil will be a real boon to farms- particularly on podzols like the lordstown and volusia soils you have here- poorly drained forest soils, but fairly fertile if limed well and drained with tile, as you undoubtedly know."

"Yes, I'm well aware of that," said Mark adroitly. "I assume, of course, that you've tested it in your field trials."

"Naturally. We've done extensive studies. Trefoil is a little slow getting started, but once it's established, it has excellent longevity, easily cured for hay, and it has comparable palatability to other legumes without any of the dangers, say..., like sweet clover. And preliminary studies make us think cattle are somewhat less likely to bloat on it, compared to alfalfa, but we aren't sure of that yet. Cows can certainly make milk on it..., high protein, and all that."

"O.K.," said Mark, in a drawn-out, almost impertinent tone of voice, as though challenging the professor, "But speaking of comparisons, what about ladino..., *ladino* clover?"

The professor stared at the young man blankly for a second, sensing a trap. There was something about Mark Gordon that was rubbing him the wrong way- he'd seen it before at other meetings, something in a man's stance, his expression, his eyes- as though about to challenge something he'd said. It was built into Mark's body language and tone of voice. Professor Brown's own expression changed rapidly from a mere frown of disbelief to one of sheer annoyance. He opened his mouth as though to say something, retreated from it, biting his lips unseen- then, shaking his head sadly as though confronting the hopeless ignorance of a buffoon, glared scornfully at the young man and said, "Ladino...? Well..., I guess that's all right if you want to milk rabbits!"

Snickers began popping off here and there in the assemblage. Then a series of giggles and subdued levity rippled through the room as the young man winced, almost cringing at first, his face reddening- which the crowd mistakenly took for tongue-tied embarrassment. As he sat there, wordless and motionless like an errant third grader admonished by his teacher in front of the class, the room exploded into cascading waves of raucous laughter.

At that, the young farmer turned absolutely livid and jumped to his feet. Addressing his antagonist, he snarled, "A few years ago you were standing right there where you are now, in this very building, and you were telling me..., and I mean *you*, not somebody else..., told *all* of us that we should grow ladino clover. It was going to be the greatest thing for us hill farmers we ever saw. I mean, like you birds at the university had suddenly unlocked some gateway that had been blocking us poor ignorant shmucks from a pot of gold all these years!

"I believed you. I grew ladino. A whole lot of it..., and so did a lot of guys around here. It was the damnedest stuff to mow I ever ran into..., one tangled mess fouling up in the knives right after another. And it was miserable stuff to dry, just as hard to cure and make into good palatable hay as mammoth red clover ever was. But whether you wanted to make hay out of it or put it in the silo, it made no real difference because it was a pain in the butt from start to finish. After four years of that, I plowed it all up. And, thanks to you, I'd seeded my whole farm with the blasted stuff.

"Nobody around here grows it anymore. Not if they've got any brains, at least. Now you're standing there and telling us about the latest marvel out of the university and expect us to believe it? Not me, buddy!" With that, he stalked out, leaving the thunderstruck professor speechless for the first time in his life, his face long and pallid. The crowd remained perfectly still. Not till the farmer slammed the outside door behind him did the inevitable buzzing begin.

The professor, thoroughly chagrined, excused himself from the room to recover, and with that, murmurs within the crowd swelled into ribald laughter, as the farmers realized there was now a juicy new tale to expand upon and spread around to an otherwise pretty tame farm community.

The meeting over, the boys left in the pick-up, stopping at Sean's clinic as they'd planned to do- just in time to see a man driving off in an obvious huff, wheels spinning and throwing mud. Sean was standing speechless at the roadside, a stunned look on his face, not unlike the professor's face an hour before. There had been an altercation. "What happened, Sean?" asked Eric.

"Don't want to talk about it," came Sean's blunt reply, as he stalked off to the clinic entrance, riled like a raging bull pawing the ground.

Eric knew enough not to bother his brother when he was having trouble. Nodding toward the house, he led Brian noiselessly into the kitchen where he had seen Nancy peering out the window through parted curtains only moments before. "What's the matter with Sean?" he whispered. "He's sure upset about something!"

"Tell me about it!" she replied, her voice low. "That was B.J.; I think you know him."

"You mean B.J. Pierce…, Sean's best good friend?" That was a form of speech that he and his brother both used, having found the farmer that invented it rather amusing.

"That's him. He just bawled Sean out. Laid him right out," said Nancy.

"Why? I mean…, what's going on? I thought…."

Nancy put her finger to her lip, commanding silence as her husband briefly popped out of the clinic and then disappeared back inside as though he'd forgotten something. Then she turned to Eric and Brian and answered, "They did like each other. *Did* is the operative word. As of now, I guess it's over. He thought Sean set him up."

It seemed that B.J. had made an appointment with the former county judge, as Sean had suggested, being as how he was the best lawyer in town. The judge, leaning back in his well-worn, swiveling arm-chair, feet on top of his desk and chewing a fat stogie, had listened patiently without a word as B.J. unloaded his grievances with his milk plant and the sanitation inspectors, citing collusion. After he'd unloaded every detail, the judge asked him if he had anything to add.

"No sir. That's it," said B.J., eagerly awaiting the judge's offer of help. "Dr. Auchinachie suggested I come here to see you about it."

"Well, young fellow," replied the judge, "I believe your vet has misled you. It happens that I'm the attorney for your creamery- the one you're squabbling with, that has been telling you over and over to clean up your place. Now you haven't lived around here long, but I'm telling you right now we don't take to trouble-makers like you in this county…, so now you can just turn around and march your puny ass right out of my office. Right now! And don't slam the door behind you!"

Shortly after that incident, Nancy had received a call from B.J., saying he was coming down if Sean was there- which he was- but she didn't yet know what was up. She had noticed he seemed a bit brusque. Later, she had overheard the conversation between the two men. In fact, the uproar was intolerable, as B.J. cursed Sean up and down, smoking mad, figuring he'd been set up with one of Sean's infrequent but infamous practical jokes, knowingly sending him to his adversary's attorney.

Sean's protests of innocence to B.J. were to no avail. After all, hadn't Sean told him he'd worked for that same milk plant for years? Didn't he know all the guys at the creamery, as well as its president- even on a first name basis? Then how could he deny that he knew the situation? "You bastard, you set me up!" he bellowed, as he got in his car, slammed the door shut and drove off.

The boys retired to Drew's farm, thinking they'd seen enough controversy for one day. And they did not return to their differences of opinion about farm finances.

On the Way Back

Eric had a little work to do on his pickup before he and Brian headed back to school the next morning. All of these things would be a lot easier to do while he was home on the farm, as well as less expensive. Everything he needed was in the farm shop, which not only had the necessary tools but had quite a lot of room- once the tractor parked there was moved outside- as well as a furnace. Though the shop could hardly be called warm, it was certainly better than crawling around outside in the cold and damp. In short order Eric and Brian had changed the tire with a bulge in the sidewall, adjusted the points, cleaned up the carburetor and poured some stop-leak in the radiator, which had recently been losing fluid. Then they greased the truck and changed the oil from the farm supplies.

Eric said good-bye to his mom and dad the next morning at the break of dawn, and the boys headed out, remembering at the last minute that they needed some gasoline- which they took from the farm pump near the shop. All in all, Eric had, as usual, saved himself a little bundle of money by doing his own work and using farm supplies while he was home, avoiding any mark-ups in the process.

Also stopping at Sean's clinic to retrieve a sweater he'd left there, and finding his brother showering in the bathroom after returning from another messy call, he chatted with Nancy and Jim just a bit before heading back to school- during which Penelope appeared, nicely dressed and ready for the school-bus, due to stop in short order. It was the first time Brian had an opportunity to meet Penny, though he'd seen her at the farm a few days before when Sean had come to see the downer. Beyond an introduction, they hardly had time to talk before they heard the bus coming down the road, so she excused herself, picked up her books and dashed outside, Brian was smiling, his eyes following her till she was out of sight.

"Nancy," he said, "what's Penny planning to do when she gets out of school?"

"Well, Brian," she said, "that seems to depend on when you ask her. Right now she's thinking of being a hairdresser. Next week it may be something else."

"When is she supposed to graduate?"

"She's a senior next year."

"She looks pretty bright, to me. How's she doing in school?"

"She always gets good grades when she wants to. As long as it isn't math, she does quite well. She's very good in English and Spanish. Not bad in science, either. Sean and I hope she'll come around after awhile and decide on the teaching college over in Mansfield, or some place like that. I think she'd be a good English teacher..., and we need some good ones around here..., in case you haven't noticed. Of course, right now, she's quite taken with the boys."

Eric had been looking at the kitchen clock. "Well," he said, "I guess we can't wait for Sean to show up, Brian," he said, "Nancy, will you tell him we stopped, and we may send down those two vet students that we know, sometime, like we were talking to him about. I know they'd like to ride along with him on some of his calls."

Nancy smiled. "I'll tell him. We'll see you in a few weeks, then. And it was nice to meet you, Brian," she said, as she shook his hand. "I wish you could have stayed longer. Didn't see much of you. But I know how it is. And take care, will you?"

In a few minutes, Eric and Brian were back on the road to the university. They rode along without saying a word- for half an hour, perhaps- each lost in his own thoughts. Finally, Brian broke the silence. "She's sure a beautiful girl."

"Huh?" came the reply. "What did you say?"

Penny. She's real pretty, isn't she?"

"I don't know. I guess so. Never thought about it."

Brian said no more.

Seeing Red

Had anyone seen him, Sean would have looked like he was scrounging through the garage shelves for hidden treasure when Jim entered the garage that morning. Without bothering to turn his head since he knew perfectly well who it was by the sound of his footsteps, he called out, "Before you go down cellar, Jim, do you know where we put the extra Sulfanilamide? Ferguson wanted some last night, and I gave him all I could find. I thought we had more of it…, just can't remember where it is."

Jim took his hand off the doorknob of the cellar door and shuffled over to the other side of the garage, pointing to the top shelf. "Did you look over here, Doc? Should be some up here somewhere. At least I saw a tub of it there about six months ago."

Sean went over to see. "Maybe," he said, "just maybe there's some there- I didn't think of that."

Jim backed away. "Maybe you can reach it, Doc, but I can't do it without the stepladder."

"Where's that?"

"Down cellar, I think. I used it to find something a couple of weeks ago."

Sean reached up to the top shelf, moved some bottles over, stood on his tiptoes and reached behind them. After groping for a minute or so, he gave up. "I'll bet I forgot to order some more. Rats! I thought I had another twenty pounds of powder around here somewhere." He walked over to the back of the garage. "Jim, would you check down cellar again. I checked it earlier, but couldn't find any."

"Ain't goin' to be any there, either. I'm sure of that."

"When did you look?"

"Don't matter. Ain't none there, like I said."

Sean's eyes quickly flared, his voice sounding a little testy. "Why in blazes didn't you tell me we were out then?"

"Weren't out till last night. You were the last one to hand it out."

Sean shut up, incoherently grumbling to himself as he went down in the basement. There were wooden shelves all over the place, loaded with boxes and bottles up to a gallon in size, a work bench covered with a piece of cardboard- bearing multiple stains from haphazardly spilled medical fluids- and a battered baby scale hanging from a floor joist overhead to weigh out various compounds. Over in one corner was a small gas range bearing an open boiler flat, its sheet metal well scorched from a wood fire during its former use to boil down maple syrup, which Sean now used to sterilize calcium gluconate and dextrose solutions poured into reclaimed glass pints and quarts that once held vinegar.

Sean had long been his own pharmacist, compounding a few simply made drugs strictly for farm use, having found them much more economical, despite some extra labor, and seemingly no less effective than commercial preparations. He gladly passed on most of these savings to his farm clientele. Even his sulfanilamide powder was purchased in bulk, having become so cheap and available after the war that he could sell a pound jar of it for a dollar or, on occasion, even give it away without real loss. And there was an unexpected spin-off for his practice. Knowing Sean had their need for thrift in mind, farmers were more apt to call before their sick cow had become a lost cause. As a result, their recovery rate was better, enhancing Sean's reputation no end.

Intense frugality has long been an indispensable necessity for most farm operations to survive- their margin of profit historically compromised by a one-sided pricing system, caused by their own self-defeating independence and reluctance to cooperate with each other. The latter, of course, has historically resulted in their having only a feeble bargaining power in the market-place- unlike industries in general.

The issue was finally settled. There was no sulfa powder. Not an ounce. Nancy phoned Merck and confirmed that 500 pounds were on the way, and Sean located three bottles of sterile azosulfamide that he could use as a substitute, if needed, though it would be given intravenously rather than orally. He handed them to Jim, who put them in the Jeep. In another ten minutes they were barreling down the road again to their first call at Morris Kane's farm.

Morris was one of the increasing numbers of farmers who had lost fingers somehow, in his case by trying to yank a plug of weeds out of a chopper in motion despite precautionary signs on the machinery. Instead of half his body being sent up the silo pipe in pieces he had lost four fingers, leaving the stubs of a thumb and an index finger from his right hand. After that, he was always warning other farmers, especially the younger ones, about "them blowers…, they's awful hungry for a guy's fingers…, ya know what I mean?" Of course, Morris was noted neither for his erudition nor his public elocution.

No, Morris was noted for something quite different. Despite his handicap, he had compensated rather well, unlike many such victims, even learning to tie a bowline handily by holding the standing strand in his teeth. And he had likewise learned to manipulate some small tools between the remains of his thumb and index finger. But there was something far more notable about Morris, a singular attribute; Despite several other misfortunes, any one of which could have broken a lesser man, he remained remarkably cheerful, courageous, absolutely unflappable. The fate of his oldest son, only fifteen at the time- when the tractor he was driving flipped over and rolled down a hillside taking him to a grisly death- probably could have crushed his father, as it commonly did other farmers, with perpetual guilt and sorrow.

But after that, some of those who thought they had known Morris pretty well were saying that only a fool could remain so cheerful. Others, knowing a bit more about him during those dark days, thought him to be a splendid churchman, *his* earlier, deep convictions of faith prevailing grandly over his own miseries. Those who knew him best believed somewhat the opposite, that the subsequent example of *others* - oftentimes through inconvenient or costly, yet seemingly insignificant deeds and expressions of love- had transformed a good-natured man, once self-centered, into a well-spring of charity. But then, that all this may be a matter of the chicken and the egg, just as it is often difficult to tell a saint from a utter fool.

Morris was not home when Sean and Jim arrived to look at his sick cow, all white except the tips of her ears, which were black, a Holstein of sorts. Instead, as was the custom with many farmers, Morris had left Dr. Sean a note near her- in this case tied with a string onto the water pipe above her stanchion. Jim grabbed it, tried to read it, then handed it to Sean. "Can't read it," he said. "I wrote better than that in first grade."

The note was on scrap paper, in hard-point pencil, and barely discernible thanks to moisture from the water pipe having smudged some ink from the opposite side. "Just says 'the cow don't eat'," muttered Sean.

"That's all?" said Jim.

"That's all. Cow don't eat."

"Don't eat?"

Sean grinned. "Don't eat…! That's it, Jim! Get some urine from her, if you can. Looks to be fresh." Sean stepped up beside the cow and started checking her over with a stethoscope while Jim placed a thermometer in her rectum and rubbed her escutcheon to draw urine- if she'd cooperate.

She did, and Jim checked it for albumin and ketones as Sean moved from the cow's thorax to her rumen- or so-called "paunch"- to see if there was stomach activity. This done, he slipped on a shoulder length obstetrical sleeve, handed her tail to Jim, who held it from the opposite side curled over her back as the doctor checked her internally. "She didn't clean," said Sean. Pretty soon, he had released the last of the cotyledons and the placenta fell into the drop, all ten pounds of it- kersplat. "Must have calved a couple of days ago…, maybe even three," he added. "What's her temp?"

"One-o-three on the nose, Doc. And her urine's O.K."

"No ketosis?"

"Nope."

"How's her bag?"

"Looks O.K. to me."

"I didn't see you check it."

"I did."

"No flakes or anything?'

"Clean as a whistle."

"Good." Sean was satisfied. "Metritis. Where's the calf? Have you seen it?"

"Think so. There was one over in the corner where we walked in."

"So dark in here I don't know how you could see it. Go turn the lights on. Should have done it in the first place."

"No lights. I flicked the switch when we came in. Couldn't find any other."

"Can barely can see in here. Oh well," said Sean, "go get that Neoprontosil. Never used the derned stuff in my life. It's an old sulfa. Bottle been sitting around forever. Ought to work anyway. Pretty stable stuff. Sure would help if you knew a little more about the stability though. Maybe someday they'll print it on the label. You might know- now that we're out of sulfa powder- we'd need it right off the bat."

A few minutes later, the two men were speeding on to the next call, having run half a bottle of Neoprontosil in the cow's jugular vein and leaving a scribbled note behind the cow with instructions on a milkstool where Morris would see it. Sean would send the bill later.

About six o'clock that night and back home, Sean answered the phone. It was Morris. "Doc, you better hurry out here. The cow is a lot worse."

"Worse? I can't believe it."

"How come you didn't come to see her? I called around seven this morning. Now she's a lot worse. Never saw anything like it!" He was excited, Sean could tell.

"I was there. Didn't you see my note?'

"Your note? You mean you were here?"

"Sure I was there with Jim before nine o'clock. Read your note and treated her."

"Well, I didn't see any note."

"Left it on a milking stool behind the cow."

"You did? Ain't no note on a stool."

"The stool. Left it on a stool behind the cow."

"Oh, the stool. Yeah, There's was a stool there. Didn't see no note on it."

"I told Jim to leave it on the stool. Didn't he do it?"

The phone was beginning to crackle. Thunderstorm, most likely on the way. "Didn't see no note there. Did you see my note?"

"Sure. I read your note."

"Where'd you find it?"

Sean sensed some suspicion on Morris's part that he wasn't even there. "Up on the pipe over the cow."

"Oh...." Pause. "Must've been here then, I guess." Morris still sounded doubtful. "What'd it say?"

Sean was getting a bit impatient. "Look, Morris. I was there. I treated your cow. How's she act now?"

"I think she's dying."

"I know. But how's she act?"

"What do you mean. I said she looks like she's going to die. Get right out here. I don't know what to do for her."

"Is she down?"

"Down with what?"

"Can she stand up and walk?"

"Sure. She's can walk and all that."

"Breathing hard?" There was more crackle on the phone, real bad this time.

"No. Look, Doc, just come out and look at her."

Sean gave up. Half an hour later he was back at the farm. Morris came out of the barn. "I let her out in the barnyard, Doc. It's funny, she eats and everything. Walks around."

Sean grabbed his medicine box out of the Jeep and headed for the barnyard as Morris led the way. "Walks around, eh?" He had been busily scratching his head trying to figure what kind of trouble the cow might be having. It just had to be a reaction of some kind. She had certainly looked like a routine low-grade uterine infection that morning. Nothing life-threatening. What else could it be?

They went around the corner of the stable to the barnyard. Morris pointed at the cow. One look at the cow, and Sean's mouth dropped open, his expression went blank. "See, Doc, just look at her," said Morris, "Everywhere you look. Must be something real bad. Must be *real* bad. Ever see anything like it before?"

Sean couldn't help it. He started laughing and couldn't stop, while Morris watched him in puzzlement. "Nope..., never have," he said. Finally, after he'd settled down, he tried to explain what had happened. It wasn't easy, but when he finally got through to Morris, they were both laughing. There was nothing wrong with the cow, who stood there contentedly chewing her cud, but Sean showed Morris the half bottle of Neoprontosil left from the morning, and then explained how the drug he'd given had done something impossible to see that morning. The barn had been too dark.

The next day, Sean gave Jim a half-hearted scolding for forgetting to put a stone on the note that he'd left on the milking stool. A little breeze from the stable doorway had evidently blown it up in the manger where Morris couldn't see it. Then he told him about the cow, and how, had she been a black cow instead of white, the color change might have been inapparent. Then they had a good laugh over the pink cow; a *pink* cow as beautiful and livid pink as a fresh garden rose, picked for the prom. The same color as the Neoprontosil.

Worse 'n Ursine

Nancy peered at one of the two kitchen wall clocks, the one that had been handed down from her grandmother. It was one of those sturdy, green or yellow, round-faced G.E. electric clocks, not beautiful but functional- so durable that it outlasted the family. She noted that, barring a late call, her husband- Dr. Sean, as he was often called by his clients- should be home from his farm calls around six o'clock, not remarkable for August.

As usual, the telephone had been keeping Nancy busy though she had, for the last hour, been permitted just enough respite to sit down peacefully at the kitchen table with a much-needed cup of coffee to read, at long last, the editorial page of the morning paper, wherein the editor-in-chief was proclaiming that if his stalwart hero, Tom Dewey, had been elected back in 1948 instead of that rascal from Missouri now sitting in the White House, the Korean War never would have happened. That would delight Nancy's husband, being as how he was a veteran of the earlier war in Europe and more than a little unhappy about President Truman's "commie cohorts" in Washington. For just a moment, she thought of tossing the cussed rag out so she wouldn't have to listen to him blowing about it that evening when he got home.

Her husband had an unusually strong practice. Depending on the time of year, Nancy could expect to receive about fifteen farm calls a day, most dairymen calling in during morning milking-time, with a few stragglers through the rest of the day. A smaller surge might develop in the late afternoon, when a vet might be needed for a handful of (supposedly) deathly sick cows- usually having been missed earlier in the day either by oversight or plain old negligence.

Though it was the truth, few of his professional colleagues believed Sean could possibly carry so many calls and do a good job. Claiming only half the number of calls themselves, some of them sneered when they heard such things about him, though Sean was careful to say nothing that could be construed as tooting his own horn. In the winter, it was not unusual for him to service twenty farm calls or, on very rare occasions, even twenty-five, though that could easily mean some eighteen hours a day on the road.

Jim Holland was the main reason Sean could handle such a load. Far from making the doctor seem like some sort of a plutocrat, as some others took it, Jim H. added efficiency on calls that made the other vets look like amateurs, even allowing service to be less expensive for the client. As a team, Sean and Jim combined a speed and proficiency that earned them the respect of farmers who, themselves being overloaded, certainly appreciated the fact that little would be required of them except to point out the cow and answer a few quick questions. Then they could get on with their other work. For them, every sick cow was an impediment to their routine. Sometimes they could even leave Sean a note and then disappear to other parts, when absolutely necessary. It is axiomatic that most successful farmers are drivers. No time is wasted, and still they can't always keep up.

There were innumerable ways that Jim saved the doctor time, knowing where everything was in the Jeep, clinic or the garage at home, knowing what he needed, how he did things, how to restrain an animal quickly yet gently, roping and casting them, haltering them, tail-pressing to discourage kicks when Sean was bent over examining a teat injury, and on and on. On those days when he was not committed elsewhere- such as at Drew's farm- Jim came to work early, loaded the Jeep while the doctor was eating breakfast, and was ready to roll out by 7:30 without fail. If there was an off-hours emergency, the doctor could count on his help, at least if he could catch Jim at home in the vacant school-house he'd recently acquired.

There was scarcely a thing Jim hadn't learned about vet medicine after a year or two with Sean. Not large, but wiry and strong as an ox, he was not considered to be a slam-bang "cowboy" by most farmers (though he could be that with beefers, if necessary) but rather, a true "*cow man*" whom a dairyman could trust to handle his bovine ladies gently, as they deserved. Being alert, he seemed to know exactly what needed to be done and was the indispensable expediter for a busy vet. And when he drove for Sean, it was for the main purpose of saving time for the doctor to make out his bills, since it was best to do so while work done was fresh in the mind; or to read a journal- while he was fresh; or should he be tired, to doze for a bit and thus last through a longer workday. They seldom stopped to eat, each carrying a lunch that could be downed while buzzing along the road. Jeeps of that vintage were explicitly not to be driven over forty m.p.h. To do so could throw a rod. Under Jim's foot, they could routinely make fifty or sixty miles per hour. The high pitched whine of the little four-cylinder beasty at that speed helped the farmer to know that "doc was on the way and in a hurry," and that he had little time to waste jawing.

Of course, all this says little about those erratic emergency calls which Nancy intercepted at any time of day or night, particularly during the two heavy calving seasons- fall and spring- nor does it speak of the daily run-of-the-mill calls for sick pets, or gratuitous advice given regarding little Patrick, the portly Pom- or Freddie the frothing feline.

Sean's farm work this summer, as expected, was a bit slow, giving his family a welcome chance to relax. Compensating somewhat for that, pet work peaked in the summer, pets being outdoors where they often get into trouble. On the contrary, when a herd of cattle was running free on pasture, as they did in the summer, it was generally at its best, health-wise. That also gave farmers more time to do their field work.

Now that it was August, calving-related cases, which peaked through the end of October, were beginning to multiply. Such parturitions were sure harbingers of the long winter months ahead when, it always seemed, Nancy would scarcely see her husband from dusky dawn to the dark of night.

Nancy had been raised on a farm. She had helped her father and brothers with the barn chores many times, as well as with the field work, so she knew what it was like having a dairy herd confined throughout the long and cold, tiresome winter dampness of the northeast, save for an hour or two each morning when the stable was cleaned. March, as a result, was the time to expect a plethora of ailments both in the barn and in the domicile. She recalled how often her ever-stoic, hard-working father- poor as he was- had said to her mother during a gloomy March, "As long as the ailments stay in the barn and out of the house, we can be thankful."

The month of May, on the contrary, begins the restoration of health in the north, marked by the day when herdsmen pause from their fieldwork long enough to watch the annual bovine "school is out" celebration. It is one of those simple pleasures that enrich the lives of farm families- when the barn door is rolled open, cows released from stanchions, barnyard gates swing wide and- "free at last" from the stable- the great beasts race en masse into lush green meadows dotted with dandelion blossoms- a swarm of ungainly behemoths kicking their heels in reckless abandon, tails high, whipping their switches in wild delight.

- - - - - - - - - - - - - - - -

Nancy jumped, startled by the telephone located close by on a small stand near the kitchen door. She answered it, took the call, wrote it down in the call book, sighed and studied the other calls to see where her husband would most likely be. She traced out the numbers she had written in front of each call reflecting her husband's planned line-up, which she had updated each time he called in, and dialed the likeliest farm. Inter-com radios were only a far-off dream for most businesses, and even then, much too expensive and unreliable in such hill country. At that time, telephones were the only practical means of communication for a country practice like Sean's.

The housewife answered on the third ring. Nancy could hear a radio in the background. Sean had left there about half an hour before. That left the Griswold farm- where they had a lame cow or two- as the farm likely to be next on her husband's line-up. Someone in the Griswold barn answered on the first ring. She had hit the nail on the head. Her husband was there, they said, standing only thirty feet away.

Shortly, her husband was on the line. Abruptly, he snarled "Whazzup?" He sounded tired, annoyed, more than tired.... Beat!

"Sorry, honey..., got another call."

"Wherezat?" he growled.

"Hennip called. He has a cow that cast her wethers."

"Yi! Which Hennip?"

"Carl."

"Carl? Carl Hennip? He never calls me. Where's his party-boy?"

"Dr. Larson? Can't find him, I guess. Nobody answers his phone, so he says. And Hennip says you've been there before. And you'll like this..., said he tried three other vets and finally figured he had to get *somebody.*"

"Sounds like Hennip!" snorted her husband, plainly disgusted. "And it's the same old story with that vet." Nancy heard a drawn-out sigh. "Great jumpin' geewhilligers! I was just headed the other way to the Newman's. Then I would've headed home. Rats!" Another sigh, then at last he seemed resigned. "Cast wethers, you say?"

Nancy realized that her husband was presently within a few miles of home, and that this call would put him about fifteen miles further out. Surely, he was exhausted, and wethers required a lot of muscle, as a rule. She decided to try a little southern-type levity. "Yup. Dat's what he say, honey chile. The-at's what the man saa-id, you heard what the man saa-id, the man said that!" Then she giggled. "Ain't you just perr-oud as a shiny na-ew navy button that Mas-ter Hennip called all the good va-its first, then thought mia-be he'd be kind and give you-all a helpin' hayand, too, 'cause you sure-ly do need *some* bus-ness now and the-in. Ain't you just as honored as a hound dog with a mi-outhful of br-er rabbit?" During the war, Nancy had lived in the deep south long enough to do a convincing, lilting drawl with split vowels, a facsimile able to fake out a southern cracker like a dinner of breaded fried catfish.

Sean laughed. "You're looney! How long've they been out? The wethers, I mean."

Now she sounded like a yankee again. "He said it couldn't have been too long. Maybe an hour. You know how he is when it comes to plain talk. But it sounds like the uterus is hanging out of her..., about two feet, and that she's a little wobbly. Straining a lot, but not bleeding too bad, I guess. Had her calf this morning."

"Probably milk fever, too. I'll head right over there. I'll be late getting in, Nancy."

"I know. I'm sorry, honey. When do you think?"

"Oh..., I'm not sure. If she's still standing when I get there, it might not take quite so long. But, with the backtracking to where I would have been going, it'll be at least two hours. Probably three.... Yeah, better figure on three. What's on for supper?"

"It's just the usual goulash. If I'm in bed when you get back, just heat it up. I'll leave it on the stove. But maybe you and Jimmy better stop and eat somewhere else. You'll need to eat something before then. Jimmy doesn't even bring his lunch with him, does he?"

"I think he did. Not sure. Didn't really notice. Well, anyway, we might just do that. We can stop in at Bob's Place and grab a bite there. I think he'll be open. We'll see. Leave the goulash out anyway. I'll put it in the fridge when I get back, whether Jimmy and I eat it or not. It'll still be good tomorrow, I'm sure. And call me if anything else pops up."

"Of course," said Nancy. "By the way, there's some nut trying.... Wants you to call him tonight when you get back. I wouldn't worry about it tonight, if you're that busy. I put his name on the book, with a phone number. But I really wouldn't worry about it. It's not urgent or anything."

"Who is he? What'd he want?"

"Somebody new, over at the fairgrounds. He has something to do with the fair. Or so he says. I'm not sure but what he's a joker..., sort of like the kids that called that time wondering if you would treat their sick giraffe with the tonsillitis."

"O.K., Nancy. But what did he want?"

Nancy snickered. "You won't believe this. He wants to know if you'll castrate a bear for him."

"A bear! A bear? You must be kidding!"

"Nope. The-at's what the mi-an said, the mi-an said the-at.... A bi-ar!"

No Bull

Nancy met Sean at the door as he returned disheveled from his calls late that fateful August night. "I was worried about you, honey, I heard about it on the radio, and I was afraid it was you! They said a man had been killed by a bull over at the fairgrounds." Nancy had been trying to call the sheriff and hadn't been able to get through. "I knew you were going there. The line was busy almost every time I called. I'm sorry if I panicked."

"I know, Nan, but you didn't need to call the sheriff. You got them all shook up, and they were already up to their ears." He took her in his arms and hugged her close, trying to soothe her nerves. That was one thing about her that he guessed she'd never get over. She was too easily alarmed. "I don't blame you, Nan. To tell you the truth, Jim and I were pretty shook up, too. We were standing just outside the show barn when it happened."

Nancy was still shook up. "The radio said some man was handling a bull, and it got loose and beat up three men and then pinned one of them to the ground. Is that right?"

"I guess that's about right. More or less, anyway. That part of it was over so quick nobody could believe it. Some of them were looking somewhere else for a second, looked back and it was already over for the handler. I didn't see it, myself. Like I said, I was just outside the barn. Luke Belcher told me about it afterwards…, he was right there near the ring when it started…, saw the whole thing. I guess he saved one of the men." Sean choked up a bit as he tried to finish. Eventually he cleared his throat and explained, "They were bringing the aged bulls into the show ring, and I guess there were four of them. They were lining them up in the usual circle for the judge, when one bull went after another and broke away from its handler.

"The two of them started banging away at each other, completely out of control, and their handlers ran out of the ring. The lad that was holding the biggest bull apparently didn't see what was going on in time- guess his back was turned. He had his bull firmly in hand on a long staff, hooked- like always- to his nose-ring, at least that's what I'm told…. You know- a big old monster, close to a ton and a half…. Maybe an eight year old. Jake told me the whole story- young fellow was on his toes, alert..., had a good solid hold on the staff.... probably he was six or seven feet in front of the bull when it started. Normally you would have thought he was pretty safe. Belcher said the handler never took his eyes off the bull or made any dumb mistakes like that. And he was all muscle, besides. He was no amateur or neophyte. Knew what he was doing.

"In all the excitement created by the other bulls, the old one jerked its head up in the air so high and so quick- its nose about eight feet up in the air- that his handler was yanked off his feet and fell under the bull's dewlap. Then it swung its head down and hammered him as he was scrambling away. That flattened him. Then it was on top of him in an instant, crushing the poor guy's chest with his head- right in front of the grandstand- where everybody..., the cattle judge..., his kids, his wife- could see it.... All over before anyone could blink." Sean swallowed hard, his eyes moist, breathing hard.

"I tell you, it was all over in a wink. Nothing you could do. You just couldn't believe it. Must have been sixty people there. A dozen or so cattlemen jumped down from the seats into the ring to save him, trying to drive the bulls off, and then the same bull knocked two of those men down. I think one guy even got a broken pelvis. The other guy had a shoulder dislocated. What an ungodly mess! Even pitchforks meant nothing to those bulls. And there wasn't a gun on the grounds!

"While the man was down there was a four-way free-for-all among the bulls. Men were scrambling away, others trying to distract the bulls, some of them rescuing the injured men. A couple of the bulls fell down, got up and started hammering each other again, until, luckily, somebody thought to bring in the old fire truck they keep on the grounds while the fair is on, got out a high pressure hose and drove them apart by blasting their faces. Cattle don't like that. Some other guys brought in a couple of tractors and chased them out of the ring into some corrals while others were trying to help the three injured men."

By now, Sean was finding it impossible to talk, perspiring, bleary-eyed, trying to keep his composure. "That poor guy!" he croaked, "Everybody was trying to find a doctor, and I guess I was the closest thing to it, so they grabbed me..., but there was nothing anybody could do. He just looked at me, his face gray, trying to breathe- couldn't say a word..., you could see in a glance his ribs were all broke… he knew he was dying- what a terrible look on his face, I'll never forget it- and then he stiffened, rolled his eyes back and died right in front of me, right in my arms." At that, his voice weakening, fading away, Sean could hardly draw a breath for himself. "The poor kid couldn't have been more than twenty-five or so," he sighed, diverting his face from Nancy as he throttled a sob.

Nancy shuddered, fixing her eyes on Sean till their eyes met once again. Softly, stroking his forehead, she said, "That's terrible, Sean. Who was he. Did you know him?"

Sean stalled for a spell, still choked up, before going on. "No, thank God. He came down here from up north about sixty or seventy miles. Married, had three little kids. Worked for the man who owned the bull, I guess. The worst thing is that the poor fellow had done everything right. Nobody ever heard of a bull doing that when he was on a staff. The stick he was using looked to be at least four or five feet long- and he had hooked it to the bull's nose ring just like everybody else does, kept the critter's nose up high and stood real solid a good way from him. Nobody ever thought a bull could lift a rugged man like that right off his feet. Must be his nose wasn't as tender as everybody expected. And probably this particular brute was just too tall."

Nancy broke away. "Honey, you're too upset to eat, and so am I. Go in the living room and sit down and I'll get you some coffee. How's Jim? Did he see it?"

"He was outside the arena with me when it happened. He's in a daze. We all are. I sent him home just as soon as we got back."

Nancy shook her head. "Nobody should ever take a bull to a fair, whether on a shaft or not. I was always scared of our bulls when I was a girl. Mother made Dad get rid of the last one we had- said she would never allow a bull on a farm again, since they came up with artificial breeding. The last one almost got my brother, you know. And that bull was only a three year old- wasn't like he was one those crotchety old things that paw the ground and beller all the time, glaring at you."

"Usually they're pretty docile when they're as young as that," said Sean as he wandered rather aimlessly into the living room and sat down, after turning on the light by his armchair. "I just never believed an animal so big can be so quick…, or so changeable. A bull can be as gentle as a cow, get the evil eye and then turn right around and nail you with no warning at all." He waved off some crackers that Nancy brought him with the coffee. He knew he would be sick if he ate, so he didn't even try. Not until two A.M. did they go to bed, where, though completely exhausted, he slept fitfully till dawn was nigh.

Sean was more at ease when he woke up. Although bleary eyed, tired looking and a bit reticent to talk, he seemed able to give Nancy a wan smile when she came into the bedroom with his breakfast on a tray- for the first time in years. "I put off a couple of calls till tomorrow," she said. "It's O.K. They were nice about it when I told them what happened. And, so far, there's no emergencies."

He protested mildly. "You didn't have to do this," he said, "I'm all right now."

Nancy insisted that he eat. She sat down on her own bed, leaned back on an elbow, lounging and watching him, just to be sure he really did so, then said, "I didn't think to ask you about the bear. You wouldn't even have been at the fair.... You didn't do it, did you?"

"Yes, I did, certainly! Believe it or not."

She sat bolt upright. "You didn't!"

"Sure I did," he said, his lips twisted into a wry grin. "Just before the... nightmare."

"I don't believe you! You castrated a bear?"

Sean winked. "Ask Jim when you see him. He lies even better than I do."

"Why in the world did you do that? Are you crazy?"

"For the money, what do you think?"

Nan was almost indignant. "Here we were last night talking about bulls and you're messing around with a bear? Do you want to die?"

"Naw," said Sean dryly, "it wasn't like that. He was a little fellow- black bear- only weighed about ninety pounds. It was a piece of cake. Just borrowed four good men to roll him over and hold him down on the grass- found a place where nobody'd be nosing around- gave him a local and castrated him. No fuss. He even yawned while I was cutting him. Amiable little fellow. Hell, Nancy, he's a *tame* bear. The owner, the guy that called us raised the cub himself; the little gink stood up like nothing happened afterward and licked my hand like he was an oversize shepherd dog."

"Why in the world...?"

"Why'd he want to have him castrated?"

She studied his face. After all, he might be putting her on. “Yeah. Why?”

“Well, it’s really pretty simple. The guy that owns him is really badly disabled. He has two trained bears, a sow and a boar. Makes his living taking them around to shows and fairs to do a bunch of different acts. Quite an interesting man, really. Been doing it for several years. The sow had the cub this spring and now he keeps messing up on stage.”

“How’s that?”

“Well…, when the sow comes in heat, he….”

“Nancy laughed. Stop right there. I get it. She laughed again, her eyes sparkling in amusement. “Just like a dirty old man!”

“Just like me, you mean?” said Sean, with mischief in his eye.

Nancy got up and fled the room, racing downstairs. “You said it, I didn’t!”

Dew On the Meadows

It was especially early in the morning when Sean got out of bed and went downstairs. He stood by the kitchen phone lining up some of his regular route on the daybook for Nancy's benefit while swilling a quick cup of coffee. That done, he ducked out the back door carrying the lunch that she, still abed, had left for him the night before. He would have to eat breakfast on the road. Looking for Jim as soon as he stepped into the garage and noting that he had arrived on schedule and was well into the habitual process of loading up everything that would be needed for the day, he checked on a few critical items his sidekick didn't know about. Jim appeared to be about to close up the back of the Jeep, double-checking one last time to see if he'd missed anything before hooking up the tail gate and closing the door to the metal-covered plywood cab above it, a convenience that had been built by a local handyman especially for Sean's needs.

Other than being a poor reader, thus never finishing high school, Jim was bright and inventive- having learned such a diversity of skills on the several farms where he had worked that there was scarcely a thing he couldn't do. When on a new job he quickly learned not to make certain mistakes, as he did during his first day or two with Dr. Sean. Unlike some other employers, in Sean's practice there was no excuse for being half-prepared: for instance, arriving at a farm, wasting time trying to find something that shouldn't have been missing from the Jeep in the first place, and then- so to speak, with a tail between your legs- having to return to the clinic to recover it so that call could be completed.

Satisfied, he closed up the Jeep's hard-top cab and opened the garage door. Sean grunted, nodding a "good morning" as he eased into the passenger seat and slammed the door shut while Jim jumped into the driver's seat. The Jeep, not new at all, but still a reliable, tough little beast- streaked with mud spatters and dented in spots- started with a noisy roar, tailpipe rattling faintly. "Meant to fix that, Doc," said Jim. "But I'll get it tonight for sure. Never seem to think of it at night when we get back. Where we headed this morning?" he asked, as he twisted around and leaned out his door, peering at the driveway as he backed the Jeep out to the road.

"I'm not sure yet," came Sean's business-like reply. While he had marked out the route for his regular "return-calls" for Nancy, he hadn't decided yet which of the creamery inspections would be first. "Head for Middletown," instructed Sean, "I'll tell you just where..., in a minute..., soon as I look," while pulling a small chart out of a breast pocket of his coveralls, unfolding it and studying it briefly, confirming that there were six herds to check today for the health department, and that all of them were within a three mile radius. Not bad at all. That should speed things up. Being almost instinctively time-conscious when running his calls- seldom even carrying a watch- it was not unusual that Sean could arrive at a farm at a fairly predictable time, as long as he remembered certain calls could well involve a "while you're here, Doc" just as you were packing up to leave.

One time, while Jim had been tearing along in one of Sean's earlier vehicles, a wheel had broken off the right rear axle. The brakes went out, the chassis began dragging and whipping around, making steering almost impossible, and they had finally ended up off the road in a barnyard, barely missing an oncoming truck and a large oak tree in the process- with Jim in a sweat, and Sean's cigar dangling from his lips, bitten almost in half. The farmer, who knew them both, came to their rescue, helped them out, showed them his phone so they could make a call for help, and then said those inevitable, infamous words that send shudders up and down the spine of the most fearless practitioners, "While you're here, Doc...," then continuing with, "I've got a couple of lame cows."

Some of the six particular herds scheduled for inspection were small enough that they could be done quickly- almost a matter of in and out. The biggest one today was currently milking forty cows, typical for the area in that day, despite the fact it was actually an awkward size, labor-wise, and probably not very efficient if a hired man was employed.

By contrast, the largest herd in Sean's practice, Freeman Farm, currently housed seventy or eighty cows. It was a low-debt farm, largely because the mortgage had been paid off by the preceding first generation. Presently, on Sean's suggestion, they were in the process of adding a section to their old barn to make room for another twenty or thirty cows. That would be, indeed, a very large dairy for that time and place, and since it had always been progressive and up-to-date, there was no reason not to make good money instead of hanging on by their teeth as so many others did.

Freeman Farm had theorized some time past that, regardless of perpetual inequities in the federal controls that effectively denied the common dairyman any direct control over the price of his raw milk, delivered at the plant, there would always be a few smart, open-eyed farmers that did pretty well through relentless hard work, while maintaining both liquidity (through reasonable debt loads) and maximum labor efficiency- which they figured meant providing one full-time laborer for every additional *"step"* of 23-26 cows that was added to a conventionally housed herd, "fractions" not allowed. Sean had noticed how well their theories worked everywhere they had been applied, even unknowingly- no more poverty and sometimes even a degree of ease and comfort. He had also noticed that dairies "out of *step*" were often in trouble without knowing why.

It was another bright, droughty September morn, dew on the meadows glistening beneath a sun barely hovering above the horizon, as the Jeep tore down the road on the way to Sean's first call, with Jim at the helm. Sean expected, from long experience, that some of the dairymen on today's creamery's list would forget they had been scheduled for inspection, even though they'd been notified the previous day by a tag attached at the creamery to one of the farm's milk cans. And they would, as usual, be itching to turn their cows back out onto the pasture as soon as milking was done, to reduce the effects of C.B.P.S. (chronic bovine polypoopsia syndrome).

There was good reason for some impatience on the part of farmers. Each September, right during their corn-harvesting season, was precisely when the milk plant decided physical exams were due. Unfortunately, in the northeast, there was a tendency for the fields to be too muddy for any kind of tractor or corn harvester- *especially* in September. Unpredictable seasonal showers had to be worked around, sometimes interfering with the harvest for several days. And since even an hour's morning delay during that season could mean further delays just to clean up a stable afflicted with A.C.B.P.S., (Accentuated C.B.P.S.), the farmers did not appreciate the vet's late arrival- not even one bit. Furthermore, the animals' rear quarters frequently exhibited A.C.B.P.S. when they returned to the barn for milking that same evening, resulting in A.B.P., otherwise known as Acquired Bovine Polypoopsia, a most distasteful evening unpleasantry for milkers of cows and similar to leprosy in its social effect on urbanized people should the poor, miserable "unwashed ones" later fumigate the bank, local library, church meeting or movie theater.

If Sean did arrive later than expected, it annoyed him to have farm clients think him ignorant of their expectations. Certainly, having been on their end of things before he got his "*Vetinary* DEE-gree," he did not expect to have his intelligence insulted with a long-winded lecture about the vicissitudes of farming. Likewise, he was not quite so ornery that he would insult them by deliberately showing up late. Thankfully, while most farmers were kind about such delays, one can still wonder why- with the world now so mechanized- the world seems to contain progressively more horse's asses than there are horses.

Sean always felt additional pressure during health inspections knowing that, any one morning, a single far-flung emergency call could mess up everybody, and some horse's rosette would be most unhappy. This would be a threat for about a month, until all the required inspections- some ninety herds- were done. And at that time of year, it was sure to happen now and then. He applied a little homespun philosophy he had picked up from his grandfather: "If a man is a real grumbler, he'll even grumble because there's nothing to grumble about."

Middletown was fifteen miles south, tiny little hamlet that it was, identifiable chiefly by a fascinating general store with a wee small post-office tucked inconspicuously inside the store on the west side, with a useless antique Gulf gas pump and an ornate iron post for tying a horse out front, which was rarely used anymore. To the casual eye, the town's handful of houses would not appear to be a community at all, blending instead into the general countryside since the farm where Sean was headed, its fields wide and long, was scattered here and there in the midst of what few houses existed.

The modest purr of a milking machine pump, as they pulled down the farm lane approaching the first dairy, told them that the farmer was still milking. And when they entered through the milkhouse into the stable, they found him and his son there, busily switching milkers from one cow to another, dumping milk into pails, to be carried off in a few moments to the milkhouse. Each cow occupied a tie-stall, a relatively new way of housing cattle. Though there remained the possibility of her fore-leg being injured by getting it wrapped in the neck-chain, it was more comfortable for a cow than a stanchion would be- and used for that very reason. More comfort, more milk.

Altogether, there were about thirty cows in the barn- mostly Guernseys, obviously receiving the best of care- five of which were not currently in milk and, from the looks of their bags and bellies, plainly due to calve in a few weeks: "*dry*" and "*due to freshen*" in dairymens' parlance. Jim and Sean, like anyone who works around livestock, possessed a nearly infallible sixth sense about animal temperament, mostly by watching their eyes. They vary a great deal from moment to moment, of course. In addition, to avoid unpleasant surprises with all kinds of domestic beasties, there's a good basic rule, old as the hills: "when in Rome, do as the Romans do," i.e., emulate the movements of their usual caretaker- the one they're used to- whether, quiet, loud, slow or energetic, whether a saint or an unsanctified rosette.

For the sake of speed and convenience as well as to avoid injury to the doctor, Jim stayed close by Sean as he slipped in beside each cow, bent over and checked her udder for mastitis. Now and then, he braced himself against the flank of some cow that was plainly rather nervous, holding others over with a little pressure from one hand on the milking-side thurl-bone or pins, sometimes physically flanking the really flighty ones by lifting the skin-fold ahead of her stifle joint- all in order to protect the doctor from surprise flips, kicks, or crowding, which can happen anytime.

Not that *dairy* cows should be considered a dangerous animal- in fact, *unless alarmed*, they are, from the moment of birth, among the most placid of creatures. That may or may not be true of some types of range cattle or beefers, where this might be arguable. But any handler of livestock has to play even the long odds to stay out of the hospital, by instinctively reading not only eyes, but muscle tension, breathing and movement, accordingly knowing when and how to move or, especially, *not* move around them. For instance, when some stranger suddenly surprises a 1200# cow by going in on the wrong side, barking like a bull walrus and squatting precipitously without the least warning next to her as he reaches out and grabs for her udder…, well, look out! At the first touch of his hand on her teat, her legs will convert the clown into a colossal Chickamauga Creek cannonball!

There were no health problems of concern at the first farm. Sean quickly filled out a health certificate indicating such, hung it on a clip in the milk house for any barn inspector representing a health department to see, and left with Jim for the next farm. There, standing by two wooden silos admiring a well-worn corn chopper/blower and silo pipe driven by a vintage Fordson tractor and power-take-off (P.T.O.) belt, were a couple of strangers, both young men, each dressed in new coveralls and shiny new rubber boots. "Who's them there two guys, Doc?" said Jim, his brows wrinkled into a frown. "They look like vets. Too spiffy, though. Look at them there white collars and ties. What do ya s'pose they want?"

Sean didn't see them at first, but when he did, he realized they must be the two vet students, friends of Eric's fraternity buddy, Brian, that had phoned him a few days beforehand asking to follow him along on his calls. "I'll be hornswoggled," he said, "they look like dudes come right out of the city, don't they?"

"Ain't a speck of barn doodoo on either of them, Doc."

"They're vet students, Jim. That's all. I'd forgot they were coming today.... Said they'd meet me either on the first call or on this one."

The two boys hadn't noticed them yet- too busy talking to the farmer's comely teen-aged daughter, who had just returned to the barn from the house. Sean appraised them a little from a distance before murmuring a subdued aside, close-lipped, almost through his nose as they do way down south in Texas, "I'll bet they don't know one end of a cow from the other. What do you think, Jim?".

"I'm with you, Doc. What are they going to do?"

"Follow us around, I guess. How long, I have no idea. I got an idea they'll quit and go home before long. Don't really know what they expect..., Eric and Brian fixed me up with this, you know. They're going to be bored. We're not doing anything too spectacular today, that I know of...." Dr. Sean opened the Jeep door and slid out of his seat, carrying some papers and a strip cup, used to examine milk. Close on his heels was Jim, bringing along a shiny new bucket, liquid soap, a boot brush and disinfectant to scrub their footwear before leaving for the next farm. Dr. Sean, unlike some older vets, didn't consider such sanitation a mere nicety. Infectious disease caused by T.B., Brucella abortus ("Bang's Disease) and Pasteurella multocida were still around, plus a plethora of other diseases- any one of which could ruin the best of herds, thus bankrupting a farmer. All these could be tracked on boots from farm to farm.

Hearing footsteps approaching them, the boys finally turned their heads. "Dr. Auchinachie, I presume," said the smaller one, standing no more than five-eight, a fresh-scrubbed looking future pet doctor if ever there was one, but with a friendly smile. Unlike Sean-type livestock vets, he would actually *need* an authentic bedside manner, though a little of that never hurt any doctor, despite what some academic, so-called "brains" might think. "I saw you drive in, but I didn't think you'd be driving a Jeep. I'm Fred Astor," he continued, motioning to his taller side-kick, "and this is my room-mate at the college, John Haverly. You remember Brian, I'm surc. John and I are fraternity brothers of him, and your brother Eric, too."

The four- Sean, Jim and the two students- shook hands, exchanged some brief cordialities and something of their backgrounds. The students were both city boys, as Sean had suspected from their demeanor, neither of them having had more than a pittance of experience actually working on farms or with farm people. No more, at best, than required at that time by the college, which expected most of the students would already have had *some* farm practice when they applied for admission. It was probable that these young men would need a little more farm time to qualify for their graduation, which would be coming up in a couple of years.

Sean noticed that the taller lad, a six-footer, seemed somewhat open to the prospect of doing farm work some day. At least, his interest seemed genuine. Cutting to the quick, Sean asked the boys if they would like to watch as he inspected the cows' bags for garget, which was a steadily growing problem for the dairy industry, and if they would meanwhile keep a sharp eye for signs of "lumpy-jaw" (actinomycosis), though of less concern. Then perhaps, they might like to try their own hands at it. "Have you ever milked a cow?" he said, almost as an afterthought.

"I have." said John. "With a machine. It was a Conde, at least I think it was.... When I worked on a farm up in Ontario County one summer."

"So have I," said his cohort.

"What kind of machine?" queried Sean.

"I can't remember. Seemed like it was a French sounding name...."

"A DeLaval?"

"Yes, that's it. A Delaval. It was a nice new one…, farmer liked it a lot. Pretty proud of it."

Sean thought he'd pursue the matter just to be obnoxious. He thought he already knew the answer as he growled, almost like a marine sergeant, "Either of you birds even milked a cow by hand?"

The two boys looked at each other, hesitating briefly. Finally they owned up to the fact that they'd had little in the way of milking experience, though they'd stripped a few cows by hand after the milkers were taken off, having been told by the farmers for whom they'd worked that the very last milk from the cow was the richest in butterfat, which was at a premium. Which was so, of course.

But it turned out that neither vet student ever milked a *full* pail from a cow by hand. Sean had suspected as much, but, hearing their admission, he flicked a disgusted frown their way, and lacking only a monocle for complete effect, feigned a spastic twitch of one cheek as a token of his disapproval as he turned on his heels and strode off.

It was purely an act. He had never done so, either.

Coming to Terms

The kid, about eight years old, carrying two buckets of feed to the hens, was on the way to the chicken coop when he stopped and listened, hearing a distant, high pitched whine- an engine screeching, revved up- coming on up the hill approaching the family farm. Scrambling to the milkhouse and seeing his older brother pouring a pail of milk in the strainer, he announced breathlessly- as officiously as a born-again bailiff- “The vet’s coming! I hear his Jeep!”

“So what if he is? And how do you know it’s the vet?” replied his brother, in his usual disparaging tone of voice.

The youngster seemed not in the least rebuffed. “It’s him! I heard his Jeep. Ain’t nahthin’ else sounds like that one!”

Just then, his brother heard what was plainly a four-cylinder Jeep approaching, engine decelerating and the sound of wheels hitting some gravel as it drew closer to the barn. He looked out the window. “You’re right, Frankie…, you’re right, by gol,” he said. “How’d you know it was the vet?”

“I told you,” said the kid. “That’s the only Jeep ‘round here that sounds like that one.”

His brother snickered. “That’s because they run it so fast, that’s all.”

“I know that, but that’s the way them there guys drive all the time. Nobody else dares to run ‘em so fast. Wish I could drive for ‘em some time.”

The kid was right. And everyone knew he had an uncanny ear for traffic on the long country lane where they lived. Even at some distance, he could pretty well tell who or what was coming up the road, maybe both. And this gift was not unusual. Some people, having noticed how observant country people are, have offered various theories as to how it works out like that.

In the first place, you have to understand that country folk almost never, never gossip. Make that a given and remember it well. You’ll need it. And among the *men-folk,* of course, it’s absolutely unheard of! Yet everybody seems to know everybody else’s business. How can that be? It can only be a gift from above, or something akin to it.

Some people think it involves some mystical clairvoyance- intuition, maybe. There aren't many think that, though.

Others think that country folk have a keener sense of smell, sight and hearing and that this is the only way such skill could possibly come about. Call it observation. What is harder to deduce, though, is trying to figure out why they are more observant than anybody else. Or even, if they really are. Anyway, it seems there has to be some sort of gift that can explain the puzzling fact that everybody seems to know everybody else's business. And immediately, if not sooner. It has to be that they are observant, since they don't gossip and aren't all *that* intuitive.

Some even think their being so observant may be natural- sort of genetic- since it is a skill developing very early among rural small fry, though one that, mysteriously, just seems to burst forth once a kid has expounded his first few tidbits of trivial observation- "I seen this...," or "I heared that...." Trivia that, for some reason or other, has created a gratifying stir among the kid's elders, such as whose car they heared driving by at an odd time, perhaps at three A.M. Or whose truck they saw a-rumbling by with a big load of lumber or hauling poorly-lookin' hay out-of-season in late winter to some improvident- guess-who who was too lazy last summer.

Whatever the cause, many of the young can, blindfolded, unfailingly identify a certain vehicle simply by its engine sound and, sometimes, even who is driving. And it was just so on the second day of creamery inspections when the "howling banshee," as some called Sean's Jeep, arrived at the first farm for the annual creamery checks.

Sean and Jim, leading Fred and John's battered but reliable old wreck, had been well on their way to that last inspection for the morning when, just around a curve, a mammoth, grossly obese woodchuck popped out of some tall grass at roadside, paused in panic, and then, unseen by Jim, dashed straight across the road in front of Sean's Jeep, somehow emerging unscathed as it passed beyond the bewildered marmot. Having escaped the first peril only to discover a new terror with Fred's *second* car already practically on top of him, the chuck froze, bolted one way, then lost his wits and scrambled suddenly back the other. Fred hit the brake hard and swerved to avoid the little curmudgeon. Instantly losing control of the vehicle as a front wheel skidded off the narrow macadam road and dropped with a thud onto a low spot on the shoulder, Fred fought the wheel desperately, gritting his teeth as he tried to prevent a roll-over. For a moment both young men expected the car would, at the very least, run off the road into a wooded thicket just ahead. Finally, after three nearly disastrous tries, Fred found a shallow access back to the hard surface and jumped the wheel back onto the pavement. They continued to tear down the road.

Fred whistled in relief. “Close one! Damn near lost it, didn’t I?”

John, still wide-eyed, relaxed his grip on the seat and looked back, expecting to see roadkill, but the chuck had escaped. “That was too close!” he snapped. But quickly realizing this was no time for rebuke, he recovered some poise. After all, they hadn’t crashed. “I don’t think I’d have tried to miss him. Just a dadblamed woodchuck.... Better to run over him than crack up, for Pete’s sake!” Then he realized that his grouchy little ad lib at the end might also be too much for Fred’s pride. John wondered why he always had a way of saying the wrong thing at a never-never time. And Fred was a sensitive sort.

Fred bit his tongue. Ordinarily not one to accept even the mildest of criticism, not even from a friend like John, yet remembering some caustic remarks only recently proffered him by his very own mother, he kept his cool. Finally he nodded in abject agreement, though he felt like he was crucifying himself, and him a Jew at that. “You’re right, John. Almost lost it, didn’t I? Not too quick, was I?”

John shut up for a moment, remembering that man need not offend by lecture alone. Perhaps he thought, I shouldn’t say anything at all. Then, more sympathetically, he commented, “I probably wouldn’t have done any better. You never know what’s coming.... Hard to be ready for some things you see on a country road..., and the roads aren’t kept up like they are in the towns.”

“But why in hell not?” fussed a disgruntled Fred. “Seems like the road men could take better care of the roads than *that*.”

John shrugged his shoulder. “I dunno. No money, I guess. A lot of road, but not many people- so they probably figure they’ll get a lot less belly-aching per mile than they would in town. Not much traffic on these roads, either. By the way don’t forget,” continued John, now relaxing a bit, “this country is thick with whitetails.... Hit one of them and it could be curtains. Might even hit a cow. Worse yet, a whole herd of them.” He gestured toward a downed fence nearby just to emphasize the point. “Fences aren’t any too reliable, you know.” He paused a few seconds, then added, “I found out quite a lot about fences after driving in the hills around here for awhile. The hard way."

Fred nodded again. "I know. I heard you hit a doe somewhere around here a couple of years ago."

"Yeah, that's right. About ten miles from here. It was at night, around nine or ten o'clock. Foggy as all get out. They're out in the fields- you know- in the morning, too, like when its dusky- early and late in the day. If you are even close to hitting one of 'em..., it might jump over your hood and come right through the windshield..., right into your face. Mine almost did, you know. Smashed the glass to smithereens. Can break your neck too..., I even heard where one went right through the glass and knocked somebody's head off- don't know if it was the exact truth or not. Maybe you saw it in the paper. Wasn't too long ago, as I remember."

Fred wiped the sweat off his brow, nodding in agreement. Then, peering down the road, he suddenly realized that he'd lost sight of Sean's Jeep. "Yi! Where'd they go?"

"Cripes," said John, "I don't know..., and now we're coming to a turn-off..., see..., just down the road- four corners..., and no road signs, of course! Suppose they turned off on one of those?" Fred slowed down the car, stopping momentarily at the intersection to look down both side roads, neither one of them paved. "I'll bet that's them right over there, Fred," said John again, pointing at a cloud of dust rising about half a mile down a side road. "Better follow it." Fred obligingly made the turn.

Unfortunately, they soon found they were following a farmer's pick-up truck loaded with bales of straw instead of a Jeep. Fred brought the car to a stop, frowning fretfully. "What do we do now? I'll bet we can't find them."

"Turn around, I guess," suggested John. "Maybe they stayed on the macadam."

"Do you suppose...?" came Fred's reply, verging on sarcasm. After all, John had been the one who suggested turning off the main road. What other option was there now?

John ignored his buddy's pique. "I don't know. Let's try it." Right now, he was cheerful, brightening up, it having just now dawned on him that he might have escaped being killed a few minutes ago. Now it was time to change the subject. "I'll tell you something, Fred. You never even want to *think* of getting lost on a country road. A year or so ago I swear I ran around in circles half a day before I even knew I was lost. And in the country, especially in *this* area, I think they assume nobody could *possibly* need an accurate road-sign, if there is one anywhere."

"Yeah, tell me about it," replied Fred as he pulled off the road into a farm lane cut through a row of towering hardwoods, turned the car around and headed back the way they'd come. "I always get confused when I get off the main roads." Glancing at his watch, he noted that they had lost about ten minutes by now. Sean could be five miles away, and no telling where. "Doc will think we're a pair of real idiots when he finds out we couldn't even follow him as far as the next place." He paused a second or two. "Well, to tell the truth," he added, "I'm not so sure he didn't think that anyway…, the first minute he saw us the other day."

John turned his head, studying Fred's face. "I don't know. I thought he was a pretty good guy. Why do you say that?"

"Oh, he was polite and all that. But I can always tell. I thought he was looking us up and down like we were some kind of bug. Or that we'd never make it…, as vets, you know…, something like that, anyway…. I mean… that was before we'd even opened our peeps."

John scratched the back of his head. "I dunno. Maybe you're right. I hope not. I guess I didn't notice anything like that."

"Well," said Fred, "As far as that goes…, I don't suppose we looked like real farm material to him…, like we knew what a *farm* was. Not sure I'd like Sean. But, anyway, I think he's pretty sharp…, don't you?"

"Yeah, I think so," said John. "Sure enough, he's been around. I've heard he's a good vet…, from some of the profs…. Like our own jewel, Jake the fake. Said I could learn a lot from him. And while I'm thinking of it, what do you think of these creamery checks he's doing?"

"Looks like Mickey Mouse stuff to me. I'd hate to spend my life doing that kind of stuff," said Fred.

"You mean, like it was a waste of time…, or what?"

"Worse than that. They only do these mastitis checks once or twice a year, from what I can tell. A cow could be okay today and rotten in another day or two. What good does that do?"

"I thought of that, too," said John. "But I suppose it would eliminate some of the chronics that shouldn't even be in the line.

Those are the really bad ones. Of course, to go along with your way of thinking, I don't think many farmers would send milk they know is bad. After all, they take their own milk from a can to the house, and, for them, it's usually unpasteurized! I don't think the exams are very important. And the creamery can pick up a lot of problems when they open the cans, you know. Just one whiff, sometimes- or if the color is off."

"Then why do they need the herd checks at all? Seems like they could figure out a better way than this," said Fred dryly. "And getting back to the doc, as far as he's concerned, I think he sort of figures you and I don't know much. Kind of like our professors. Overbearing, to say the least, like old Prof Morgan. Something I did must've bothered Sean. Told me he didn't like the way I moved around a cow- like that was any big deal! Said I was going to get hurt sometime, for Pete's sake! Does he think I'm some kind of dummy? If a half-witted hick can do all right around the cows, sure as bejeepers I can."

John let that pass. After all, Fred, a highly sophisticated city boy- and not just in his own mind- tended to underrate the intelligence of farm people- especially if they were shabbily clothed, lacked vocabulary or mispronounced words. Many of the older farmhands, even the owners, had never gone beyond eighth grade in a primitive one-room school house with fifteen kids and a teacher either right out of high school or, at most, with two years of normal school. John, on the other hand, found country people not only interesting, quaint at times, but usually surprisingly perceptive and quick-witted, with a remarkable aura of authenticity oft lacking in supposedly urbane citizens. Though some of them, initially, seemed a little withdrawn, he found that most of them were very genial once they looked you over a little, and only rarely pretentious. That, he concluded, seemed to be the rub- does the countryman trust *you*?

Having turned, going back to the route they'd mistakenly left, Fred stepped on it, catching sight of the Jeep at the next farm just as it was ducking out of sight behind the corner of the milkhouse near the boy who had recognized their oncoming Jeep by the engine sound. The two vet students quickly parked next to the Jeep and followed Sean and Jim to the barn, where a disagreeable-looking, bewhiskered old codger in faded blue bibs, assumedly a hired hand, was eyeing them suspiciously, his long face frozen into an expression of perpetual sour. And as Fred drew nearer him on the way to the barn, nodding and smiling wanly to the man as a dubious token of civility, he was greeted with no more than a contemptuous sneer, followed by a streak of brown chaw from his bulbous cheek- spat directly in his path. Fred passed by him, ignoring the affront, noticing a slimy brown drivel clinging to the old bugger's whiskers and a hostile, menacing glint in one eye as it followed his every move to the barn entrance. Fred went on into the barn without a word, whispering to John, "Somehow, I take it that old mutt doesn't like me."

This time, Sean permitted the two vet students to check the cows for him- subject to his approval. They wanted the experience, even as simple as the job was. The barn contained two rows of cows locked in their stanchions, each row facing center toward the other, so John took one row and Fred took the other. They knew this wouldn't take long, as there were only about thirty or forty cows in all. Sean stood near the milkhouse filling out some of the paperwork with the help of the farmer.

Loitering near an Ayrshire cow about half way down his line, Fred noticed the same old codger he'd just seen outside, nonchalantly leaning on the wall with a younger hired man, each of them glancing at him in amusement as he approached. Some private joke, Fred figured. Having similar build and features, he assumed they were father and son, evidently waiting for him to get there. He casually wondered why they seemed so relaxed, completely idle, yet with such obviously fiendish grins peeking through their wiry, unkempt beards, all the while plainly whispering some arch mischief to each other- like a pair of benighted, whirling dervishes.

It happened that the walk between the barn wall and the row of cows was only a little more than four feet wide, barring a foot-wide drop for the manure. This allowed little room for maneuver, but worse yet, it made a kick from a nervous cow inescapable if she were so inclined. Fred didn't worry. This herd seemed very placid, and sometimes, he'd been told at school, you just have to take your chances. A vet was a stranger in 'most every barnful of cows and you just had to get used to it. Fred knew how to handle himself.

Eyeing the two oddballs, Fred smiled absently as he brushed by them, in close quarters, watching them from the corner of his eye as he stepped in alongside the next cow, who was reaching down for a mouthful of forage, oblivious to his presence. He scootched down to a squat and reached for the cow's teats and started to draw milk.

There was no warning. Almost in one motion, she tensed and hammered his face with her tail- covered with enough dry-wet dungballs to simulate a baseball bat covered with chocolate. Without pause, she then swung her body hard against him, knocking him off balance and pinning him against the cow to her right, who reacted with a nervous blat and jumpy jig. Finally, having primed him for the coup de grace, the Ayrshire, horse-like, dropped her head for maximum power while hopping both her hind feet high off the floor, then connected Fred's belly with both hocks, splattering the now chocolate-coated man against the barn wall like a flying turd. With that, she turned her head around in her stanchion so she could admire her handiwork, wild-eyed, snorting like a bull about to go mad- as though to ask Fred if he wanted another try.

Dazed, feeling like he'd been overrun by the entire Notre Dame football team at its best, but not seriously hurt, Fred crawled away, aghast not only by the two-legged power-kick, not characteristic of a dairy cow- but puzzled why the two men had offered no help at all, not even to help him back to his feet or help him clean off several layers of stale cold doo-doo. They just stood there, still leaning nonchalantly on the barn wall like nothing had happened, a silly grin on each of their faces, studying him, each chewing his cheeky cud of good old Kentucky tobacco. The younger fellow commented, hands in his pocket, with a wry grin and a drawl of feigned concern, "Do you suppose he'll live, Dad?"

After snickering, then sobering, almost as casually as an undertaker mentioning the recent death of a rival undertaker, the old codger beamed maliciously and, through stained teeth, eked out the words, "Hee-hee Amos..., you suppose we should've told him about that one?"

Merton

Even though the hours hadn't been unusually long for him, the day had been a galling, strenuous ordeal for Sean. He was tired and ornery, and Nancy knew it. Sensing an uproar, she handed the phone off to him like a hot potato without so much as a word the instant he slouched through the back door into the kitchen. At least, she was thinking, he can't dance all over me for the way I handled *this* one. Some guy named Merton, claiming an emergency, had just called.

Nancy fully expected Sean to fly into another fit at the prospect of heading out again. He had just left the same area. Had the call come in half an hour sooner, he would have been near-by. Sean gritted his teeth at Merton's very first words "Is this here the vet what has the four-wheel-drive?"

"I suppose so," he replied, chafing that he'd ever bought that blasted Jeep. Many roads were now impassable, some plugged with snow up to the ears. Since no other vet deigned to have four-wheel drive and this guy rarely called him, it took little imagination to know exactly why he had suddenly become popular. Ever since dawn, near strangers had been crawling out of the woodwork having somehow heard of his wonderful service for the very first time that very day, vowing they would stay with him evermore because of the veritable wonders he was said to have performed. Donkeys fly.

As he talked to the farmer, trying somehow to worm out of going, it became more and more evident that Sean was struggling to keep his cool, while evading anything resembling commitment. Was there something the farmer could do on his own? Could the cow wait till morning? Or, under the conditions, should he go at all? Heavy snow had piled up from storm after storm that week, followed by heavy blasts of arctic air- even creating drifts touching telephone lines while blocking numerous roads. Vehicular shunts through farm fences had been established at a few places in order to bypass the many mountainous drifts over barren fields swept clean which were, fortunately, frozen hard rather than muddy. Some farms had been completely stranded for days.

During the week, his own farmers had mercifully spared Sean their usual number of calls. Despite that, what calls remained were tough. Tough to do, and tough to get at. He and Jim had lost over an hour and a half that day freeing their Jeep- hung-up, with tires a foot off the ground on a snow pack after attempting to power blindly through a white-out into a deceptively deep but level-looking drift where the road dropped away. Sean had long made it a practice to carry two small shovels on top of the Jeep in snow conditions, as well as tire chains. But had it not been for a good-natured farmer that noticed their plight from a distance and- braving the elements and howling wind- pulled them out with a tractor and chain, they might be sitting there still, with snow drifting in as fast as it was shoveled out.

The call itself was not an uncommon scenario for a vet: a first-time call by a relative stranger- late in the day- pleading urgently, with many complications. Sean asked a few pointed questions, none of which were answered satisfactorily, and finally wrote down the man's name on the call book after reluctantly conceding he'd be there in an hour or two. After learning where the Merton O'Brien place was, and the round-about path he was being advised to follow instead of the more direct route he would have chosen, Sean winced. Knowing rather well which roads were apt to be impassable, he doubted O'Brien's advice, sure that his own way to the farm would be better, and much, much shorter.

Merton's farm was located on a wooded back road derisively but accurately dubbed "Poverty Hollow" by the locals, originally named "Posterity Hollow." It was a place where Sean had once assumed every operating farm had been vacated long years past, in an area that a crops professor from the university, speaking at a county extension meeting, had waggishly suggested returning to the aboriginals. They would have liked it, as he said..., "being a very good place to hunt deer, make maple syrup and maybe keep a few bedraggled goats- since they take pleasure eating all kinds of weeds nothing else will touch- like nettles and burdock and even thistles."

Cynicism is pretty good proof of bitter past experience- the latter being the source of all wisdom. Of course, if it is not born of wisdom and experience, then the guy must be just a plain old sourpuss. Sometimes hard to tell the difference. A novice vet might have been more cheerful about the call than was Dr. Sean Auchinachie. It was not that he was *getting* hard- he was already there. His ears had long ago turned into shoe-leather through repetitious assault and battery incurred by *run-on* and its sequel- *run-off.*

Run-on: After a few years in practice most vets can detect even the faintest suggestion of a new deadbeat. Certain kinds of animals, certain situations, areas, certain tones of voice, certain *run-on*, well-rehearsed statements, attitudes and dramatics- usually built around a dogmatically proclaimed life-threatening, happened-just-now, damn-the-cost almighty-emergency, adroitly designed to bring the hardest professional to tears of repentance, begging on his knees to join the order of the kindly St. Francis of Assisi, live in blessed poverty, to be famously revered thenceforth by all mankind after dying of kindness-induced malnutrition.

Run-off: *Run-off* out of sight and/or sanctimonious outraged melodrama when the fee is due. How could a vet be so heartless as to harass me about mere filthy lucre for this poor helpless creature, especially when it's just a stray I found the other day and I've been feeding it out of the kindness of my heart for a year and after all, it's not as though a vet was a *real* doctor, or that he was saving something precious like the life of a child, but do your best, it's your duty- money's no object anyway. If you do a good enough job I'll pay you something, if I win the Bingo game this week.

But Sean was mystified. This man had not rehearsed the part. At least, not well. He lacked the finesse, the intricacies of the accomplished con artist. Of course, if he'd actually spent his life in the country or on a farm, most likely a run-down farm at that, he probably would still have a lot to learn about such an accomplished craft. The poor guy actually sounded half-way decent; might even be trustworthy- surely not an aggressive blow-hard demanding service-no matter what. Not only that, he had apologized for calling late, while explaining that the cow hadn't been eating much for the last day or two, but was suddenly in desperate straits, needing "a good vitinary like I done heared you waar, and right away, Doc, don't know if she'll make it to marnin." His regular vet was unable to come out. At least that's what the man said. Seemed genuine. But Sean was suspicious about any and all adulation, having heard that same flippant flatus flipping from the quivering lips of many an unctuous rascal expecting fulsome praise to suffice for payment in scrip- after all, what more could a mere vet want?

Sean hanged up the phone, plainly annoyed but speechless, and sat down to supper with his wife and daughter, plus Jim- who had stayed on rather than going home. Just to help out.

The Way What Was That Wasn't

"Doc," said Jim, "I don't see how we're going to get out to that there O'Brien place. Ain't no way I can think of! You and me was out there this mornin', not more'n a mile or two from where I figger his place must be..., and you saw what it's like out there- flat land, nothin' to break the wind, and it's blowin' like there's no tomorrow. It must be driftin' in like crazy on top of that there hill. Ten, fifteen feet in places, I'll bet."

Sean, musing, reached into the closet next to the kitchen stove for his Mackinaw jacket, then started putting it on as he replied, "Well, Jim, I agree with you. Merton seems to think I can get in there that way. But there's bound to be some big drifts. Of course, he claims the plow just went through there and opened it up."

"Hell," said Jim, "as far as I can see, he couldn't have gone out there to see for hisself..., not where he lives! How would *he* know?"

"Well, I don't know, Jim. Maybe a neighbor told him when he called in. He said he was at a neighbor's house when he was talking to me, 'cause his own line was down."

Jim shook his head. "I dunno, Doc. I'd just bet that road will be plugged full on top of that hill by the time we get there. Some of those drifts fill right back in twenty minutes after the plow goes through. I never seen such a miserable wind." He reached for his own coat, hanging on a hook by the back-room entrance. "I just don't see how we can get in there way it is, 'specially where it's so flat and windy."

"I think you're right, Jim."

Jim rubbed his nose, thinking for a second. "Say, Doc. Maybe we could try going in the back way, over by Norris's place. Not so flat over there..., and a little more cover from the wind, as I remember."

"No, I don't think that would work either, Jim. It's still on the windward side of the hill. Besides that, it's even farther around that way than the way O'Brien was telling us to take. I'd figure that was out of the way quite a far piece..., wouldn't you? It'd waste us another half hour, I'll bet..., each way, and I don't know about you, but I could really use some sleep tonight. You need it too, I think, from the looks of you."

"At least," said Jim by way of rejoinder, "it sure ain't agonna drift as bad as the other way."

Sean shook his head in disagreement. "Bad enough, I figure. But I have another idea. It just came to me. How about taking that short-cut we use in the summer? It almost goes to his house..., goes right by his road..., turn left at the first corner, up at the top of the hill- and you're there in a few hundred feet."

"What short-cut you talkin' about?"

"Oh, you know.... The one we took to go over to Tracy's farm. A couple of summers ago. You were with me. I know you were. That's the guy that had the crazy horse- Theilerosis..., liver screwed up. Remember?"

Jim thought a minute as Sean stuffed a scarf around his neck, inside his coat, and started buttoning up. "Oh...! I think I know. You mean that road that goes through the woods? A dirt road. Goes up a steep hill at the far end?"

"You got it," said Sean, as he reached for his cap with the ear-flaps. "I figure that road won't drift. Not with all those hemlocks and pines just off the road. And it'll save us time, if it works- it's at least eight miles shorter each way."

"Yipes, Doc!" said Jim, his face plainly consternated. "They don't even plow that road in the winter, Doc. It's closed clear until May."

"I know," replied Sean, "that's what the sign says, but they have to plow out each end of the road because there's people living there. And I'll bet the middle section is plowed out, too- at least as far as the bottom of the hill on the far end. They've got the only turn-around on the road there..., so the plows have to go that far, at least, from the low end. There's no other way to turn around- road's too narrow." Seeing a little bewilderment on Jim's face, he continued. "I know what you're thinking. It's the hill, isn't it?" Jim nodded, and Sean continued as he slipped his boots on, over his shoes. "That hill isn't very long, Jim. It is pretty steep, but if there's no snow I think we can make it."

"That's pretty iffy, Doc."

"I guess it is. But the trees there are real thick. There's a pretty good chance there won't be much snow on the road- it's apt to be on the branches, hanging right over the road."

"Doc, the wind'll have blown it off the branches."

"You may well be right. I know that. But the road is kind of down in a hollow along a creek bed, and on the leeward side of the hill to boot. Worth a try. All I can say is, it might work, and if it does, it's our best chance to get in and out of there. Once we get up off the slope, Mert's farm is only half a mile away, on the first left. Right in sight of the corner." Sean reached for his heavy mittens and shivered as he peered quickly at the thermometer outside the kitchen window- just from thinking about it. "Brrrr! Five below right now. And I'll bet the wind is illegal, too."

"Illegal?"

"Over the speed limit. Wanna bet?"

Jim shook his head. "Nope."

"You got a better way to go there?"

"Nope."

The bitter cold wind, once they faced it, gusting near fifty miles an hour, convinced both Sean and Jim that O'Brien's chosen route would certainly have to be a last resort. The main road was pretty clear, as they expected. The plows had done a good job there, where commercial traffic, including eighteen-wheelers, was pretty constant. Turning off it onto the first leg of the secondary roads into the hills, and then once again onto another, they reached a road where a sign was posted, saying "closed for the winter." Turning off onto the lower end of it, they quickly passed the last of a number of isolated dwellings, dim Christmas decorations of the month before cheering them on their way. Beyond that there were no tracks on the road as their wheels crunched their way into a silent white wilderness of scrub brush through crusted virgin snow that lay on the road only about six inches deep. Evidently the town plow had passed through a few days before, going only as far as a turn-around, eventually abandoning further effort as the storms continued.

In another mile they entered an isolated three mile stretch through dense woods- snow-laden evergreen branches overhanging the road- as they approached the challenging slope, short and straight, not quite a mile below the O'Brien farm, and which, once surmounted, would culminate on a good open flat next to the homestead. Sean suspected, remembering the lay of the land, that any drifts there would be small. The questionable part would be that last climb up the slope.

Jim needed no coaching from Sean. He got some anyway. The trick, he said, would be a good running start before hitting the slope, just in case there was a patch of ice somewhere on the slope that required extra momentum. “At worst,” Sean explained, “I can’t see any more hazard going this way than through the flats on top of the hill…, that open country Merton was talking about.”

Jim was beginning to sweat the approach to the steep part of the hill, as he gradually picked up speed. He was sure there would be ice on that rise, and lots of it. Sean had said no, not all that much, because it was a slope. Besides that, the shoulders had been washed out into fairly deep gullies on both sides of the road that summer. That meant there could be a rough ride on stones, in spots, perhaps something like a creek bed, but no ice on top.

“What if we slide into one of them there gullies?” said Jim, somewhat worried. That was unusual for him.

Sean urged him on. “We won’t- if you get up all the speed you can,” he predicted, staring ahead as he studied the road while nervously chewing on a perpetually soggy cigar stub that had long ago needed relighting. “If we have to shift, though- on the hill- then we’ll be in trouble. Put it in second as you start to climb, leave it there, and keep your speed up.”

“Ain’t goin’ to work, Doc.”

“Sure it will. I’ve done stuff like this lots of times.” He looked ahead to where the road rose sharply, the sturdy little steed humming, its four wheels pulling ahead together. “Keep it steady, Jim, don’t accelerate like that, or we’ll lose it!” he barked as he felt the Jeep suddenly losing momentum, its engine revving. His cigar was half falling out of his mouth before he caught it, just in time.

They were on the slope and the Jeep was losing momentum. Jim was panicking. “We’re slipping, Doc! We ain’t goin’ to make it.”

Now Sean really barked- sort of like a Parris Island D.I. with the pope standing at his elbow- or more accurately, like Sean’s wife- Nancy- who’d been trying to cure him of his foul language for years. “Gah…! I mean…, oh bah!….Hold it steady boy, for… Cri… for Pete’s sake! Oh shit! Keep ‘er straight or we’ll end up in the stinkin’ ditch!” At least he tried.

It was too late. Jim was, as he’d predicted, slipping, losing momentum- despite following Sean’s advice- and then they slowed to a halt, wheels spinning, engine momentarily racing before being shut down, followed immediately by a slight slipping back down the hill even as Jim shifted his foot to the brake, slowly picking up speed backward- helpless, in the darkness, to steer out of trouble. Sean was yelping impossible orders, like a captain on a rapidly sinking ship, simply adding to Jim's confusion.

Jim exploded. "Doc, dammit! Shut up, for the love of Pete! The whole road is nothing but ice under the snow…, like a creek bed- just like I told you!"

Sean had visions of a backward slide deep into a ditch. If they didn't roll over then, it would be a wonder. But realizing he'd better leave Jim alone, he toned down, keeping his mumbling to himself, having just now completely bitten his stogey in half, as he had the time the axle broke, "…had to be run-off from last week's thaw; gullies must have plugged up with twigs or something; can't believe it…, just can't believe it; gullies a foot deep on each side…. At least they were when I went through here last summer!"

Suddenly, with a shudder, the Jeep hesitated and came to a stop, Jim having accidentally steered the right rear wheel onto to a high spot, gravel protruding through a thin veneer of ice on the edge of a foot-deep drop-off into the gully. His hands were frozen, locked on the steering wheel. He used them to brace himself as he pushed his foot on the brake pedal- lifting his body off the seat, rigid- practically standing on it. The brakes on Jeeps of that vintage, a surplus WWII Army Jeep, weren't much. It continued to slide. But, slowly, the front of the Jeep began to slide to the left, pivoting off the right rear wheel till, at last, the Jeep was almost completely broadside to the road with the nose pointing slightly uphill, where it came to a rest. Jim shut the engine off and put the Jeep in first gear, not daring to release the brake for even an instant.

"Now what we gonna' do, Doc?" said Jim, sweat pouring off his brow. He was still guessing how fast they might have been coasting backwards down the hill if they'd slipped all the way down on the ice. A quarter mile. Maybe forty, fifty m.p.h.??

"Mon dieu, la fume!" said Sean, holding his nose and staring at Jim in disgust. "What's that?" said Sean.

"What's what?"

"What you just said…. What did you say?"

"Never mind, I'll live. Even cigar smoke couldn't kill *that*." He crossed himself reverently as he studied his broken cigar for a second, opened the window and threw its remains casually out of the Jeep, glad that Nancy wasn't there to record his lack of cool for a taunting future play-back. "Sit tight, Jim. Keep your foot on the brake, like you have it right now. I'm going to get out and see what it looks like. Don't change a thing till I've looked around." With that, he opened the door, stepped cautiously out into the dark and immediately landed on his lunar limbo. "I'm all right, I'll make it," he said, as Jim helplessly tried to reach over to steady him when, trying to stand, he slipped again. "Keep the Jeep right where it is. It's slippery as hell out here. Snow, on ice, everywhere!"

"I tried to warn you, Doc," came the retort from the Jeep. "Got any idea what to do? Can't hold this thing forever."

"Aw, shuddup," said Sean innocuously, trying to get up, slipping three more times beforc he finally grabbed the side of the Jeep. "Can't see very good, Jim. Where's that dad-blamed flashlight?"

Jim turned to his right, reaching around in the Jeep to the wooden shelf built across the Jeep high behind him- basically to hold boxes of medicine- fumbled in the dark briefly, felt the flashlight and handed it to Sean. "Shut the door as soon as you can, Doc" he said, "I'm freezing." He was already starting to shiver as the frigid night air filled the Jeep, penetrating his clothing. The heater at his feet, had it been as effective for heat as it was for noisy clatter, might actually have warmed his feet. As it was, they'd been as cold as ice for the last half hour or so. This time, he vowed, he wouldn't forget to cover that inhospitable, bare metal floorboard with some cardboard when they got back..., if they got back alive. Right now, he was wishing he'd worn rubber boots over his shoes like Sean always did.

Doc had shut the door, but was taking quite a while. Jim could hear him shuffling around outside, muttering to himself. Finally, getting impatient, his brake foot weakening, he shouted out, "Hurry up, Doc. My foot's goin' to sleep. Whataya doin' out there, anyhow?"

"Melting ice. Just emptied my bladder, if you need to know." Finally Sean was at the Jeep's back door, hinged above the tailgate onto its homebuilt top and, having opened it, was now pawing around in the heap of bottles and paraphernalia in a cardboard box directly behind the passenger seat.

"What ya need, Doc?"

"The rope..., and the peter warmer, if you know where I can find one."

"I'll let that one pass, Doc," said Jim, snorting. "You want the foot rope? What for?"

Sean was sarcastic. "Yeah, the foot rope. The one we use to pick up a cow's foot." He pawed around a little more. "Never mind..., don't need any help. I've got hold of it." He started pulling on it, then yanked harder. Apparently it was caught on something.

"What you gonna do with that?"

"Put it tight to the left rear wheel. Under it if I can, where it belongs."

"Where it belongs?" he replied in wonderment. "For what?"

"Traction. Just a little traction."

"Hell Doc, we ain't gonna get any traction to go up that hill. The only way is back down."

Sean laughed. He wasn't tired anymore, having just now found his second wind. "That's right. I'm going to turn us around, if I can, so you can go down the hill front-ward."

"How ya goin' to do that? Put it under the wheel?"

"Yup."

"Won't work, Doc."

"Maybe not. But what else we goin' to do? Sit here all night chattering our teeth?"

"I don't know if I can control this thing, even if we face around."

"Well, we can't do anything else but try. I can't get in *your* seat, or I would..., unless you can tell me how to pull *that* off without losing the show. I think you can do it..., in fact, I *know* you can," he said evenly. Sean regarded Jim as the best driver around, though he would never think of saying it out loud- at least, in his presence. Recently Jim had been racing a friend's stock car at the local dirt track, winning rather easily.

Being careful not to fall again, Sean moved gingerly to the rear of the Jeep thinking of the many goofy things vets run into- continual challenges to one's ingenuity. Ever conscious of his personal danger should the vehicle resume its slide, he grasped the side of the Jeep wherever he could find a hand-hold as he crept around it to its left side, intending to wad the rope, 3/4" and about twenty feet long, tight to the left rear wheel on its downhill side. He wasted no time accomplishing his purpose, hoping the tire would ride up on top of the rope enough to provide a temporary pivot point for the Jeep till it faced downhill. And then, as an afterthought, he tied one loose end of the rope to the tailgate so, afterward, the rope would trail the vehicle to the bottom of the hill. No telling but what the rope might be needed later that night.

When he returned to his seat in the frigid interior, Sean was a spectacle. Snow had fallen from an overhead bough and landed on his head and shoulders. Jim guffawed. "Doc, you look like Santa Claus!"

Sean laughed, then turned more serious. This would be something they might remember for years, each of them, but right now they had to get down to business. "Never mind that, we gotta git out of here, Jim. Cow'll be dead time we get there."

"Ain't out of the woods yet…, are we?"

"Not by a dam site, Jim. And, come to think of it- if you look out the window- no, literally. We're in woods all right. Now this is what I want you to do: When I get back out, I'm going to try to push the front end to its left over the ice, so it's pointing downhill. I hope the rope will hold the back-end where it is…. It should if the wheel slides over it. If it doesn't you'll probably end up in the ditch- but hang on good and try to steer out of it. I know you can do it if anybody can."

Jim didn't seem worried anymore. Nothing, in fact, stirred him more than a daring adventure. "All I can do is try," he said, seemingly confident.

"Got that right." came Sean's reply. "I'm going to go out in front and try to push the front end around. Hold onto the brakes, like you are, unless I wave you off. If you can't stop to let me in, ride it out. I'll follow you down, somehow, if that happens. I've still got the flashlight. Might take me a while, of course…, on this ice. O.K.?"

"Got it!" said Jim.

"O.K., now start the engine. You're sure you're still in four-wheel drive?"

Jim felt the gear shift lever. "Yup," he said. "And I put it in tractor gear, too."

"O.K. That's a good idea. As long as you're in tractor gear, I'd put it in second. Want the wheels to be rolling a little- But you know all that better than I do. Second gear O.K. with you?"

"Sure. That's where I put it before you said anything."

"Good, then! Keep it in there. Let's give it a try." With that, Sean closed the door and poised himself beside the right front fender. He could hear the engine turn over, start, then idle. Nodding to Jim, he bent over, pressed his shoulder on the uphill front fender and, bracing one foot against a small dead bough frozen into the ice, gave it a strenuous downhill push. It was easier than he expected. The Jeep pivoted nicely on the rope, nose now downhill, Jim signaling Doc Sean to jump in while he continued to hold his foot on the brake. Back in the passenger seat, Sean slammed the door shut and waved Jim onward without another word.

Thanks to Jim's driving expertise, they made it to the bottom of the slope without further event other than a couple of brief slides, which were quickly corrected. Sean hopped out, gathered up the rope, which had trailed behind, rolled it up speedily, reloaded it, and jumped back inside. They were, once again, off to see O'Brien's cow. But now they were both wide-awake.

Inanition

There was none of the usual tirade, blankety-blank this or that. Jim had expected the doctor to be firing off in disgust over his failed attempt to make it to his late emergency call through the short route. Even more to his surprise, he seemed serene, not the least bit troubled by their escapade. Evidently Sean was simply grateful that nothing more serious than loss of time had come from his botched plan.

Moreover, it was becoming clear that he was not going to abandon the project and head back to base. Chalk one up for grim bull-headedness. Whatever his faults, Sean was never one to quit. There were still two possible ways to reach O'Brien's farm. Now the question would be which one to take. Sean decided on the one the farmer had suggested, despite his earlier misgivings about it. It wouldn't be nearly as far and the risks were about the same.

This path turned out to be at least as perilous as the earlier one Dr. Sean had elected to try. Hit by unrelenting, howling winds and blinding white-outs, the Jeep shuddered with the impact of each blast, sluing left and right through tracks plowed scarcely an hour ago, having carved out only the narrowest of single lanes and forging- here and there- sheer, ten foot piles of compacted snow. And each pathway thus created was already rapidly refilling with wind-blown snow. Had they mired in one of these canyons, they'd have been so confined that they'd be hard put simply to open the doors of the cab, say nothing of slipping out. Not only that, each drift was disguised beneath its own cascading white-out- building it steadily higher. Had another plow burst into the drift with the Jeep there, unseen…, surprise, surprise!

Not only was the visibility to the front being smothered by snow well beyond the capacity of the windshield wipers, but the heater was losing the battle with interior frost. Both men's' gloved hands were busily scraping such frost off the inside- barely able to keep a meager peep-hole to the front on the inside, barely four or five inches wide.

Even then, visibility was minimal. The windshield wiper on the right side, unlike the vacuum-operated one on the left, was run manually- which was advantageous in heavy snow. Thus Sean, on the right, was able to sweep away the snow faster, allowing him to see a little better through the windshield than the driver could. When all else failed he even reached to his left a couple of times, briefly taking the steering wheel from Jim. All in all, it was not exactly a pleasure trip.

By now- feeling like an absolute sucker, or maybe a plain idiot- Sean was furious at himself for having gone out on such a night for a cow that was probably long past hope. Not only that, she was owned by a sometime-client of uncertain solvency whose regular vet was, he pictured, probably reclining comfortably in an easy chair at home, relaxing snugly with his family- in slippers, bathrobe, perhaps an ascot, sipping his bourbon, toasting his feet on a footstool by a blazing fireplace- knowing full well that some altruistic imbecile like him had assented to cover a nightmare for him. The delinquent vet was one more of the fair weather, easy buck kind that seemed, to Sean, to be accumulating as the years went by. Once the chirp of a robin told him that it was safe to come out of hibernation, he'd be back in practice doing the easier stuff.

Finally, they arrived at the farm. As they pulled in next to the milkhouse, the dark form of a man carrying a kerosene lantern- evidently heavily bundled up- appeared from the dimly lit farmhouse and carefully picked his way out to the barn around mounds of sparkling snow that had filled the path. "You the vet?" he called out, as he drew near.

"Yep, where's the cow?" responded Sean.

"Took you long enough to get here," he replied, acidly.

"You're lucky I came at all, on a night like this," snapped Sean, not pleased to find an ingrate after what he'd just been through- as he slogged to the barn, slipping now and then- Jim, behind him, carrying the usual pair of grips. Unable to see a latch, he waited for the farmer to open the door, which was white with snow, as was that whole side of the barn. Like the farmer's whiskers, too. Sean vaguely remembered the barn, once he was inside with the lights on. A real old-timer.

O'Brien still seemed unhappy about something. Rather than facing Sean, he turned his face aside and asked him, rather testily, "Get stuck somewhere?"

Sean was matter of fact, thinking he could dismiss whatever was bothering the man and get down to work. That should be the end of it. "Tried to come the short way, up the hill. Would've been a lot shorter."

O'Brien wasn't buying it. "That road is closed all winter. I've lived here a few years and I'm not stupid. If you could've made it that way, I'd have told you so. Why didn't you come the way I said? I've been waiting nearly three hours for you. Cow could be dead by now."

"That way didn't sound too good to *me*. I was over this way earlier today, and I saw what most of these roads are like. As it happened, we could just as easily have gotten stuck coming *your* way." Hearing a disgruntled snort from O'Brien, Sean stopped in his tracks, locked his eyes with the man's, and then- after a suggestive pause- continued, his voice rising steadily. "Look fella. Yes, it took me awhile, and it's late. And you *called* me late." There was a real edge in his voice now. In fact, hc was about to blaze away. "The two of us were kind enough to come out late in this miserable weather to help you out if we could..., and we've just had three long, hard days. I didn't need your work, but I thought I ought to help. Now I can look at your cow, or I can go back right now..., if that's what you want! I could stand some sleep, and so could Jim, here. Now what do you want?"

Stunned, realizing this was not a man anyone could bully, O'Brien looked like something that had crawled out of a rat's nest, with his scraggly, snow-flecked beard, long, uncombed hair drooping from under his ear-flapped cap and raggedly patched clothing, bedraggled, smelly and not fit for a dog to lie on. Quickly deciding he'd rather get his cow looked at, he cooled off. "Well," he said, almost apologetically, "I guess your chances were about the same whichever way, when you get down to it. Come on and look at my cow."

Though he was an imposing man physically, Sean's eyes alone, fixed coldly on an upstart, had a long history of quickly reducing an inflated ego to status pesticus, as though toying with the idea of swatting no more than a pesky fly.

As O'Brien led Sean down the line to the sick cow, Sean quickly sized up the herd. Most of the cows were still lying down in their stalls, though a few rose when he entered the barn. Oddly, not a one was chewing her cud. The barn was surprisingly clean, with very little manure in the drops, and evidently the cows had finished eating what had been left in their manger, having cleaned up very well. Only a few little scraps of hay were visible, and those were out of reach.

It had been a few years back and a different owner- an old man- and Sean remembered there had been no electric lights in the barn- a few undersized cows locked into stanchions. It had been a night call then, too, with a single kerosene lamp the only means of seeing a draft horse with the colic. Dimly lit now by the only two light bulbs in the stable that worked, each of them encrusted with fly specks amidst a few strands of dusty cobwebs, he saw that the same fixed, wooden stanchions were still there, that the horse stalls were empty and then he counted sixteen cows locked in, all dry, most of them red and white scrubs. Not your average dairy farm, by any means. Somewhat less.

In his off-duty reflections on how farms had changed, he saw this as one of those pioneering farms that was doomed to oblivion from its first day, despite the best efforts of any good hard-working farmer. Its fields of two to four acres were meant for out-dated horse-drawn implements and were too small, too far apart to join together into larger ones- each obstructed from another by woods and stony upland swamps- with such poorly drained hard-pan soil that spring planting would usually be late in the season. Poor crops would be its legacy, and its only future would be as a subsistence farm or a nature conservancy. Many such farms had been abandoned during the depression and subsequently converted to state lands for hunting and camping and, if a pond was dug out, fishing.

The cow was down- it turned out she had been down three days- her sunken eyes, weakness and debilitation obvious even to the uninitiated. He drew blood and then proceeded to treat the animal with what I-V fluids he had- which was scarcely enough. Tight-lipped, Sean glanced at Jim and saw his expression of dismay, as though he was about to blurt out something better left unsaid. He nudged Jim and, catching his eye, held a finger unobtrusively to his lips while O'Brien's head was turned away, all the while keeping up an ordinary conversation. From a previous incident, Jim, had learned that when Sean gave that particular signal, he'd better not open his peep on pain of death, or something even more radical like a cold-turkey orchidectomy. But seeing the grave expression on Dr. Sean's face, his lips pursed, concentrating and plainly troubled, he knew something unusual was up. And after treating her, Sean checked the cow again, over and over, concentrating on her heart and lungs, checking the color of her gums, and finally putting away his stethoscope and going to the house with O'Brien while Jim loaded up and waited for him to get his fee.

As they drove away later, Jim couldn't resist. "What's the matter with her, Doc?"

Sean seemed unduly cautious. "I'm not quite sure, Jim. I think it's probably either inanition or cachexia. I can find out, I think, from the blood."

"What's that?"

"What's what?" replied Sean.

"What you just called it?"

"You mean…, inanition and cachexia?"

"Yeah, I guess that's what you called it."

"A little hard to explain till I do the blood work, Jim."

Jim was fairly bursting at the seams. "You know what I think?"

"What's that?"

"It sure looks like…, well, like starvation, to me, Doc."

"That's not what I said, Jim. It's exactly what I told you, and I didn't say starvation, even if it looks like that to you. It's either inanition or cachexia. Let's leave it at that. And remember to keep your trap shut, like I've told you before about any of the cases we see. Don't want some ugly, unfounded rumors running around."

Jim stared at Sean briefly, unable to discern- in the feeble light- any sign that would convince him that he was kidding. It had been a long, hard day. He shrugged his shoulders in disbelief and focused on the road, heading back home to bed and the sweet, sweet repose of slumberland.

A Ride with Buck

Buck Braddock seldom missed a regional vet meeting. Sean rarely went. Yet, just in case the weather should change back to winter, Sean was sitting on his porch steps, dressed in a rarely-worn suit, winter coat in hand watching for his old class-mate's sleek, low-slung Hudson, having decided to bum a ride- since the interior of his Jeep smelled like a cow stable and Nancy needed their car for her own purposes. Buck, of course, was flabbergasted that he would actually attend a meeting, Sean having mentioned on numerous occasions that his worst fear was that he might hear a lecture so bad that it even failed to anesthetize him- quickly adding that this was not likely. Lectures, Sean believed, were God's natural anesthetic, the Lord's special provision for a fine mid-day nap, though he admitted that it was better not to snore too loudly unless the lecturer deserved it.

The meeting of the great minds was to be held fifteen miles north of Sturgis, so it was not out of the way for Buck to pick up his old friend, since he lived twenty-five miles due south of Sean. Unlike Sean, Buck- who did no farm work- had a compatible colleague nearby who was able to cover his pet practice for him when he was away, but this was virtually impossible for Sean due to the shortage of farm vets acceptable to his clients. Instead, Sean had arranged for Jim to come get him if a crisis came up.

Sean was well aware that a farm vet's reputation largely depended on his availability in time of emergency. Whatever else farming might be, it is usually intended to be somebody's livelihood- so a loss of a cow eats into what can already be a meager income. Likewise, he had learned from personal experience that a farmer with a gripe, whether real or imagined, can be merciless in broadcasting and even embellishing his grievances, especially after losing- as is certain to happen somewhere, sometime- two or three cows in succession. Sean had thus concluded that even if his patients were recovering quickly, inexpensively at a spectacular 99% rate, the 1% that ended up as something less would eventually erode all of that success- given enough years with the same old crowd and minus a steady flow of new clients to replace the disgrunts.

Finally, he saw Buck's Hudson coming up the road. Pulling over, Sean jumped in, finding Buck's oversized mitt already extended to greet him. Grinning broadly, plainly delighted to see each other, they shook hands and quickly sized each other up. "You're looking good, Buck," said Sean.

Buck nodded. "So are you, Sean. I was afraid you might change your mind about going. Can't believe it. How long since you've been to one of our little academic blah-blahs?"

Sean closed the car door. "Oh, a couple of years, I think," he said.

"I think it's been more like five. Never mind. It's about time you came to one of our seminars again." Tongue in cheek, Buck went on, "Got to keep up, you know. I was just surprised you called last night." A big fellow, six foot four, currently about 240 pounds, Buck had played first-string football at the university, where he had been a shoo-in as team captain partly because of the kidding he took so well about his big, big, elephantine ears whenever he was struggling to slip on his helmet. "Sure is good to see you again, Sean. How's Nancy? Haven't seen her in awhile. I don't have to ask how you are." He glanced at Sean a moment, eyes running up and down as though about to purchase a horse. "You look just as miserable as usual so I figure you're still monogamous. No girl friends?"

Sean laughed. "You think I'm crazy? And Kathy? How's she?" Kathy was Buck's wife, of course. Sean threw his coat in the back seat as the Hudson eased away from the curb.

"Oh pretty good. Had a hysterectomy last fall and had me worried for a bit, but she's pretty tough, you know. You knew about it didn't you?" The motor purred like a kitten as he smoothly shifted into second gear.

"No, I didn't, Buck. Sure glad to hear she's coming around. Kathy's a real jewel."

"Don't know what I'd do without her. We were made for each other, Sean."

"I always thought so, in fact, everybody did." Sean had been Buck's best man.

"Not quite. Her mother wasn't any too sure about me, you know."

Sean chuckled. "I remember. But then, don't you expect that from a mother-in-law? Say, how long have you had this car? It's pretty neat."

Buck grinned. “Isn’t it a beaut? A Commodore. Nicest handling car I ever had. I got tired of bumping my ***ass***ets around in a Ford. Straight eight, you know. Rides like a Caddy, and a lot more zip. Listen to that engine- ain’t it sweet? You’ll have to see that engine.”

“Yeah. it’s quite a car, all right,” said Sean as he looked over the interior. “Look at the upholstery. And the dashboard…, and these seats…. It’s like you’re sitting in a living room. And so quiet. How’s the heater? I hear a lot of good things about these cars in the winter.”

The heater? Just like you said- it’s like a living room. There wasn’t a cold spot in the car even in the worst weather last month. No cold feet. I didn’t even need to wear a coat.” Having now turned onto the state highway, Buck stepped on it. “Feel that power!”

“Say, not to change the subject, but do you ever see old Doc Greeley, over in Heath? Haven’t seen him in quite awhile.”

“Funny you asked, Sean. Sure, I saw him a couple of weeks ago over in the garage. He was looking at a Hudson, too. I had to laugh. I remember him saying, one time, that a Hudson’d go by anything except a gas pump.”

“That true?”

“I don’t think it’s bad at all,” Buck replied, “I’ve heard about the older ones being gas hogs. Solid, but thirsty.” He paused, trying to recall what it was he wanted to say; brightening up as he thought of it. “Yeah, Doc Greeley. He’s quite a character. I gotta tell you this one. He told me quite a story while I was there.”

“Go ahead. I’d like to hear it.”

“Well, this was back in the depression years, when Greeley still had a practice instead of being the milk sanitarian for the city board of health. There was this old guy- retired, I guess- that lived with his wife on that hill road that runs straight west out of Heath. Had a Beagle dog that his wife was always harping about. You know the scene. Kept it tied up to a doghouse most of the time and didn’t pay much attention to it. All it did was eat and spread turds around the lawn.

“Well, his wife kept nagging him to take the dog down to Greeley and have it put to sleep. I met her a couple of times myself and, to tell the truth, I’d hate to have her nagging *me*! In the first place, her husband didn’t want to do it at all, but even more, he didn’t want to pay the vet a dollar or two to put it to sleep. Times were tough, and that was all the money a lot of men could earn in a day, as you and I know.

"Well, he happened to remember he still had a couple of sticks of dynamite left over from when he worked on the roads. Guess he was an explosives man. So he happened to think…, all he had to do was tie a couple sticks on the dog, light them and run. So that's what he did. Trouble was, he forgot to tie the dog up, and when he lit the fuse, the dog got scared and started following him…, for protection, I guess. Well, he ran faster and faster, and then so did the dog. Right on his heels. Then he ran into his barn- he had a small horse barn where he stored things- with the dog hot on his heels…, tried to shut the door behind himself but the door wouldn't shut and the dog followed him right into the barn. He was so scared he dived out of the barn through a window pane- the only way out. And then, blooey! No dog, no barn."

"Yow!" said Sean, gritting his teeth. "This is for real?"

"Sure is. I got the story directly from Greeley. And he said he heard it directly from the guy's wife a few days later. Guess she was still fuming, ready to kill her husband. From what I knew of her, he probably would have been better off if he'd stayed in the barn with the dog, instead of divin' out the window. Can't imagine he ever heard the end of it."

Sean doubled up laughing and, accepting the truth of the story, said "Well, Greeley'd never kid you, at least without telling you afterward, I'm sure…, especially another vet." Sean knew the old gentleman and had the highest respect for him. "He's as honest as they come. Might even make it through the pearly gates, unlike you and me." Then he went on to tell Buck about "The Trip to O'Brien's," as he'd officially dubbed the story of his drive to that farm- following which he would allude to the cow itself.

At the end, Buck was a bit puzzled. "Then, I take it, you never told anybody about the cow…, I mean…, dying of starvation?"

"Well, I told Nancy, and O'Brien, of course, and Jim knew it died, but I never wanted him to know why, because I was afraid he'd spread it all over the neighborhood and stir up a lot of trouble. That's the only thing about having a driver…, though Jim is pretty good about it. Slips up once in awhile, though. I sure didn't want that to get in the papers or I never'd have heard the end of it."

Buck laughed. "So you finally told him it was inanition, and not cachexia? Pretty cute, ain't you? Did he even know the difference?"

Catching Buck's eye, Sean winked, "He still doesn't know that's just a fancy word for "starvation."

"Pretty fine difference between the two, anyway," said Buck. "Nobody else knew, though?"

"Well, of course," continued Sean, "there was the cattle dealer I contacted about the problem. He was the only other one who knew. But I needed his help, and I could trust him. He's a real good guy, you know. Done a lot of work for him when he's shipping cattle out of state."

"Oh, yeah- you mean the inter-state tests, and all that. But anyway, you didn't call somebody..., like the S.P.C.A.? The sheriff? A justice of the peace? Somebody in authority?"

"Nope."

"Didn't you just tell me the rest of the herd was starving, too?"

"Yup."

"Sean, if I didn't know you better, I'd say you were taking quite a risk. I wouldn't flirt with trouble like that. Some people... I mean..., well, they'd think it was your duty to report such things. Or is there more to the story?"

"Nobody ever paid me to be a policeman, Buck. Let me go on- there's a whole lot more. I didn't let Jim see me looking in the hay-mow..., afraid he'd figure the whole thing out, if he did. Anyway, I checked out the mow when he wasn't looking. There were, so help me, only ten bales of hay up there. Not only that, it was old hay, maybe two or three years old, and not much better than straw."

"Is that all? You sure?"

"Absolutely sure. That's why the mangers and drop were so clean. He was feeding the herd one lousy bale a day- I mean, for the whole herd!"

"You're kidding!"

"Not a bit, Buck. Those poor critters were getting no more than two pounds apiece, once a day."

"I've kind of forgotten how much a cow eats- but it sure must be a whole lot more than that," said Buck.

"Well, unless they are getting something more, like silage, you generally figure a little more than twenty pounds of *good* hay a day for a 900 pound cow- like a Guernsey- just for subsistence and of course, if they're milking, some grain besides."

"You don't need to tell me how much a bale weighs but I know it sure wouldn't do for a whole herd."

"I figure those bales might have weighed fifty or sixty pounds. No more than that. They were baled with wire, I think from an old Case two-man baler, so I think they weighed a little more than some of the others..., you know, the ones that are baled with string. Nevertheless...."

Sean went on to explain that he treated the dying cow as best he could, meanwhile seething at the farmer's negligence, but figuring to bawl him out when he had him alone. He still didn't want Jim, or anyone else, for that matter, to know about it until he'd really given the nitwit a chance to explain himself. Beside that, there were some blood tests to run back at his lab, to be a little more sure of the diagnosis.

Buck acknowledged that would probably be the best course, while admitting, had it been his own case, he probably would've sailed into the fellow immediately. Forget the ritual.

Sean was now getting into the remainder of the story, starting with how he'd then left Jim at the barn, followed O'Brien from there through the snow to the house to collect his fee (which he chose to ignore, as it happened) and, *for sure*, find out what was going on. "I went in the kitchen," said Sean, "all set to raise absolute hell. I was afraid the whole herd would die. But then I saw an old man sitting there at the kitchen table, patching his shirt with a needle and thread, skinny as a rail. I thought he must have cancer, or something. Figured he was the farmer's father, which he turned out to be. But then, the son took off his heavy coat and I couldn't believe my eyes. He was just as skinny as his dad was. I mean, those guys were *skeletons*, about as scrawny as a Ravensbruck rat!

"I guess they saw the look on my face, because they apologized for the way they looked. Said they'd had nothing much to eat for a few days..., couldn't get out because of the storm, and so on. I didn't ask permission..., I just checked the kitchen shelves and saw there were two boxes of breakfast cereal, one nearly empty, and half a loaf of bread. It floored me. The refrigerator hadn't been used in a long time, years, I'd say- actually, it was an old ice box, not a fridge. Two boxes of breakfast cereal. Half a loaf of bread and a little butter. I suppose they might have had a little unsavory meat if they waited for the cow to die. That was all there was. They admitted it. But I'll bet neither one of them weighed much more than a hundred pounds. Grown men, not shrimps!"

Sean continued. "Well, Buck, you're probably about to ask me what their problem was? I asked a few questions. In fact a whole lot of questions. And I was glad I hadn't flipped off like I almost did. Turns out they were nearly penniless, snow-bound, no vehicle. Sold their old Model-A pick-up to buy a little hay for the cows back in December. Nobody had put any hay in the barn that year- sick. Real sick. Both of them. Boy had emphysema, father had cancer- liver, I think..., sclera yellow- terminal case. Neighbors too busy to help, or didn't care. Don't know which. O'Briens did have a telephone, but the line was down.

"They finally got hold of one cattle dealer just before the lines went down. Just one. Must have been listening to his heart instead of his head, unlike the others- offered to bring them some hay for the winter provided they would settle up in the spring. Supposedly he said he'd buy the herd as 'grassers,' restore them on a good pasture in the spring, get them bred, and then put them on sale to recover the cost of his hay and grain. Now I know that guy real well, and he was no fool. He had to know he'd lose something on the deal, even though grass is cheap. Then, as it happened, the blizzard hit the very day he'd planned to bring the hay. O'Brien's cattle were already in trouble, of course. For ten days, one blizzard after another, no truck could get in or out- cows couldn't be fed or hauled away. The whole county was that way, but other folks had stocks in store."

Buck broke in. "What did you say about the old man, Sean? I guess I missed that."

Sean responded, "Well, the old man was emaciated, like I said- slowly dying of some kind of cancer. Hadn't kept up with the doctor. Can't blame him too much for that. And I almost forgot..., there was one more twist in the deal. It turned out he was the actual owner of the herd. as well as the farm itself. Refused to ask for help from anyone- least of all the welfare people, who knew absolutely nothing about him or his son. Independent as they get. Insisted that he'd stay on the farm- where he'd been born- wanted to die there peacefully. Turned out his son was mentally handicapped due to a difficult birth- and he knew little or nothing about farming. He'd left a real low-paying construction job, miles away, to come back home when he found out his father was real sick."

Buck's expression changed from astonishment to absolute dismay as he listened to the story. "Talk about complications!" he said. "Sounds like something out of the distant past, when they still had famines around these hills. I don't know what to say, Sean. I didn't know stuff like that happened around here. For one thing, I can see you had a lot more to think about than I would ever have guessed. Now the question is..., what became of the case? How many cows died, and all that...?"

Sean filled him in. "Well, of course, the cow that was down that night was dead the next morning. I knew it was coming.... She'd been so weak she couldn't even lift her head up off the manger. I figured, for the rest of the herd, some concentrate was the only thing we could get in there through the roads- so I bought some sacks of grain at the feed store while Jim scouted up an old four-wheel drive truck, think it was a Dodge, anyway..., small enough to get through the drifts. Then he took it on his own and delivered a little over half a ton of that grain bit by bit until the dealer's big truck- we got hold of him, of course- could squeeze through the drifts with a load of hay, and then he took over responsibility for the whole deal. My wife got some groceries for the men and Jim delivered that too.

"They lost two more cows during the next week. And then the others slowly began to gain. The cattle are still on the farm, as far as I know, but the dealer will be taking them, come a good spring day." Sean paused, looking squarely at Buck as he asked him, "Now tell me..., and tell me honestly. What would you have done?"

"I don't know, Sean. But I tell you one thing. If I took the time you did to figure out what was going on, like you did, I'd sure think twice about turning anybody in. And I can see a number of things that could have happened that would have made things a whole lot..., and I mean a *whole* lot worse than they were. How would a guy look dragging two men like that into court? And how would that help the cows, under the conditions? I suppose they'd have gone in there and shot them all and called it mercy. On the other hand, the way you handled it, most of the cattle survived."

"Well, Buck, I see things like that...," said Sean, "of course, not as bad as that one..., but I see them now and then out on the smaller backwoods farms. People don't seem to believe it, but you don't have to go far around here, like out in the hills, to find Appalachia. And, if you ask me, I think you can find Appalachia all over this country, if you open your eyes. And I've seen do-gooders come in like a big wind and thoughtlessly disgrace little people that are helpless, or sick, or incompetent- people who need just a little help, an ounce of charity instead of being publicly embarrassed by self-righteous know-it-alls.

"I've watched certain of these do-gooders for a time, and I think, after their first success, they can't get enough blood, like sharks in a feeding frenzy. They keep looking for more.... Turn into attention-seeking, self-appointed heroes without a scrap of real wisdom or compassion for the people themselves, even when all the signs of misfortune are there.

"Take another kind of case: it isn't very often as simple as they make it out to be when an animal is supposedly abused. I've known some dog-owners convicted in court of starving a dog that I'm pretty sure has a case of hookworm, where nobody even stopped to think about the fact the problem might have been poor observation-sickness- not abuse or negligence- maybe just ignorance, childishness maybe, or lack of intelligence. But, in spite of that, no lab tests or anything. Just like that.... Guilty!

"People like that sometimes need to be given the benefit of the doubt, taken aside and taught; needing help themselves as much as the animal does. What good does it do to brand them as witches and, like, burn them at the stake? I haven't seen very many people that are negligent or abusive by choice, at least out here in the sticks, and when I see somebody with a stray dog that they say they took in, and that they claim was 'abused,' I do a double take. Most of the time it's just a matter of one guy building himself up and strutting around pounding his chest at some other guy's expense, and to hell with the truth. Just wants to be a big shot."

Buck had to enter in at this point. "You can dot the 'o' in that, Sean. Well, I know what you mean, but you will have to admit, especially with some of these dirty, crowded, wormy little puppy factories, that there are some people that shouldn't have animals and need to be hauled into court."

"Yes, I will. You're certainly right about that. I've run into some like that, too, although I don't see so many pet cases as you do..., I'm sure. I'm only saying there are people that exploit animals, as you say, and then there are people that ruthlessly exploit people, even innocent people, for their own advantage, sometimes just so they can pose for pictures in the newspaper as saints. Which is worse? And the worst thing is that so many vets are called in on such cases and don't even do a cursory exam of the animals to be sure their testimony is accurate. After all, a lot of things can look like starvation and abuse. And the ordinary layman is not qualified to know the difference. Nor is a judge."

"Yeah, Sean, but I think you're asking for a lot of trouble. You can burn yourself out trying to solve the injustices in the world."

"Well, you're probably right, Buck. You know perfectly well I'm no flaming activist. But I get a little riled when I see the arrogance of self-appointed watch-dogs who don't know diddly-squat, haven't enough to do, so they're running around looking for a chance to make trouble just to bolster their own egos! If there is no consideration, no humanity shown, they are just plain phonies..., at least in my book!"

"On the other hand, I don't think I'd have gotten so involved as you did," said Buck, a bit dryly.

Why not?" inquired Sean. His face reflected some hesitation to go on.

"Now don't get mad, but I'll tell you why. Veterinary medicine is a business, after all, Sean, and I became a vet to make money. There's no money in what you're talking about. Just a lot of fuss and bother-and you're even losing money on that deal, besides sticking your neck out."

"You must be kidding," said Sean, a look of consternation creeping across his face. He and Buck were always like the best of brothers: no disagreements- in memory, at least.

"Nope. Can't blame you, or anything like that. But I guess I'm just being a realist. Their problems are their problems. Haven't you got enough problems of your own?"

Sean couldn't believe what he was hearing. "You mean it, don't you?" he said, totally perplexed.

Buck couldn't keep a straight face, a grin slowly fighting its way till it spread across his face practically to his big ears. "April fool, you dummy."

A Thought for Your Penny

Nancy was making a pumpkin pie for the Sunday dinner as she heard the Jeep approaching, slowing down, then rolling onto the gravel on the clinic's driveway. As soon as Sean popped into the kitchen, still dressed in his farm clothes, he went over to the call book, saw there were no more calls and breathed a sigh of relief. He turned to Nancy. "Well, it's good to get home. Nothing new in the clinic either?"

Nancy was crimping the edge of the crust, almost ready to put a pie in the oven. "No. Just that the Fosdicks came and got their dog…, at last."

"Well, good! Won't have to hear it barking tonight."

"I wish they'd come when they said they would. A few days ago. Maybe I can get some sleep tonight," said Nancy, as she opened the oven door and slipped in the pie. "I always hate to have that dog boarding here."

"I know. It's lonesome, that's all. They treat her like a baby."

"Well, I wish you'd give her a tranquilizer or something next time she comes. Or else give it to me." She nodded towards the next room, "Oh…, the postman brought you something different today- you got a letter from Brian Miller. I put it on the dining room table with your other mail. Bunch of bills there from Haver and Jen-Sal, too," said Nancy, closing the oven door. "And, of course there's the usual bunch of ads. I separated them for you…. I suppose you'll just want to heave them out."

"No doubt," said Sean, as he headed to the table and picked out the letter. "You're right. It's from Brian. Wonder what he wants?"

"Usually you have to open the envelope to find out," said Nancy as she went over to the sink and turned on the faucets to fill the dish-pan. "When are you going to get me a dishwasher?"

"Can't afford one. If I get another, they'll get me for bigamy."

"Not if you don't marry her."

"Then they'll call it adultery."

Nancy laughed. "They don't have to know. I won't say anything, if you don't. Anyway, I could use a vacation like that."

"Well that's interesting!" said Sean.

"Interesting, eh?" said Nancy. "I might know- you dirty old man!"

"No.... This letter, I'm talking about this letter," said Sean, having opened up the envelope and unfolded it. "Brian wonders if I could use him this summer. Guess he needs a job, and thought maybe he could work for me two or three months. Seems to think riding with a vet on his calls would be a good education if he should end up a farmer."

"What would you do with Jim?"

"I'm not sure. Probably Dad could use him."

"Will he need him? Won't Eric be back at the farm too?" asked Nancy.

"Sure, Eric'll be there, but I'll bet he'd like to have Jim help, too. I'll ask Dad." said Sean.

"Where would we put Brian? And I suppose I'd have to do his wash and cook for him..., and all that."

Sean studied her face for a moment. She was serious. "Maybe it's not such a good idea, at that. What do you think?" She still seemed a little uncertain, maybe half-willing. That was a good sign- changing her demeanor that quick. Sean went on, "I suppose he could do his own wash, if you could cook for him- or maybe Penny could help you out. That makes me think, couldn't we give him the room next to Penny's if I clear out some of my stuff?"

"What would you do for an office? You don't have enough room out in the clinic for all those books and things." replied Nancy. And all we have is a day bed for him."

"I don't know, Nancy. Guess we'll have to mull it over, won't we? By the way..., where's Penny?"

"Went up to the farm for the night. I let her take my car."

"Well, that's good. That'll make Mother happy- she'll treat Penny like a queen. I don't think she's seen her much the last few weeks, what with exams and all that."

"I think most of those Saturdays she didn't go up to the farm weren't because of her studies half so much as going out on a date," said Nancy, just to set the record straight.

"Really? I didn't know that," said Sean.

"You ought to pay more attention to your daughter, Sean. She's been getting a lot of attention the last few months. She gets two or three guys calling her up for a date almost every week."

"Hmmm.... I guess that doesn't surprise me," said Sean. "She's a real pretty girl and, beyond that, she's got a nice personality to go along with it. Don't think she'd ever say anything unkind to anybody."

"Well, not that most people would know, anyway- not even you. She just thinks things.... Doesn't usually say them. If you were around her as much as I am, you'd see another side.... She isn't as shy as she used to be."

"Well, getting back to Brian..., what do you think, Nancy?"

"It's O.K. with me, if that's what you want. He seemed like a real nice boy when he was here with Eric. But you better not lose Jim, that's all. I wouldn't want him to feel bad about it. I don't think you could replace him."

"I don't think he'd be upset..., really. I know he really likes to work in the field, drive tractors, repair, and things like that. I think it'd be a welcome change for him.... But I'll find out before I say anything to Brian."

"Wonder why he didn't just call you instead of writing?"

"I dunno, Nancy. Probably thought I'd be hard to catch on the phone. But, getting back to Penny..., when did all this stuff start? I didn't even know she was going out on dates- at least not regular, like you're telling me. Last I knew she was crying the blues because nobody was noticing her."

"Ever since last fall when Erna came to the school. They're good friends. And Erna is a year ahead of her- real popular, and all that. Erna introduced her to some boys and they all went out together on double dates. Foursomes. I guess they still are."

"That sounds safe, to me," said Sean. But he was puzzled. "Erna? Who's she? I never heard of her."

"Like I said, Sean- you better notice things a little more. You've seen her. She's been here four or five times while you were here."

"Erna..., Erna who? I don't remember her. Oh..., is it that real buxom girl- the blonde?"

Nancy gave Sean a disapproving look. "Yes, honey. That's Erna Vries. You know her dad. He has a farm over on the other side of Damon."

"Who? Not John Vries?"

"Of course, honey! Get a life! Pay a little more attention to something besides what's at the end of your nose! You've been to his farm enough."

"The guy that has three or four daughters?"

"That's him. Erna is the youngest one."

Sean was not happy. "Betty Vries her mother?"

"Yes, of course. What's wrong?"

"That's the one I was telling you about a few weeks ago. For one thing, she and her husband are barflies, always hanging out down at George's Tavern. I know that for a fact. And Betty is a real first class get-around gal, if you know what I mean."

"Oh…, who told you that, Sean? One of your gossipy friends?"

"No…, he's no gossip! He saw her one night when he was taking the side-road off the Kipper road. There's a parking spot there- a lovers' lane in the trees. You see cars there all the time at night. As he was turning off Kipper, his headlight caught this woman running to her car…, surprised her- she was trying to hide her face but said he recognized her plain as could be- only about-half dressed- some guy ducking down low in a pick-up next to her car."

"Oooh…, you guys just like to think that kind of stuff. It probably wasn't even her. She's pretty and he just wished it was true. Guys tell stories like that all the time. Sometimes I hate men!"

"O.K., but I don't think he made it up. He described the car pretty well. Anyway, if Penny's running around with one of those girls we better look out! I hear all her sisters get around too, just like mama. Jim knows a guy that went with one of them. Said mama told all of them, as they got to the age, to go out and have all the fun they could- just don't get pregnant. Then she gave them some rubbers and made sure they knew what to do."

"I don't believe it. No mother would tell her girls that! I don't believe it…, some guy with a dirty mind saw those pretty girls and just made it all up."

"Don't believe it? Not even from Jim?"

"Well, maybe somebody told Jim that- Jim didn't see it, so it's just hearsay. I don't believe any of it! I know Betty a little, and I like her. She's really a good mother, and she loves her family- always talking about them. And she's always talking about her church! I *know*!"

"All right, Nancy," said Sean, having been irritated enough for that day. "Have it your way, my dear."

The Auction Barn

Sean looked down the line. The barn was full, which meant he had fifty cows to do in the next hour or so before the auctioneer would begin barking away. That was enough time. He had his usual coveralls on and a pair of rubber boots- ready to work. The cattle were locked in stanchions, two rows facing out. "O.K. Penny," he said, "go get me a bucket of water while I go look for Austin. The sink is right over there by the door, where we came in. Hot water doesn't work…, cold is all right. I'll go get him and be right back." Pointing to the spot on the floor that he had in mind, he said, "Set the bucket right over there in the middle of the aisle. I'll be starting there…, and go up this row," he added, motioning with his arm, "and then right back on the other side to where we started. Got that?"

"Got it, Dad." said Penny as she picked up the bucket. "Do you have a sleeve, or do you want me to get you one out of the Jeep?"

"Right in my pocket, kid. And I'll be back as soon as I find Austin." With that, Sean scurried off, turning the corner just around the far end of the first row of cattle, passing through a short hall and into the office near the cafeteria and auction ring, bedded with nice clean shavings. "Hi, Maud," he said to the clerk, "Glib around?" Glib was the name everyone knew Austin by, for the obvious reason. Glib had bought the sale barn five years before from the preceding auctioneer- who had looked almost as old as Methuselah and upped and died a month later with his boots on- literally- while he was trying to buy back a cow from a guy who was asking too much. Or so they said.

Maud lifted her eyes from an account ledger as Sean bopped into the office. She was expecting him. "Hi Doc," she said. He was a regular there every week on sale day to check cows for this and that, as well as make out local health papers and those required of each cow going out of the state. "Yeah, Glib's around here somewhere. He was just here a minute ago. I think he might have gone out to the dock. Buster just backed in with another truckload of beefers…. Think Glib must have took some sale-tags out to Denny and Carl." Maud, a little past her prime, was a hefty woman, about forty-five, and had been the head bookkeeper for years before Glib had taken over from the old gink. She'd supposedly been an extra good, very, very special friend of the old boss- as well as his accountant, head of the office for the last fifteen years- without her kind and simple cuckold ever suspecting a thing. When the old auctioneer died, everyone that worked at the sale barn sent her flowers. That was a lot of flowers- her house was full of them, and she cried miserably. Her husband still didn't get it.

Sean ran into Glib as he was heading for the loading dock, just ten feet outside the office. "Ah, you're here!" said Glib. "I was beginning to worry. I'll meet you out in the stable soon as I get the book from Maud. I think most of the cows are bred. Pretty good farmer- seemed to know what he was doing." He started to move off to the office.

"You using Dave today, or are you the auctioneer?" asked Sean.

Glib paused, coming back for a couple of steps. "I'm on till he gets here. He called this morning, said he'd be a little late, Doc. See you out there." With those last words still dangling from his mouth, Glib was intercepted by a farmer wanting to know something about the herd. "See you in a minute, Doc," he said as he turned to the farmer and rattled off, "good herd, Seth- real good herd. On test, making 15,000 pound average, some nice cows up close, and a bunch of them just fresh a month or two…."

Sean went back to the stable, where Penny was standing by the bucket of water she'd gotten, talking to some young buck that should have been washing out tails and combing them instead of standing there gabbing away, while another one, a younger dude, about twenty feet away, was ogling her hopefully- meanwhile brushing off a cow, albeit half-heartedly. An older man- one of the regulars- was throwing hay down in front of the cows, and the whole herd was greedily filling up on it. That was always a good tactic. Makes a cow look filled out, happily chewing her cud later on- prosperous- whether at a sale or at a show. Meanwhile, small groups of farmers were drifting idly up and down the two rows, sizing the animals up, trying to bump calves, checking bags, and writing down sale-tag numbers of prospective bids.

This was not new to Penny- she often filled in for Jim. And it certainly wasn't anything new to Sean. He had been doing about two or three hundred of these exams every week- not just at the sale barn, of course. Sean put his sleeve on, watered and soaped it good, and arced the first cow's tail around from her left up and over her back to her right topside where Penny grabbed it, while standing on the cow's right with her hip braced against the cow's flank to steady her- holding the tail just tight enough to keep its base off her father's arm. Sean then dived in with his left arm and checked for a calf. This one only took about fifteen seconds, if that. "Five months, sale-tag T67," he said, as Glib, who had just arrived, pulled a ball-point pen out of his shirt pocket and wrote the info down in his book. As soon as Sean and Penny moved to the next cow, Glib wrote the same data on the card hanging over the cow for the buyers' benefit. The stage of gestation- if such there is- is always a significant factor in the value of the cow.

Glib, though all business, gave Penny a brief look of appraisal. "How come no Jim today, Doc? Of course, I'd rather see your daughter, any day. How are you doing young lady?"

"Just fine," squeaked Penny, as she stepped up alongside the next cow and took the bossy's tail from her dad's hand.

A medical career of any kind is not for the squeamish. Whether one is a physician, a dentist, a surgeon, a nurse- or a veterinarian, which is often a combination of all four of the other skills- some things are *necessarily* done by them that most people would find impossibly offensive- including, at least till they get used to it, the professionals themselves. Certainly such almost unmentionable things would be appalling to the usual wimp or, perhaps, some lily-livered preacher- unless he'd earned a few beneficial calluses or, at the very least, dirtied his hands somewhere along the way. All of which can quickly alter a fancy feast attended, in part, by a group of unabashed medical professionals- should any of them shamelessly forget the presence of others of more sensitive natures.

Several years before, Sean had been doing pregnancy exams on another herd in this very same place when a towhead from town- perhaps nine years old- appeared from nowhere, just as, opere citato, he was thrusting his arm into something or other- clear past the elbow. How long the lad had been watching the procedure before Sean noticed him is hard to say, but he was standing there transfixed, with a sickish, yet ghoulish look on his face. Their eyes met and, forthwith, the kid bolted, running off outdoors through the open doorway, legs flailing wildly like another Jackie Robinson on his way to stealing second base, disappearing in a wink without a word. Sean went on blithely down the line, did a few more checks, when hearing a rustling sound, he turned his head to the right where, behold, stood not one, but three more small fry accompanying the original descrier- each with the same sickish look- fascinated at the sight of what must have been, to them- the utmost in fiendish depravity.

The herd checks done, with only a few of the cows that had been bred found open, all the rest pregnant in excess of forty days of their normal 282 day pregnancies, Glib knew the selling farmer would be happy- just as he was, since he was on commission. Both of them could smell dollars. But in the process, one heifer- a two year old- was found not only open, but in heat- much in need of a bull or an artificial breeder. And it happened that in the far end of the barn was a sturdy stall made of iron pipes whcrein lay a large and experienced bull who was eager for more experience. A match was made, and, with Penny removed from the scene, a certain agreement was consummated.

Now it happens that such a simple service rendered by a bull is often referred to as the heifer having been "bred." This does not yet mean that said animal is pregnant, by any means, although it is also commonly said that a cow is "bred" when what is meant is that she is, in fact, certifiably carrying a calf. The latter, of course means more bucks for the bang, for the seller of said pregnant animal. And as Sean was passing by the ringside somewhat later, the self-same heifer appeared in the ring, much to his chagrin, as it soon turned out. While at first there was stout bidding from the stands, it soon dropped off. Nothing had been said about whether the heifer was pregnant. Plainly the bidders were assuming that she wasn't, their bids having been much too low for a "bred heifer" of her obvious quality. Someone in the bleachers, evidently a bidder, yelled out- as a point of information- "Is that heifer bred?"

Glib, from the auctioneer's post, never hesitated a bit. "*Yep*," he said. "*She's bred.*" Was that a lie? Well, was it really? Then, because of the ambiguity, the bidding got hot, then hotter and hotter. Well, she *was indeed* a beautiful heifer. Nobody thought to ask how far along she was, nor if she'd been checked for pregnancy. Most cattlemen can tell that, in a glance, when a heifer starts to "*bag up.*" And this heifer, while not "bagged up," was..., well..., *maybe* bagging up- the way one sometimes does by her third month. Anyway- foolish or not- *up* went the sale price by a good hundred dollars, then more- going..., going..., GONE! And Sean was mortified. Would somebody think he'd certified her as pregnant? Well, it wasn't anything he'd personally done that was wrong. Anyway, by the time he made his mind up to say something, it was already too late- the heifer was sold, chased out of the ring to a holding pen out back and another introduced to the ring. Come to think of it, as he realized shortly, there was nothing in writing about it. "Glib" had pulled off a slight increase in his commission by this little deceit, and the seller would be happy, too. The buyer was somebody out of the territory never seen before. So what?

Penny hadn't been to a cattle sale in a long time. And when she'd last been to one, she was too small to know what was going on. On one occasion, sitting beside her dad as the bidding was going on, her dad completely distracted by the fierce action going on under his nose, Penny, in her innocence, asked her dad, "If I raise my hand, do I get the cow?"

Now everybody knows the hawks in the ring have sharp eyes. You don't dare wink, much less wiggle when the bidding goes on unless you are a bona-fide bidder. You certainly don't want to sit there at ringside if you have a nervous tic or you may end up owning the whole herd. Unfortunately, Sean wasn't listening to Penny. "Yes," he had said.

Up went Penny's hand. "Hup!" yelped the barker, loud and clear, standing there in the ring steering the animal around with his cane. Then there was someone else bidding, and another, before the barker realized he'd taken a child's bid. Stop action. Hold. Awkward moment as the bids were scuttled and started over, with glares at Sean from the auctioneer and ringmaster. When bids are going hot, rapid-fire, and then there is a pause for any reason, it can be hard to get the bids moving again. Bad. Bad.

Except for one scrawny heifer, probably wormy, it turned out to be a real hot sale. There had been a lot of good advertising, the herd was well known, and the crowd was large- drawn from four or five counties. Rather than leaving as soon as the vet work was done, as would ordinarily have been done, Sean and Penny decided to take seats up in the stands to watch for a bit as the sale progressed. It wasn't long till Sean spotted a certain cattle dealer across the way- a man by the name of Hoban- who was crooked as Capone, thus referred to his face as "Cicero" Hoban, without his ever figuring out why, nor anyone recalling who invented the name, appropriate as it was. Should have been given an award.

"Cicero" and Sean had crossed paths many times. He had a nice barn- one of the few that actually had tile laid up half-way on the interior walls, sort of like wainscoting. But he was always trying to chisel Sean on his bills. Nancy would send out his bill every month, but no pay ever came back in the mail, like it would have with someone less wily. What "Cicero" wanted was to wait till Sean came to his farm on one of his calls- when he was there himself, bill in hand, to chisel him out of few bucks. He wasn't happy unless he could gain even a measly five bucks on a three hundred dollar statement. His favorite tactic was to call Sean from his work on a cow, standing in the middle of the barn under a good strong ceiling light, pencil in hand, as he pointed to the bottom line on the statement. "See this?" Cicero would say, as he touched the figure with his pencil. "Yes," Sean would say- while still in his greener years as a vet. Then Cicero would slowly, deliberately round the figure down with his pencil to the nearest five or ten or fifteen dollars expecting Sean to say, "O.K.," at which point he would make out a check, pleased as a sailor in a Siamese cat-house.

On a few subsequent occasions, Cicero would point out a minor mistake Nancy had made in totaling his bill, which was not uncommon for her. Although the errors were always small, Sean soon noticed that Cicero said nothing at all if the mistake was to Cicero's *advantage*. Regardless if there was a mistake or not, he would never pay a bill without trying to find something wrong with it. Eventually, realizing that this was a game- yes, an obnoxious one, and tiresome, Sean put a stop to it by totaling the bill himself, instead of having Nancy do it. In the process, Sean would deliberately, facetiously "overcharge" some pharmaceutical item by a small amount right after leaving the farm. Cicero didn't know the usual cost of such items. So Sean would add up the statement's total minus that same "overcharge" so that when Cicero added it up he'd think the addition was off, favoring himself. That was the end of the dickering. Of course, Cicero thought he was beating Sean- using Sean's own mistake. He never caught on- just figured Sean was a lousy mathematician. That was O.K. with Sean, as long as he won the war.

As Sean was watching Cicero from across the ring, he noticed the man sitting next to him was bidding for cows, plainly with Cicero's financial backing. He was accustomed to take some poor ninny to the cleaners with a chattel mortgage on the cows he bought at the auction, or better still- if he could work it around- a mortgage on the farm itself. This meant, if there was a default, as he half expected there'd be, he'd gain on the recovery through a foreclosure because the cows would never bring the same price again if they were resold. The poor dope would then have no cows, and still owe the old skinflint money. He'd made scads pulling that, sometimes ending up with the title to the farm, or at least an onerous lien which meant he could buy the farm cheap some time in the future. Of course, this was always preceded by running up the price of the cows on the poor sucker.

Sean hadn't figured how old Cicero could get the farmers he backed to pay so much for the cows he, in effect, bought for them on their credit. Why wouldn't they realize they were sticking their necks out? So, today, he had been watching the old skinflint as his sucker of the moment bid consistently higher than he should have done. Finally, he said to Penny. "I want you to see something Penny."

"What's that, Dad?" she replied.

"You see that old guy across the way with a hat on, got a cigar in his mouth, a black suit and glasses? Looks like Vito Genovese?"

"Yeah."

"Well, Penny," he whispered, "that guy is a crook. A cattle dealer. Not that they're all that way. We call him Cicero, because Al Capone lived in Cicero- out in Chicago, you know."

"Yeah. I know that. I've heard of him. Valentine's day massacre?"

"You got it, Penny. Anyway, he's got a guy across the way bidding the sucker up, so he'll buy the cow for more than it's worth."

"Why's he doing that?" said Penny.

"Never mind..., do you see him.... There! Right now..., he just winked! And..., there, see the auctioneer just took another guy's bid! He just signaled that guy across the way to bid him up. Did you see that?"

"Yes, but I don't get it," whispered Penny.

"That's all right. Old Cicero is putting up the money for the guy sitting next to him. He wants him to owe him more than the cows are worth, then he won't be able to pay him back, and he'll end up with the cows again, plus some money because they won't sell again near as high as he paid for them. Most of them are just cull cows- not really milking. In other words, Cicero will take them back- and then file a claim on the dope's land for whatever wasn't paid off. Then, eventually, if the guy can't pay it off- he hopes to get the farm on a foreclosure. That's how he gets rich. He only invests money in places he figures the guy will lose out. Suckers, in other words. Do you see?"

"I think so. He's a crook then?"

"He's a crook, honey. But I want you to see how this kind of stuff goes on in an auction. Any kind of auction can have somebody in there bidding you up, for one reason or another."

"But I'd think they'd get caught, if the guy they're bidding up quits bidding. Wouldn't they be stuck then?"

"Yeah, of course. That's the trick here. Cicero knows how far the guy that's sitting there with him will go. So then he signals across to his buddy to bid up again."

"Oh. I get it. Is he rich?"

"Cicero?"

"Yes."

"Filthy rich, Penny. He's worth at least a million."

"I'd think if everybody he backs up loses, other people'd figure it out, after awhile."

"That's why I… think it is…, that he has a few of his good friends he backs up- ones he knows are good for the money. He can always point to them, and they'll stick up for him. They really think he's been good to them. And, I guess, he really has been."

"Boy, he's smart."

"That's what I wanted you to see, Penny. Someday, if you ever marry a farmer- remember to be careful when you're in an auction. You can really get burned. There are all kinds of tricks go on here that nobody knows about. Sometimes, if another farmer doesn't like you- jealous or something like that- he'll try to bid you up and then drop you when he's got you too high on a bid. You don't see much going on here in the stands, do you?"

"You mean…, like people bidding?"

"That's right…, some just wiggle a finger. Some wink, some just stare at the ringmaster. And some have a special code the ringmaster knows. There! See that one? Over there in the straw hat?"

"Yes, I see him," answered Penny.

"Did you see him tug his ear lobe?"

"Yes. Just now…, he did it."

"He bids that way. Auctioneer calls out a price, and he just tugs an ear. That means he accepts it. But if you don't know what to look for, you don't even know who's doing the bidding, do you?"

"I sure couldn't tell," said Penny.

"Well, I hope you remember this little lesson, Penny. It may save your neck some day…, when you have a farm of your own."

Penny

"Do you want to drive, Penny?" Sean, of course, knew she loved to drive his Jeep, though she'd had little opportunity in the past except around the farm lots at her grandfather's farm. Primitive as it was, Sean's Jeep was a marvelous little buggy that could go almost anywhere. There was something that fascinated Penny about those rugged little four-wheel-drive vehicles, as she had learned on a few occasions when she'd driven for her dad, particularly the time she'd driven her dad up a steep side-hill pasture lot to reach a downer- a cow with heat stroke. Aside from the desperate clinical aspects of the case, just getting to her side had been a enough of a challenge, particularly where a hidden spring crossed the roadway next to a cornfield, already hampered by interlacing tree roots. That had been a rough and slippery spot requiring use of the Jeep's tractor gear. No telling what you might need once you got to a pastured case, either; Much better to take everything to the field with you than to switch only a few likely items from the back of a car to a tractor-drawn wagon, as most vets did.

Penny didn't need a second invitation. She scrambled into the driver's seat with her dad on the right and tore off down the road. "Did you have any more calls?" she asked him, as she slid open the glass panel on her door to get a little more air. "You called in just now.... At the sale barn, didn't you?"

"Of course," replied Sean, "One more. That's all..., so far, anyway. Do you know where George Blake's farm is?"

"I think so," said Penny. "Isn't that where you and I went out in the woods to look at a whole bunch of dead cows last year? The ones that were killed by lightning? I remember they were all covered with tree branches and leaves, and there were at least twenty trees blown to splinters- looked like a bomb went off."

"No, that's the next farm just beyond Blake's." said Sean, almost flinching as he recalled the grisly scene. "That was the worst lightning case I ever saw. Wasn't it twelve..., I think it was.... Twelve cows laying there under what was left of the trees? I remember there was at least an acre of trees blown to bits. And there was one tree- I never saw anything like it- where it had been blown completely into splinters, and they were all driven into the ground like little spears radiating around what was left of the trunk..., sort of like iron filings around one pole of a magnet. I think I showed it to you."

"Yes. You did. But I think there were fourteen cows," said Penny, "and one of them..., remember..., we found on the other side of the fence, down off the bank- landed on the road..., about twenty feet away. That was *really* strange!"

"You're right. That was really freakish! She never even hit the fence or the bank," added Sean, "neither one! High fence, too! Got hit, made her jump- one last super jump, and she just leaped up and over, fell twelve feet or so and landed right near the center of the macadam. Not a sign she'd ever hit anything on the way! By the way, take the next road to the left. Blake's farm is on that one. We'll be there in a jiff..., you'll see it off that road a ways, on the right. Three or four miles to go, I'd say. Hard to see the buildings, long driveway, a lot of trees. Don't miss it." He took off his glasses, steamed them with his breath and wiped them clean on his handkerchief before continuing. "Probably you remember Blake's barn? Where the whole roof was gone? We went by the same day. Big roof, too- maybe eighty feet long."

"Yes I remember it. Blake was in the barn milking, too, when it happened. It's a wonder he didn't get killed."

"Yeah, it's a wonder all right. Killed some of his cows, where the end of the barn collapsed. That sure was quite a storm- seem to be getting more storms like that all the time." Sean looked ahead, and saw a stop sign. "Better slow down, Penny. See the stop sign?" Four-corners were dead ahead.

"Oh, Dad!" replied Penny, a little annoyed. "I can see it."

"Well, dammit, Penny!" grunted Sean, "don't push your luck! For the love of Pete, *slow down*!" It was too late. Penny buzzed half way through while braking, gave up, and throttled on out of it, straight through, like a student pilot doing touch and goes in preparation for a private license. Sean was furious. "How many times have I told you not to...."

Penny picked up the litany, loud enough to drown her father out, in sing-song sarcasm, "...wait till the last minute to slam on the brakes! Is that what you were about to say?"

"Yes!" growled her dad, "especially a Jeep loaded down like this one is.... Doesn't have very good brakes, in the first place! And don't get fresh with me!"

"Gee, Dad!" protested Penny, her dander up. "I wish you would.... Let...! Me...! Drive...! You scare me, yelling at me like that! I might have had an accident! Suppose somebody'd been coming along and I got stuck out in the middle like that, trying to stop, and he ran right into me?"

Sean shut up, withholding the temptation to strangle the girl, turning his head aside so she would not notice any bruxism a-brewing. Juveniles must occasionally be granted the privilege of folly. After all, of such license are some of our most prominent journalists made, if not earlier dissuaded by some undiscerning elder.

Soon, they were in Blake's barn- practically all new since the big wind had passed over. His cow was lame in the left hind foot. Very lame. Sean drove his grabs- a bit like ice-tongs, but with a ring- into one of the joists over the cow, roped her leg up and, with Blake's help, had her foot up in the air where he could work on it, well restrained, with a minimum of discomfort for the cow. Unlike some cows, she made little effort to struggle. Penny watched from a safe distance as Blake stood alongside the cow's foot facing Sean, steadying it, holding it firmly between his hands. Sean cleaned it off, examined it and started working away with a hoof knife, careful not to nick Blake or himself. Or the cow. The hoof material was hard as stone. Though the knife was sharp, it was therefore useless. He put it back in his box. Instead of trying to trim the hoof material, which was barely overgrown, he palpated the bulb of the medial heel, firmly pressing it with his thumb. Nothing. But as he pressed the outside claw, she flinched in pain. Big time pain. In fact, had the ropes not been tied up somewhat as the Swiss do- preventing her lashing away- she might have kicked somebody's fool head off; even more likely mushing the doctor's jewels; then slipped and fallen on one side, possibly luxating her uppermost hip, a most serious injury. Prognosis then: Beefer.

"Boy," said Sean, "she sure hurts, doesn't she?"

"Hasn't put it down since you looked at it last week. You didn't help her a bit, Doc. All she does is stand on three legs and hobble around- never puts the foot down flat- just keeps it cocked up like you saw it just now."

"I saw that. Flexed. Didn't look like this last week," commented Sean.

"I know it," said Blake in his rasping voice, with a wry grin, "if I didn't know better, Doc, I'd say you made her worse!" Sean reached down into his hoof box and pulled out a different knife- straight as a lance. Actually, it was an old-fashioned lancing bistoury, made before anybody had replaceable blades. Not near as sharp, but sturdy and virtually unbreakable. And sharp enough. "I can't figure what's the matter with 'er, Doc. One of my best cows, too. She ain't ate more'na smidgen past three days. Only gave a couple of quarts this forenoon."

Sean washed off the heel and scrubbed off the manure, using an iodine soap. The cow flinched again. "I think I found the trouble," he said.

"Where?" said Blake. "You sure?" He sounded pretty doubtful. "You know, I paid you eight dollars last week and you told me the same thing then."

"Right here," said Sean. "Look right here," as he pointed to the painful spot with the old scalpel.

"I don't see it," said Blake.

"Get a little closer. Do you see that spot?"

Blake's nose lacked only about a foot of the cow's heel. Sean could see that the cow had backed up just a bit when he'd tested for pain thus tightening the forward throw of the foot rope. It was impossible for her to kick now. With a gleeful grin he quickly thrust the blade into the abscess. He'd found the spot, all right- and he knew what Blake's reaction would be. He was squeamish as they come. A goodly amount of laudable, stinking, thick pus, the consistency of custard, blew out through the incision- maybe half a cup, under enormous pressure- right under Blake's nose- then landed in a long streak on the floor about five feet away. Sean was an expert marksman. None of it actually hit Blake. He just wanted it close, where Blake could really *see* what was bothering the cow.

Blake ran off, retching, headed for the drop- where, without even apologizing for his immodesty, he tossed his cookies. Sean irrigated the wound with some furacin, calmly counting Blake's disgorgements (there were seven real good ones) then let the cow's foot down, unbandaged so it would drain well.

"Damn you, Doc," snapped Blake. "If I was big enough, I'd whup you for that!"

"I wanted you to see for yourself, that's all," said Sean. "You know, I half-figured last week it might be an early abscess. Thought I told you that. Can't do a lot about those except wait till the damned thing's ready to break."

Blake was indignant. "Hell, I coulda give her a dose of that there penicillium, if I'd of known that," he sputtered, wiping off his chin on his dark blue workman's handkerchief. "You didn't tell me nothing like that last week. No way." Then, seeing the pus on the floor, he turned back around and barfed again. Sean was thinking once again how there would be no kids if it was up to menfolk to deliver them.

"I thought I did," said Sean, "But I couldn't be sure, then..., that it wasn't something else. Anyway, you might be right. But lots of times, all penicillin does is delay things when you're dealing with an abscess. Sometimes you can win if you give it a long time, but then you'd have had to throw her milk out. I didn't want you bitchin' about that. Cow'd get better, then it's bad again. This way, we most likely finished it off."

"I sure as hell hope so," said Blake.

- - - - - - - - - - - - - - - -

"Where we headed now?" asked Penny as she drove out Blake's driveway and headed down the hill toward Sturgis.

Sean had called Nancy from Blake's barn phone. "Nothing new, Penny," he said, looking up from making out Blake Farm's bill, "so I guess we can head back. What time is it, anyway?"

"You've got a watch, haven't you Dad?" she replied.

"Yes, but it's a pocket watch and it's hard to get it out from under these coveralls when I'm sitting down like this. I keep it in my trousers, side pocket."

Penny glanced at her wrist watch. "I'm sorry, Dad. I was just curious. I thought you had a watch somewhere." She stared at it a little longer. "It's four o'clock. That's all." She rubbed her nose, as she often did whenever she was trying to find a solution to a problem. "Why don't you use a wrist watch, then?"

"Not with all the sleeve jobs I do. That's for sure," said Sean.

"Wear it on your right arm, then. You don't use that one for your sleeve jobs."

"True. I tried that years ago, Penny. But when I give shots, herd vaccinations, I use that arm. That's a matter of bang-bang, rapid fire-down the line. Sixty cows in ten minutes if they're in stanchions. Watches don't take too well to repeated shocks, and that's what would happen if I wore it on that arm. So I just use pocket watches. Besides, I only need a watch once in awhile, like when I have an appointment or a meeting somewhere."

"Oh, I see." said Penny. "Well then, I won't get you a wrist watch."

"Say, Penny..., I was just wondering what you think about something. This is a good time to ask you. Your mother doesn't seem to know either. What do you think you'll be doing a year from now, after you graduate? It'll be graduating time before you know it."

"Oh, I don't know, Dad. I haven't thought about it a whole lot."

"Well, you have good grades. In fact, they're very good. I think you could get in most colleges without a bit of trouble."

"I'm not too sure I'd like college," said Penny.

"Why not?" said Sean.

"Well, I talked to Millicent Kierney..., she graduated two years ago and now she's going to Penn State. She said she and her first room-mate didn't get along very well. A lot of girls say the same thing. And she said most of them really weren't very sure what they wanted to do after they graduated from college- unless they took something like nursing or teaching. Most of them just meet somebody in school and get married afterward. I guess it's hard for a girl to get into something else, like law, or medicine. Besides, that would take a lot more time, and a lot of money. I don't think you ought to spend a whole lot of money on me and then have me go off somewhere and never really use it."

"Well, what about teaching, or nursing? Seem like real good careers for a girl. It's a good part-time job, too. You know, like a private nurse or a substitute teacher. You can still use something like that when you get married..., and a lot of women go back to it full time if their husband dies or leaves them. It can be bad for you to just rely on a husband. Suppose it doesn't work out, or he dies.... Something like that...?"

"I don't know, Dad. Sometimes I think I'd just like to be a farmer's wife, like Gramma is. She loves her home, and seems so happy all the time. But if I have kids someday, do you think I'd be a better mother for them if I've been to college?"

"Well," said Sean, "that last thing might be debatable, but there's certainly nothing wrong with it. I suppose you could work there at Gramp's farm with Eric. You have a good way around animals. But that probably wouldn't last long- he'll get married some day. Do you think you'd like something like that?"

"I think so. But sometimes I have big ideas..., like I'd like to go to music school. Maybe be a music teacher or something like that. Maybe even a concert pianist."

"Well, you certainly play well- better than most people around here. But do you think you could really succeed at that? It's very competitive, you know. And besides that, it's a tough way to make a living, no matter how good you are- that is, unless you are one of the very lucky ones in huge demand..., and that seems to be largely a matter of good luck..., opportunities, the right agents, and all of that. Most people that get into music can hardly make a living. I had some buddies in my frat that tried it. Didn't last long, either."

"I've heard that too, Dad. But if I got married, it wouldn't matter so much how much I made playing. For all I know, I might end up marrying a minister- and I could really be an asset then."

"Well, I don't know honey. But, you better begin thinking about it. By the way, what are you planning to do this summer?"

"Oh, I thought I'd work with Eric and Gramps, up on the farm- at least some of the time. I love it up there. I just don't know if they'd need me."

"Have you asked Gramps?"

"No. But when I was there last Saturday, Gramma said she'd ask him..., if I didn't want to. She said they probably couldn't pay me much..., but I don't care if they pay me anything at all. I just love it up there..., it's so peaceful and quiet. It's like heaven to me."

"It is to all of us, Penny. For me, too, you know. I grew up there, after all. By the way, I think Brian is coming to work for me this summer. I got a letter from him last week-end."

"Oh!" said Penny, abruptly. She didn't seem to be pleased.

Detecting something in her voice, Sean asked her if there would be a problem with that. She hesitated before she admitted she wasn't sure she felt easy around him, and when Sean asked why, she said he was a nice man, but too smart for her, and not only that, she thought he was attracted to her. Something about the way he was always looking at her. She thought that she would rather go with somebody her own age. After all, he was four years older than she was.

Sean laughed. “Four years might seem like a lot right now. And it is. But lots of women are married to men four years older than they are. Even older than that. By the time you’re twenty-four, a man twenty-eight will seem just about right to you.”

“That’s what mother said.”

“Oh. You’ve talked to her about Brian?”

“Yes. Back when he was here in March. She said she thought he liked me. Liked me a *lot*, if you know what I mean.”

Sean chuckled. “Well…, it could be worse. You don’t know how pretty you are…, at least I don’t think you do.”

“My nose is too long.”

Oh, baloney. Look at all the boy friends you could have. Even if it was true, you’ll get over that…, especially if you go to college. Girls learn a lot the first year in college about how to fix themselves up. I’ve been amazed how they’ve changed when they come home the next summer.”

“Then you think I need to be fixing myself up, too! I knew it!” Penny seemed hurt, acting as though her worst suspicions had just been confirmed.

Knowing he’d said the wrong thing, Sean decided to change the subject. At least, as soon as he could. First he figured he had to reassure her. “Penny, let me tell you something. I don’t see anything wrong with your nose, for heaven’s sake. You are a beautiful girl and everybody says so. But even if you weren’t, there are far more important things. I don’t want you to get into this business of running yourself down because of some little thing you think is an imperfection. In the first place, it probably isn’t even an imperfection. At least…, not the thing that *you’re* looking at. Everybody has things like that- depending on what’s ‘in’ at the moment. And then, I remember one girl- most beautiful girl I ever saw- but, as time went on, she looked more and more like a dairy cow. Kind of spoils that first impression. But most of the time, you won’t even know the real imperfections- like in your character- which is far more important, as you’ll see in years to come…, and all the while you’ve been focusing on something else that nobody else would notice. Why, sometimes, your mother has even told me this same kind of baloney. And what do you think of her looks?”

"Daddy, she has the most beautiful eyes I've ever seen."

"I'm glad you said that, Penny. You may not know it- but the eyes are the first thing somebody notices, whether it's a man or a woman. You can tell if somebody is kind, or crafty, or a schemer, or loving, or selfish- it's a window right into the soul. At least, that's what it is for me. You're right. Your mother's eyes are beautiful. After you see that, you know something about her character..., her soul, like I said. And your mother will always be beautiful, no matter how old she gets to be, especially to you and me- because we see even more than her eyes. But her eyes never lie to us, do they?"

"No, Dad. Especially when she's mad at me."

"Well, while we're driving along together, there's something else I wanted to ask you about." He looked straight at her to sense her reaction. Was this the time?

Penny suddenly seemed to draw away- almost as though there might be something she wanted to hide. "What's that, Dad?" she said, plainly apprehensive. Not like her, at all.

Sean thought maybe some sudden, unintended change in his demeanor had telegraphed something to her. He was careful to speak more casually now, as he went on, "I understand you have a friend who's a daughter of someone I know."

"Who's that?"

"Erna Vries?"

"Oh..., Erna! Yes. What about her?"

"I've seen her a couple of times, and her sisters. Pretty girls." Sean didn't mention voluptuous, though he was well aware of it. "Of course, I know her father and mother better. They live quite a ways off from us."

"I know. Her father told me he'd had you there a few times to look at a cow."

"I don't go there regular..., but, yes..., I've been there. Not often. Mostly the distance, I'd say, or they'd call me more often. At least, I think so." Actually, Sean didn't like her dad much, knowing he had said some pretty nasty things about him to other farmers. The word usually gets around, and you can tell if it's a valid story or not when they are quoting a situation you'd never discussed that had only one other witness. Sean had lost a couple of cows there- both desperate cases.

"How did you know Erna was my friend. I never told you. Was it mother?"

"Of course. We were talking about you the other night, while you were gone up to see Gramma. And by the way, where were you Saturday afternoon? You took your mother's car about noon, but Gramma told me you didn't get there till pretty near chore-time."

Penny suddenly seemed alarmed, her voice almost strident. "Is this an inquisition?"

"I don't know," said Sean, plainly troubled by her reaction. "Should it be?"

"I told mother not to tell you Erna was my friend. Well, she *is* my friend- the best one I ever had- and I like her! She's a lot of fun."

"Back to my question. Seems reasonable to me. Were you at Erna's Saturday afternoon?" Sean was afraid that Erna's reputation- even if inaccurate- would affect his daughter. Or anyone else's for that matter.

"No, I wasn't at Erna's."

"Oh! Where were you then?"

"I don't want to talk about it. It doesn't matter. I was just driving around."

Sean was getting a little ticked by now. He wasn't used to Penny being evasive. "Well, my dear..., I'm beginning to wonder. You take your mother's car..., say you're going to gramma's. It takes twenty minutes to get there. And you get there about four hours later. Where were you? Did you go shopping, or what?" Sean was trying to ease the tension.

"Yes"

"Did you buy anything?"

"Yes."

"Where did you buy it? Over in Damon?"

She was close to tears. "I can't stand anymore of this, Daddy. Yes. I got it in Damon. It was supposed to be a surprise for somebody. Now you're spoiling it."

"Penny, I'm disappointed in you. I know you just lied to me, and I don't like that. You were seen going up the road the Grange hall is on. And that is the wrong way to go to Damon- you were way off course. And it was nowhere near your gramma's or anywhere else that I can imagine you'd want to go. Why were you going up the Settlement road? There's not much up there- except the Grange hall and a lot of woods." Sean also knew about a couple of isolated parking spots that, judging from the tracks, were well used- and obviously not for midnight mass.

"I don't like this. I'm not a little kid anymore! I didn't do anything wrong. Don't you trust me?"

"If you trusted, *me*, Penny, you wouldn't be *lying* to me." said Sean, trying to cool it down. I can only think you don't want me to know something…, whatever it is. What's the problem? You may not be a little kid, but you aren't grown up, either!"

Penny was now in a pout. "I don't want to talk about it!"

"All right, little girl, that does it. Stop the Jeep!" said Sean. He'd had enough.

Sean, boiling mad, took over the Jeep and drove back to the house with Penny- cringing in her seat over against her door. Not another word was said, but as soon as the Jeep stopped in the driveway, she jumped out and ran to the house, breaking out in tears. And Sean felt like hell…, a lousy rat. But something was going on and he had to get to the bottom of it. Nevertheless, he wondered if he should have figured she was past the age when she had to account for her time.

Then he thought about her borrowing Nancy's car, and swung back the other way. If she had said nothing about where she was going and Nancy had allowed her to take it on those terms, that would have been all right. But that had not been the case. Yet Nancy had asked him not to press the girl about it. She thought they ought to say nothing about the time lapse- at least not yet. After all, lots of kids ran around wild and parents never knew where they were, either.

Sean had a sinking feeling that something had been lost to him forever. Yes, he said to himself…, I think I really screwed up. I'm a lousy rat!

Ex the Ground Hog

It was a hellish hot day in July. It was so hot that the trees had started steaming, creating a heavy haze visibly lifting off the forested hills into the sky, dimming the sunlight on an otherwise cloudless day. All the creeks had long since dried down to a few puddles beneath 'most every rural bridge- swarming with desperately trapped minnows- as birds, weasels and mink eagerly gulped down their scrawny little carcasses. The Susquehanna region was suffering such a drought that many of the farm wells had gone dry- virtually all of them in trouble, at least to some extent.

Even dry cows- those that aren't milking- are guzzlers when it comes to water requirements. And they require enormous volumes of water when they are also giving sixty to ninety pounds of milk a day- one good reason not to drill deeper and deeper wells trying to maintain milk cows in nevergreen desert country instead of where things are greener. During the current drought, a few farms- in great difficulty, but lucky enough to be near their creamery- were meeting their needs by hauling truckloads of water day and night from the plant back to the farm's water trough- in milk cans. Of course, that wasn't fast enough for the thirsty bovines. Between trips, cattle milled around the water tank- restlessly bawling and battling for position each time the truck arrived. As fast as it was filled the trough was sucked dry, some animals- usually the smaller ones- anxiously looking for some more, licking up the bottom of the tank with their long, narrow tongues.

Even those accommodating creameries that had the best of wells were finding it necessary to ration their water among their patron farmers. And though some well-drilling outfits were being called in from a hundred miles away, they weren't keeping up with the demand for new or deeper wells. Pastures were short and, though what little hay that was put up was of excellent quality, hayfields were yielding only half their usual tonnage. Field corn, normally drought-resistant, looked great at first. Local yokels had never seen such fast-starting, robust corn till, suddenly, when it reached about four feet in height, growth stopped, the leaves started curling, rapidly turning brown. In no time at all, the leaves of corn on well-drained gravel ground were so dry that, when struck by a mild breeze, they were suggestive of skeleton bones hanging up from some gallows and rattling in a stiff gale. Thus what had started out as an impressive crop that would balance out the shortage of hay, was now an impending disaster.

And the river was also low. In spots where the Susquehanna would normally, in summertime, be five or six feet deep, people could easily wade across. In fact, one adventurous young buck even drove a vehicle across the river, claiming it was a short-cut, but really just to show that it could be done.

Though it was only nine in the morning, it was plain to Sean and Brian as they approached the old schoolhouse where Jim lived, that this was to be another sweltering day. Turning the bend, Sean was surprised to see that Jim's car was still there. That wasn't like Jim. He should have been up with Drew and Eric by now, working there, maybe getting ready to do some field work. Then, seeing him draped over the fender of his car, reaching under its uplifted hood, they pulled in with the Jeep to see if they could help. Obviously, something was wrong with the engine.

Sean and Brian clambered out of their seats and walked over to Jim, who was fiddling with the carburetor, his shirt soaked in sweat, and from the sound of his cussing, evidently not having much luck. "What in haa-il's goin' on fella?" said Brian. "Hain't yo' got no pee-trol in that there thing?"

Jim responded in kind, imitating a friendly Tennessee stock car driver he had once raced against, "Oh, ah think I jist about got it fix-ed, if you can just la-end me a hand here, for a minute. Just hold that...."

"Say, Jim," said Sean, "Where can I get a drink of water around here? I'm sweating almost as bad as you are."

"Crap!" replied Jim, as his wrench slipped, skinning his knuckles. "Doc, I ain't had enough water here for a cat to drink for the last fortnight or two. And you know how much water a pussy-cat takes. You can try to get something out of the old hand pump out back. You might get a pint or so."

"By that time Sean was standing by, looking down the well. "Don't see more than a puddle there. Looks like your pipe doesn't reach down far enough, Jim."

"Yeah..., I know." said Jim. But I already added a section of pipe. Then, after a little while, that wasn't far enough down, either. Need a force pump, I guess. Finally, I started hauling enough in here from Eric's place to at least be able to wash the dishes and drink. Had to stop running the electric pump quite a while ago, so I wouldn't waste so much. I kinda' found out you're more sparing of water when you have to pump it the old fashioned way. If you want, there's a milk pail with some water settin' on the sink, inside. Won't be very cold, though."

Sean went in, got a glass, filled it, returned to the back porch and slugged it down. "Well, I'm pretty impressed with that old hand pump you got, there, fella," said Sean, as he studied it. "Brian, you like to age old things like this. Take a peek over here. Got a real long handle with a couple of curves in it..., kinda rusty lookin'. How old do you figure it is?"

Brian lifted his eyes from under the hood, where he was holding a wrench for Jim. "Oh, I'll bet it says on the handle. Looks like around 1890, to me."

"Doesn't say anything on the handle," replied Sean as he worked it up and down. But from the sound of it when you work it, sounds to me that it would pump pretty good if the other end was down in some water."

"Yeah," replied Jim. "The rubber is good I guess. When you prime it a little, the piston sounds like it's still sucking- just ain't any water. But I get along all right except I can't flush the toilet- don't have enough water for that. And I have to swim up in the farm pond if I need a bath. Though that ain't any too good, anymore- smells real fishy- maybe half full, probably not even that. I'm goin' somewhere else to swim tonight- over to the lake."

"Maybe I'll go there with you again tonight. Had a real good time last time." said Brian, immediately switching back, saying, "What do you do about your toilet, then?"

"Well, do you see that can over there next to the corner of the porch?" Brian nodded. "That's the can out of the old back-house you see over there behind the elderberry bush. Can't use that. It's full of bees, and they're mean as hell. Stung me on the ass a dozen times when I sat down. And, I'll tell you- don't get too close to the can. It stinks. I was just going to dump it."

"Don't worry, I won't." said Sean. "Where do you dump it, anyhow.?"

"Well, probably I hadn't ought tell you this, but look up there. You see that pile of dirt and stone up there back of the out-house- just a peekin' out through the pigweed?"

"Yeah. I see it," said Brian.

"And so do I," said Sean.

"Well, I make a delivery up there once a week and dump it down that woodchuck hole. So far, I ain't seen it fill up and run over."

"How long you been doing that?" said Sean.

"Well, I don't rightly know, Doc," said Jim, "but I reckon it's been quite awhile, 'cause I see'd the old woodchuck layin' a fur piece from the hole ta other day, deader'n a smelt. He was my tenant there for a couple of years, now."

"What'll you do for rent, now," said Sean, "now that your tenant is dead?"

"I dunno, Doc. He didn't pay me too good. I know my cat is gonna miss him. They been playin' ring around the rosary with each other for quite awhile, now- kinda sizin' each other up, touchin' noses and stuff like that. I think they was buddies, of a sort."

Brian laughed, looking like he was about to split. "You don't suppose he was killed by that there crap you was pourin' down his hole?"

"Ya know, sir," said Jim, a comical expression creeping across his face. "I just gotta wonderin' about that bein' a bare possibility. All I know is when I found his worthless carcass, it lay about twenty feet from the hole and he were in runnin' position, evidently running away from the port-hole full-speed when he dropped over dead. Whada you think? Say, why'd you fellas stop by anyhow?"

"Just hoped you'd be here so Brian here could see your house, and what you've done to it. Besides that, we thought you needed some help with your car."

"Well, I reckon I can do that. Come on inside. It's a little cooler in there. You got any calls, Doc?"

"None that can't wait. Let's take a look."

Big S

The instant he saw him, Sean knew that Strickland, dubbed "the big S" by those who liked him little and loved him even less, was not very happy. He had mood smeared all over his face. It was almost as though he had called Sean so he could register another of his incessant complaints. Sean was guessing what it would be this time. He had treated a cow with the bloat- a common ailment in pasture season- about two weeks before. It had looked like a routine case, one that he'd had no doubt about making an uneventful recovery. And, suspicions confirmed, as soon as "the big S" was within talking distance of Sean, he unloaded, in his usual sparse and officious manner, "That last cow died."

"The cow with bloat?"

The great one grunted, almost sneering. "I told you it was hardware. That's just one more you've lost," he said, sarcastically. "Now I've got another one. Maybe you can lose that one for me, too. Only this time, I expect you to *operate* on her! I've been a dairyman for thirty years, and I know hardware when I see it. When I had old Doc Swanson, he didn't wait even a day. When I told him to do one, he did it- right then and there- 'cause he knew I'd know if anybody did. And he never lost one of them. This one, today, I want you to know, is the best cow in the state."

Sean, as usual in such situations, pretended not to notice his perpetual insinuations. It was useless even trying to tell Big S that he'd personally seen more hardware cases in his first two years as a vet than twenty farmers like him would see in a lifetime, or that Swanson, by not waiting two or three days and then re-examining the cow, probably was operating on many cows that had something as common and unmenacing as simple indigestion. That would certainly account for a splendid recovery rate from "hardware." But, regardless of right and wrong, a professional had to act like a professional, unless a good tongue-lashing was worth losing some business.

He'd done all of Strickland's work for the last ten years, and "the S" had paid his monthly bills without fail. And without any real slip-ups on his part, though Strickland would invariably try to find something that could have been done better- "old Doc Swanson's way." Instead, he heard things through the grapevine like "my best milker ended up with a sealed 'pencil teat' and lost the quarter," just because Sean "didn't do it right..., the way I told him." This despite Sean having laboriously repeated from the first that, heroics aside, such a crushed teat was best treated very conservatively. Efforts to open a streak canal sealed by massive hematomas and adhesions might seem to work for a day or two, but under farm conditions, almost invariably expose the cow to even worse problems, such as a deadly bout with gangrenous mastitis. In other words, it was better to lose the teat, than to risk losing the cow. Some farmers, nevertheless, couldn't believe that she could give just as much milk on three teats as she had on four, a bit like the few who consistently prefer heroics to common sense.

Sean was quick to respond, in kind, except he had a smile on his face, as though he was joshing the great one. "How come you get all this 'hardware?' What are doing? Feeding your cows nails, or baling wire, or what? I've never seen a place with so much hardware. Boy, I'd get after somebody. You must have a hired man..., walks up in the mangers with holes in his back pockets, while nails are falling out." Then, before Big S could respond he slipped beside the cow, on her left, and started listening to her rumen with a stethoscope placed high, just behind her rib cage, saying "she sure has the bloat. No question about that." He continued to examine the cow: temp, pulse, lungs, heart, urine, sternal flinch and so on, as Big S stood by, watching suspiciously to see what fault he could find. Sean wondered what it must be like for Big S's wife. Maybe there was, in fact, some justification for her running around on the old goat.

Sean had completed the exam, and resisted the urge to scratch his head. That would trigger some cynical remark from old eagle-eye, standing there, watching his every move. The cow's paunch was only slightly bloated, but there hadn't been one rumination in five minutes-only an occasional pinging, tympanic burp. The only evidence for "hardware" was the fact the cow was depressed, her G-I motility essentially absent, no cud-chewing, some weak tympanic sounds from the rumen plus the fact she hadn't eaten a thing in two days. Nor drunk much, if anything at all- judging from her eyes, which were sunken a bit. Nothing pathognomonic, at any rate. The diagnosis was uncertain, so Sean caved in.

He motioned Brian to bring in the surgical equipment and, after sedating her in her stanchion with a saturated solution of chloral hydrate- given orally in a one ounce capsule; tying her tail off to her right- on her hock; head to her left with a halter as a form of gentle restraint to minimize any tendency to bop around left and right; clipping hair from her left flank; prepping the site and numbing her with procaine in a regional block. Then he was ready for his own scrub.

Sean's barnyard surgery was antiseptic, rather than aseptic as it was with pets. He had tried both methods. Cows never seemed to do much better one way or the other. For one thing, surgery in a dusty, dirty barn made absolute sterility nearly impossible, and Lister's original method more reasonable to Sean. Stripped to the waist, he scrubbed up in a pail of soapy water with a surgical scrub brush, then rinsed off in another bucket of water containing lysol, soused his skin with alcohol and fumbled among his hemostats for the scalpel in his instrument tray, which contained another disinfectant solution. The cow was in standing position for the whole procedure, without feeling a bit of pain.

In short order, he had entered the body wall, exteriorized the upper part of the rumen and fastened it with towel clamps after folding it over onto the animal's hide so as to block contamination of the body cavity through the incision, sans drapes, opened the rumen with an incision large enough to admit his naked right arm- which was scrubbed and disinfected clear to the arm-pit and shouldertop, and inserted his arm- after moving or removing rumen contents- forward, clear into the first "stomach" (reticulum) which lay tight to the diaphragm, forward of the rumen itself. There he groped through the contents till he found the esophageal groove, and feeling around that and the diaphragmatic area, where the "junk" that cows accidentally ingest usually lodges and is removed manually, whether or not it pierces the reticular wall.

Sean brought out some scraps of iron- wire, and one 6-penny nail, as well as six or seven nails that had been dissolved down to nothing more than little discs- former nail heads. None of the junk had pierced the stomach wall. Nor was there any palpable abscess or adhesion. That made the diagnosis problematic, unless the junk had, on its own, retreated from an earlier position piercing the stomach wall. Where piercing has occurred, pericarditis sometimes ensues. Otherwise, the surgery usually succeeds- though it may sometimes require a few days of anti-biotics.

After removing his bare arm from the cow's body cavity, Sean scrubbed up again, disinfected thoroughly with lysol and then alcohol, and then cleaned the stomach detritus from the exteriorized rumen and body wall before final closure- first suturing the now disinfected rumen, then- when that was replaced into the body cavity- the peritoneum, muscle, fascia and skin with through-and-through stitches of stainless steel wire.

"Well," said Big S to Sean, as Brian was cleaning up the instruments in the milk-house, "that went pretty fast."

"I take some short cuts. How long did this one take?"

"I happened to be keeping track, Doc," he said, effusively magnanimous now that his orders had finally been properly carried out. "It took you just twenty three minutes from opening her to closing her."

"That didn't count scrubbing up and all that, I assume."

"No. Just the surgery. Even good old Doc Swanson wasn't that fast. Usually took him an hour or more."

"Well," said Sean, having waited for a riposte of a gentle sort, "that's probably because I've done enough so that I have learned some short-cuts. Other vets use rubber sleeves, special drapes, even sterile drapes, and even loops to hold open the incision. I used to do that, too. But I get just as good results this way. And it's a whole lot simpler, quicker, and so…, it costs you guys less."

"Guess I never saw where you did it very cheap. Least…, not like old Doc Swanson," muttered Big S.

Sean gave up. Big S was irredeemable. Swanson had practiced long before the economy had inflated. And as he and Brian drove away, Sean sighed and said, "I don't know, Brian. I did the surgery to make him happy, but I really don't think that the cow had hardware disease."

"I know you use farmer language a lot, Doc- like "hardware." But what is the medical term for it? Or should I say- the 'vet' term?"

"I suppose I ought to be more scientific-sounding. Nancy thinks I should, too. But if you want to get along with farmers, they'd rather hear you talk their language. That is, unless you're working for some gentleman farmer or a snoot in a suit." He yawned. Then he yawned again. "Anyway, there are several names for 'hardware,' as the farmers call it, but what they call it covers them all, because they're getting at the cause itself rather than the area affected. It's usually called 'traumatic gastritis or reticulitis,' or 'traumatic peritonitis,' or 'traumatic pericarditis'..., in school.... All depending on whether the infection involves the stomach tissue alone, or also the peritoneum that lines it, or, if it has pierced about an inch through the diaphragm, to the heart sac. For practical purposes, that last one is eventually fatal, because the heart sac gradually fills up with infected serum and compresses the heart muscle till it can't pump."

"Nothing you can do for that one?" queried Brian.

"Can't say that. We did one at school on a valuable bull, and he lived. But it's more likely to kill them than save them, because the lungs may collapse when you open the chest. We vets could use some special equipment nobody can afford, but in terms of money, it makes no sense anyway, with ordinary livestock. Maybe a high-priced animal like a race-horse. There you're not talking dirt-farm language. It's more like Hollywood. Foolish, but they'll pay the big bucks because there's a bigger demand for some dam-fool thing like horse-racing, gambling, and booze, and sports- not that I don't like some of that, too- than they ever would for the food-industry. Makes me sick when I think of it."

"I guess I never thought of it. That might change someday, I suppose, when times are tough." said Brian.

"Well," said Sean, "all you'd have to do is look at how it was in Germany after the first world war. They sure found out where the real value was- could hardly afford to buy a loaf of bread. No wonder the country blew up, when people over there couldn't even get enough to eat. They were a sitting duck for a Hitler or Stalin. Imagine! A whole wheel-barrow of money to buy some little thing! My dad thinks the day may be coming for us after a few years..., the way peoples' priorities are headed today."

That Same Afternoon

"Doc," said Brian. "What do you think could have been the matter with Big S's cow, if it wasn't hardware?" Sean hadn't said a word for the last ten minutes.

"Take the next turn right- about half a mile down the road," said Sean. Then he went on. "You're probably wondering why I operated on her, especially if I didn't think it would turn out to be hardware." He sighed with an air of resignation. "Well, I guess I'll have to admit it.... Sometimes you have to do what the client wants, whether you want to or not. I don't usually do that, as I think you know by now. I certainly think a professional judgment is better than a layman's- at least over the long haul. But the other side of it is to ask yourself the question what this guy will do if you don't go along with him."

Brian turned his head toward Sean as he spoke. "Well..., what do you think he'd have done?"

"The odds are he'd call someone else. I suppose, then..., I might lose him as a client, regardless of how the case came out. Now..., I don't really think he'd do that..., but he might. I think he'd trust any other vet around here even less than he does me, if you see what I mean."

"Sure, I understand," said Brian. "Seems to me you're the real farm vet around here."

Sean frowned as though he had his doubts, at least at the moment. "The real issue is that the guy just might have been right. Not all hardware cows fit into the usual syndrome- maybe I should call it the usual 'mold.' For instance, there is such a thing as vagal paralysis in hardware cases. Those aren't common, but it did cross my mind that it might be the case here. Now, my operation- let's face it- probably won't help the cow a bit. But if she gets better on her own, it'll *look* like it did. If she doesn't get better, which is probably the case, he can hardly blame me for operating on her. After all, he insisted on having it done. But, if he raises a fuss anyway, you can be sure I'll remind him that I did it just to make him happy- because I was figuring, at least, it might be good to do it- simply as an exploratory operation. One time I did an exploratory where I found no metal at all, but instead found a big greasy reticular ulcer from necrophorus infection.

Symptoms on an ulcer can be quite a lot like what we saw in this cow. Are you following me?"

"Yes, I think so. At least, most of it. I guess you're saying you were operating to find out the diagnosis."

"Well, not exactly. I guess I'd say I was trying to eliminate some possible causes before I could narrow down to the right one. After all, it didn't cost him an arm and a leg to have it done. The cow is a good one. She's worth the cost. Then at least, knowing a few things it *isn't*, I can start reading up a little. Meanwhile, I expect to be going back in a few days to see how she's doing. By then she may have developed some other symptoms that will clue me in. Right now, I'm sort of inclined to think it's 'something she et', as the farmers say. When the pastures are down like this, the cows start eating things they ordinarily wouldn't."

"Like what, Doc? Poisonous plants?"

"Very likely that's just what it is. But it's hard to prove. Around here, this time of year, it could well be nightshade poisoning, or just possibly bracken fern. The trouble is, they usually have scours. Not always, though, if the exposure is mild.... She hasn't had diarrhea, as far as I can tell. Her tail doesn't show it, anyway. In fact, she seems to be a little constipated. Did you notice how she was straining today?"

"Yeah, you're right. I did see her straining. It sounds to me like cows have a lot more complicated digestive problems than you'd expect in other animals."

Sean nodded in agreement. "Yes, they certainly do. Especially the more milk they are expected to produce..., and of course, that's for economic reasons. And we still have a lot to learn about the intricacies of their digestive processes- the bacterial flora, protozoa, the pH, fiber content, protein and carbohydrate balance- things like that. Ruminant animals have highly specialized digestive tracts. And we aren't exactly feeding them the way nature...." Sean stopped suddenly, slapping a hand against his brow as though he'd just recalled something. "Dammit! False hellebore! It could have been that! It just came to me! She looks like that cow I saw years ago."

"Hellebore? What's hellebore?" asked Brian. "I know what nightshade is- sort of related to potato vines, isn't it? But I never heard of hellebore."

"Yeah, potato..., and tomatoes, too. Grows wild along the hedgerows. Little red berries this time of year. And Bracken? You've seen that kind of fern all over in the woods around here. They don't go for that one unless they're hungry as hell- nothing else to eat." He stopped a moment before going on. "And Hellebore? Hellebore is the name for skunk cabbage, and false hellebore looks like it, grows along creeks and swamps. Saw a cow ten years ago; a lot like this one today- even found where her feet were planted in the mud next to the creek..., and where she'd eaten off the plants. It helped that she was the only cow in that pasture lot, of course- right close to the barn- heavy in calf. Of course she died- no stopping that one, if they get enough of it. In fact, she died about three hours after I saw her. Massive melena."

"Melena? Never heard of that. What is it?"

"Oh, you know, Brian. Blood in the stool. In that case, connected with scours; bloody scours." said Sean.

"That makes me think.... Tell me something, Doc. I never say 'scours' in college. Farmers know it's diarrhea, of course..., but would they think I was a dummy or something if I said 'scours' to one of my... high-falutin professors? I got to thinking it might just be a colloquial expression. I don't want to get laughed at."

"No, of course not. Anybody connected with animal husbandry, like your profs..., would think nothing of it. They'd sure know what 'the scours' are.... Common vernacular. I think you'd even find it in a dictionary."

"So I take it you're going to look up something about this case when you get home?" said Brian.

"Just as quick as I can get to it, Brian. You never want to be afraid to admit that you need to brush up on things now and then, especially when it's something you don't see very often. And, I have to admit, there's something about that cow that disturbs me. It's no ordinary case. I'm not sure she's going to make it."

"You might know," said Brian, "that a guy like that one that would have a case like that."

Sean smirked as he uttered his next words. "It's always like that in this business. But, now..., to change the subject, are you planning to go to the lake tonight? Like I overheard you saying to Jim when we were down there."

"Yeah," said Brian. "But I goofed. I don't even know where it is. And I didn't think to ask when they'd be going there."

"Usually they do that after they're done milking. I think if you get to the farm by six o'clock, you'll be safe. Do you know who's going?"

"No. Jim didn't say. Sounds like it's quite a lake, from what he said."

"It is. Nice lake. I used to swim there pretty near every night in the summer. It's up on top of a hill…, well, almost at the top. The town built a dam on the creek where it starts to run down the gorge. Beautiful place, but it's pretty well built up around it now. Fancy cottages, and all that. Trees- big trees- all the way around the lake. Good fishing, too."

"Sounds like rich folks. Doctors, and lawyers…, guys like that." Said Brian.

"Yeah. They've got some boats there. Don't worry. There's a nice place to swim right by the dam where nobody'll bother you. It's pretty deep there, so you can dive off the dam. And I'll bet there'll be a lot of young people there besides you guys. You might even see some nice girls there. Makes me wish I was young as you are, all over again. We had some real good times there- a lot of fun. And if nothing else, it'll cool you off." Sean, perspiring profusely, wiped his brow on his sleeve. "Sure is hot, isn't it? I'm sweating even worse than I was this morning- maybe I should go with you!"

"Hasn't cooled off a bit since we saw the woodchuck this morning at Jim's," replied Brian. "By the way. Do you really think that can of crap killed that woodchuck?"

Sean laughed, then snortled. "I don't know. They're pretty tough little fellers. And they don't just have one entrance, you know. I kind of doubt it's what Jim was suggesting. But it sure makes a good story, doesn't it?"

For awhile, there was no more conversation, each of them lost in his own thoughts. Then Sean motioned down the road. "Don't miss our turn. The next right. Got a cow- up there a mile or so- that is in heat and won't catch. The breeder's coming this afternoon, so we better hustle…."

"What's up…," said Brian. "I mean- what's the big rush?"

"We have to get there a little before he does, anyway, to check her over. Then, if we're lucky…, maybe I can let you go a little early today. You sure don't want to miss the swim tonight, do you?" said

Sean. Sean was no fool. He had heard that Penny was going there, too.

Brian said nothing, but as he turned his face away from Sean, there was a smirk on his face.

Events At The Swimming Hole

Lulled by the sweltering humidity and the steady soft pulsations of a tired old Hinman milker he was using, Jim was half dozing as he squatted next to the cow he was milking. A voice from nowhere said, "Hi, I see your car is running again. Must be you knew what you were doing this morning." Startled by the sudden appearance of the huge shadow looming over him, Jim looked up and, seeing Brian standing there, realized he'd just been spoken to. He grinned, nodding in recognition as he rose, detaching the milker from the cow as he did so. Then, tipping the milker pail over from bent knee, he dumped its contents into an empty pail parked in the alley not far from Brian, who watched appreciatively as he was pouring. "Man, she gives quite a mess, don't she?" he opined. "She must be fresh."

Jim smiled and nodded towards another cow across the way. "She's a good cow, all right. Not quite as good as old Molly over there- don't hang on quite as long- but she's still a good one. Freshened last week. Bull calf. We were hoping she'd give us a heifer. Bred her to Lochinvar Segis, that fancy bull Drew bought at the Spicer sale- the one that dropped dead a few weeks later." Pausing till he'd poured out the last dregs from the milker pail, he continued, "I'm glad you made it tonight. Wasn't any too sure you'd make it. Sometimes Sean seems to slow down a little when he thinks you want to be somewhere at a certain time.... Least, it seems so." He brightened up and went on, "I've been dying for a swim, and I'll bet you are, too." He paused again as he put the lid back on the milker, trying to think what it was he wanted to say next. "Oh yeah," he said, "And, before I forget, I wanted to tell you- you must be good luck. After you left my place this morning, the car started right up. Ran like a top again, all the way up here this morning after you and Doc left. I'm still not sure what was the matter." He bent over alongside the next cow in line, actually a heifer in her first lactation- shifting uneasily a little left and right as young cows often do until fully acclimated to the milking routine. Applying the teat cups. he continued. "Sean all done for the day? Or is he finishing up the calls without you?"

"Yup. We got done early today. Let me go about three o'clock."

"That's one of the nice things about working for Doc in the summer- you get a few days like that, when you get off early. That is, if he don't drag his feet just to make a nuisance of hisself. Of course, he may be getting a call or two right now, for all we know. He must be in a good mood today- must think if another call or two does come in, he can do it alone- no need of having you hang around." He stepped out from the heifer's stall, reached down and picked up the pail he'd just filled with milk as he inquired, "You *are* going swimming with us when we get done? Maybe I just assumed you are."

"I was sort of figuring on it. How much longer you going to be?"

Jim stood there, pail in hand, momentarily looking down the line to see where Eric was on the opposite line. "Oh, about half an hour, I'd say- yeah…, about half an hour before we finish up. Can't wait. It's so blamed hot milking these devils in here on a day like this- sure need a swim. You get in between these cows and you feel like you're pressed between two radiators."

"Well, I see you're smarter than a lot of guys I've seen. You're letting them out of their stanchions just as soon as you're done with them. That cuts the heat in here a little, I'll bet."

"I'll say! Why, if they was still in here, we'd be hotter than Beelzebub's brood of bawdy broads. Miserable, miserable hot. Even though we took out every window in the barn back in June, to let a little more air in here." With that, Jim moved on toward the milkhouse, picked up a second bucket of milk along the way and headed to the milkhouse.

- - - - - - - - - - - - - - - -

The lake looked even better than Brian had expected. It was small- perhaps equivalent to sixty or seventy acres, and judging from the reeds and lily pads, not terribly deep. The water, he judged, should be just about right- not too cold. Near the dam- which was the only public site- was a bridge crossing the overflow over which a narrow road passed, circling around the lake through a naturally cool and refreshing glen of splendid shade trees- oaks, elms and maples, with a few birch trees here and there at water's edge- most of them nicely spaced around some well-kept period cabins. Most of the cottages, he saw, had a small boat of some kind tied up at a modest dock, gently bobbing- slapped by waves rippling across the lake stirred by soft vespers from the west.

There was no need to ask if the cabins were reserved for upper crust. Once seen, they spoke for themselves- even if you missed the sign pointedly stating that property titles were exclusively limited to members of a lake society descended, years back, from certain influential families, all townies. Since the lake was out of their own territory, that plainly meant one thing: No Local Rubes Allowed. Not that the owners were snobs, or anything like that. After all, on only one occasion had these persons of great consequence ever gathered the umbrage to confront these inconsequentials, not having, by a damsite, driven them off.

It being the hay season, and a scorcher of a day at that, the yokels were really out that evening. A cool swim was the best way to wash hay chaff off a sweaty body at the end of a long day slinging bales off the ground onto hay wagons or, even worse, inside a haymow. And by the time Brian and Eric emerged from Jim's car, they found there were already a dozen other inconsequentials in the water, all hicks, most of them being farm folks they knew at least remotely. Among them were a few married couples, but it was not until Erna Vries arrived with two of her sisters, accompanied by Penny- whom they'd picked up at the Auchinachie farm shortly after the men had left, that things livened up a bit. Brian's spirits lifted at his first sight of her. Though she was certainly any man's dream girl, especially when wearing her swim suit, she always seemed incognizant of it. But Brian, being a college senior starting in September and fearful of scaring her off- after all, she was four years younger than he was- tried to play it cool around her. Not that she was fooled much. Whenever he was around, there was something inexplicable about him that made her just a little nervous.

- - - - - - - - - - - - - - - -

As though their arrivals had been preplanned to synchronize- while the sun was just starting to sink down to horizon's edge behind the towering trees- another car arrived. Out jumped four boisterous bare-footed yahoos in swimming trunks who, despite the stony beach, raced boldly to Penny and the Vries girls, acting as though they owned them. The one named Cashidy stood nose to nose with Penny, who'd approached him with an amorous smile that Brian, who was watching unnoticed from the water, could hardly miss. Worse yet, their conversation was suppressed, almost intimate in familiarity, their eyes locked on each other while he fondled her pretty chin admiringly with one hand.

Jim, who seldom missed much, took it all in from the pond where he was paddling around- being not much of a swimmer. Brian had looked, to him, like some smitten stag the very first time he'd set eyes on Penny- before he'd even had a chance to talk to her. That was the time he'd come to Sturgis with Eric during college spring break. Likewise, the very first week of Brian's arrival in Sturgis, Jim had noticed how crestfallen he'd seemed when he learned that Penny would be at her grandfather's place rather than at home with her parents- where he would now be encamped for the summer. Seeing that, Jim had suspected that Brian's principal reason for working for Sean during the summer was a good deal more than just making a little money.

Courtship is a strange mixture of hope and misery. And there seems to be no solution, as long as one party or the other is, as is customary, playing that unreal game of putting only their best foot forward. Jim himself had played such a game to the fullest at one time- unsuccessfully. So, as Jim was watching Brian's face, it was as though he saw himself in a mirror, once again- absolutely crushed- having himself lost such a girl to a slick lothario much like Cashidy, a phony, selfish make-out artist, a master of only one thing- gainful flattery. And, knowing something about Cashidy personally, Jim was sure that Sean, in one glance, would never have approved of her dating such a blatantly manipulative scamp. So it was that Jim suspected, with no real proof, that Penny must have been arranging secret trysts with him, deluding her parents in the process, either by lies or half-truths.

Certainly Penny had not been the same since she'd tied in with Erna Vries. It was through her that she'd met pretty-boy Cashidy. Jim knew that, though they were regular church-goers, neither Erna nor her sisters were pillars of virtue- and even less, their mother, whose husband seemed to be oblivious to her infidelities or perhaps encouraging them, since she made no effort to conceal them from him. Strangely enough, father, mother and sisters were all active church members in a good church led by a good pastor, noted for its piety, either taken in by them or without the guts to deal with the issue.

\- - - - - - - - - - - - - - - -

A shout of alarm went up from the roadside. "Hey, look at this!" Then another voice yelled, "get out of here!" as though trying to drive off a wild animal of some sort. Every face turned to the scene unfolding in the dusk, over near the dam. "Hey, there's a crazy cat over here, going after my dog!"

In no time there was a furor, people scurrying around, a cat screeching and a dog yelping, evidently terrified. Jim saw a dog weighing at least forty pounds fleeing a cat- streaking after it, tail fluffed up, over the embankment by the dam and into the woods- where the furor continued for about a minute off and on. Voices of a couple of men yelling back and forth finally concluded with, "I killed the damned thing," repeated three or four times, and then there was silence for a minute till two men came out of the woods with the dog, breathless, lifting it into the back of their truck. It seemed that a calico cat had been poised to get a drink of water at the edge of the lake, saw the dog, sailed into it without evident provocation, and chewed the living hell out of it, even going after the men before being clubbed to death in self-defense- so he said- with a tree branch he'd picked up in the woods.

Jim, Eric and Brian, being the greatest experts with the mostest on the scene, figured the cat, being calico, thus a female, must have been trying to protect her kittens- probably hidden somewhere nearby. "They'll fight to the death for their babies," proclaimed Eric, as brother of a vet, when he was queried by a number of the other people still at the scene. "Especially with a dog around." So a few of the people, out of compassion, started looking around through the brush, along the road, and every nook and cranny for the nest where mama cat had hidden her babies. To no avail. Finally, they all gave up. It was getting late, and people were going home.

Jim had lost track of Penny during the fracas, and he'd sort of forgotten about her for awhile as he was pontificating to other people about the decision of the three trial judges regarding the cat and dog. Then he noticed her coming out of the woods, slipping across the road back to the lake quietly and quickly as though wishing to remain unnoticed, over to the Vries girls, striking up a subdued conversation with them. In a little while, they all piled into their car together and drove off. Shortly after that, as Jim was getting in the car with Eric and Brian, who were about to return to the farm, he happened to look over near the dam, and saw Cashidy coming out of the woods on the same path Penny had left, joining with his buddies in a group, soon laughing together over something or other.

Jim and the other two returned to the farm. Eric had to check on a cow to see if she'd calved all right before he went to bed. She had been standing normally and then broken water about the time they meant to go swimming, but he'd left after confirming that the calf's nose and two front feet were visible and not oversized, assured that she'd probably deliver the calf all right.

- - - - - - - - - - - - - - - -

"Well," said Erna- with a suggestive grin- as the Vries girls drove off with Penny in the back seat alongside Erna, "how'd it go between you two out there in the woods?"

"I don't want to talk about it," came Penny's reply. "He's rough."

"Oh, honey just tell me a little about it. I'm dying to hear. You never want to feel embarrassed about it- it's all natural, you know. People have been doing that forever. My mother told me that's how she knew she wanted to marry my dad."

"I know. You told me about that. How she told all you girls never to marry somebody till you find out *everything* about him. I don't think that's right." Plainly, Penny was upset.

"That never hurt anybody, honey. But you don't have to talk about it right now. Later on, you'll feel better. Some girls feel pretty bad about it the first time, though none of us ever did…," as she raised her voice teasingly, "did we girls?" There was coarse laughter from all the Vries girls. "Well, Penny, I'll leave you alone, if you don't want to tell us about it just yet. We can wait."

"I'm telling you, Erna," snapped Penny, "I won't ever talk about it! Nothing happened!"

"Okay, okay. I believe you, Penny. You were just necking, weren't you?" said Erna facetiously, "I see you got a hickey on your neck that wasn't there a few minutes ago. I'll just say that you caught your neck in a stanchion somebody'd thrown in the lake while you were swimming, if anybody wants to know. Of course, they won't know but what you caught your neck the time you were supposedly taking your mother's car up to your gramma's place. It's a good thing your dad and mother didn't find out what really happened up there, isn't it?"

"Erna! You're nasty. Sometimes I detest you!"

The Vries girls all had a really good long, raucous laugh. An evil laugh. "Tell me, Penny," said Erna, "why did you cry during the sermon when your gramma took you to church the day after that?"

"How'd you know about that!" blurted Penny, in effect confirming something Erna had heard, nonetheless needing some verification. With that, she broke down and sobbed briefly, protesting bitterly, "It's not what you think, damn you Erna! I thought we were good friends. Now I can't ever trust you again."

"Oh, baby..., pul-ease, please don't make me cry! Spilt milk is spilt milk."

"I *hate* you, Erna Vries. I hate you!"

Erna laughed. It was cruel laugh. Then she started singing a childish mocking song: "Penny *was* a goody-goodie..., Such a *prissy* goody-goodie" - as her sisters joined into it, sounding like a trio of harpies.

A Certain Rhabdovirus

Sean and Brian returned to check out Strickland's cow two days after their first call, when they'd done an exploratory rumenotomy. They'd had her scheduled on the book at the office, but the "Big S" had called early to be sure they came. Nancy answered. "Sturgis Veterinary Clinic. What can I do for you?"

"Strickland!" he snapped, like an army sergeant calling roll, following up with a growling, "The cow is worse!" Click. He'd hung up.

Nancy was disgusted. Turning to Sean, who, like Brian, was just finishing his pancakes, she said, "That Strickland is about the rudest man I ever ran into."

"He's strange, all right. What did he do now?" said Sean, elbows on the table, his mouth full of pancake.

"Never says hello, how are you, or anything like that. Just yells out his name and expects you to get it the first time, and hangs up before you can say a word. Suppose I needed to know how bad a cow was, or what she acted like? How would I know how urgent it was?"

"Well, you have his phone number, if it's even necessary. Personally, I'd forget it. Hell, Nancy...," muttered Sean, finally getting the mush out of his mouth, "that's his way of getting me there first. If I don't know if it's an emergency or not, then I suppose he figures I'll have to treat it like one. Pay it no mind. I'll get there when I get there."

Nancy grimaced. "I wonder what kind of a wife he has. How can she stand him?"

"Don't worry. She can't. Old man Bender told me that he was there one time with the threshing crew and they were all taking a break on Strickland's porch one afternoon, and she was getting some ice cream out for the guys. She was asking them what kind they wanted, and had gone all the way around till she came to her husband, and when she asked him what kind he wanted, he just let out one of those nauseating 'harummphhs!' of his. Anyway, according to Bender, she sailed across the porch and- right in front of everyone- walloped him right across the face! Screamed at him like a bawdy banshee- 'Don't you harummphh me, you miserable oaf.' Guess she pretty near knocked him out of his chair."

Nancy cackled in glee. "I'd like to have seen that! Then what did he do?"

"Nothing. Nothing at all, according to Bender. And he's a guy that doesn't stretch the truth much. Strickland just sat there speechless. Didn't even move. From what he says, she can sure take care of herself. Hot tempered, quick on the draw. Outside of that, pretty likable."

"Anyway I guess you know what Strick wanted today," sighed Nancy. "I sure don't."

"Yeah. I was going there anyway. And he knows that. He just called so he could think he was ordering me around, like he does everybody else. If I went on my own, that would mean he hadn't ordered me around, you see."

"I guess I see," said Nancy. "As long as you don't mind playing games with him, I suppose it's okay. Seems so foolish. Guess I'll never understand you men."

"Well," said Sean, grinning impishly, "anything for a buck. Right?"

"Yuk!" said Nancy.

- - - - - - - - - - - - - - - -

A couple of hours later, Brian and Sean arrived at the handsome, well-tended Strickland farm. "Big S" was champing at the bit, nervously pacing around his sick cow, evidently trying to figure out what was the matter with her. "I don't know what in hell you did to my cow the other day, but she's going to die. I might have known you wouldn't find the problem. Now you better get some results today! If you kill this cow too, there's gonna be hell to pay!"

Sean, focusing his eyes strictly on the cow, pretended he neither saw nor heard his would-be antagonist- calmly, deliberately, ignoring him- that being his customary strategy with overbearing clients. When ignored, sooner or later, they give up. Then, still not acknowledging Big S, he started examining the cow from one end to the other. Fake 'em out, as old Prof Wilson had advised his class- let 'em think you're preoccupied. At first that went routinely. But when he put a thermometer in her rectum, she hopped her rear end up in the air and nailed him with a lightning-fast, one-legged all-out trip-hammer kick, nearly knocking him down- and enough to break his leg had it not been a glancing blow. As he stepped back, rubbing his bruised thigh bone, she turned her head in the stanchion, wild-eyed, seemingly mad with fright. Then she started to dribble, and it didn't stop. Meanwhile her tail, barely raised, was constantly switching in the urine, feebly slinging it everywhere behind her like a dirty, wet rag mop maliciously whipped around in the hands of a juvenile prankster.

When it was time to remove the thermometer, Sean reached his arms out cautiously, full-length this time, ready to spring back if she so much as wiggled, and managed to retrieve it without stirring her up again. Wiping it off, he saw that she had a fever. Almost 106 degrees. Oh Lord, he thought, not an infection somewhere! If so, he hoped it was not from the surgery, or he'd never hear the end of it. Then, strangely, she started to tremble, perspiration quickly building up and visibly dripping off her- the latter not too common in cattle. Another glance, and he was even more puzzled. She'd started treading back and forth from one hind leg to another, almost like a milk fever case about to go down. Then he recalled another oddity that he hadn't really noticed at the time, due to being kicked. When he'd initially lifted her tail, putting in the thermometer, the tail had seemed abnormally limp, though not completely paralyzed. So, on closer examination, he cautiously palpated the top of the pelvic area, soon assuring himself that there was no sacro-coccygeal injury or abscess-common causes of such a paralysis. Nor was there any sign of injury to any other part of the spine, nor to the pelvis itself.

As he worked, the Big S watched, no longer as dubious, scratching his head at times, trying to figure out what Sean was looking for. He had never before seen Sean do this kind of exam. The thought was occurring to him, for the first time in his life, that a vet might actually know what in hell he was doing. He would think better of it later- no use of making a mistake like that.

But, without question, the most critical and noticeable thing Sean had found was how deeply the animal's eyeballs had sunken into their sockets, unquestionably a sign of severe dehydration. Often, in the past, that meant curtains- so to speak, for an animal- literally so, were it a man being discussed. Turning to Big S, who had, for the most part, shut his big mouth down ever since Sean had been kicked, Sean asked him if he'd ever seen the cow drinking. It turned out that was a mistake. Necessary, but still a mistake.

"Nope," he said. "Not once. I figgered I'd better keep track of that, even though you didn't tell me to..., like you *should* have done. She puts her nose in the drinking cup now and then, and turns away quick, shaking her head like it was poison or something. Hasn't et a bite, either. Been four days. Jus' look 'n see how gant her belly is. Whatever you did to her, you..."

"Look," said Sean, having had enough. "Will you let me do my work and... *shut up*..., while I'm doing it? Either that, or I'll get out of here right now. I think I'm onto something now."

"What's that?" said Big S, hardly taken aback. "What is it?"

Sean glared at Big S. "For crying out loud!" he barked, "Let me figure it out, will you? I'll tell you when I'm done, and not before! I'm not going to give you a running account. You're acting like..., like a..., spoiled brat!" He started to put the stethoscope on his ears, thought better of it, and then sputtered, for good measure, "How in the world do you expect anybody to think, or hear with a stethoscope, with you yammering away like that?" With that rejoinder, Big S finally left Sean alone. Sean could now listen to the cow's paunch. Absolutely quiet. And the incision looked fine. Nor was there any sign of pain, as would be the case with peritonitis, a possible but unlikely result of Sean's previous surgery. Yet, she had the fever. Anything from 100.4 up to 103.1 would be considered normal for a cow.

Sean listened to lungs, heart, then checked the cow's bag- careful not to get whaled again. All normal. He took a sample of her urine and found it to be negative for ketosis- another possible cause of the jitters, though the effects of dehydration were evident in the urine's specific gravity. Finally, Sean turned to Big S and suggested he close up all the barn doors because he wanted to turn the cow loose, inside. He wanted to watch her walk. Sean had a lingering thought it might be Listeriosis, a common disease in the area sometimes called "circling disease," even though neither ear was limp, hanging down.

With the doors shut, Sean went up in the manger and released the cow from her stanchion. That was a bad mistake. The cow immediately went into a frenzy and bolted forward out of its stall and into the manger- bawling, hot to kill Sean. Absolute bedlam resulted as the cow, frothing at the mouth, raging mad, with a low-down throaty roar, punctuated with shrieking screeches unlike anything Sean had ever heard, even from a cow in heat, pursued first one man, then another from one end of the barn to the other, her mouth foaming like soapsuds.

"You have a gun?" yelled Sean to Strickland, as he ducked behind a post for the umpteenth time.

"A shotgun!" came the reply.

"For the love of God, go get it! We've got to kill her."

"Can't you do anything for her? She's my best cow!" hollered Strickland as the cow left him and tore off down the center of the main alley hot on Brian's tail, chasing him into the silo room. He scrambled up the ladder, just in the nick of time, as she tried to climb up after him with intent to kill, goring the silo itself- in lieu of a human being- to the point of breaking off her horn.

"Go get your shotgun. She's got rabies, you damned fool!" shouted Sean.

With that, Big S said no more, high-tailed it out of the barn like a Big S bird, leaving Brian and Sean to whatever the fates would bring. Finally, the animal tired, so exhausted she sank to the ground, bawling in absolute terror, frothing and coughing, choking on her own saliva, since she was, of course, unable to swallow and, momentarily, hardly able to breathe; spreading small piles of infectious froth all over the floor.

Strickland finally arrived outside the barn, trembling in fear. "It's my twelve gauge. Here, you can take it. I've loaded it. But you ain't about to get *me* to come back in there." He tried to hand it to Sean through an open window.

"I don't know anything about your gun. Get in here and shoot her."

"Oh no, you don't. It's your job, Doc. You shoot her!" Big S was no longer quivering; he was now absolutely shuddering. It pleased Sean, somehow, to see it.

Brian zipped by Sean with the cow hot after him again, having recovered her breath, snorting like a mad bull. "Give me the gun, and I'll shoot her!" he hollered as he started to run by again, back the other way, as the cow ran head-long into a post, fell down, dazed as Sean handed the gun to him, admonishing him to shoot her in the neck, not the head. Brian looked the gun over, unlocked the safety, aimed and hit the cow just as she was rising for another chase. She dropped like a rock. Brian had hit her perfectly, breaking her neck. The battle was over.

After removing the cow's head, Sean soon had a sample of hippocampus from her brain, which he'd obtained through the foramen magnum with long thumb forceps and scalpel, plus a long ice tea spoon he'd sneaked away from his wife, which she never seemed able to find again despite having repeatedly looked for it. Big S, by now thoroughly deflated, brought him an empty peanut butter jar from his wife's kitchen, sparkling clean, into which Sean placed the tissue, which he then transferred to a special kit in his lab refrigerator at his office. He mailed the specimen to the lab the next day.

Sean didn't expect the nasty phone call that came from the lab the day it arrived there. It was as though the director of the lab had, himself, caught rabies. Almost foaming at the mouth, he proceeded to chew out Sean. "You mean to say you don't know better than to kill an animal that might have rabies?" he roared.

Sean minced no words, roaring back, thoroughly p.o.'d. "What in hell would you do if that cow was chasing three guys around in a barn trying to kill you or somebody else?" Silence reigned. Then all Sean heard was a feeble, "Oh." After hanging up, without exactly apologizing, the lab man went ahead with the usual procedure and found the Negri bodies which confirmed Sean's diagnosis.

This case was unusual, in that fever is not expected in a case of rabies, as any vet will tell you. In this case, Sean had theories about the cause, but he never discussed it with other vets because they would think he was full of bull.

Sean, of course, knew that the Negri bodies the lab would be looking for under the official rules at that time, might be inapparent on microscopic study unless the animal died naturally in the late stages of the disease. Thus it followed that it would be a real no-no to shorten the life of a suspect animal- that is, to *kill* it before Negri bodies would develop. He also knew that there was an alternative, though slower, way to prove rabies virus without even resorting to Negri bodies.*

* *Eventually, the Negri test would be supplanted by the less exacting F-A test, also performed on brain tissue. No longer were suspects to be held till natural death occurred. Instead, once the clinician had determined the probable diagnosis, the official recommendation was to euthanize the animal immediately rather than hold it, as formerly done. As of the year 2001, no case of human*

rabies has ever been conclusively traced to a cow- but the failure to find something can never be taken as proof that it does not exist.

At Summer's End

The rabid cow at Strickland's farm was only the beginning of a much larger problem. A week later, when Sean encountered another case at the same farm, it dawned on him that the first cow that died of unknown causes had symptoms much like the last two- initially rather vague- a cow off feed, seemingly a G-I problem, then not drinking, and progressively dehydrating. Death had, in each case, followed within seven or eight days of the initial call to Sean's office. Of course, two of the cows were typical "dumb" or "paralytic" cases, rather than the "furious" type that had chased Sean and Brian around the barn.

The disease, of course, was reported to the state Health Department, since it was an anthropozoonotic disease. From there it went to the press. From the press, it went to widespread panic, particularly when the paper disclosed that Doctor Sean Auchinachie, much to his embarrassment, as well as his aide, Brian Miller and a farmer by the name of Strickland were taking the standard series of shots to prevent development of the disease. Then it spread to the radio and surrounding communities. Pretty soon, Sean was getting calls from his colleagues to get the real specifics, since some of his remarks when interviewed were misquoted or exaggerated at the expense of less dramatic, but more significant facts.

At that point, every vet and physician in the area was getting calls from panicky people, mostly mothers of small children who had petted, or were thought to have petted an unknown- or stray- dog or cat. At first, this was easily disposed of, since it had not been detected yet in anything but cattle.

That ended when the dog that had been attacked by the calico cat at the lake (the same cat that had been clubbed to death in the woods) developed rabies about three weeks later. This then led to shots for not only for those *probably* exposed to the dog, but also the men that had dealt only with the mad cat. There was the *assumption*, reasonable enough, that the cat actually had rabies- its body never found after it was killed- though actual exposure of the men involved was very uncertain. They just knew they were near it, and though not bitten- unable to recall if they'd been scratched or even touched the cat.

Beyond that, even those *possibly* exposed to the rabid dog- i.e., indirectly- were given post-exposure shots- even for such things as petting the animal long before it could have reached the contagious (overt) stage. In the absence of concrete information from those supposedly exposed, what else could a doctor do with a hysterical patient? After all, better a safe and live nervous ignoramus than a dead one. This, despite the fact the vaccine used at that time was, like its predecessors, still suspected of having the potential to cause neurological problems in those it was supposedly protecting- such minor things as brain autolysis and subsequent long, drawn-out death after turning into a vegetable.

Soon, farms not far from Strickland's were having more cases of rabies, though only two more were cows, the rest being cats or dogs, and, of course, a couple of sheep. By that time, they were finding dead foxes along roads in that area, where those dazed by rabies had been clipped by a vehicle. Since that is not a common occurrence for foxes, a few of the dead ones, freshly killed, were examined by the state, under the assumption they would not have been in the road if they weren't rabid- wandering aimlessly, as they often do with the "dumb" form of rabies. Supporting that theory were many reports of foxes seen close to houses and barns during daylight hours when, normally nocturnal, they are rarely seen.

In connection with all this, it was not until the week before Brian was to leave Sturgis Valley and head back for his last year of college that he happened to think of that hot day he'd been at Jim's house, when Jim's car wouldn't start. As he was riding with Jim one evening, headed for the small town of Damon to get one last beer together, they had started talking about all the pandemonium that had developed since that day- thanks to the rabies enzootic.

"You know," said Brian. "I was just thinking…."

"Thinking? What about?" Jim inquired.

"Do you suppose that woodchuck you found at your place might have died of rabies?"

"Rabies? I didn't know they'd get it, too."

"Sure. Sure they can. Sean said he'd checked up on it just to be sure it was true, and, in the process, read that *any* warm-blooded animal can get it, and yet he wasn't too sure himself, for instance, whether they'd been thinking about birds when they wrote that. Said he'd never heard of it in one of them, though it might be because there wasn't much chance of their getting an exposure outside of a laboratory. Sure…, woodchucks can get it."

"By gol," said Jim, "I didn't even think of that. I'd kind of forgotten about the woodchuck. Maybe he was the first one to get it. And come to think of it, I *did* see a fox hangin' around a couple of weeks before I found the critter dead, right near his hole."

"Did you see him after that, by any chance? The fox, I mean."

"No, come to think of it, I didn't. He disappeared just about the same time as the chuck must've croaked," said Jim. "Never saw him again. And…, come to think of it…, he'd been scooting around in broad daylight, acting kind of funny, like he didn't hardly know where he was. You don't suppose…?"

"Well, anyway," said Brian, "it's a good possibility. The doggone epidemic might have started right around your place. When you think about it, your house was awful close to being the center of the whole blamed outbreak."

"Dad gum, if you ain't right. Yessir," said Jim, "I really think you're onto something." Jim rubbed his nose briefly, before he thought it proper to say the next thing that came to his mind. Finally, he opened up. "Brian, you and I been hittin' it off pretty good this summer, and I take right kindly to that…, seein' as how I'm a guy never even finished high school. If you figger I'm as good a friend to you, as I think of you…, seems like maybe I could ask you about somethin' that's been troublin' my mind a little the last few weeks. But if you don't want to talk about it, just say so. I never like to butt my nose into other peoples' business, though I suppose I notice a lot more goin' on than most people do."

Brian had no idea what was coming, but he said, "Go ahead and shoot. If I don't want to talk about it, I'll tell you. Okay?"

"Well, like I said, it ain't none of my business, but I been through somethin' like I think you're goin' through with Penny, and I just wondered how you feel about her. Somehow, I just got the feelin' that you was hopin' she'd talk to you a little more than she did. 'Course, you hardly had a chance, what with her up on the farm with her gramma most of the time instead of being down at her mama's house, where you probably thought she'd be. Or am I sorta' misjudgin' the whole thing?" With that, Jim turned his face toward Brian, to see his reaction.

Brian bit his lip, sort of uneasy like, and cleared his throat-hesitating briefly. Finally, he went into it, describing how he'd expected he'd see Penny more, and how that was the main reason he wanted to work for Sean during the summer, since he could have had a summer job at the university in an animal nutrition lab and made a little bit more. Yes, he liked Penny. Trouble was, the more he saw of her, the more he was attracted to her- but he was "feelin pretty poorly" about his chances with her. Not only was she pretty, but the best thing about her was she was a peach- and she was the same way with everyone- friendly, kind, helpful, intelligent and, something more he hadn't expected would ever happen: Somehow, he had changed, since he'd seen her and her family. Where once he'd scorned churches, he'd even gone to church with her three times that summer, after she'd invited him. All out of respect for her family. But lately, she seemed to be cooling off more and more. He wondered what he might've done to cause that, granted that he'd never expected to sweep her off her feet. Their age difference, he knew, was too great for that. But lately, she seemed to be ignoring him, like at the lake.

Jim got the picture, but he didn't quite know what to say. He knew what Penny's father thought of her new friends, Erna in particular, and he knew exactly why he felt that way. He could see that Penny had changed a great deal since her friendship with Erna the previous spring, but he thought it best not to get into that.

"Tell you what," said Jim, again lapsing back into that contagious dialect of West Virginia where he'd been raised years before till the sixth grade, and that he still slipped into whenever he was most wound up about something, "if I was you, I might just think about writin' her a letter every so often while you're up in school. Just to let her know you're around. You gotta keep your presence known to a young girl like her, you know, and then someday, when she's tired of all the young bucks that's maybe more excitin' but got nothin' deep down compared to you, it may dawn on her that you're the man she should be interested in. From there on, it's up to you. I think that was my mistake with the girl I liked. I knowed she liked me, but when she seemed to ease off, instead of fightin' a little for her attention, I let her slip away out of my life altogether. Didn't even know I was doin' it, Brian, till I seen it were too late. Best chance a pol-tician got to get elected, you know, is for him to keep his infernal name and puss in the paper. Don't even have to say nothin', even if he actually happens to know a little."

"What would I..., write to her about?"

"Hell, Brian, I jus' don't know. You're the one gotta figure that all out. But I suppose, you gotta let her know some interestin' things goin' on where you are. She won't know anything about the football games, and all that. But if she sees something about that in the paper, she'll think maybe, that's pretty impressive. She likes to play the pianni, you know. Ask her how she's doin' and what she's up to. Best of all, tell her about some people there, in school, and what you'd like to do when you get out on your own. Can't hurt, can it?"

"Suppose she won't write back?"

"She will, believe me, Brian. I know the girl, and I knows her dad and mama pretty good too. Doc likes you. I can tell. And, it's a little harder to tell, but I think Nancy has her eye on you as a future son-in-law. In fact, I knows it as sure as I know I'm a-sittin here talkin' to you that you got somethin' goin' for you there."

Saving Mankind

Once again, snow was drifting on the hills surrounding Sturgis Valley, and, as usual each year at that time, Sean received his personal communiqué from the state agriculture department. This year, they announced, there were some eighty herds in his assigned territory due to be tested for tuberculosis- by intention, only a fraction of the total population. And, as usual, they'd provided him a list showing each owner's name, location, size of the herd, status, and date of last test.

Being primarily a bovine practitioner, he had- for years- been authorized to cover, not the usual one or two, but five townships where he practiced. That was no small responsibility, and it required some management skill. For one thing, he had to be especially careful that his private practice and his state work didn't interfere with each other. State work was a boon to his income, but it was only moderately supplemental to his much more remunerative private practice.

For years, veterinarians, far more than physicians, were pretty much on their own. Unless they were near a city, where vets were more numerous, there was little opportunity for case referrals. Nor were there emergency clinics, though they'd been tried in places- financially unsuccessful, for the most part, due to collection problems. (For some reason, clientele seemed to have a most casual illusion of entitlement when it came to *pet* emergencies.) To sum it up, cooperation among vets was nil- in most places.

Cut off more than most vets from any cooperative effort, problems for *farm* vets could be greatly multiplied. In general, virtually nothing was done on a mutual basis. Unless a partnership of some kind was established, there was no genuine relief time from their responsibilities: no shifts, no week-ends, days or evenings off- nothing but a voluntary sort of slavery to their work, akin to what it was like for dairy farmers. For Sean, there was an additional problem in having to conjoin considerable state work with a very demanding private practice- manageable only if done efficiently. The unpredictable daily demands of his practice, being largely therapeutic, greatly outweighed anything else- sometimes even his family. State work, on the other hand, was rarely anything but prophylactic, and so it could be done most anytime. That helped.

Whenever T.B. testing was done, *all* the mature animals on the farm were involved. If herds were done otherwise, piece-meal, or day after day, a few animals at a time, there would be enough confusion to make countless underpaid and starving bureaucrats and attorneys smile in ecstasy.

Second, if a doctor- especially a solo vet- were to pre-arrange an *appointment time* for state work- the unpredictable, untimely emergency demands of his private practice might force him to negate some or all of the T.B. tests that had been pre-arranged for the day. That simply would not do. Doctors not there for an appointment on time? It would be anathema. Breaking an appointment is a perquisite routinely permitted only people of unfailing irresponsibility. Any physician, dentist or vet can tell you that.

Third, if the vet, as the last option, instead of making an appointment, just walked in like he was going to take over the place, a farmer just might be a little put out about it. Testing could well take enough of a chunk out of his day to upset a whole week's plans. Ignoring time- the sacred province of college kids "working on a term paper" while imbibing nightly in Joe's bar- was anathema in the farm world.

For Sean, there was an obvious solution to the problem of state work. *Jim.* Jim displaced much of the need to use farm help, especially in the smaller herds, by going up in front, lightly grasping each cow's ear and calling off her official eartag number while Sean, standing behind the cows, was writing them down on an official state chart. Far speedier at the job than any of the farm help, Jim seldom read any tags wrong. Once tags were recorded, Sean injected tails intradermally with tuberculin while Jim flanked them to prevent sashaying. Then they were done for three days, when they would return so Sean could check tails for blebs. That was the easiest part.

The beauty of it was that, in most places, they could do all this without using any farm employees, and by doing the work in the winter months, they could be pretty sure all the animals would be in the barn. Therefore, when in the vicinity, he and Jim could just "drop-in" when the work-load of their day permitted. If it was a bad time for the farmer, well, all right! They'd try another time. The method worked reasonably well for Sean as well as his farmers because he could fill up some of his slack days with state work. Meanwhile, his private practice was not jeopardized.

It didn't always work- having no farm help around. One time in particular. The lighting in the barn was inadequate and, instead of stanchions, the cows were standing in tie-stalls- many not tied at all- so Jim was encountering a good deal of trouble reading tags. Some animals were very skillful at flipping their heads away from Jim, or from one side to the other, or backing out of reach with their hind feet in the drop. Some cows went even further, backing out of their stalls and nearly knocking Sean down as he tried to drive them back in, handicapped by a chart and pen in hand. After wasting five or ten minutes trying to corral a couple of runaway beasts, they managed to proceed with the next cow.

After an hour and a half at a job they'd ordinarily have finished in half the time, they started to pack up. Jim noticed Sean was looking for something, a puzzled look on his face. "What's the matter, Doc?" he asked.

"Looking for the papers I made out. I thought I left them down low on that ledge over by the door to the milkhouse, where they couldn't get splattered by bovine doo-doo." said Sean.

"I saw you put them there," said Jim. "I know you did."

"Gee, I don't remember putting them somewhere else after that. I must be cracking up."

"No, you aren't," said Jim. "I noticed they were there when you were injecting that cow right near her. She wasn't one of those that got away, was she?"

"Naw. She's tied in. I was real careful about not putting it where she could reach them. Or any other, for that matter."

It was at that precise moment they saw one goat, previously unnoticed, running around in the barn with a wad of paper in her mouth. She was in the very act of swallowing the last of them as they rushed over to catch her. That didn't help. It was now a game, and she ran off, belching in fiendish delight. It was no use. The papers were all gone. She hadn't left one. After a moment of helpless rage and cussing, they faced the inevitable and began to read the tags all over again. Only this time the cows had wised up and were even harder to deal with.

\- - - - - - - - - - - - - - - -

Perhaps one of veterinary medicine's proudest achievements in the United States was the great national effort to eliminate bovine T.B. Tuberculosis is caused by vicious acid-fast bacteria- three different strains of Mycobacterium tuberculosis- infectious to many kinds of animals and birds, as well as humans. Over the years, raw milk had infected huge numbers of small children with T.B., more often with the bovine strain than the human strain.

Children infected from drinking raw milk were more likely to develop lesions in the lymph nodes of the neck and abdominal region, unlike the human strain- which usually causes thoracic lesions. Nevertheless, bovine T.B. was scarcely less serious in its debilitating, often fatal consequences for small children. The best that could be done, since there were no really effective medications for such patients, was considered to be supportive care in a sanitarium. So it was that T.B. ranked, for many years, near the top of the national mortality and morbidity lists.

A solution was there. But it was a difficult choice. The only practical recourse for farm veterinarians would be, first, to identify infected cattle- through periodic testing of entire herds- condemning and shipping those animals found positive to an abattoir, where veterinary inspectors would decide what, if anything, could be salvaged from their carcasses. A draconian measure, vets knew this would be the ruination of many cattlemen. Conspicuously identified, papered and relentlessly traced to their post-mortems by the state process, bidders at an auction would give next to nothing for their cattle.

Vets knew that the first herd test, even if negative, would seldom be the end of it. Even a herd that was supposedly cleaned up could, months later, reveal positives, so that farms where most of the cattle were tested and deemed negative could still be wiped out, piecemeal, following recurrent herd tests. They also knew that the more faint-hearted farmers, discouraged after one or two tests, would probably give-up and sell out.

The second measure that would have to be taken was pasteurization of all commercially sold milk- a process that required precise temperature control so that bacteria of all kinds, not just T.B., would be killed without spoiling the taste of the product. Up to that point, most milk had been consumed "raw," i.e., unpasteurized. To accomplish this, many local health departments, urged on from higher up, concocted strict sanitation rules and enforced them rigidly through the whole process from cow to bottle. There were further administrative improvements as time went on.

Nevertheless, despite the many draw-backs of the prospective program, Congressional bills were moved authorizing action, whether farmers liked it or not. Unlike so much that Congress does, this time it was not- once again- a case of "we don't know what in the devil to do, but we're sure going to do it." Much thought had gone into it. The medical community was behind it. Radical measures were required. The disease had been running rampant, and seemed to be going more and more out of control. After much rancor, the bill passed.

Thus, to accomplish eradication, a mandatory federal program was begun in 1917, and even though funds were provided for testing as well as indemnification of condemned cattle- the latter being a minimal amount, a mere sop to their owners- the program was extremely unpopular with most farmers. Opposition soon became so ferocious as herd after herd disappeared, that some veterinarians, once again, had to learn how to duck bullets, deer-slugs and buckshot, not to say the more common hard right cross to the jaw.

Despite all this, more and more herds were tested clean, each of them given a much-deserved "accredited herd" certificate. Thereafter, strict isolation of the herd had to be maintained. There could be no exposure to cattle not proven clean. And, in the long run, the farm community gained. By 1940, the program had reduced the overall incidence of bovine T.B. from about 4.0% country-wide, to about 0.46%. Progress continued till it was indeed rare in most of the country by 1950, which, together with the strict health dept. rules for milk pasteurization and meat inspection, practically eliminated milk or meat as a source of tuberculosis in this country. Nevertheless, the need for testing remained for many years, as a single flare-up resulting from an illicit importation or an infected human being could quickly infect large numbers of cattle. There was no federally-approved vaccine to prevent the disease, of course.

- - - - - - - - - - - - - - - -

"Let's drop over to O'Brien's farm and see if he still has some cattle," said Sean. "I heard he still kept some, even after the cattle dealer hauled them off to the auction last summer. Guess they fattened up better than you might think."

"Just on grass?" queried Jim.

"That's what I hear, anyway. Guess they didn't look too bad. But I see O'Brien's never been taken off my list from the state. Guess I forgot to write him off. Anyway, since he doesn't have a phone, I figure- since we're over this way- we might as well stop and see if he still has a few heifers or something like that."

It was only five miles to O'Brien's place. Nobody was home, so they drove over near the barn door. "Wait here," said Sean. "I'll go take a look in the barn." Jim nodded in approval, keeping the engine running. In a moment, Sean was back, red-faced, his eyes bugged out.

Jim was mystified. "What's the matter, Doc?"

"I can't believe it," he exclaimed, "I just can't believe it!"

"What happened? Get bit by a rattlesnake in a snow-pile?"

"Don't be a smart-ass," said Sean as he climbed back into his seat and slammed the door shut. "I guess I wasted my sympathy on that guy. You remember the cow that had inanition? Saw her last year, during that big storm?"

"Yeah. I remember," said Jim. "I still think you were giving me a line. She sure looked like plain old starvation to me. What about her?"

"Well, Jim, I'll admit it. It *was* starvation. I just didn't want anybody to know about it. I felt sorry for O'Brien, and his dad. Having a tough time. They didn't even have enough to eat, themselves. So I went to a lot of trouble sticking up for them, spent some money of my own to help them out- and then what do I see..., just now?"

"I don't know. What did you see?" asked Jim.

"The barn is empty...."

"No cows? So ....

"Yeah there's two cows in there. Skeletons, both of them..., laying right there in their stanchions. Full grown cows. Stanchions still locked around their necks, their heads curled around and their noses resting on the concrete manger right where they died. Didn't even have enough ambition to open the stanchion and haul the poor critters out of the barn! Must've been dead half a year or more. Just bones."

"So what now?" said Jim.

"They don't have any cattle." said Sean, plainly mad as could be. "No tracks out in the snow, or anything. So much for bleeding hearts. Let's go."

Penny's New Friend

Shortly before Eric and Brian had left the scene at Sturgis that summer, heading back to endure their last year in college, a new hired man and his family had arrived to replace Eric at his father's farm. That was because Jim Holland- as planned- had once more left Drew's farm to work with Sean in his veterinary practice. Distantly related to Jim, Hank Breslau had brought his family of four north from the Shenandoah after he'd sold off the small dairy farm he'd been working to an urban tycoon- a developer who was planning to build a money-grabbing, competitor-gobbling shopping plaza. Just what the consumers had desperately needed since the time of the Indians, though for the more rural folks, it would soon mean a lot more gas-guzzling mileage to get a simple item like a pair of shorts or some new shoes. It was the first such major boondoggle in that area- soon to be a national trend- abandoned and torn down in a few short years for bigger and bigger such boondoggles, and on and on in an endless cycle to hog the markets "for the benefit of the consumer," and.... No one else, of course.

Hank had been barely scraping along, anyway. The trend to survive was for larger and larger farms: efficiency would save the farm home. But land prices in his area were becoming far too high for the meager income a farmer could make off such fields. And so, unable to rent land at a decent price and lacking enough land to enlarge his herd like others were doing, he could see that there was no longer any future for him there. Not only that, but he wanted to be nearer to the peach country of Pennsylvania where he'd been born, and to the generations-old family homestead his ailing mother and sister had never left. Drew's farm was only a reasonable morning's drive away, to the north. He could manage to see his mother without missing chores at the farm.

As a start, Hank would be getting $300 a month, with automatic increases of $20 a month for the next five months, at which time a new deal would be negotiated based on his performance. In addition, Drew provided his family use of his two-story tenant house; what meat and milk they required; electric service; firewood and coal for the stoves; as well as use of some furnishings and enough paint to pretty up the interior, if they would provide the labor. There was also a sizeable garden plot behind the house for their use. The deal was not at all that bad for hired men at the time- having been for years used to being mere serfs on a fief, at the bottom of the national payroll. Actually, it was about what he'd made in Virginia as a self-employed farmer without all the risk that entailed.

But Hank Breslau, it turned out, was no ordinary hired man. Like Jim, he was dependable and hard-working. He knew what he was doing, having run his own farm for many years. And he had no vices except that he chewed tobacco. Drew didn't mind that. Like many farmers, he had also chewed earlier in his life, and he figured if that was- in fact- a vice, it was probably among the least of them. And if a man had to spit, which seemed to be the chief objection of womenfolk, other than stained teeth and foul breath- incidentally reducing the repopulation rate- there were plenty of places where he could spurt his spittle on a farm. Might even kill some insect pests if you spewed enough around.

Once the Breslau family moved in, it didn't take Penny long to find a good friend in Hank's daughter, Betty, who was slightly older, but like her, a senior in the same high-school. Betty was a gentle, petite blonde, her quick smile accented by her bright, blue eyes- almost azure. Having been born in Virginia, both she and her brother sounded the part when they were speaking, as did their mother- born near Harper's Ferry, not far from Jim Holland's birthplace in West Virginia.

Penny's only really close high-school friend had been Erna, and that had ended abruptly on that sweltering summer night at the lake. So now, she needed a good friend, one that she could take into her confidence. Having been drawn to Erna's verve and ways of the world, Penny had envied her most because of her coterie of male admirers. And, unlike herself, Erna was never at a loss for words around them. It seemed, at times, utterly impossible to embarrass her. Most of all, she was always reckless- a devil-may-care. Nothing dull about Erna. Penny could discuss boys and things freely with her that she would never even think of mentioning around her mother- much less her dad. And while she respected Gramma Rache most of anyone she knew, and really loved her, she was, like Grampa Drew, deeply entrenched in traditional ways and more than a bit too religious. It would be unthinkable for her to discuss openly with Gramma Rache most of the things she and Erna had pondered over together. That Erna had a reputation had made her even more fascinating- a primal soul of the glorious years lying in wait just ahead- when freedom, though godless, would reign: outranking wisdom.

It was only after she realized Erna considered her some sort of awkward goose, good for laughs because of her innocence- eventually mocking her at the lake- that Penny turned away- discovering, at last, that Erna was a rebel without conscience: shallow, cruel, calculating and untrustworthy. Penny had shared with Erna some of her innermost feelings about certain boys she liked. Not long afterward, she began to suspect those same boys had been apprised of what she'd said- things she would never havc wanted anybody to know. Unaccountably, some of them had suddenly become very bold with her.

Penny, like most teen-agers, had been testing the waters after a period of skepticism about many of the things she had been raised to believe about life. Having now come to despise the cynical and sordid life that once intrigued her and that Erna so ably represented, she was now ready to retreat to the way she, ostensibly, had been raised.

Her new friend Betty had been raised in a Calvinist sort of church and acted the part she'd been told to expect. But there really was nothing at all stuffy about her. And she seemed to know a lot of things that Penny knew nothing about. In fact, she could talk most unabashedly about those wonderment related to the birds and bees. Penny decided that, despite what she'd heard, Calvinists might be human after all. And by Eastertide, after a little push from Gramma Rache, Penny joined Betty several times at services given in her modest little country church with white clapboards and a traditional steeple. None of this "holier than thou" stuff. Simple, practical, and germane to the times. The pastor preached the Bible, stayed within the guidelines of the Bible and did so naturally, without any theatrics. Before long, Penny was rethinking some old prejudices of hers about the faith of her fathers. Perhaps it was not meaningless bunk, after all.

- - - - - - - - - - - - - - - -

"So you've been getting letters from Brian, then?" said Betty, her eyes sparkling. "That's cool, kid- I mean, like wow! Getting a college senior interested! You must be pretty excited about that!"

The two girls were sitting in the school cafeteria, off in a corner by themselves. "Oh, I don't know, Betty," replied Penny. "He's a nice guy..., and I like him, but I don't know how to take him. I think he might be, well..., just a little too serious- for me. I don't want to go steady or anything till I'm older. If you know what I mean?"

"Sure," replied Betty. "You're like me.... Want to look around some, and see what the world is like before you make some big commitment you can't get out of. Not that you'd get married yet.... I didn't mean that at all. But, you know..., just going steady can get pretty serious, and you don't want to get into something so deep that you have to hurt somebody to get out of it. I think it will all get a lot clearer to us in three or four years. What's the hurry, anyway?"

"Well, my old friend Erna didn't look at it that way at all. She thought you ought to *try* all the boys out- get hooked up and then dump them till you find the one you want. And don't waste any time, or you might lose Mr. Right to another girl."

"I know. You told me about her." said Betty. "That makes me wonder..., I don't think she likes me. I don't know why, but she hasn't said a word to me. Walks right on by. Do you suppose it's because *I'm* your friend now?"

"I don't know. She sure doesn't like *me* anymore," said Penny. "She's been saying a lot of dirty things about me, you know. I'm almost getting so I hate her, anymore."

"You mean..., like, *dirty* dirty?" replied Betty.

"You won't tell anybody will you..., if I tell you something?"

"I'd never do that, Penny. I think you know me. I know I'd tell you most anything, because I trust you too."

"You sure?"

"Honest to God, Penny."

"Well, she's been telling everybody I'm not a virgin..., and that it was with a boy she used to go with, when we were up at the lake this summer..., and even before that. And I've noticed how the boys look at me now, and how they sort of stand around and whisper when I walk by them in the corridors here. Some of them even leer at me. I hate it! I'm just not quite sure what's going on. Maybe I'm imagining things."

"That would be awful. You didn't, did you?"

"Of course not, Betty! I wouldn't do that. Oh I've done some pretty heavy necking, but I know when to stop. If they get too pushy, I go straight home. And I never go with them again. That's what happened up at the lake. But we never *did* anything."

"You think Erna has been telling lies about you, then. She must really be mad at you, if she's doing that."

"I don't know. Maybe she thinks I'm a prissy because I don't trip and fall down every time a boy comes along, like she does. I think she wants everybody else to do the things she's done, and then she won't feel so dirty and cheap when she's around the rest of us." Penny looked around to see if Erna was gone from the cafeteria. She was. Yet, instinctively, she whispered, "I know we aren't supposed to gossip, but you know what she told me she did when she was twelve years old?"

Betty knew it was wrong to tell tales but, naturally, she was curious, so she bent her ear a little. Penny looked around and then, seeing that nobody in the cafeteria would hear, whispered in Betty's ear.

"Ooooh! That's awful." said Betty. "And she never told anybody about it? I mean, she should have told the police!" Betty, horrified, went on, "That must be against the law!"

Penny bent over and whispered a little more, then sat upright. "You won't tell anybody, then?"

"Oh no! But I can see why she didn't do anything to stop…. Oh, I don't want to hear anymore. That's just *awful*! And she said she led him on?"

"What would you do if that had happened to you?" said Penny.

"I surely don't know, Penny. I just don't think I'd ever get over it if that happened to me. I'd die, I think!"

Penny could see that Betty didn't want to hear anymore. She quickly changed the subject. "I forgot to tell you something. You were asking about Brian. He wrote me and wanted me to come up to the college on a big prom week-end. Just got the letter yesterday. And I hardly know how to dance. I don't even have a good dress for a prom. What do you think? Billy King asked me to go to our high school prom with him, and its on the same week-end. Of course, I think he's nice, but…."

Betty interrupted. "Gee, Penny. Brian must *really* like you. I'll bet you're excited!"

"Well, sort of. But he makes me uncomfortable sometimes. He seems so serious. I just want to have some fun. A good time."

"Yeah, I know. You said that before. What do you think you'll do?"

"I don't know. I think I'll talk it over with Mother."

"That's what I'd do..., honestly. I'd be a whole lot nervous if a college senior asked me for a date. You know, I've only had three dates in my life. And all of them belonged to my church."

"What did you think of them? I mean, being from your church."

Betty laughed. "One of them was the preacher's son. What do you think?"

"Dullsville." Seeing it was time to go to class, Penny started to rise from her chair.

"That's what I thought, too," said Betty, also rising. "Not very exciting. Sort of like going to a party with your brother or something like that. And, for some reason, that makes me think of something. Have you seen your mother again?"

"My mother? Just this morning," said Penny, a bit puzzled till she caught on. "Oh! You mean my..., my...." Penny was floundering for words.

Betty suddenly realized someone was approaching. She hushed down to a whisper as she explained, "Your real mother..., your *birth* mother. Have you seen her again?"

"Shhh!" said Penny. "I'd die if my mother found out. I meant my *adopted* mother. She and Dad still don't know that I went to meet her that afternoon I got in trouble with them. I told you about it. It was when I borrowed mother's..., I mean my *adopted* mother's car."

"Then they still don't know your mother..., I mean your *real* mother- found you?"

"Heavens no! And be sure you keep your lip buttoned. Nobody but the family knows I'm not really their kid- nobody at all. That is, nobody else but you. Not even Erna..., luckily." By now the girls were walking hurriedly down the hall, headed for their classes. "We never talk about it at home! And as far as I'm concerned, *they're* always going to be my *real* parents."

"I know. I'll be careful. I still don't know why they've kept it so secret, all these years," said Betty, almost dropping her books as she tried to keep up.

"I do. I'll explain it sometime. I've got to get to class," replied Penny, turning off down the next corridor as Betty continued straight on. "See you later, alligator."

- - - - - - - - - -

Later that day, as Penny and Betty were riding home together on the school bus, sitting alone in the back seat where nobody was likely to overhear them, Penny was about to fill in some details about her adoption, quietly, of course.

She was beaten to the punch. "You were going to tell me about your parents." said Betty. "I still can't figure out why they still keep it so hush-hush that you were adopted. And didn't they think, someday, you'd like to know about your *real* parents?"

Penny was a little miffed at that last remark, but she let it go. She studied Betty's face for reaction while whispering, in a conspiratorial manner, "Mother and Dad- and whenever I say mother and dad, I mean my *adopted* parents- were down south at the end of the war, where dad was stationed. They'd been married three or four years and they'd found out Mother couldn't have children, for some reason or other. I guess they just figured they were out of luck. But some chaplain at the camp knew about it, and heard from the Catholic chaplain that a baby had been left in a wicker basket somewhere just outside the entrance to the house where a priest lived. There was a little note with it that said my name was Penelope and when I was born. And that was all. Nobody had any inkling whose baby it was. They couldn't find any records of my birth. She must have had me alone, without any help."

"Wow," said Betty, "that's like something out of a romance novel…! So I expect your mother and dad got wind of it and adopted you?"

"Yeah. I don't know the details, but there was some state law or other about foundlings where they were and I guess it wasn't all that easy- some sort of ritual you have to go through to be sure the mother hasn't come back looking for her baby- to protect her rights, or something…, don't really know much about how it works. Anyway, after awhile, they found a lawyer and, lucky them, they got me. By that time, I'd been in a Catholic orphanage for awhile."

"But why didn't they want anybody to know you were adopted?" inquired Betty, whispering, still a bit uneasy that someone might hear.

"I think Gramps had a lot to do with that. I guess when he was a boy, he had a friend who was adopted, and everybody in town knew about it. Some busybodies in town started a story about him being illegitimate- which wasn't so. Guess they didn't even stop to think he could be anything else. Nobody except the people that adopted him knew that his mother and dad and older brother had been killed in an automobile accident, and that he'd been adopted out of an orphanage fifty miles away. Anyway, the story got around about him having no father, and after that, all the other kids sort of looked down on him and made fun of him. You know how kids are. And even the grown-ups figured he would be a no-good after that. When he grew up and was trying to find a job, he brought along his birth certificate to some of the places where he went, but nobody would hire him because even then they thought he could hurt their business, what with all the rumors flying around about him being nothing but so much rabble. Nobody thought he was worth hiring.

"He'd never done anything wrong but once. He and some other boys stole some apples out of some man's orchard, just for fun, and when they got caught, all his buddies pointed at him. It was no big deal. But, the lies just kept building until, eventually..., he had to move away to somewhere else before he could find people who would treat him right. I guess Mother and Dad didn't want something like that to happen to me, and since they found me way down in Georgia, they figured the best thing was to say I was their own child. They were just trying to save me the trouble Gramp's friend went through. I think they were right in doing that. I knew another girl in school here- she's graduated already..., older than me- she was adopted, too. She doesn't know I was adopted, though. And she's always been treated like she was riffraff. She told me how people would just sort of draw away from her when she came around. I always thought she was pretty strong, but she told me once that she felt like she was less than anybody else, and she finally ended up married to a man that was a good-for-nothing, I think it was because she didn't think much of herself either."

A tear formed in the corner of Betty's eye and ran down her cheek, as she fought to maintain her composure. Downcast, her voice low, she simply said, "that's one of the saddest things I ever heard. It's *so terrible* that people could be like that! Now I think I know a little better how black people must feel. And for them, it's even worse, because what they are is written on their faces..., no matter where they go!"

Penny continued, "And I told you about how I kept seeing this strange woman driving by our house, slow-like, looking me over real funny as she went by. That was last summer, just a little while before the thing at the lake. Then, come September, while I was coming out of school one day, she stopped me, and asked me if I was Penelope. I told her I was. And then she asked me what my last name was, and I told her. She said she knew that I was a veterinarian's daughter and where I lived- I guess I looked kind of funny about it all…, and why she was following me around- and she asked me to sit down on the bench with her for a minute. Then she sat down beside me and told me she'd been looking for me for years and years, and was so glad she'd found me, and that she was my mother. At first I didn't believe her. Then she told me when I was born and things like that, and finally, I knew it was true. Then she asked me if she could kiss me, and I said okay, and she did and then she pulled out a handkerchief and started crying. I guess I didn't feel like kissing her, at least not yet."

Betty was taking it all in, spellbound. "Did she tell you anything about why she left you there at the church?"

"Oh, yes. We talked for awhile longer, and then she asked me please not to say anything about her coming around- especially to my parents, because they might be real mad that she'd come back like that, without saying anything to them. So I promised I wouldn't and then she said if I could meet her up on the road that goes by the Grange Hall, come Saturday, she'd found a place where we could park, real quiet like, and talk- if I could get there somehow. I told her I'd try to think up something and maybe I could borrow mom's car, and I'd try to be there like she said, that afternoon. And if I couldn't get there, she said she'd try to get hold of me again. But I had to keep it all secret about meeting her. That's why I could never tell mom and dad what I did that afternoon, and so they caught me in the story I made up. I don't think they trust me yet. But I promised not to tell."

"But why did your real mother abandon you? Did she say anything about that?" asked Betty. "That's an awful thing to do! She must have said something about it!"

"She did say something about that, but I'm still not clear what really happened. The more she talked about it the more confused I got," said Penny. "Sometimes, it seemed like her story was changing while she was going on about it."

Betty sat bolt upright, sensing maybe she should quit asking questions. "Maybe you don't want to talk about it anymore, Penny. I hope you don't think I'm prying. I don't need to know anything more. It's just that I've read about things like this, like in Reader's Digest, but I never actually knew anybody…."

"That's all right, Bet. She was rattling off a lot of names. It sounded to me like her husband ran off with someone else just before I was born, and she never saw him again. She didn't really know anybody down south- hadn't been there very long, and she didn't have a job, didn't know how she was going to support me and work, and just went to pieces and ran away. She said she'd regretted it all her life, but after she finally remarried to a nice man, she spent a lot of time trying to find what happened to me. But she couldn't get any state records. They told her it was illegal to do that, and before anything could be done, she'd have to prove she was really the mother. She knew that was nearly impossible for her, seeing as how she hadn't lived in the state for so long, and couldn't stay there while they were piddling around."

"How did she find out then?"

"I guess she finally slipped somebody in the court system some money to find out."

"A bribe?"

"I guess that's what you'd call it," said Penny. "But she didn't want to say much about that. I think she was afraid she'd get the woman that looked it up for her into a whole lot of trouble. The adoption records were supposed to be sealed. In fact, she said the office worker could go to jail for it."

Three Strikes and You're Out

"B. J." was back. B.J. Pierce, that is. The one who had parted company with Dr. Auchinachie because Sean had sent him to old judge Clancy, the attorney for the very creamery he was going to fight. B. J. was going to sell out, and he called Nancy to ask, as though nothing had come between him and her husband, what time he could come up. The herd was to be sold in another week.

When Sean returned that evening, the first day of summer, he was not sure he'd honor the call. Penny, who had recently graduated from high school second in her class standings, was standing nearby as he discussed it with Nancy. She listened to her parents arguing about what to do. Her dad was against it. He'd been royally insulted- never given a chance to explain during the confrontation with Pierce- his best good friend at the time. Nancy thought he ought to go ahead and do it, acting as though nothing ever happened.

Penny, considering herself now fully adult, broke in. "Dad, I think you ought to go."

"Huh?" grunted her father, not used to taking advice from a kid, even his own kid. *Especially* his own kid.

"Yeah, I think you ought to do what you always told me to do when something like this came up."

"Whuzzat?" growled the scowling Sean.

"You told me once that you never want to be too proud to make up with somebody."

"I did not!"

Penny stood her ground. "Oh yes you did, Dad! Do you remember the time I had Joanne over here and we had a fight? I was only about ten then, but I remember it like it was yesterday."

"You're full of prunes, Penny," said Sean, a trace of a grin crossing his face.

"Oh yes you did, Sean!" said Nancy. "I remember that day too."

"Aw, baloney!" he growled, "You two are just ganging up on me."

"We're right and you know it, Dad," said Penny in her teasing voice, starting to giggle.

Finally, Sean looked to his right, out the kitchen window. “Beautiful day out there, isn’t it?” he said, walking away whistling to himself as though nothing had happened, or if it had, as though he’d won the game handily- without hearing the titters of his womenfolk. Somewhat later, Nancy noticed that B.J.’s name was written on the book for a Wednesday morning call, to blood-test and T.B. test the herd and then vaccinate the whole kit and kaboodle for shipping fever. All in Sean’s writing.

Jim was disappointed when Sean and he arrived early that morning. He’d expected some fireworks. Instead, B.J. acted as though nothing had ever happened between them. The two old goofs, once again the best of friends, just picked up where they’d left off up to the time of the imbroglio, B.J. even helping to manhandle some of the heifers that were loose-housed so their tags could be read. Once the testing was complete, Sean fished some pasteurella bacterin from his supplies and walked down the line of cattle, sticking them with a pistol-grip syringe. The same was done for the heifers running around loose in the pens, bang, bang, bang, though that soon became a bit of a trick once one of them cleared the gate and ran up and down the barn looking for a way to get out. Seeing that, others followed. In the process of chasing them down, they darted from mangers, pushing through the stanchions and to the main alley, then back and forth till - finally, Jim bull-dogged some of them. Then, as usual, Sean had to pregnancy check some of the cows. All in all, it went quickly, without breaking any windows, knocking down any doors or finding a heifer galloping around in the milkhouse. Time elapsed? An hour and a half.

Sean, coveralls splattered with brown doo-doo thrown from fleeing hooves of the heifers, was in the milkhouse being hosed off by Jim- being careful to hit the floppo with glancing streams of water to minimize the soak-through. Regardless, Sean was getting soaked in the process. Coveralls aren’t water-proof. But what else could he do? He’d forgotten to put in an extra pair of coveralls that morning, and he couldn’t very well go on any more calls looking and smelling like something that crawled out of a sewer.

B.J. watched, amused, offering to take the hose to Sean, himself, “so Jim can do something else.”

“This is something they don’t tell you about when you apply to vet school,” said Sean, plainly untroubled by the water. “I haven’t been soaked like this since I was in the service, in Piccadilly Square.”

It was a warm June day, and he'd dry off in an hour or so. The only trouble was the water in his overshoe boots. He hadn't thought water would get in those, being stuffed full of cloth. So he took them off, dumped out a pint from each and dried the inside with some paper towels, hanging them up and letting the clodhoppers he was wearing dry on their own. That, of course, took all day and part of the next. All just part of the process.

"While you're here, Doc," said B.J., "I've got a sick one over in the heifer barn that I found wandering around by herself in the pasture, like she couldn't see. I don't figure we can do anything for her, but I wonder if you've got time to look at her? Otherwise I'll send her off for beef tomorrow."

Sean, of course, while a little annoyed, went over to the "other place" half a mile away, and looked at her. At first, when he saw her, he thought the rabies scare of the last year hadn't died off, after all. That time, the impact had been minimal, with the few rabid cattle he'd seen being the only ones around- their owners indemnified by the state. The whole scare was over in a matter of a month.

The heifer was not quite blind. While her vision was poor, she could respond occasionally to a shadow passing over her eye when in the sunlight. But, she was having a great deal of difficulty walking. She staggered and almost fell three or four times. Furthermore, her neck was extended, almost rigid, her nose high and she was frothing slightly from the mouth. *Slightly*. Corners of her mouth. That's all.

Sean saw a bucket of water in a corner of the pen. "She drink at all?" he asked.

"I didn't think so at first," said B.J., but this morning she did manage to suck up a little after I splashed my hand around in it."

Sean tried the same stunt. The heifer, a large yearling, pricked up her ears. Sean carried the bucket over to her and splashed in it. She stuck her nose in and sucked up a couple of quarts and then quit as she went into a mild and temporary seizure- opisthotonus, as it's called. Finally, after a rather lengthy examination involving some neurology, he ventured to say that it might be lead poisoning, and that neither the history nor the symptoms were quite like the rabies cases he'd seen- admittedly infrequent.

"Where would she get any lead?" asked B.J.

"Got any junk around where she could get into it? Been painting somewhere? Any putty, old discarded batteries, or empty paint pails?

Maybe a tractor sitting around where she could lick oil or grease or, maybe the battery?"

"Nope," said B.J., emphatically.

"Where do they get water, when they're out in the pasture?

"The creek. You can see it over across the field, where the grove of trees are. Comes down off the hill up there where you're looking- the woods near the pine grove."

Sean admitted he wasn't sure it was lead, but gave her a half bottle of versinate I-V to play safe, after drawing some blood for the lab. "I'd keep her, if I were you. I just have a hunch she'll make it. Besides, if you send her to slaughter, they'll condemn her. If not that, somebody'll probably think it's rabies and start acting like a chicken with its head cut off."

"In other words, I might better hang on to her and see how it goes," said B.J.

"I would. She might not make it, but I think there's a pretty good chance. Meanwhile, see if you can get her to drink. And I'll be back tomorrow to take a look at her, if you want."

"Might as well, said B.J., "it's on the bank."

"The bank?" said Sean, mystified.

"I thought you knew," came the response. "They're selling me out- lock stock and barrel. Foreclosure."

"Who? The bank?"

"No, the F.H.A. They were my bank. They own everything now. I'm out of here in a few days." Seeing Sean's look of distress, he continued, "Doc, I'd like to talk to you if you've got time. Could you come in the house for a few minutes and have a cup of coffee with me? I guess I need some company right now, and you're the best friend I ever had. Jim can come along, too. I've got no secrets to tell."

The Prophet B.J.

Sean hadn't been in the sun-room in B.J.'s house for several years. It was a bright, pleasant room with most everything white: wicker furnishings, windows facing the south with six panes per sash, as well as the interior wall toward the kitchen, on which were hung various mementos of the days when B.J. had lived in Venezuela, working on a cattle ranch for a North American tycoon. Scattered around the wall were some shelves bearing interesting artifacts of the Indian and Spanish periods- the result of diggings by B.J.'s wife during her college days as an amateur archeologist. There were framed photographs of B.J. with various notables, including his wealthy employer from the U.S.A., one in particular catching Sean's eye: B.J. and a native on a river-bank standing astride an enormous anaconda.

"Good grief," said Sean, "was that thing alive?"

"Sure. It was just sleeping there enjoying the sun. We ran across it while we were out there working in some sugar cane."

"How big is that thing, for Pete's sake? I wouldn't get within a hundred feet of it. Can't stand snakes. It looks like it could wrap around an elephant, if it wanted to."

"Yeah, it's big all right…, about as big as I ever saw. We figured it was over twenty-five feet. They've seen some, now and then, thirty or more. We even saw one that had just killed a medium size cayman."

"A cayman? A *crocodile*, for the love of Pete?" said Sean. "And I suppose you had venomous snakes down there, too."

"You had to be careful, that's for sure," said B.J., as he pointed to another photo. "There's a bushmaster. One of the Indians had killed it and hung it up. Only about eight feet long, that one. Hadn't grown up yet."

"What did you birds do with that anaconda? Kill It?"

"No, no. Just stepped over it and went on our way. It wasn't bothering us any. They aren't as bad as you might think," said B.J. "Of course, they swallow a pig now and then, but everybody expects that. No big deal. Makes me think, you ought to go take your family down there sometime. I have some good contacts at that farm, and they'd really show you around. It's a huge ranch, you know- I think it was ten or fifteen squares. Say, speaking of family, how's Penny doing? Didn't she just graduate from high school? Seems like I saw something about her in the paper." At this point, the coffee having finished perking, it was poured into cups and the three men sat down at the table to talk a bit.

"Penny just got a job working as a teller in the bank," said Sean. "She starts next week Monday, unless I'm mistaken." Sean turned to Jim. "That's what she said, wasn't it? Next Monday?"

"That's what she was telling Nancy, anyway. Maybe you weren't there, Doc, but I think she was waiting on a call from the bank," said Jim.

B.J. seemed a little surprised. "Isn't she going to college? I supposed, with the grades she had, she'd probably start college this fall."

"I did too, to tell the truth. But she isn't sure she even wants to go to college yet," said Sean.

"Didn't I hear somewhere that she got a scholarship?" asked B.J. "Won't she lose that?"

Sean sighed, shrugged his shoulders and grimaced, as though to say he couldn't do anything about it. "She wasn't sure she wanted to go to that school. It's the Oberlin school. Out in Ohio. But I think she's still kind of tied to home. Didn't want to go that far away. And I suppose that could be for the best, right now. I think she'd get pretty homesick. Nancy wasn't any too sure she was ready for the move, anyway. So far Penny doesn't really seem to know what she wants to do. One thing one day, another the next. Maybe she'll be happier being a housewife..., at least I think so. But she could do anything she wants, that's for sure."

"Nothing wrong with that, is there?" said B.J. "By the way, I understand she's going with Brian Miller. Does that have anything to do with it?"

Sean knitted his eyebrows briefly, then looked down and rubbed his forehead before looking up again. "Now then..., what do you know about that?" he said. "Do you know something I don't, or what?"

"Probably I don't know much at all. But I heard Brian took her to the spring prom at the university."

"Well, yes. It was a surprise to me. I didn't think she really wanted to go with him, but when she got back she was all gaga about the place. It sure changed her view about college. Nancy said, since then…, she's rethinking the college issue. But I don't think she'll be going anywhere this year…, too late, for one thing…, and I think it might be just as well. I really don't think she's mature enough. By the way, B.J., who told you all this stuff?"

"Guess."

"Cripes, how do I know?"

"It's somebody you know."

"Who…? Not… Nancy?"

"No…, it's Brian."

"I didn't know you'd talked with him."

"Of course. I know Brian. He was with you here a time or two. You probably don't remember it…, but, yes…, I've been talking to him quite a lot. He's thinking of renting my farm after they kick me off. At any rate, he's been talking to the F.H.A.- the same guys that are foreclosing on me. Right now he's talking to a cattle dealer that might buy the farm from the F.H.A., and then, maybe…, make some deal with him. Of course, it's all real tentative, right now. And of course, you must know he's got himself a job as ag teacher over in the Damon high school."

"I'll be doggoned! I didn't know any of this."

"Don't feel bad. I just ran into Brian yesterday," said B.J.

"Who's the cattle dealer, anyway?" In a flash, a change in thought hit Sean, like a premonition. "Man alive! You don't suppose it's Glib…, or Cicero! It sounds like them, and they've got their hooks into the goings on in the F.H.A., you know. They know what's going on there long before the other wheeler-dealers. Why, those two skin-flints would be the last he'd ever want to get mixed up with. They're in league with each other, you know!"

"I think Brian knows that, Doc."

"How would he know?"

B.J. rubbed his mustache, then went on. "Lots of ways. For one thing, your daughter told him. I don't know how she knew, but she did."

Sean was almost staggered. "Well I'll be damned," he said. "She's got more on the ball that I ever thought she had. It must be she actually listened to me…, at least, on one occasion!"

"When was that?"

"That day I took her to the auction barn. I pointed out old man Cicero to her, when he was bidding up a cow on one of his suckers! Well I must say..., Penny's sharper than I thought!"

B.J. thought he'd better tell Sean another tidbit he'd recently heard. "Well, I can't say as I know who might be dealing with the F.H.A. for the farm, but it might bear looking into..., at least- if I were you. Whoever it is, knows one of the farmers on their board pretty well..., *real* well..., if you know what I mean."

A knowing look came across Sean's face, as he leaned back in his chair. "Ahhh..., yes! Say no more!" Seeing B.J.'s cup was nearly empty, Sean reached for the coffee pot and asked, "You want more?"

"Sure," said B.J. amiably. "Say, fella, I hope you've forgotten our little..., umm..., you know. It sure is nice to sit down and talk with you again, like we used to do."

Sean didn't seem to hear. He was pouring more coffee. "You too, Jim?"

"Sure."

Sean refilled Jim's cup and then his own, practically empty. "Now, what I want to know, B.J., is what in hell are you going to do with yourself now? And how's it going with your wife?"

"That's the hard part, Sean. My wife." B.J. shook his head sadly. It really hurts her to leave this place. The kids all grew up here, and she'd spent so much time fixing the place up.... And her flower garden! Did you ever see anything like those flowers?"

"Not around here, anyway. It must really be hard on her."

"Doc..., I want to tell you something." B.J. shuffled his feet- knees spread out a bit- leaning forward, resting his forearms on his knees, hands folded as a grim look came across his face. "Most of the world doesn't give a flying flak jacket about a farm like ours going under. Now, I know I've not been the best farmer in the world, and most of this trouble is my own fault. But you talk to anybody about losing your farm- and I've heard this from other guys that have lost out- and all most people think of is that it's just another business going under, like a store, or a garage, or something like that. Can't they see that, it's *a home*, not just a farm, that we're losing? Don't they know how hard it is for us- even the best of us, the ones that make out pretty well- that if we all had a fairer return for our time- our labor, hours and hours- and for our investment, most of us so-called 'failures' would have gotten along without any trouble? And a few of us might even make what the city twerps make. But, hell, there's no mercy."

"They don't know, B.J." said Sean. "They don't know what it is."

"I know. And as long as they've got food in their mouths, they don't give a shit!"

"I'm with you, B.J. I've thought a lot about it. But I think, someday, the time is coming when the world is going to ask where all the food went."

"Or they'll say, "Why does it cost so much all of a sudden?" said B.J.

Sean nodded, as he added, "And then, they'll look around and ask where all the farmers went."

"I hope I live to see that day," said B.J. "And then they'll start asking the politicians what happened, and they won't know the answer. After all, how many of them ever did any real muscle work in their lives?"

Sean added a comment. "And then, do you suppose there'll be hell to pay…? Like- 'off with their heads,' with a few refurbished guillotines imported from France? And think of Ireland- the potato famine. You know, I've read that farm production was a real concern for our founding fathers. They had seen what had just happened in France, and they wanted to be sure we had plenty of food over here. Did everything they could to encourage production. Better too much, than too little."

"Well," said B.J., "isn't it still that way? Even now our ag colleges keep pushing that idea. Now, I must say, surplus food is great. I'm all for it, but when there's a surplus, what happens to us farmers?"

"Of course," said Sean. "Then they try to tell you that if you'd only *stop* overproducing, you'd make more money! It's like I heard a smart guy say once- he was an immigrant straight from Holland, most gifted farmer I ever knew, no less- and I think he was dead on…. Over in Europe, he said, the nation subsidizes the farmer. Over here, the farmer subsidizes the nation. I guess what he meant was that our farmers are subsidizing…, by accepting less than their produce is worth. No fight, no protest. Feeble at best. And it pretty well applies to all kinds of farms, not just dairy…, from what I've seen. It doesn't work that way in Europe. I was talking to a Norwegian. Said he knew a family over there that had fifteen or twenty cows- that's all- and living as comfortably as anyone else. Of course, they were subsidized, but at least they don't have to live like paupers or work like slaves."

"Sometimes you wonder, don't you?" said B.J. "Well, whatever will be, I guess. But you asked me what I was going to do now, so let's get out of the maudlin stuff. Did you ever hear of the Farmer's Organization?"

Sean's face lit up. "The A.F.O.? Sure. My buddy Buck Braddock- he's a vet, too- knows the A.F.O. secretary pretty well, even though he doesn't have a cow practice. Guess their wives are old college room-mates, or something. Sure. I even met the guy once. He sure is a live wire, I can tell you that. And a damned good dairyman, from what Buck says. Top notch. Got money out of the ears and, somehow, made it in farming."

B.J. seemed satisfied. He'd been half afraid Sean, being a vet, would be kneeling, like many of the more prosperous, fatuous farmers, at the altar of that sacred cow- survival of the fittest- Cooperation? With my competitors? Phew…! Or, Ye gods, not a union!

He went on, "Their secretary- I forget…, I think Jack is his name- is one of the few who has his head screwed on straight, I'd say. I've been talking to him on the phone. Now, Doc, I don't want this to get around- and that means you too," he said, glancing meaningfully at Jim, "but he wants me to go around this part of the country and see how many farmers we can get signed up. They're looking to get enough membership so we don't have to sit back anymore and let the bureaucrats in Washington and the milk processors *tell us* how much we're going to get *after* they've run off with our milk. It's the craziest thing I ever heard of! Gone on forever! And by the way, the reason Jack has money is because he was born with it. Third generation…. Farm all paid for. Why wouldn't he have money?"

"I don't know, B.J.," said Sean. "I don't think many farmers around here will go for it. They're too independent. What you're talking about is getting enough producers unified so they can *negotiate* their price, isn't it?"

"Of course. That's where I have to do a lot of convincing. And I'm just hot enough right now…. I mean…, they can call me a damned communist or whatever they want, but I don't know any other business where the guy has to sell his stuff for what somebody else decides for him."

Sean was dubious. "That's because food, especially milk..., is perishable. You either sell it quick, or you lose it. And it's always been that way. I don't see what you can really do about it, either..., if you go on strike.... Then if it isn't a big enough strike, they'll bring the produce in from somewhere else, where there isn't a strike, and probably pay them a premium, to boot. Meanwhile your stuff rots."

"Unions call them 'scabs,' I guess. If that happened, I can see it could get pretty rough," said B.J. "By the way, did you hear about that milk strike down south of here?"

"Not recently. What happened?" said Sean.

"One of the milk truck drivers got shot. He was trying to push a load of milk into the creamery through a farmer's picket line, and somebody shot him. Guess he thought he was tough enough to break through. Now the authorities are breaking up the strike, arrested a couple of suspects. Just heard it on the radio this morning."

"Killed?"

"Maybe. Real bad wound. According to the radio, he's in a real bad way."

"See? That's what I'm worried about. It could end up like that strike at the Ford plant some years ago. I don't think," said Sean," that you'll get enough backing to make it work. Farmers don't like agitators. But, let's say you work for the A.F.O. Can you make a living doing that?"

"Nope. Of course not," said B.J. "That'll be part-time. But I got another job all set up, besides that. That'll be my real job. But let me finish.... there was something more I was going to add. Imagine a car dealer, and he's got a pickup truck and sells it to a buyer. Then after the guy has driven it 10,000 miles, six months later, the seller decides on a price, and sends him a bill."

Sean shook his head in disbelief. Wait a minute, B.J., that isn't the same thing. You got that one turned around, if you think about it. The farmer is the seller..., only of milk, and not a truck. And *he* sure isn't sending out any bill to the milk plant months later. He doesn't even send a bill. He just takes whatever trickles down to him from above-last man on the totem pole..., except, maybe for the hired hands."

"Of course," said B.J. "That's exactly my point. Would the milk plant let a farmer get away with sending a bill for his milk after they'd used it all up, processed it and sold it to the Grand Union or whoever?"

"Not in a blue moon!" said Sean.

"Well," said B.J., "I'm no idiot. I know this may not fly. I know that. But I'll tell you something. If the darned fools won't work together, and cooperate somehow- if they won't try to unify, and the A.F.O. doesn't work out, I'll try to start a real labor union. Teamsters, Garment Workers, something like that. Maybe the A.F.L. Even if it kills me. And, by the way, did you ever hear of Taylor Caldwell?"

"Sure. I've read a couple of her books. Everybody thinks she's off the wall. But, myself, I think she's onto something. Don't know as I'd say it too loud, though. What do *you* think?"

"I'm *sure* she is." said B.J. "Though not quite the way she thinks. I don't think it's a plot. It just happens, automatically, in a society where money is everything…, where altruism has died. I don't think half of this country knows what a bunch of cut-throats big business is, when you peel away the facade of happy faces. I was talking to a retired fellow- a big-time exec. You know what he said? And these are his exact words: 'Don't kid yourself. They put on a pretty face. But businessmen, when you get up at the top, are all a bunch of whores. Everyone of them. And I'm one, too.' They'll do whatever it takes to make a buck. All in the name of the 'American Way.' And wave the flag. For instance, the first and greatest commandment is, 'you must always charge whatever the market will bear'."

B.J. was really wound-up now, as he went on, "There's such a thing as reasonable profit. And there's mercy, like I said. If something doesn't change, some day- maybe fifty years off, it'll get so a handful of cut-throats…. Might as well call it a Mafia…. I don't know as I'd buy Taylor Caldwell's blah about 'Bilderbergers,' 'Rothschilds,' 'Rockefellers' and all that bunk- but like I said, a handful of cut-throats will rise to the top and virtually dictate production, processing and merchandising from start to finish- probably world-wide. And when his last big-time competitor has been routed by the last 'Big Boy,' we'll all be at his mercy. And our Congress, and all the other politicians, will be kissing a 'Big Boy' royal rosette because his consortium, if they take it over, will surely fail, ending up run by a bunch of state-farm type soviet idiots that don't know beans about industry- or maybe a bunch of pencil-pushing lawyers and judges, professors and bureaucrats who always seem to know what's best for everybody else. And the industry would collapse, just like it did in

Russia. 'Big Boy' will have more power than the military. You can't do without supplies, even the military. I think it's inevitable."

"An apocalypse, then?" said Sean.

"If you want to call it that. You know me. I've never read anything about the apocalypse. Never touched the Bible, as you probably suspected already. It just adds up, to me. All the trends are pointing that way. This twentieth century, with two world wars and all of that, is still just a prelude to a bigger disaster- and I think, if somebody doesn't wise up, it will end, and I mean *overnight*, like lightning, with high prices for food, once the critical minimum of food supply is breached, and people everywhere have to scramble to find what they need and then start fighting each other for it. Like Germany in the 1920's. They may have lots of cash, just like the Germans did, but you can't eat cash. And the farmers will be gone, simply because they couldn't take it, with no youngsters anymore- even those that love the land- no young ones coming on to replace the old ones who are dying out, knowing they could make more money doing almost anything else. Why bother?"

"Man alive," said Sean. "And I thought I was a pessimist! Wow!"

"Let me tell you something, Sean. This isn't something new for me. I've thought and thought about this for years. And, as you know, I'm a little older than you are. I think there are a lot of farmers right here, close by, that would get out today, if they thought they could do it without losing everything. For instance, they'd have to find a new home. Where? With what? If they sell, they'll take a big licking. I think most of those guys are looking for some sucker who will buy them out. I know I was. For a long time. And I loved this farm, even if sometimes I didn't act like it. Guess I was running out of will power, or stamina, or faith, or something."

"You were depressed, that's all. A lot of farmers are. My dad sounds like you, sometimes," said Sean. "He thinks mechanization is the answer for farmers. Don't you think that will eventually make farming more attractive to the young guys?" said Sean. "They seem to be crazy about machines. Some guys say there will always be farms."

"Yeah, all that might be true. I could see some hope in that, if they could get robots to feed and milk the cows, instead of just doing field work and the like. But I don't think they could ever give cows the kind of care that a good herdsman would. The best cow men I've known seem to treat their animals with the same kind of individual attention a good parent would do with his kids. The more you robotize, it seems to me the shorter the cows' longevity would be. Each animal is a little different. I don't think you can get away from that. Do you?"

"Well, I think when they start that," said Sean, "they'll probably shorten the life spans of the cows. You can't treat a living creature like a machine and get away with it for long. And, as far as that goes, some of the new ideas I've seen seem inhumane, to me. Like chickens stuffed in pairs in dinky little cages all their life. What creature was meant to have space more than a bird? Don't we have any regard for other creatures?" Sean thought a minute, before adding, "As far as the other machinery- field work, and so on, I think it would be a big boon. Wouldn't need near as much help, but there's one drawback."

"I can see it coming," said B.J. "Cost. Right?" Sean nodded in agreement, and B.J. continued, "Once again, they're buying farm machinery retail, bucking steadily increasing industrial labor cost, driven by unions composed of city boys where prices are always inflating fastest- like property- and at the same time, taking a diminishing return on their own produce, sold wholesale while reducing prices because of the ruthless pressure of consumerism and marketplace competition- middlemen being squeezed more and more- passing the squeeze on down to the last man in line- the poor damned fool farmer. Why shouldn't he just fold up and quit? More and more debt, more and more risk, for less and less."

Sean chuckled. He couldn't help it. "I don't think you could get much more than half the farmers to agree with you, B.J. I don't know as I would agree, either. At least, it really isn't that bad."

"I think you're right about one thing, Sean. But that leaves half of them that *might* agree. That's because they're goin' to fold soon. After they're gone, then there'll be another half. And it will keep going like that once it starts, half by half. Mark my words. Finally, when it gets down to some big corporate farms being all that's left, the labor unions will see some ripe picking and organize their farmhands. Will the government fight that? Hell no. Farmhands are votes, not filthy capitalists, like the owners. Then, for sure, the prices of food will blow sky high. Politicians will try to solve it. They won't be able to. In desperation, the privately owned farms might be replaced by some kind of state-run system, like I was talking about. But it would be like sending somebody out, today, with a harness to put on a draft horse. Or trying to spin flax into linen at home. Nobody will remember how to do it. Socialized farming will never be as efficient as it is with farmers owning their own places."

"Why not?" said Jim. He'd been fidgeting more and more as B.J. sounded off.

"Why? I'll tell you why, Jim. It'll be like any other bureaucracy. Don't rile the waters. Do no more than you need to for the day. Save your own neck, and stay out of sight as much as possible. Stagnation. No progress. Comfort. In other words, don't be a target. No risks are taken till somebody has a pitchfork pointed at your behind. A farmer takes risks every day, as does any entrepreneur. Without risk, no progress."

"Well," said Sean, as he pushed back his chair from the table. "I've really got to go, B.J. I'll be back in three days to read tails for T.B. By the way, you didn't tell me what you were planning to do other then recruit farmers for your A.F.O. cause. How are you going to make any money?"

"Oh, that's right. I started to tell you and got side-tracked. I'm going to work for a bank as a farm loan specialist. Can't say who just yet, but they're hot to trot. Want to filch some business away from some rival bank that does farm loans around here."

"What's that entail, exactly? I mean..., for you?"

"Pretty much what I did as a farmer. Figure out if the guy can make payments on a loan, and if he'll be successful. Look over the farm. Evaluate the potential. Risk-evaluation if you will, and determining how much we can safely lend a guy."

Unseen by B.J., Jim's mouth dropped, then he gritted his teeth, making a face with his personal message written all over it.

Displaced

Hank Breslau was working in the stable cleaning out mangers and drinking cups when he heard a great clattering in the milkhouse, like somebody was battling his way through the outside door while carrying a whole load of stuff. Then he heard booted footsteps and the sound of metal pails banging in the milkhouse sink, followed by the sound of water running and, in short order, the water pump inside the barn turning on. Jim's tell-tale voice clinched the deal. Sean had arrived and was setting up to operate on the cow he'd diagnosed with a displacement the day before and that had been kept in the barn that morning. Hank dropped what he was doing and hollered up the silo chute to tell Eric that his brother was there to do the operation. "All hands on deck."

Hank could hear Eric's voice sort of wafting down from the top third of the silo. "Tell Sean she's down in the far box stall, all bedded down nice and clean. She's all ready, clipped, ropes on her and everything. I'll be right down. Almost done here." He had been making some adjustments to the silo unloader.

Jim appeared from the milkhouse carrying some of Sean's gear and- hearing the exchange- asked the obvious. "Something wrong with the unloader?"

"Yeah," said Hank. "I don't know what's the matter with it. I never worked with one myself, you know. I always pitched it out by hand. Couldn't afford one of those things anyway."

"Well, if you had to pitch silage with a fork every day twenty feet just to the reach the silo doors instead of fourteen, like you had down south, you'd pretty near think you could afford an unloader too, wouldn't you?"

"First off," said Hank, smirking at his cousin, "that 14 by 40 wooden upright came with the place. It ain't what I'd have ordered. Then, when I needed more silo, I got *smart* and put in trench silos. Never could see why a guy would blow all that stuff up into a fifty foot silo and then chase up and down a ladder every day so's he could pitch it back down, when you could dig yourself a silo in the ground, like mine, a whole lot cheaper. I even had one of mine set up with a rolling gate so my heifers could eat their way into the silo and...."

"Yeah, I know," snickered Jim. "You told me about that before. We saw one of them things put in over in Fulton township. Guy said he'd never try that again! Cows were eating sand…, got a bunch of them real sick."

"That's the reason you put in a concrete bottom and wood sides, you dummy," came Hank's jovial retort.

"All right you guys," said Sean, laughing- following them to the box stall. "Stop your bickering." Like everybody else, he too enjoyed bickering. Done with tongue in cheek, sticking up for a long lost cause can be a most enjoyable sport.

"Now, Doc…," said Jim, "this here be a *family* feud. I've a mind to…."

"Okay, Jim," said Sean. "I'll stay out of it. Hate to, but I will…, I *think* I will."

The cow was not hard to get up, even though she lay there, at first, looking like death was on its way- eyes a little sunken, belly hollowed out, an anxious, pained look on her face- not hard to discern when you're a vet. Sean checked her over briefly with a stethoscope, found the displacement still high on the left where he'd found it the day before, with no sign of the distention typical of torsions. A displaced abomasum can move around a lot or come and go day after day- willy-nilly- making a perfectly good vet look like a monkey's uncle. He was very glad this case wasn't one of those.

The only actual anatomic counterpart of the human stomach that a cow has among her total of four so-called stomachs, the abomasum normally lies low on the right side of the cow's belly, though it does move about a bit- not having anything really keeping it there. When it fills with gas, it can float upward- becoming a "displacement" unable to empty normally, and the cow goes "off feed," i.e., not eating. No eating, no milk, and a high probability of other complications such as ketosis if allowed to continue that way. After his brief check-up, satisfied that she was a good subject for the surgery required to "tie" the abomasum in its proper place, Sean put away his stethoscope.

He'd brought along a couple of bottles of Kemithal, a general anesthetic intended for horses. Rather than using the usual local anesthesia and, perhaps, a tranquilizer of some kind, he had plans to use it on a cow someplace, sometime- whenever it seemed to be fairly safe to try. As far as he knew, no practitioner had ever used Kemithal on a dairy cow- and this seemed to be as good place and time as any to experiment, right on his dad's farm. He hadn't, of course, forgotten the admonitions of his professors, years before, about using *any* general anesthesia on mature cattle due to the danger of inhalation pneumonia.

Of course, as every doctor now knows, such a dangerous event can be prevented, among a few other ways not available at that time, by either using an intratracheal tube with inflatable cuff or by parking the scalpel until the last meal has emptied from the stomach. (i.e., fasting) Not only was the first option inconceivably awkward under barn conditions at the time, Sean would have laughed derisively had anyone suggested the alternative- to go twiddle his thumbs until the enormous bovine stomach emptied. That could be days.

Cows, of course, regurgitate all the time to bring up their cud from the rumen, so they can chew it more completely- under a shade tree if they wish- before swallowing again. Though they belch uneventfully and often, when *conscious*, it's quite another story when normal belching is inhibited by general anesthesia. If such anesthesia is prolonged, bloating can be the result, so severe that it forces a profuse reflux, consequently drowning the beast in its own vomitus when tied up on its back- the supine position greatly favored by Sean despite some added difficulties. Unfortunately, an optional standing operation using local anesthesia had, for him, been somewhat less reliable, especially with respect to a large Holstein or Swiss cow.

Having already determined there was no pre-existing bloat or torsion, he was banking on a rapid recovery from anesthesia before bloating could be significant. Even if not fully conscious at the conclusion of surgery, once she was rolled back over to normal resting position, the threat would be minimal. Considering the crew he had at hand to roll the cow and tie her up and scrub her, Sean figured a simple abomasopexy on the cow at hand shouldn't take more than thirty minutes. In this case, it would take only twenty from initial incision to the last stitch, though he had allowed an hour or more for it.

As previously indicated, an abomasum is the only anatomically "true" stomach among the four so-called "stomachs" a ruminant animal has, the other three actually being highly specialized esophageal compartments entitled the reticulum, the omasum, and the rumen, the latter vat occupying most of the left side of a ruminant's abdomen. These three "extra" stomachs, common to all ruminants (moose, elk, deer, sheep, goats, giraffes, camels, llamas, caribou, antelope, cattle, bison, etc.) are fermenters and processors of cellulose and hemicellulose. These carbohydrates are found in grasses and are virtually indigestible to most mammals, including mankind. It is that "vat" that makes the cow- and other ruminants- uniquely valuable. Cattle, in particular, are *major* converters of those indigestible substances into milk and meat- which *are* digestible to man- making them increasingly useful where the growing season is short- e.g., the north- or anywhere the land is unproductive of major crops edible for man. Though some have tried it in the past, man cannot live on grass alone.

With Jim's cousin watching enviously, Sean administered Kemithal I-V. with a large syringe. Hank had never seen a vet operate before, so he was astounded to see the cow being cast- going down like a rock- the men bracing her fall so she landed on her right side and not her left, feet pointed toward Sean, spine close to the stall partition. While two men were hurriedly tying her feet to the stall ironwork, Sean stripped to the waist and began scrubbing his arms while Jim prepped the operative zone, slightly posterior to the animal's ventral rib cage about where a human gall bladder would be explored, on the patient's right. Since he had no tracheal tube for a cow, Sean saw to it that the cow's neck was straight and fully extended to provide the maximum airway while she was anesthetized. Even cows, strangely enough, cannot live long without air. There is really no need to learn this the hard way, as some folks have done.

In one respect, this operation would not go quite the way Sean liked. Once their work was done, the casting crew had started gabbing about not much of anything. It went on and on. Brian wasn't there, so they chattered about Brian. How was he doing with Penny? Now that he'd finished college, was it true he was going to rent a farm? Whose farm was it? Where was he going to live while he was teaching over in Damon? Did Penny like him? Did Nancy like Brian? Would they get married some day? Sean kept his mouth shut as they figured it all out for themselves. He had already made an incision- long enough for him to admit his thoroughly disinfected arm into the cow's belly (peritoneal cavity) well past his elbow. Of course he would have preferred that they would all shut up. But previous experience had pretty well deafened his ears to idle talk when he was trying to concentrate, the latter being an absolute necessity when doing major surgery.

Then Brian walked in, so the other men began pumping him about his ag class for the fall session. Brian, it developed, already had his teaching plans figured out. First off, he asked Sean if his fall students, whom he was currently going around to see, could watch him sometime when he was performing another displacement operation. Sean, of course, simply nodded as he was applying hemostats- sweat pouring off his brow from the heat of the shop lamp overhead, close enough to roast his brains. He paused to lengthen the abdominal incision- not quite long enough- very carefully ligating several huge, critical mammary vessels before cutting through them- most of which had been obvious to the eye during the prep.

Sean was crouched down, his knees bent to spare his back some pain as Hank, being eager to see everything up real *close*, was breathing down his neck asking questions: "Is that the stomach, there?" and "You got a couple vessels squirting blood!" Things like that. Sean already knew about the squirters. They'd just splattered blood on his face.

"Maybe you ought to work for me as a scrub nurse," said Sean to Hank, intending to be sarcastic. Hank practically had his nose in the incision by now. "Or maybe if you watch real close, you could do the next one of these, yourself."

The sarcasm was lost on Hank. He was fascinated. "Yeah," he replied," I suppose I could, at that."

Sean smiled at Hank's naiveté. It reminded Sean of how easy the first surgical demonstrations at school had appeared to be, until he tried it himself. Not only was it important to learn the surgical principles out of a book, but you had to learn the hard way about the feel of tissue in each animal, the relative strengths of them, as well as identifying things that somehow didn't much resemble either the pictures and diagrams in the texts or the cadavers dissected in anatomy class. And then there was the matter of suturing- an art in itself, and especially critical on the ventral surface of a big, heavy animal like a cow. The skill of a surgeon, he'd learned, did not require unusual dexterity as much as great tactile sense and lots of experience. And each species, in that respect, was different.

He reached his right arm into the cow's abdomen, groping around blindly a bit till he had in hand what felt like the cow's true stomach, bringing it to the incision where he examined it under the shop light- which, though hot as can be, never seems quite bright enough when you are doing surgery in a barn. He pointed out the faint longitudinal striations on the abomasal serosa to Hank and, having thus confirmed its identity, commenced attaching it to its *normal* place along the belly wall.

Sean temporarily replaced his needle-holding forceps in the surgical tray. Not in the least knowledgeable about surgical protocol, Hank reached for them, only to have Jim grab his hand by the wrist in the nick of time before he could contaminate the instruments, followed up by a stern lecture about touching *anything* without permission. Sean took it all in stride. Many times, barnyard "guests" at surgical gatherings had pulled gaffes like that. Even though his bovine surgery was antiseptic rather than aseptic, the same principles regarding contamination applied. But you had to be alert when a new man was around. Sometimes watchful, well-meaning clients would unthinkingly put their grimy hands or fingers where they didn't belong.

Sean started closing the muscular and fascial layers of the belly wall with two layers of absorbable #4 medium chromic catgut and then, finally, the skin- which is very tough in cows- with a strong non-absorbable plastic suture. Closure had to be tight and firm, yet not overly tight. All the weight of her viscera would be on the incision. The least flaw and it could be a lost cause: guts underfoot or a fistula draining stomach contents. But given a week, the visceral and parietal peritoneum would have melded, forming a durable adhesion so the abomasum would thereafter remain where it belonged. When the surgery was done skillfully early in the course of an uncomplicated abomasal displacement, it was a sure winner.

Despite the party atmosphere, Sean's surgery had gone without a hitch. Scarcely had the last suture been placed, when the cow was stirring. And when untied from the box stall partition, she immediately rose and- staggering just a bit- helped herself to gallons of water at the drinking cup. But the show was not quite over. Brian, who had been taking pictures during the operation, wanted to know what caused these displacements in cattle. His class would want to know. After all, such problems were virtually unknown until a year or two before. And since he'd only seen two while he was driving for Sean the previous year, he considered them an oddity. Sean had acknowledged that he'd already seen ten this summer, a time when displacements were relatively unlikely. Such disorders were soon to become so common that they were a major nuisance in some herds.

Sean admitted he didn't claim to know what caused them, but told Brian there were a number of vets that could tell him all about it, as they knew all things. "One of my esteemed colleagues," he said, with a tinge of irony, "thinks it's too much corn. Another tells me it's the lack of good fiber, like we used to get when we were feeding 'them there mixtures of grass hays like brome grass or timothy with clover instead of all the high protein stuff we're feeding now', like straight alfalfa. Another vet thinks it's a mineral problem- probably calcium or potassium, or something like that. Another one says we imported it from the great dairy state of Wisconsin, when we started using those burly Burke-bred bulls instead of the good, angular Ormsby lines, and Dunloggins and Rag Apples we always had here in the east."

"What's with the Burkes?" said Eric, not content to stay out of the fray should one, hopefully, develop.

"Nothing as far as I can see," said Sean. "They seem to reach their peak production earlier than the eastern cattle do. And while they aren't as big sometimes, they sure are a lot more rugged. Tough. Cows look like barrels on legs- big-barreled things. Of course, that's why that one vet thinks we're getting more trouble with displacements- big, rounded ribbing instead of the flat-ribbed, pear-shaped bellies our cattle around here once had. He thinks it allows more empty room up high- if the cow is off feed- for a bloated abomasum to float into. But, like I say, I don't know the answer. And as far as I can see, all these guys might be right at the same time. Personally I think it all adds up to the fact that we're just pushing them too hard. Feeding too much in the way of grain derivatives and concentrates instead of whole grain."

"A combo of grain by-products, you mean?" asked Eric.

"A combo," said Sean. "Yes, and they aren't processed the same as they were when I took nutrition. Some of them, anyway. Try soybean oil meal. And we never saw these d.a.'s when we fed according to Morrison's standards. Didn't feed them as much as we do now, of course. Now we feed some cows forty pounds of grain a day. Back then, twenty or so was tops. But of course, they didn't milk as hard back then. Not near as much stress. At the same time, cows lived longer. Nine, ten years back then- that was common. I even saw two cows in a barn when I started practice, one was twenty-one. I told the lady that owned the farm she was the oldest cow I ever saw, and she laughed at me. She said, no she wasn't. The one standing right there next to her was her mother! Six or seven years is about it now, for a cow, and it's getting worse. And a lot of it now is because their feet go bad. And if that doesn't look like the founder that horses used to get, what is it? And what caused it in horses? It was eating too much concentrate. Take your pick. And it wouldn't surprise me at all if it gets worse if we keep on building these free-stall barns that are going up all around the country."

"Why's that?" said Hank.

"Simple. You don't really know what the cow is eating or not eating when she's running around loose. She might be eating all her grain but not enough forage- the fiber she needs. Put them in a stanchion and feed them individually, and then you know what they're doing. But that- the ag school boys now tell us- is not efficient, so you're losing money. The first thing a good a vet wants to look at when he's trying to figure what's the matter with a cow is what's in her own private manger. Maybe they're picking over the feed, and not really getting the balance the rest of the cows are getting. Especially when she's close to calving time, when they seem to go off feed anyway and their serum calcium is probably down. Someday I'm going to have somebody try boosting the calcium and phosphorus in their ration, maybe the vitamin D too."

Sean saw Brian wandering off with Eric. "Say, Brian…," he said. "Hang on. I wanted to ask you something while I've got you here."

"Sure, what's up Doc?"

"What's up, Doc! Pfooof!" said Sean in mock disgust. "I just wanted to know how you're coming with that farm of B.J.'s"

"Oh that! Well, Doc, I still don't know. But I might be putting some heifers in the barn this fall. I think I've got a bite. There's a fellow who's going to build one of these free-stall barns you don't like and put in a couple hundred cows, for a start. If he does get the money to build, he wants me to raise his heifers for him at my place. He'll pay me in heifers, if it pans out like he thinks it will. Then maybe I can have some milkers in a couple of years."

"Who's that you're talking about?" said Jim.

"Can't say just yet. He doesn't want the word to get around till the deal is closed."

Sean said no more, but his heart sank just a little. The day of the hot-shot, big-boy farmer might be here sooner than he expected. It would mean a lot of change. But could farming survive without it? Or with it? Farm land was steadily disappearing around Sean's practice area. Fewer farmers, fewer cows, more good land sitting idle, growing up to brush lots, being held by speculators in the real estate business. More and more money was pouring into the area for housing, developing- all of it raising the price of land. Rentals were up for those farmers needing extra land and unable to buy any. They were competing with each other, and the farmer with the most bucks was gradually pushing the other fellow out.

In addition, a new interstate highway was in the wind, expected to open the area to realtors, developers and industry of one kind or another. Some farmers were already selling out. And why not? The price was right. Others were buying up the smaller ones. The O'Brien farm that Sean thought was doomed to be no more than a brush lot, had been bought by someone who was planning to build a horse farm, paddocks, stalls, stud barn, fancy fences, trainers, track and the works. To him, that was a speculative sport, not pragmatic agriculture. Where would it end up? A vote on a proposition to build a new high school was in the wind only a few miles from Damon. And retired people from the city were learning that their urban residence, if sold, could buy twice as nice a homestead in that area with the same money. Suburbia was arriving, with its nice homes, lawns, swimming pools and golf courses. And they were planting themselves all around the very hills where farm families had long lived, raised their kids, eventually abandoning the farm due to hardships of one kind or another. As it is said, one man's meat is another man's poison.

In his dreams that night, Sean found himself again a uniformed soldier in post-war Germany, wreckage everywhere, driving an army truck into a compound where the Nazis had housed innumerable prisoners for their nearby labor camps. It was nothing new to him to have this same tormenting nightmare. But he could never get it out of his mind. The same old horror came back to him, seeing once again the starved bodies, the hollow, lifeless eyes of the near-dead, their gaping mouths, their shuffling gait. And he witnessed, again, their countless hands outstretched to him and his buddies for food and for help, their hopeless cries in languages unknown to him begging to be restored to their homes- as though there was still a home to go to.

They were the D.P.'s, the "displaced persons," the chaff, the pitiful remnants of a nation gone mad in the hope of reaching a Greater Germany, the third Reich, a paradise prospering at the expense of non-Germanic chattel. But then, for the very first time something new to Sean's dream occurred- the same outstretched hands remained, but the faces were gradually transforming into the weary, gaunt faces of various people he'd known that had, by now, passed away. A respectable, honest working class, these were blue-collar, unprivileged, solid types like railroaders, truckers, carpenters, tradesmen, toolmakers, shoemakers, carpenters, contractors and farmers. These faces, in turn, gradually faded away, replaced by a new generation, like B.J., O'Brien, Eric, Jim, Brian, and even crotchety old Strickland- wearing coveralls- their hands also reaching out, in his reverie, to soft, affluent, gutless-looking, pasty-faced, heavy-jowled office drones, with their uncallused hands doing not a thing all day but sorting, shuffling and fondling mountainous, superfluous reams of paper with their corpulent behinds perched on desk chairs, while others greedily counted stacks of folding money- all of them watching the clock for the minute they could escape their meaningless work and head out to the greens away from the bleak stares of the prisoners.

Then he woke up with a start. Someone was shaking his shoulder. He opened his eyes. The room was dark as pitch, and Nancy was saying, "Sean! Wake up! Wake up! You're having a bad dream."

Sean shook his head, his dream fading rapidly away into a distant realm, no longer real, as the prison camp disappeared. He was sweating, just as he had when he'd been in the Ruhr that day- the day that would torment him the rest of his life. "I'm sorry, Nan, did I wake you up?"

"I'll say. You were flopping around, saying something over and over in your sleep."

"What was that?"

"It was strange. It was like you were seeing a ghost, or something. And you kept breathing real hard..., mumbling something, that sounded like 'displaced, displaced', over and over. Was it that nightmare again?"

"Yeah, that's what it was. Only worse this time. It's coming here, and it's going to stay. Sorry I woke you up, honey."

Pure as the Driven Snow

What with no car being in sight when Betty Breslau pulled into the parking lot- and then finding the front door to the church locked- the girls were afraid the pastor had forgotten his appointment with Penny. "Maybe he's out back," said Betty. "There's a small spot out there where the pastor parks once in awhile." That, too, proved to be fruitless- neither the pastor nor his vehicle was there, but the nearby church door, fortunately, was unlocked.

Penny, her voice betraying that she was a bit uncomfortable, asked her, "Which way do we go, Betty? I mean…, Beth."

"Down this hallway to the right, over past the sanctuary," said Betty. "Just follow me." She went on, "Most people call me Betty, but I like 'Beth' much better, that's what my best friends all call me. How did you know?"

"I heard your dad call you that the last time I was at your house," said Penny, laughing.

"Ahh, I see," said Betty, casually. A few paces on, there was another hallway to the left. "Ah, I see a light in his office," said Betty. "I think he's here."

It turned out that the pastor's wife had run off with the missing car to go get some groceries. All highly commendable, it would seem. But after apologizing obsequiously for his wife not being there as he'd planned and for having forgotten to unlock the front entrance, the pastor offered them a pair of arm-chairs next to his desk and then closed the door to his office. Then he returned to his desk and seated himself, after pointing out for the girls' benefit the magnificent scene of rural splendor framed by the picture window behind his chair. An elderly, kindly looking man- Pastor Lewis was tall and lean, yet not gangly- with a rather long face and big ears, wearing a pin-stripe suit that had seen its best days fifteen years or so before- obviously not a man of great wealth or ostentation.

He removed his bifocals and started cleaning them as he began, looking at first one girl and then the other in a fatherly sort of way, smiling, "It isn't often I have two such nice looking young ladies here, especially on a beautiful day like this."

"Thank you, pastor. It certainly is beautiful out there," said Beth. "A lot nicer than it was yesterday."

"Yes," replied the pastor, "but it's something like life. Without clouds and rain, it wouldn't be so beautiful later on, when the sun comes out- with all that gorgeous greenery we take for granted around here. It's just as green here as it is in Ireland. My wife and I, you know, went there a few years ago. We think this area is one of the best-kept secrets around- and it's so *peaceful* here.... The birds singing, the locusts and crickets and things like that. We love it. That's one reason we've been here so long. And by the way, I expect she'll be here in a few minutes. Something must have delayed her. I usually have her sit in with me when I'm talking to ladies..., if you don't mind?"

"Oh no, Mr. Lewis," said Penny. "I don't mind. It would be nice to have her here."

"And I expect you know, Penny, that anything personal we talk about here is kept perfectly confidential, unless you say otherwise. You do understand that, don't you?" he said, as he looked first at Penny and then Beth. Both having agreed, he opened a desk drawer and pulled out a note pad and a file card, and reached into his coat pocket for a pen, which he then held poised in his hand. "Betty," he said, "it was thoughtful of you that you brought your good friend to see me," then turning to Penny, quickly detecting some tension on her part and addressing her, he went on, "I know you've been to some of our services here with Betty a few times, but let me be sure if I remember right..., it *is* Penelope..., isn't it? Your full name, I mean."

"Yes, pastor," said Penny. "I hope I'm not imposing on you. But I really need some advice, and I appreciate your taking the time to see me. I'm in an awkward situation right now, and I just don't know what to do. Beth thought I ought to talk to you as soon as I could."

"And I'm honored that you decided to come here, Penny. I just hope that I can be of some help," he said. "Betty said you might want to talk to me about a family problem you're having. I'll be glad to help, if I can, but I just want you to know I really haven't had a lot of training as a counselor. And, by the way, do you belong to a church, Penelope?"

"I go to the Greenville Community Church with my gramma Auchinachie now and then, but I'm not a member, myself."

"May I ask you..., how do I say this...? Is there some reason you aren't going to Pastor Williams, over there- to talk with him? He's a fine pastor..., and I have the greatest respect for him. And I don't want to intrude on his ..., ah..., territory. He and I are good friends, of course- often have lunch together."

"Well, pastor," said Betty, "maybe I shouldn't butt in, but Penny doesn't want her family to know about her problem, and I thought she could confide in you. Maybe that was the wrong thing to do."

Pastor Lewis, pursing his lips, his eyebrows raised quizzically, leaned back in his chair, clearing his throat. "I take it, then, that this is something rather..., personal..., Penny?"

Penny knew what he was thinking. "No, it's not a boyfriend or anything like that, Mr. Lewis. It's something that goes way back to when I was born, that I don't want my folks to know about."

Lewis was puzzled. He had half expected the appointment would be another unwed pregnancy consultation. There had been a rash of them in the last few months. "That strikes me as odd, Penny. Did I hear you right? At the time you were born? What could it be that you know about- then..., that your folks don't?"

Betty interrupted again. "Pastor, Penny was an orphan, and she was adopted when she was a baby. I think that's what she's referring to."

"Ohhh!" said the pastor, looking at Penny. "Is that right? You were adopted?"

"Yes, Pastor Lewis. That's what it's about. You see, my natural mother came back and found me a few weeks ago. I never knew her because she left me on the steps at a church parsonage down south, and my father and mother- I mean, my *adopted fa....*"

"Let me guess," said Pastor Lewis. You were adopted by somebody that lives up here- in the north. It just came to me. You're Penny, the daughter of..., it must be Dr. Auchinachie and his wife! Everybody knows them! And, for that matter, I've heard of you- quite a pianist, I hear. So they adopted you! God bless them, what big hearts they must have! How come they were down south? Or weren't they?"

Penny felt a little awkward. This was something she seldom discussed with anyone, having been told repeatedly, at home, to keep it mum. "They *were* in the south, Pastor. Dad was a captain in the army, somewhere in Alabama. He and Mom were living near his base- just a couple of miles away, I guess. They said they found out about me about the time the war ended. Anyway it was after he'd finished his tour in Europe and was about to be discharged."

"Okay," said Lewis solicitously, as he made a few notations, "and I take it you want to have Betty here with us while we talk this thing over?"

"Oh..., of course, pastor. She's the best friend I ever had. And she wouldn't ever break a confidence...," she quickly glanced at Beth and seeing her nod, finished, "...I know she wouldn't."

The pastor started making notes about her family history, inquiring where Penny was born, where she now lived and the like on a standard church form. He came to one line and paused, pursing his lips again. "What is your mother's name, Penny?"

"Nancy. Didn't I tell you that?"

"No, I mean your birth mother's name."

"Oh. It's Frances Durst."

"And your father's name? I mean, again- your actual father."

"I don't know Pastor. Supposedly James Fallon. I may be confused. She told me so much when she was talking to me, I'm not sure what his real name was."

His expression seemed suddenly skeptical, "What did she tell you? Were they married?"

"Oh, yes. In fact, she brought me a picture of him." She reached in her purse. "Let me show you." Finding it in an envelope, she handed an old print to the pastor.

"Oh," said Lewis, "this is a nice picture. An old one, black and white, of course, and I see it was taken at a lake somewhere. Three people sitting in a rowboat..., evidently tied at a dock..., two young women and a man, looking at the camera. Trees on the other side of the lake. Looks like they were having a good time- judging from their smiles. Now, who are they? I take it the man is your father." He looked it over again, flipped it and looked at its back. "Oh. It says here, I think- James Fallon, Frances D. and Polly M. Let's see, your mother must be Frances. Sure, Frances D- for Durst. Did she still look like that, when you saw her? She certainly was a very beautiful woman when she was young."

"Yes, Pastor, I'd say so. She's absolutely glamorous. And she's always so well dressed and real classy looking. And I could hardly *believe* all the people she knows down in Maryland and Washington-politicians and everything- first-name basis. I figure she must have money, what with the clothes she wears, and the jewelry and ear-rings and perfume. She drives a Cadillac, too, you know. A red convertible."

The pastor wanted to be sure there was, in fact, a marriage. "How come the initial on the picture- for her last name- is a D, instead of an F for Fallon?"

"Oh, I think she said they weren't married yet when the picture was taken. They were on a double date with another couple, and Polly, the other girl, was a good friend of hers. The other man was taking the picture, I guess. She said she took back her maiden name, Durst, after my father died in a motorcycle accident. I guess he used to beat her, and she didn't want to keep his name anymore. I was born after he died. She really didn't want to talk about him."

"I see. Now the tough one. Did she say why she abandoned you?"

"I asked her about that, Pastor. I don't really understand, even now. She said all her family up north, where she came from, was gone- and she didn't know anybody down south, and that she just lost her head- no friends, or family, or job, no money- not even enough to pay the rent. The landlady was going to kick her out on the street, and I guess she just panicked and left me where she thought I'd get good care."

"Seems to me like there might have been other options," said the pastor. "They must have had some sort of welfare down south, or foster homes, or something like that."

"She said that if you sounded like a Yankee, which she did, they'd treat you like dirt. If you were black or from the north, they just shut you out. That's all I know."

"Shhh," said the pastor, listening as he heard a car driving into the parking lot. "Ahh, that's my wife. I could tell that car anywhere. She'll be in here with us in just a minute. Have you ever met her, Penny? I know that Betty, here, must have. She's a very loving woman. You'll like her, I'm sure."

The introductions completed, Mrs. Lewis remarked on how much she'd enjoyed hearing Penny play the piano during her graduation exercises. "I didn't know anybody so young could play so well. And I understand you might be going to Oberlin. Is that right?"

Penny looked a little abashed. "Nooo," she said, "I decided not to go to college till next year."

"Won't you lose your scholarship then? As I remember- maybe I'm wrong- they announced that you'd won an Oberlin scholarship…, during the commencement. We were there because some of our kids here from the church were in your class- like Betty, here."

"I'm afraid so, Mrs. Lewis. But I didn't think I wanted to go out so far from home right away. I guess I'm a sissy."

"Well, Penny, don't feel bad. God will make it right if you just listen to what He tells you. And I think he must have told you that the time wasn't quite right for you."

Penny wasn't quite so sure about all that. She and God seemed to be on rather uneven terms anymore. At times, even Gramma Rache had noticed a falling away from her earlier days. But she thanked Mrs. Lewis, and said, without sounding too lame about it, that she'd try to pay more attention to God in the future.

Pastor Lewis spoke next, addressing his wife. "Penny, here, has just told me that she was adopted by Dr. Auchinachie and his wife when she was a little tyke, somewhere down south while Doc was in the service of his country. And she says she has some sort of problem that I think she's just about to tell us. I take it she has been talking to the mother of her birth, and I think she's about to tell us what the problem is. I'm sure she's very happy with the doctor and his wife." With that, Lewis paused, rather expectantly, and there was an awkward pause before Penny seized the moment, realizing she'd just been cued.

"Well, Mr. Lewis," she began, "I've been seeing my birth mother without telling my folks about it, and I feel guilty about it."

"That's odd. Why don't you just tell them? And why do you feel guilty?" asked the pastor, wrinkling his brow.

"Well, you see…, it's like this. It's a long story. Nobody in town except my family, and Betty, and one other person, even know that I'm adopted. When they came back home with me from the south, everybody just supposed that I was really their baby. And they wanted to keep it that way so I'd never have doubts I was really their own kid, like some adopted kids do when they get older.

"They seldom brought it up, though they were always open about it when I asked them. So it wasn't like they ever hid things from me- I just sort of forgot about it…, and I think that's the wisest thing to do, when you can. You know how stories get around. They thought it would be better to never mention it to anybody, then there wouldn't be a lot of gossip just because one person assumed I was… ummm…, illegitimate or something like that. They'd known of cases where someone was treated like a pariah if someone even *suspected* they were born out of wedlock."

"But Penny," said Lewis, "you just told me that your birth folks *were* married. Certainly you have no reason to be embarrassed about it."

"They- my adopted parents- never knew whether there'd been a marriage or not, Pastor. And even if they had known, my dad- Dr. Auchinachie- would say that it doesn't seem to make any difference sometimes. That just as soon as some gossip hears you're adopted, they spread the word all over town that you were illegitimate."

"But that isn't the truth, in your case. Your birth parents, you said, were married."

"But Pastor, don't you see, my adopted parents still haven't found that out! They always *assumed* there'd been no marriage. Nobody knew anything at all about my real parents until my birth mother got hold of me a few weeks ago. I'm the only one that knows. And she insisted I never tell my folks about her seeing me."

"You didn't tell them about Frances? That's odd. Why is that, Penny?"

"Frances said that lots of times, the folks that adopted you resent having the real mother come around…, like she was going to steal you away or something. Like then I wouldn't feel like I was part of their family anymore. She didn't want to hurt me, or them either. But she said she just had to find me, after all those years, and she knew I was old enough so there wouldn't be any legal battles about it. She even cried when she found me."

Lewis sighed, pursing his lips again. "Well, there's some substance in all that, for sure. I guess there are some things like this…, that most of us don't even think about. And I take it you don't want to do anything that would hurt Doc and his wife. I assume you are their only child?"

"That's right. They couldn't have any kids after Mama miscarried one time. If they lost me to Frances after all these years, they'd be heart-broken. And it would be hanging over their heads forever, wondering if I will always be their daughter. And could they count on me when they are old? You don't know how lucky I feel to have them as parents. And the way I've been raised, I wouldn't *want* anyone else to be my parents…, I love them *so* much. I'd hate myself if ever something came between us."

Penny's sincerity prompted Mrs. Lewis to get out her handkerchief and touch her eyes. "It makes me think of that story in the Bible about Naomi and Ruth. That's my favorite story. You don't often see that kind of devotion, honey, and God will bless you for that, don't you see?"

"But there's one catch, Mrs. Lewis."

"What's that, my dear?"

"I lied to my folks. And they know I did. They still don't know I went to see her, or that I even met her. See, it was like this: I borrowed my mother's car and told them I was going to Gramp's farm, but I didn't get there till late in the day and they found out about it, by accident. So then, they wanted to know where I was, and I lied, and they knew I'd lied. They still don't know what I was hiding. I think they're wondering if I was fooling around with my boy-friend, which I wasn't. It hasn't been the same since, and I feel so bad about it that sometimes I think I've ruined everything."

"Why don't you just tell them, my dear?" said the pastor. "Surely they'd understand. It seems so easy to me."

"I *can't*, Mr. Lewis!" moaned Penny, her voice rising, "My real mother made me promise not to say anything to them, and I *promised.* I didn't think it could end up like this! They don't trust me anymore…, and sometimes I feel like I've hurt them so bad- by being dishonest- and I never wanted to, don't you see? And if I do tell them now, about what was going on, they might be hurt thinking I met her at all, especially without talking to them about her."

There was a moment of stunned silence before anyone knew how to respond. Finally the pastor looked at his wife, and seeing she was nonplused, managed to eke out a feeble but heartfelt word of praise. "Would to God, that all of us were so troubled by a so-called white lie. Honey, haven't you ever lied before?"

"Not that I know of…, except maybe when I was a little girl, Pastor. Certainly not to them. I love them too much. And I've always known when I've done something wrong, I can tell them the truth and they'll forgive me and tell me how I could handle it a little better if it the situation ever happened again."

"They sound like wonderful Christians, Penny."

"They don't even go to church, Pastor."

"But I know Doc's parents go. It must have rubbed off. Or am I wrong about that?"

"No, you're right. Grampa and Gramma are the kindest, most loving people I've ever known. And they go to church, of course. Gramma said to me when I was a little girl that it wasn't church that made you good, it was just a place where you could hear about Jesus, and He'd make you good if you asked Him to help you and stayed with him. And I know both of them read something out of the Bible every day. Even mother and dad- I've seen them reading the Bible, when they have a little time. Of course they're awfully busy."

"Are you a Christian, then?" said Mrs. Lewis.

"I've been to the altar a few times. Sometimes I think so, but I still don't know. I've just been so mixed up about things the last year or two!"

"Why don't we bow our heads, now," said the Pastor, "and we'll pray about it. Okay? I may not have the answer, but God does, and we know He'll hear us."

All four bowed their heads. And when it was over, Penny realized- for the first time- that while she used to pray that earnestly on a regular basis, it had all come to a halt the day she first became a close friend of Erna Vries.

Bondage to Self

It turned out that shortly following her meeting with the minister and his wife, Penny summoned the courage to tell her folks about her secret meetings with her birth mother. Initially, she thought it would be well to have an assist from Beth or even the parson himself, but the opportunity presented itself one evening at the dinner table, and it went off surprisingly well. There would be no repercussions, and no need for repentance, as far as her folks were concerned.

"After all," said Sean to Nancy, who was naturally apprehensive about losing her long-standing maternal status with Penny, "she was caught in a real dilemma. We both expected this might happen someday, when we adopted Penny- and what better time could it have been? She's a young woman now- practically grown up. And after awhile, we might be gone, and she'd like to know her mother better. Penny isn't going to leave us or anything."

"I know that," replied Nancy. "I just wish her mother hadn't done it the way she did, that's all! It seemed so sneaky." Turning to Penny, she went on, "And I don't think I ought to meet her right away, Penny, I hope you know that. I'll need a little time. I know it must have been a hard thing for her to do, and probably I'd have done the same thing if I'd been in your mother's position. But just give me a little time to change."

But a change was not long in coming over Penny. Her friend Beth noticed it first. She was slowly slipping away from her resolve, after a few weeks, to do many of the things that Pastor Lewis had gone over with her- things that could give her the strength and endurance that quick converts to a religion so often lack. While, at first, she'd never missed a meeting for Sunday services, even attending the Wednesday evening meetings regularly, she was becoming steadily more laggard as time went on. And Penny herself, in her conversations with Beth about it, sheepishly conceded that her lapses had begun when she started skipping some of her morning devotions- as they were called- reading from the scriptures and praying privately. And she realized that her prayers began to weaken even before that, when she tired of intercessory prayers for others, simply asking the Lord to deal with the *outcomes* of her personal temptations- to which enticements themselves she simply would not confess, neither to her maker or herself.

And what were those temptations? No decent girl would ever admit she had such wild and wanton fantasies. They just don't happen to *ladies*, do they? Yet the more she pushed those lascivious impulses away, the more urgent they became- a classic case of the turbulent struggle between id and superego, so strong, at times, that she was terrified she might go absolutely mad. And the worst of it was that Erna Vries- her belated strumpet friend, now foe- in a moment of malice, sensing full well her boyfriend's attraction to Penny, had vowed that she would steal him back from her by deliberately getting herself pregnant and entrapping the fool into marriage- which she did very easily.

And that, of course, left Penny- more than a little crestfallen- with Brian. Brian would be the ideal provider, real husband material, and she always expected she might marry him some day, but he would never excite her the way Erna's lover- now husband- had, despite their bitter lover's quarrel in the woods by the lake. It was as though Erna had drawn her into a circle of fire from which she could never escape. She was now convinced that she would have to settle for a life so many other women knew, dreary and lifeless by comparison. How romantic it would be to be a goddess- worshipped eternally by the one and only man of her dreams.

Yet, in her heart, she knew all such thoughts were simple vanity, unrealistic. Perhaps she should do what so many clever women had done, and marry that droll man who is solid and manly, a good provider, and then secretly sleep with the man who would worship her, be it only for a day or two. She would be his goddess and he would be her god; they would worship each other recklessly and they would go to hell together but, at least, they would have lived life to the fullest, having known it from its greatest heights clear to its dismal, dreaded depths, mistrusting that there were such things as pearly gates, or a heaven or hell- or anything of the kind waiting for you when you pass from the scene. Suppose all of that churchiness was sheer fantasy, a vain hope, an artifice to diminish the social dangers entailed with brazenly daring to live life to the fullest, selfishly, since that is truly the only life that we will ever have. What fools we would be, if all that is true, for not enjoying it to the very fullest, artistes, libertines all, and as long as we can, hoping still that we can at least be gracious while stealing what we want from others.

On the other hand, if a door to a far greater, everlasting existence exclusively for those who are qualified lurks behind the curtain of death- turning out to be gloriously real- and that higher order can translate each of our earthly lives through a metamorphosis, like a butterfly from a cocoon; or a release, as a child from the womb- aren't we fools who cannot, for these few short years, dismiss what now seems fulfilling but is evanescent, for that which now seems imperceptible, but is actually lasting and real? But there's the rub. Though we cannot know, but only trust, we can still bet our lives on the path to that metamorphosis. And if we have done so, what have we *really* lost? Only those things that, in our vale of years, will seem but pitiful tokens substituting for reality to all but the unwavering fool.

So it was something of a struggle for Penny. She cursed the very sunrise of the day she had met Erna, that being the last time when she had truly felt free. Now she was becoming a slave to the master, whoever it is, of things she cursed. And she hadn't the strength to free herself. Could such a slave be bought back by some other, more beneficent master, and freed from this bondage to self?

Heading South

In the old days, most parents figured their kids, at a certain age- maybe even twelve years old- should learn to shift for themselves rather than lean on the old man every time they wanted something. Weaned, in effect. As a result, by the time they were cut loose, they had developed an instinct for survival that brooked little frivolity. In Penny's maiden days, there existed vestiges of that process, though the day of endless nonsense- the next stage between frivolity and insanity- was fast gaining momentum. Not so much in the countryside. Countryfolk, fortunately, had a virtuous way of being more than a little behind current fads. Untrendy, unless you count spinning wheels and chasing girls- which will never go completely away until Old Man Decrepit creeps into the seat- front or back.

At any rate, in the early fall following her graduation, Penny bought a sporty little Chevy coupe, a second-hand two-tone yellow Bel-Aire, having earned enough as teller at the bank for a down-payment beside having some mysterious sort of insider status regarding a loan. And the main thing she decided she would do with it, when the time was right, was drive south to see her natural mother, partly to know her a little better and partly just to see the south. By that time, Nancy was confident her own vicarious motherhood was neither about to be displaced nor even threatened, though the things she was hearing about the "other" woman caused her, at times, to wonder. Apparently she was a real whirl-wind.

According to an earlier letter she had written to Penny, she was an executive with considerable financial backing, owning some vague business of her own and having personal contacts with numerous big-wig politicians, journalists, and celebrities in the area around the District of Columbia. It did strike Penny as odd that Frances' comments about her present husband were so sparse- and terse- until her next and last missive stated that a separation was in the wind, and that he probably wouldn't be around by the time she came south. As Frances had so eloquently stated in that same letter, such had long been the sad fate of so many hugely successful women like herself. To wit, she said, never does a good old boy like to play second fiddle to the woman he's fiddling with. That, she added, was *one* reason she had decided, after her first marriage, to never again change her maiden name, the *second* being that it had acquired great value as a professional moniker. None of this was forthcoming, however, until Penny had declared her intention to head south.

Penny hadn't yet had a chance to head south before there was another matter, noticed by everyone in her family, as well as her new friend, Beth, and even the minister at the church she had started attending. *Especially* the latter. Her attendance was *really* falling off at church. Nobody knew quite why. Initially, she'd seemed so zealous. Had someone offended her? Apparently not. If anything at all was bothering her, she certainly wasn't inclined to talk about it. When questions were asked, she would simply brighten up, smile, and say she was just *fine*, and not to worry about her. And as soon as you were out of her sight, her face resumed its forlorn expression, as though suffering some constant unrest. Certainly Penny just wasn't herself. Even Brian Miller, who was now dating her more frequently- not yet her "steady," but hoping to be so- commented on it. Some that only slightly knew her were puzzled, while others were more than a little concerned about her, yet it hardly seemed severe enough to be called depression, clinical or otherwise. The standard assumption was that it must be one of those incomprehensible "moods" that are best not addressed if you value your head.

At any rate, if Penny had any real problems she was definitely keeping them to herself. Nancy was one of the few who even came up with a theory about it. Perhaps her birth mother's ultra-high social position might be making her feel deprived- living, as she was, in an uneventful, rinky-dinky little town among a bunch of happy-go-lucky, unsophisticated bozos. After all, Penny was a budding and brainy piano *artiste*, and was, as such, entitled to a measure of eccentricity. Yet she still seemed eager to see Gramma Rache up on the old family farm, and to help with the farm work on week-ends. Maybe even more so. Many times she'd been called to substitute for Eric or Hank at milking time, and had seemed to be cheered by the opportunity. Perhaps, thought Rache, Penny just found it boring to be a teller.

At last, the opportunity came at Christmas time, and so- with the bank officers agreeable and the weather suitable- Penny took off from her job as teller, bought a few items to give her new-found mother for Christmas, proudly loaded her car and headed south. It would be one of the most memorable experiences of her life.

The Raid

In her wildest dreams, Penny had never expected to see a place like it. Her natural mother Frances had operated her business in an expansive old mansion in the heart of D.C.'s ritziest neighborhood for the last ten years. She gave her daughter a tour, introducing her as though she were a duchess to the cortege preparing for the upcoming evening. The dining hall- with a huge, hand-crafted oaken table imported from Germany and capable of seating thirty people, with a low-set stage for entertainers and musicians as well as a dance floor- seemed akin to a night club. But when you entered the several parlors, each distinctively furnished and appropriately named on a plaque, it was like you were stepping back into Victorian Britain, Napoleonic France, a Viennese opera house or some such, with classical paintings, the finest of drapery and carpets, elegant matched chairs and settees and spectacular crystal chandeliers hanging from lofty ceilings, all of which would have done justice to a palace.

Next to one of the parlors, acquired from some disreputable ghost town among the bandit mountains of Wyoming, was an unusually long, highly decorated chestnut bar with a wild west decor- complete with its original mirror, same length as the bar, and bearing the unmistakable mark of a bullet reputedly meant by the *firer* to be the last rites for a *firee* that had been too attentive to a certain voluptuous lady in red, one of several easily available by going up some stairs, well-worn by cowboy spurs, to the second floor. The stairs, unfortunately, could not be removed to Washington. But nearby the bar and its adjoining pool-room, Penny noticed that some of the washrooms were equally unique, bearing immaculate, well-polished period fixtures resembling those of the 1890's, and baroque figurines continuously spouting or pouring a slender stream of water into merely decorative porcelain basins.

Moving to the kitchen, Frances introduced Penny to each of the chefs and dining room attendants, who lined up as though she were royalty, bowing as she took their hands and tried to behave like the ultra-sophisticated, urbane lady she wasn't. And off in another section were several posh, heavily mirrored overnight guest rooms, soundproofed against traffic noise in the streets below, for those, she said, that came from out of town and wished to stay for the night.

Frances, really getting into the swing of things, explained to Penny how she had bought the old, run-down mansion through a tax lien, for a song, envisioning the most truly *exclusive* rest-club in Washington, reserving membership for the cream of its elite- based on the nomination of two members and the approval of a board of directors with herself as administrator. Since she actually owned the principal share of stock and had enough connections to keep the property taxes down, there was no argument about her authority, and she made sure that the annual dues, obscenely extravagant, were paid in due fashion- in hard cash. The board had named the club the "Hooker Institute," in remembrance of a brave and capable- but mostly hard-luck- union general during the Civil War, who had briefly lived at the site.

And in Maryland, only a few short miles away, an associated facility on the Chesapeake Bay provided a casino, a large marina, tennis courts, two golf courses, swimming pools and horseback riding facilities, as well as squash and volleyball courts for members of the club. Functionally, it was not unlike a private golfing club, but far more exclusive. There was little that was lacking, she said, for the comfort and security of the gentlemen and their ladies.

Finally Frances took Penny, by now completely awestricken, to her personal apartment, in which were several smaller upstairs bedrooms with outside balconies- including the room where Penny would be staying- overlooking a view of the Capitol a few miles away. "Now, Penny," said Frances, in her most dulcet tones, "I want you to make yourself comfortable here tonight while I'm tending to the clientele. I didn't really plan to have this happen right now, while you were here, but something came up. Tomorrow afternoon, after I've rested up, I'm planning to take you around the city and give you a nice tour and introduce you to some very prominent people. But, I must warn you that my guests tonight would be nervous about having strangers in their midst, for fear of a foreign spy or a leak, or something like that..., where, you know..., very confidential matters might possibly get into the wrong hands. Invariably they are trying to make political decisions here, or at least discussing politics. Unlike what the electorate thinks, most of their decisions are made in places like this, over drinks late at night, not in the Capitol. Most of them wouldn't even want it to leak out that there was a private gathering here, at this level, much less who was here. So…, top secret…! Okay? There are, as I said, some very prominent people coming tonight, in fact, if I told you who they were, you wouldn't believe it."

"Don't worry, I'll stay out of sight," said Penny.

Frances continued, "And I know you must be dying to see them, but please stay in the apartment. You never know but what national security is at stake- at least they think it could be. And if that's what my clients think- anything they want- is what they get! Okay?"

Penny was almost quaking at the thought of her, the naive little country girl, being near so many people of the world. Far from wanting to mingle with them, she dreaded the thought of it. "Okay, Mum," she said, with a wan smile.

"You're a sweet girl, aren't you darling?" cooed Frances, as she touched her daughter's face gently, "And I think that's cute…, the name you're giving me- I like it…, 'Mum.' You're a smart girl, too, I can see that…, but then, I'd expect that of any daughter of mine." With that she introduced Penny to her Persian cat, named Cynthia, showed her a few more things she could do to amuse herself during the night and left her alone, saying she'd probably be occupied till three or four o'clock in the morning, sleeping till about eleven- that being her usual pattern.

Penny, somewhat put out, warmed up the can of spaghetti and meatballs her mother left for her, eating it with some bread and butter and a cup of instant coffee for beverage. Otherwise, she decided, there wasn't much of anything to eat at all, after looking around in the kitchen cupboards. There wasn't even any milk. Frances had said that anyone wishing to remain a ravishing beauty, implying herself, should never drink milk! Indeed, as Penny looked around the kitchen, she saw little evidence, such as implements, that her mother had ever even *planned* to cook. Figuring maybe she ate in the club, or had her meals brought in to her apartment, she still knew that Mum was definitely not a domestic. She hadn't even thought about her daughter needing some supper when she arrived, simply improvising on the spot. That might fly in Washington, thought Penny, but it surely wouldn't fly with Gramma Rache, back home, or with Nancy.

At least, someone was doing a nice job of picking up and cleaning her apartment. It hardly looked lived in. She studied some framed photographs on a table in her bedroom and didn't recognize anyone at first, though she saw a picture of Frances with a bunch of very pretty girls much younger than herself, taken at a beach somewhere. But when she looked in Frances's own room, she found three framed photographs of her father that she'd not seen before. He seemed to have been a roguish looking fellow, with a wry grin, attractive, sparkling eyes but otherwise perpetually unkempt. And she realized that she didn't resemble him in the least, though she looked a bit like her mother. She already knew, of course, that he'd been killed in a motorcycle accident about the time she was born.

After awhile, she gave up trying to make friends with Cynthia, the saucy cat- who lashed out savagely if touched, ears laid back and snarling at her- in effect saying don't bother me or you'll bear the scars. She couldn't figure out why anybody would keep a pet like that, although she probably was something of a showpiece. In fact, it dawned on Penny that everything her mother valued might be merely a *showpiece* to her, perhaps even *herself*- when her mum was introducing her to the staff of employees.

So after watching the T.V. for a couple of hours, she went to her bedroom and undressed, crawling under the covers of her bed and burying her head in her pillow. It was the softest, most luxurious bed she had ever slept in, and in no time she was fast asleep, with the cat- no longer untouchable, even purring- curled up by her feet, evidently having decided she was a friend after all. We lonely ones must stick together.

First waking up at the sound of drums, she heard a combo playing some rocking jazz, dixieland, and low down-blues in the dance hall, besides some standards from the thirties and forties. So, half asleep as she listened, she amused herself trying to figure whether the arrangements were like those of Woody Herman, Artie Shaw, Goodman, Kenton, Basie, Ellington, Tommy Dorsey, Harry James or Glenn Miller- or actually inventive. While she was considered a classical musician, the spontaneity and complexity of improvised jazz sometimes mystified her, and she listened intently trying to figure out how it was done. Everything she had ever played had to be written out for her. But eventually she yawned, beginning to feel drowsy again. In the morning, she decided, she would have to play something on the piano for her mother. She just hoped her playing would meet with Mum's approval. At least as another of her showpieces.

She didn't know what time it was, but it was still dark when she was startled out of her dreams by a sound in the room, and the cat fleeing the bed in panic. It was simply impossible, but there was someone in the room with her. Larger, much larger than Mum. To her horror, she realized that it was a stranger. Then, not only that, but a man! And he was groping around in the dark, trying to find the bed and having done so, to crawl in with her. Paralyzed in frightful horror, unable to scream, she fully expected she was about to be raped. And by the dim moonlight coming through the window, she was shocked to see he was as naked as a new-born baby- in addition to smelling strongly of booze and muttering like he was half-looped, trying to explain where he'd been to someone named… Frances! Then her mother appeared out of nowhere, wearing a nightgown, standing in the doorway as though she were an Amazon ready for mortal combat, thoroughly aggravated, yelling at him to get the hell away from Penny and, scolding him like a fishwife, dragging him off literally by his ear somewhere down the hall- without a word of comment to Penny- where more muffled contention went on. And when it stopped, a door somewhere slammed shut. Then there was silence.

She baled out of bed, quaking, scared stiff, and peeked out the bedroom door to see if anyone was hiding there, and seeing nobody, crept down the hall by the night light, to see what had happened. Where had that man come from? Where did he go? And, why was he unclothed? She thought he had simply forgotten where his room was after, maybe, going to the bathroom. But why was he in her mother's apartment in the first place? Had he wandered in from some other part of the house? The club, maybe? But seeing her mother was no longer around, she crept back in her room and shut the door, locking it this time, wondering what would happen next.

It didn't take long- about half an hour of quiet- before another commotion began. This time, it was all over the building, like the house was on fire. Women screaming, men shouting, more pounding on a door somewhere nearby, and then shouts of anger and panic. Suddenly another man was turning the doorknob to her own room, then battering on the door, demanding she open it immediately or he'd smash it in. Penny, trapped in her room, was afraid he would actually do just that. Then she heard another man's voice, saying the magic words that explained all, "This is the police! Vice squad! Open up the door, or we'll smash it in!"

The subsequent ride in the paddy wagon would be an unforgettable education for a naive country girl like Penny. Clothed in little or nothing but a robe and slippers, like the other girls in the wagon, she wept in bitter despair, tears running down her cheek, sobbing. Nobody had listened to her, nobody believed she wasn't a hooker in the aptly named Hooker Institute and nobody even cared. Her mum was nowhere to be seen. The other girls in the wagon with her didn't seem to be too concerned, like they'd been through raids before. Gradually, as her senses returned, she realized, despite their dishabille, how classy, smart and gorgeous and unconcerned each of them- even when caught in flagrante delicto- still looked, and started listening to them a little better to find out what was going on.

First, she discovered that, far from being common crib-service debauchees, they were highly educated- sometime call girls, sometime escorts- each having her own apartment, very much in demand and well-off, not residing in the mansion except during "party time," confining themselves to that facility for their own security as well as that of their highly esteemed- and notoriously lecherous- guests. Detailed records on all transactions were encoded- placed on file in "Mother" Frances' office- where all arrangements were made for the closely guarded trysts the elite membership of the club required- mostly congressmen or bureaucrats who, naturally, demanded the utmost discretion and paid handsomely for it. Being just one of the Institute's many available accommodations, and being part of a package deal, there was no extra cost. This of course, would make it difficult for the law to prove procurement, since there was no evidence of an exchange of money even for escort service. The girls accompanied their "johns" as dates. And, of course, Frances, the madam, was simply running a dating service. Nothing illegal about that. And, like all hotels, the Institute had rooms available. Not that all the patrons availed themselves of such activities.

It was precisely those last members- the crafty ones- that used the service as a means of power, occasionally "setting up" one of their balky colleagues for political extortion. These clever devils, of course, were the older ones for whom blackmail was a way of passing certain pork-barrel projects and other legislative boondoggles in their favor. More than one majority leader in the history of Congress had acquired quite a company of loyal "friends" among the "independent young turks" by so doing- most of whom would have danced in glee to see him drop dead. Frequently the extortioner would even "help out" the very man he had entrapped, by "fixing it up" with the police station- after their raid at his own secret request- so that the fall guy's name wouldn't appear on the police blotter for the media to pick up, thus making himself a most gullible and grateful ally for the rest of his life.

Though frequently booked, Mother Frances herself was often handsomely reimbursed for her participation in the game, as were certain corrupted members of the vice squad- all kept under the protective wing of the Institute, rapidly becoming the center of the ugly web that was coming to run the country.

One young woman had been briefly detained but never actually arrested three times in the last two years. Seeming to like Penny, she spilled the beans rather freely to her as they rode along in the paddy wagon, despite dirty looks from the other ladies of the night. The police, it seemed, made regular pre-arranged raids on the place, and any fines were paid off by the Institute- checks signed by Mother Frances. But, for some reason, this raid was unanticipated, proven by the simple fact that there were no embarrassing photos taken of a girl with her political "target." Unexpected raids were a no-no, and whoever engineered it would soon find out where the chips lay. His immediate superiors were all on the take, and the budget and salaries for the D.C. police department could well be affected by a "federal change of heart" regarding expenditures for Washington. From her, Penny learned a couple more things, once she had settled down. The man that had tried to crawl in bed with her was Frances' current boyfriend, just too drunk to know where he was. Being in high demand, she had a new "boyfriend" every month or two, then she'd kick him out and get another. The madam, Penny's mother, was the head strumpet of the house. And the more she heard about her, the deeper Penny's heart sank.

"What's your name?" asked Penny.

"Oh, I'm sorry," she said, "Just call me Fanny. That's not my real name. I'm married you see..., and my husband would kill me if he ever found out about me."

"Married?" said Penny. "That sounds so dangerous. I think you *could* get killed!"

Fanny laughed. "Not if he doesn't find out. He's out of town right now. Usually I don't come here at night, because he's home then. He's easy to fool. What I do is go 'shopping' some afternoons while he's off boozing somewhere. We live about thirty miles from here and he never suspects what I'm really up to. When I go home I take him some little token..., a gift of some kind. Besides, I really do love him, despite his faults. This stuff doesn't mean anything, anyway. It's just a job."

"I don't see why...."

"I knew you'd ask that. Well, honey, since we lost the farm over near Hagerstown and moved into the city he just got to drinking so bad he can't hold a job anymore. He was a real good man before that. When we came here, I tried to get some work so we could keep the bank from foreclosing on our town house, but I couldn't make enough. Then I had a friend that lived down the block from us that said she used to work here, and told me to give Frances a ring. So here I am. And I've nearly got the house paid off now, in just a couple of years. My husband hasn't even noticed, he's so far gone. Once that's done, I think I'll quit working here."

"I'd think you would," said Penny. "That would be awful..., having strange men...."

"Oh, I don't know. You get used to it. It was kind of bad at first. I remember I cried the first two or three times, but I don't think anything about it anymore. It's just natural, you know. And you can meet some pretty nice guys, too. Especially here. No rough stuff or anything like that, and lots of times they're having a mess of trouble too, and we can talk about it. Sometimes I actually feel like I'm a therapist." Seeing Penny shudder in disgust, she said, "Well, honey, you may be Mother Frances's daughter, but you sure aren't like her. By the way, don't believe a thing she tells you- she couldn't even remember how to tell the truth, she's been lying for so long. She probably told you she was married. Didn't she?"

"Yes, she wrote me a letter, said she was, and then she wrote me later and said he'd left her. That was after I said I'd be down to see her."

"Well, let me tell you something honey." said Fanny. "I'd get out of here just as fast as I could and don't look back. She's no good. She's smart, but she's cold, and she takes advantage of people all the time. How do you suppose she got all this money- she's rich as Croesus, you know."

"Is she really?"

"You bet she is. And you know how she got it?"

"How's that?" said Penny.

"Not like I'm doing. She just does that for fun. She's a con artist, that's what she is. And she can talk the Bible like a preacher's wife, too. You'd think she was a saint or something if you didn't know better."

"That's terrible," said Penny. "But I'm not exactly sure what you mean by a con artist."

"A swindler, honey, a confidence woman. How do you suppose she got enough money to start her business here?" Sensing that the vehicle was braking, she looked out of the paddy wagon. "And I see we're at the police station now. They'll be booking us here in a minute. I'll stick up for you. They'll think you're one of us, but I know some of these cops pretty well…, the sergeant here, if he's on tonight, he'll listen to me. I don't think he'll book you if I tell him what happened. The other girls here will stick up for you, if I tell them to. We're all friends. Kind of like a sorority house, we are. We stick together when we have to. But remember what I said. As soon as you can, get out of here, and stay away from your mother. She'll never be anything but trouble for you. Don't ever be like me. It's too late for me now- I know I'm going to go to hell. But I can tell you're a good girl, and you ought to go back and get married and have kids. By the way, somebody said you have a serious boyfriend. What's he into?"

"He's going to be a farmer someday, I think. He teaches agriculture in high school right now. But he really wants to be a farmer. He owns some heifers already."

With that, Fanny's face disintegrated. "Really?" she said, then suddenly bursting into tears. "Oh, honey, that's so good…. Those were the happiest days of my life, when Steve and I were married and he and I bought that farm. We had such a nice home, and we were really in love. But we had to keep borrowing more and more just to stay afloat, and finally we couldn't get anymore, even when he started driving school-bus and I went to work in the school cafeteria." Tears were still streaming down her cheeks as the paddy wagon stopped and the police started unlocking the cage. "Go back there and stay away from people like me, and your mother…, and God will see you through."

A Moment of Malice

"Honest, sergeant, it's like I told you before. I don't know anything about it. I just came down here to see my mother, and arrived early yesterday afternoon, and I don't have anything to do with all this." Penny was trying very hard to keep calm, but she could feel the hackles on her neck beginning to rise. Was there any justice, any decency in Washington? "I just walked into something I know nothing about!"

"Oh, is that so?" sneered the sergeant, leaning over his desk and looking down at Penelope. "That's a new line around here. I suppose you're the Virgin Mary, and now the Pope sent you over to this here convent to help out the Sisters of Mercy. Now just who in hell is your mother? Which bawd is she?"

Penelope was not about to give up. No way was she going to let them put *her* in a cell, like they already had done with "Fanny" and a couple of others. Yet, after ten minutes patiently trying to make it plain, she still hadn't been able to penetrate his thick-headed skull. "You don't have to be sarcastic, officer, but like I said, I don't know *where* she is. Her name is Frances Durst, that's who it is. And you can ask me a hundred times and I still won't know where she is right now. I was asleep in her apartment there when one of your officers pounded on the bedroom door and made me open it. Then I tried to explain but nobody would listen to me and they put me in the wagon with all these girls…."

"Yeah, I know. You don't even know who they are. All strangers. Yeah, yeah, yeah! Honey, you're a cute little trick all right, but don't try to push that kind of crap down my throat. I ain't buyin' any of it! One girl gave me some line of crap about you being Frances Durst's daughter, too. Nobody else seems to think you are. And I know Frances pretty good. She ain't got no daughter, sweetheart, or sure as hell I'd know it! We've dragged her in here a dozen times over the years. And if she had a daughter she'd have said so, and she'd have had her working in the mill like these other broads, only at a premium."

Penny was getting desperate. "Please, sir. I've never been in Washington till yesterday, and all I want is to go back home to mother and dad. I haven't done a thing wrong. And if you'll let me call home to my mother, that'll straighten it all out. You can talk to her."

The sergeant leered at her, "Now look, sweetheart, you're trying to fill your story with even more poppycock. You say you got a mother here, and you got a mother there, and the Pope sent you here to reform these sweet little hens. Do you think I'm some damned fool, or what? So now you got not one, but two mothers. Maybe another one somewhere else. Sure, sure. Well, you can tell it to the judge tomorrow. Meanwhile, you're going in the can with the rest of these lovelies. Maybe he'll fall for your sweet little face and then you can feed him that same line."

Penny was in tears. "I can't believe this! Isn't this America? That's not fair!"

"It's nothing to me. I'm just here, doing my job like I'm supposed to. I ain't got enough time in the day for such baloney!" He motioned a rookie standing nearby to take her away. "Put her in the cell with those hookers we picked up yesterday, and then she won't think she's so important."

So Penelope soon found herself locked in a cell with four unlovelies, uglier than anyone she'd ever seen in her life, none of them from the Institute- each of them coarse, lewd-looking Amazons, blessed with a blasphemous vocabulary that would make a Marine sergeant wilt. Maybe, even, run for his life!

Penny went over to one corner as the cell door was locked behind her, and sat on a wooden bench, shivering. One of the other women handed her a well-worn blanket she'd claimed to use for herself, the only one left in the cell. "Here, honey, use this. It's all we got. It's cold in here, ain't it?"

Penny hesitated. It didn't look like it's been washed in a year. And it smelled like it might have been two years. But she covered herself with it and sat on the bench, shivering.

"What they got you in here for, baby?" said another one, swinging her jaw on a wad of gum, casually, like a cow chewing her cud.

"I don't know, and they don't know, but when they find out the truth they'll let go of me like a hot potato- and then I'm going back home where I came from and never coming back." Then she felt something crawling on her, scratched herself and came up with a louse, wiggling feebly under her fingernail. She held up the blanket to the light and realized that its relatives were having a convention there.

She curled her lip in disgust and threw it on the floor, then looked up to see each of her cell-mates grinning from ear to ear, their beady eyes fixed on her, greatly enjoying their moment of malice.

Cackles in Hell

As the hours passed away with no rescuer in sight, Penny became more and more apprehensive. In fact, she felt so helpless in her bewildered brooding that she was nearly inconsolable. How could this be happening to her? They don't put innocent people in jail cells- not in America. No matter how it now developed, the stigma would be there the rest of her life, like a big brand, whenever someone wanted to wield it as a weapon. Never before had she considered the life-long importance of a person's reputation, and hers was now in jeopardy. Once that is gone, nothing remains to prevent your sinking deeper and deeper into murkier waters.

Being parked helplessly in a jail cell was bad enough- with nothing to do, nothing to read, nothing at all to occupy the time other than cold and nasty cell-mates. In jail, time became an enemy. Already fearing claustrophobia, suspecting she would surely go insane within four or five hours, she realized for the first time what enforced idleness and passivity could do to anyone's mind- precisely as she imagined herself spending a week or two in stir before her innocence was established- a mere nothing to a hardened criminal.

Then she began to sense why the other women had immediately disliked her. In the first place, she was obviously of a different social class. Maybe she didn't look like a girl they could dig, but she needn't have acted like a stilted old prig. At the first report of a louse on her hide, she should have been a good sport and laughed about it. After all, she'd certainly seen lice- from cows- and even shared them at times- briefly, of course: sometimes so numerous, so thick on a section of a Holstein's white hide that she'd initially thought it to be just another big black spot the cow was born with. No doubt she'd seen more lice than these women would ever see- just a little different variety of pediculosis.

And would they still think she was just another frilly Milly if they'd seen her coveralls plastered with bovine dung, or seen her pitch hay, or spread manure, or perspiring heavily while raking hay on a fifty acre meadow under a hot afternoon sun with a tractor and side-delivery rake? What would they think if they saw her cleaning the drop, or milking a cow, or even, as she'd done on occasion, delivering or bull-dogging a calf? Was she conveying in her body language that other people were beneath her, that they were mere “animals?”

Some gentle advice from her Gramma came to mind regarding how to handle people who, seemingly without reason, were cold to you. Gramma Rache had said that most of the time it was because they sensed your own disrespect for them, maybe through what you said, but more likely what you said without *saying*- your body language, as it were. She applied Gramma’s cure. She relaxed and began talking *with*, not *to* her fellow inmates in a more natural, unassuming manner as though they mattered- and as though she was more than willing to pick their brain, to learn something both *from* and *about* them. After all, Gramma had said, there will rarely be a time you find another human being you can’t learn something from.

Much to her surprise, her cell inmates responded quickly. In the process, she found that while one girl was about to be released from jail, all of the others were former penitentiary inmates expecting to be returned to what they referred to as their “home” that day, either through some new conviction, or jumping bail or probation. That was only the beginning. Before long it was as though the sun had penetrated the walls and illuminated their dismal cell. There was even laughter. And, in the process, Penny was learning what it is like to be born into a family without a trace of privilege- a fate she had narrowly missed when an infant.

Still, every time she heard the steps of a jailer walking their way, Penny expected her own deliverance. After a few walk-on-by’s, her confidence no longer ebbed and flowed, it simply sank to the depths. Why hadn’t Frances shown up? She had money, power. Or did she? Was she locked up too? Then too, why had the police denied her an opportunity to phone her folks up north or, at least, a lawyer? Supposedly that was the law. And where were the patrons of the “Hooker Institute,” those powerful men of imposing posture in Washington? It seemed they had disappeared- in the words of one of the more eloquent girls arrested- like “darting donkeys and zebras zooming off at the first nicker, kicking up clouds of dust just as high as possible to keep their behinds out of sight of any pursuing predators…. Every braying ass for himself.”

It was precisely when Penny expected it least that a jailer came, rattling the keys that would open the cell. “You’ve got company, Miss Auchinachie,” he said as he proceeded to unlock the gate and led her out, holding her elbow. Locking up again, he started walking her down the hall like a mare on a halter. "Got your mother out there in the office waiting for you. I think they're about to let you go."

Penny, now on good terms with the other women in the cell, turned and gave each of them a nod as she was led away, collectively wishing them the best and thanking them for chatting with her. "She's not so bad, at that," said the one that had given her the louse-ridden blanket.

"Yeah," said another one. "They got nothing on her. I don't know what's the matter with their heads. I hope she sues the buggers."

"I do too," said the first one.

The jailer opened the door to a cramped little office with four chairs and a single desk, a scattering of shelves packed high with disorganized piles of paper, leaving Penny there, shutting the door again and departing. An officer was standing at the desk, evidently having a rather heated argument with someone on the other end of the telephone line. Seeing Penny, he signaled for her to be seated, finished up his call and hung up. "More damned fools around here…," he muttered, as though to Penny, while he fumbled through the files on his desk, "gets worse all the time. Have a seat. Let's see, you're Miss Auchinachie, aren't you?"

"Yes sir," she replied, as she sat down.

"Well, our own saint Frances is on her way here to take you home to her bordello…, I've known her for a long time. It ain't the dog that's *man's* best friend, it's Frances- at least, that's what they say around here. You related somehow to her?"

Penny didn't quite get the joke. "Yes, she's my birth mother, sir. That's all."

"Call me Lieutenant Dearborn. I'm head of the vice squad. So you're her daughter, by birth…." he said, with a tinge of sarcasm. "I supposed all girls were daughters by birth."

"Yes, that's right. But I never knew her all my life till just recently…."

"Funny I never heard Frances had any kids. Never saw you before. That's funny…, real funny. Seems I'd have seen you before, as many times as I've run into Frances. And your last name isn't same as hers. How come?" He was sizing her up with his eyes. Not a bad kid, he figured. He guessed he'd lighten up on her.

"I was adopted, Lieutenant. Auchinachie is my adopted name. I'm Doctor Auchinachie's daughter, and my mother..., my adopted mother, that is... her name is Nancy. I just can't get used to this kind of thing- having two mothers, but I don't really think of Frances as my mother. At least, not yet."

"How'd they get you? Frances give you to them?"

"Not exactly. Right after I was born, she left me on a Catholic priest's doorstep. Nobody knew whose baby I was, but there was a note in the basket with me- with my given name, and when I was born. That was all. Frances, I guess, was having trouble and didn't know what to do with me. I'm still not sure what the story is. And then I was placed in an orphanage for a few days and put up for adoption. My dad was stationed down there at the end of the war. I never knew who my real..., that is, my birth mother- Frances- was till a few months ago."

"Let's see," said the lieutenant as he looked at her file, "looks like your home is quite a ways north of here, according to what you told the desk sergeant last night. How long you been here in Washington?"

"One day. That's all. I came down to see Frances. She found me a few months ago. I guess she'd been looking for me for a long time, and wanted us to get together sometime."

"How'd she find you? That can be hard to do."

"I know. Well, I guess somebody slipped someone in the courthouse a little money to get the records. They were sealed- or supposed to be, anyway, by court order."

"Sounds like Frances, all right. She always finds some way to get things done. I take it you really don't know much about her, then."

"Not much. I'm learning," said Penny, "and the more I learn, the more I want to go back home."

"Don't learn too much," said the officer, "she'll teach you more than you'd ever want to know."

"I'm finding that out. Last night some guy walked in my bedroom- a perfect stranger- and was trying to get in bed with me, until she saw him and yanked him away somewhere."

"Believe me when I say I'm not surprised. Who was he? Did she say?"

"No, but somebody told me later it was her boyfriend." Penny, being suspicious he was much more than that, watched the officer closely to see his reaction. She got it- suspicions confirmed: the officer shook his head in loathing, a little involuntary tic jerking one eyelid indicating he knew more than he was going to admit.

At that point the desk phone rang, and he answered it. "Dearborn, here." Pause. "She's here, right under my nose." Pause. "Yeah, I know that. She told me." Pause. "Okay, consider it done." Another pause. "I just said I would..., now get off of my back!" Then he hung up, muttering to himself, "Snafu. Always some snafu. That was our law department." He ran his hand through his hair, gritting his teeth for a second, evidently thinking of something more. Was he wondering about a law suit for false arrest? Finally, he came to and, turning to Penny again, lied through his teeth. "That had nothing to do with you, Miss Penny. I mean Miss Auchinachie." Then, seeing her dubious stare, he opted for the naked truth. "Don't mind me..., of course it did. It's been a madhouse here ever since I came in this morning."

"Now you know how I felt, ever since I came to Washington yesterday, officer," said Penny. "The whole city seems like one big madhouse to me. By the way, what's snafu mean? My dad is the only man I ever heard say that, but he was always pretty vague about what it meant."

The lieutenant laughed. "I can tell you've been around another G-I when I hear something like that. I was in Italy, you know- Salerno..., Naples."

"I figured it was G-I lingo," said Penny. "But what's it mean?"

"Ummm, umm..., it just means things are sort of..., fouled up, like the army has sent your quartermaster a ton of shoes with, let's say- all of them for the left foot, nothing for the right. Or a ton of cartridges and no rifles. Sort of like what happened to you last night."

Penny was well aware of the literal meaning of the word. She had just decided to play a little game with the lieutenant, and he'd sort of circled around it. There was something she liked about him the minute she saw him- reminded her of her dad. She watched as he opened a drawer and rummaged around for a chart of some kind before he continued, "Well, I hope your troubles are over. Your mother is out there waiting for you- your mother *Frances*..., that is. And all charges are dismissed. I'm sorry for all this mess. If the usual sergeant had been on duty last night, this never would have happened. But, as luck would have it, his wife was having a baby and he had to rush her off to the hospital. Or if we could have found Frances, since she's the only one that could verify who you were, it sure would have helped. After all, they found some half-naked drunk coming out of the suite where you were. They supposed you were part of the crew. We couldn't make any contact with her till this morning. Now, if you'll excuse me just a minute, I've got to leave you for a minute and get some papers made out. Won't be long, and you'll be out of here." With that, he disappeared, leaving the door to the hall open.

Penny heard him talking to another man somewhere on down the hall. Lt. Dearborn was asking the other man something about her case that the other man was responsible for, and then they were talking back and forth. Then she heard mention of Frances's name a few times from the Lieutenant, to which the other man replied, "Why, she always says she's married to this guy or that. If she had a quill for every boyfriend she'd had, since I've been here in this district, she'd look like a porcupine."

For once, Frances seemed abashed when she saw Penny. "I'm so sorry, honey," she said, "This never would've happened if Stanley hadn't got drunk and wandered into your room last night. It was a good thing I happened to be there. He was my groundskeeper… roomed here- at one time- but I had to fire him because he was drunk all the time. He didn't know where he was last night, and I had to run him back to where he's been living. And I'm sorry about all the other commotion after I left. I think somebody called the cops thinking there was a fight going on. I don't know why. It was disgraceful the way they treated the ladies brought in by the gentlemen as though they were some a bunch of tramps. How could they be so stupid! But it's over now. I couldn't figure where you were at first, when I came back…, until I got a call from Fanny. The police certainly should have let you use the phone. That's the law, and they're going to hear about it!"

"That's what I thought. But what I think is that the sergeant didn't like me, for some reason or other," said Penny. While she said nothing to offend Frances, she knew now what her mother really was, and just let her babble on self-righteously with her rationalizations, concocted stories and outright lies. Nor did the torrent diminish for several minutes. But as far as Penny was concerned, it was all over between them- now that she knew some of the truth. She would leave D.C. as soon as she could without ever looking back: Goodbye to rubbish.

Penny drew her first deep breath of fresh air thankfully as she accompanied Mother Frances through the front door of the police station and paused on the top of the steps. Suddenly there were two flashes of light, then, just as she saw the photographers standing at roadside, there were two more flashes. They'd just been photographed together.

Penny was startled, of course. "What's that all about?" she asked Frances, "Was that a cop or what?"

"Well, I know one of those guys. He's a press reporter for the..., well never mind. I'll fix that as soon as I get back. The other guy, well..., I've never seen him before. Don't know where he came from. But don't worry. Can't a mother and daughter walk in a public place anymore? What's to be ashamed of?"

Penny turned around and stared at the sign over the door. "But Fran..., I mean Mother, look at that. If that gets out, people could know I'd been in that police station."

"Me too, honey. So what?" said her mother. "Is that against the law?"

"No, but suppose everybody knows I'm...."

"You're what, kiddo?" said her mother.

"Never mind." Penny was going to say something, but thought better of it. Some things were better left unsaid, such as "a daughter of a cathouse madam."

"Well," said Frances. "Don't worry so much. I can handle it. Your precious reputation won't ever be smirched, believe me."

"Okay, okay," said Penny. And as soon as she got back to the Institute, she was gone, headed back home without a word to dear Mother Frances, the call-girl madam. And all the way back she thought about it more and more, until she was steadfast in her belief that the past conflicts in her mind had been a war between her better, selfless nature- exemplified by her Gramma Rache- versus her instinctively far more potent impulses- little different from those of her former friend, Erna Vries, whom she had envied and admired. And she knew that Rache had just lost the war with her granddaughter- by *adoption* only, mind you- now a jailbird, her name on a police blotter, photographed and fingerprinted, thus officially contaminated. Suspicions confirmed. She was carrying the same bad genes- the genetic proclivities that Frances had. There were some things that nature designs, she was sure, that God cannot or will not change. And the worst of it was, she felt a sort of glee at the very same time that she felt such revulsion at what might lie ahead of her, now that she recognized the stark truth about herself. For her, all that had happened to her in church was now but a transitory illusion. Why fight it? She was, so she thought, free. And there were all kinds of cackles in hell.

Besmirched, Benighted and Bewildered

At first, after Penny's return home from Washington, she seemed to be recovering from her traumatic experience. While she did confide in her mother and dad, keeping nothing from them about the unsavory mess she had encountered there and accordingly receiving their utmost sympathy and support, they had no quick solutions for her loss of face, which seemed to deepen as the days passed by. They were both, of course, insistent that she never have anything more to do with the reprobate woman that had given birth to her. Sean, having sensed trouble when Mother Frances first appeared out of nowhere, had been upset, in the first place, to learn that Penny was planning to go Washington, and was now vowing, suspicions confirmed, to either personally tar and feather the woman or run her out of the county on a rail if she ever appeared there again. He even placed the local sheriff- a friend of his- on alert, in the process learning from him that the dear soul had a long record of petty arrests going back even before the time when Penny was born, eventually spending a couple of years in a Maryland state pen for fraud. Nancy, as one would expect, was calmer about it, devoting much of her attention and time to comforting Penny, watching her closely as she slowly recovered from her painful depression. Foremost in both of their minds was preserving her self-esteem and her personal identity in their family as *their own* daughter- not someone else's. And, since there seemed to be no one else in the area that had an inkling of her embarrassment, they thought the whole thing would blow over. Consequently, Penny's self-confidence seemed to be gaining as the weeks went by.

But as time went on, the fear that she would eventually be the subject of malevolent gossip began to take its toll. Her sleep was plagued with dreams of debasement, where she was fleeing from crowds of hateful people- all pointing accusatory fingers at her, scornfully rejecting her every plea of innocence until she, in despair, knelt submissively before them, confessing the guilt they were, like ravenous wolves, virtually salivating to hear. Even when awake, knowing full well her feelings of inescapable shame were pretty senseless, she sensed a veritable ax hanging over her head that could drop at any moment- simply for having been born the daughter of such a disreputable woman. Bad genes. And how was she to know that her sire was one bit better? So she steadily, though unconsciously, began withdrawing from all her friends, for fear that they would, somehow, learn of her disgrace and spill the beans- even her most reliable friend, Beth.

Perhaps things would have corrected themselves in time, had not a most unfortunate thing occurred. The local newsstands regularly carried a tabloid newspaper that reveled in anything the least bit salacious. On a certain Sunday just such a story arrived, all about the recent raid on the Hooker Institute. Though it had missed most of the sordid political machinations that would have made the incident an absolutely sensational headline story in the more prestigious newspapers around the country, it did allude to the fact a handful of Washington power-brokers had been regulars at various whoopee parties, though actually naming only one them- evidently an uncooperative individual the schemers had decided to whack as an example to the others should they fail to toe the line.

Of course, none of this would have been a problem for Penny had it not been for the full front page photograph- a picture identified as "That Marvelous Madam, Mother Frances," as she was shown standing "side-by-side with her daughter," left unnamed, at the entrance to the police station with the precinct number plainly visible in the background at the top of the steps. Further on, the lead story added that while two girls were not arrested, seven of the madam's "other" call girls had "just been released from jail." The daughter, of course- though unnamed- was unmistakably none other than Penny. Everyone that knew her would recognize her. So it was that the news of their distinguished "celebrity" spread through-out staid, conservative Sturgis and Damon- overnight.

Mother Frances had failed to provide the cover-up she had intimated would be such a cinch. And when the publicity first hit the Auchinachie home, there was shock, and there was grief, and there was rage. Things had been looking up till that paper arrived. What would happen now? Sean, in particular, was beside himself. An attorney was immediately contacted. He was unable to see more than a slim chance for a libel suit to succeed. So he called the former judge, Judge Clancy. He agreed. And, even if there was a monetary settlement, wouldn't it just drive the thorn deeper?

Meanwhile, Penny, mortified, aghast at the news, huddled alone in the dark of her room day after day, shades drawn, door shut- shunning the world at large. And then, when she was watching the television with her mother and father just after supper one day, a strange thing happened. During a T.V. ad, a strange look came across her face, as she stared at the screen and whispered, accusingly, without the slightest reason to do so, “They’re talking about me again, just like they were last night!”

Not long after that, her parents saw similar episodes- more and more often. It was then that their initial denial vanished rapidly in the face of the heart-breaking suspicion, that their beloved and gifted daughter might be on her way, after all, to losing her mind.

Kyesis

Doctor Rosenbaum was ingratiating as he discussed Penny's problem with Nancy and Sean, after examining her at the hospital and deciding that Penny would not need institutionalization at the sanitarium- at least, not if things went as he expected. Her symptoms, he said, of "paralogia," "blocking," "delusions" and "hallucinations" might be symptoms of oncoming schizophrenia, but in the light of her recent experiences, he said, he thought she could be treated at home. Recently, he said, an experiment on some college students had been cited in a medical journal which had suggested another possibility that could be the cause of similar behavior- even a cause of overt schizophrenia.

"What's that?" said Sean, sitting at one side of the shrink's desk, with Nancy on the other.

Rosenbaum smiled, then said, "You won't believe this- and I'm not sure that I do, myself- but it's called insomnia. Plain old *insomnia*, no more."

"Insomnia!" said Nancy. "Lack of sleep?"

"Yes, ma'am. In a nutshell," he said. "They took a small group of normal college students, forced them to stay awake as long as they possibly could and found that they displayed many of the symptoms of schizophrenia after a period of 2 or 3 days, depending on the kid."

"Two or three days and no sleep?" asked Sean. "This is for real?"

"That's right, Doctor," said Rosenbaum. I don't remember for sure, but I think there might have been a couple that went even longer than that. But I want to add that this is only a preliminary study. You know what I mean? No controls or anything."

"Of course," said Sean. "But I don't know how you'd control an experiment like that, anyway."

"Well," said Rosenbaum, "I don't know either, other than you'd let the control group get only some set amount of sleep, and perhaps group the subjects that were denied sleep into specific time spans so you could show some sort of a curve in the degree of schizoid symptoms. And I would expect you'd need more numbers."

"Yeah," said Sean. "That's usually the problem in preliminary studies. Where are the numbers? Sounds to me like they were just keeping them awake to see how long it'd take them to crack. Sort of like when I was cramming for finals- taking caffeine pills to stay awake. After a couple days of that, I thought I was going to crack up, too."

"Well, anyway," said Rosenbaum, "I thought it might be encouraging to tell you about that. As I understand, Penny hasn't been sleeping well for many days- ever since she left Washington. And, as far as that's concerned, I think she went through enough down there- at least for someone as young as she is, to make 'most anyone crack up after living in such a stable and quiet environment around here. She was really under a lot of pressure."

Nancy gave a sigh of relief. "I hope that's all it is, Doctor. And she *has* had a whole lot of trouble getting to sleep, lately. But what are we supposed to do to help her, when we take her home? I don't know if we can handle it."

"It's not all that hard. At least, you ought to try it. Personally, I hate to institutionalize patients. By and large, they don't seem to do very well in a strange environment." He reached in his desk drawer, pulled out a mimeographed sheet and handed it to Nancy. "There are two categories here, with some detail underneath them, if you look. And by the way, Dr. Auchinachie, you better study this too while I'm explaining this to your wife. You're a real important factor in how this comes out. Your daughter puts more confidence in you than most young people do with their fathers, so I expect you must have had a lot to do with raising her."

"I didn't think I did nearly as much as I should have, to tell you the truth, Doctor. But I tried," said Sean.

"Well, it must have been quality time, because it sure rubbed off. And you too, Nancy. I think, if anyone can pull this off at home, you two can. But let's get into the directions. By the way, don't forget to remind me to give you something to help her sleep."

Sean was studying his paper. "What's this mean..., here? Where it says 'Repudiate an imagined hostile environment.' How can I do that?"

"Said Rosenbaum, "Hasn't she been *afraid* of people since that newspaper story came out?"

"Of course. But the fear is real- people have even called our house- crank calls. It *exists* doesn't it? How can I repudiate that?"

"It's probably not as real as she..., or you and Nancy think, Doctor. At least it probably isn't very significant. Don't you suppose, once they know the truth, that most people will stick up for Penny? It's hard for me to think there are many people that wouldn't be very kind toward her, wanting her to overcome her problems. After all, she wasn't to blame for any of that. But if she's in hiding, that won't come easily."

"Well, I suppose so. But when you throw in the fact that nobody ever knew she was adopted...? Do you know how people are when they think somebody's a bastard?"

"They'll get over it. And so will you. She's a wonderful girl."

Nancy spoke next. "What about this second group of instructions?"

"All of those come down to trying to get her off of her inward, subjective concerns and focusing on objective things- outside herself."

"How do we do that?" said Sean.

"I think it should be simple, for people like you. First off, try not to leave her alone too much. Company will be a big help. And be congenial, invite her friends in, plan some recreation for her, take her on trips with you, or even a vacation. Something physical, like tennis. Try to keep her attention focused on things going on around her, even if its just a bird singing in a tree. And if she says something weird, don't tell her that it's weird, but say something like this- that her thoughts will probably change in a little while. Don't let her get off by herself and start brooding again. And whatever, don't get exasperated with some of the things she does, no matter what it is. You have to be very patient. If you can do what I'm saying, I really think she'll come out of it. Otherwise, she may end up in the mental ward. I expect you don't want that."

Nancy was gaining in confidence. Sean less so as he said, "I'm not going to be home enough to do some of these things. My work is mostly on the road, you know."

"Well, Doctor, I think you should try to engineer something so you can spend more time at home. Maybe you can get somebody else to do some of your work."

"That's doubtful. Cow vets don't grow on trees, you know."

"Well, second best would be to find some peppy young folks, friends of hers, to come in and keep her thoughts off herself. That's the whole object. It's sort of like something I've heard now and then on the radio from some of your Christian preachers."

"What's that? I don't go to church, at least not if I can help it," said Sean, grinning as though it were quite an accomplishment, considering his background.

"Well, it sort of goes like this. As I understand it, Jesus never seemed too concerned about himself. He was a 'Man for Others,' and- from what I gather- exclusively so. I think my own people would do well to pick up on that idea, whether or not they buy Jesus. It's very good- it's healthy- for people to quit studying their own navels and focus all they can- if not exclusively- on being kind and helpful to others. Don't you think so?"

"I suppose so," said Sean. "Never thought much about it, I guess."

"I'll bet you do it all the time without thinking about it," said Rosenbaum. "Well, personally, I think it's the road to a happier life..., excellent psychology, you know, comes from excellent philosophy."

"I think you're right," said Nancy. "I've even read articles that say you live longer, more contented lives if you live like that and, Sean..., just think about your own folks. Aren't they like that?"

"Hmmm," said Sean. "Guess I never thought about it. Maybe that's true. I never thought I was half as strong a man- when there's difficulty- as my father is, nor half as big-hearted as my mother, nor as happy- despite my having twice the education. Nothing ever seems to bother them as much as it does me. They both just seem to take things in stride."

"Well, then, Doctor," said Rosenbaum, a bit uneasily, "That brings me to this. There's one more thing I'm obliged to tell you that I wish I didn't have to do, but I hope you both will take it in stride."

Nancy's face was apprehensive. "It's about Penny?"

"Of course." said Rosenbaum. "And I want you to stay calm when I tell you this. Do I have your word?"

Sean looked at Nancy, puzzled. Nancy returned the look, puzzled. Almost simultaneously, they agreed that they were all set. "It's something bad, isn't it?" said Nancy.

"It doesn't have to be, Nancy," said the doctor, "but you'll probably think so, at first. With time, I think you'll get over it. Most grandparents do."

Nancy looked at Sean, her mouth open, then turned to the doctor. “Don’t tell me…, she’s…, Penny’s …, pregnant…? Are you trying to….”

Rosenbaum’s face was sad, but kindly. He saw the pain crossing their faces, as they looked back and forth, speechless, at each other-the word “grandparents” sinking in, and he reached out his hand, in sympathy, to touch Nancy’s arm as Sean rose from his chair. She’s pregnant?” he roared. “My God…, that’s what you’re trying to tell us, aren’t you!”

“Yes, Doctor, your daughter is pregnant. About two months. It must have happened a little while after she came back home from Washington.”

The Pendulum

There was a quiet wedding in Gramma Rache's rose garden that June, amidst picture-perfect weather, setting the farm off so it looked like an idyllic New England calendar picture- the last flush of dandelions ornamenting the grasslands, and the rolling, wooded hills back of the barn, off in the distance, displaying delicate shades of fresh greenery that rivaled the subtle shifts of color precursing autumn. Rev. Lewis officiated, joining his wife and some twenty other guests afterwards in a simple reception at the rambling old farmhouse. Brian was at his best, evidently untroubled by Penny's past mental affliction, which had passed off, as Dr. Rosenbaum had theorized it might, by resolving her anxiety-driven *insomnia*. Plainly, the doctor said, she was not psychotic.

Sean held Brian in high esteem. Certainly he was a promising sort of marriage prospect for any man's daughter; hard-working, temperate, well educated- a man's man with a mission to succeed at whatever he did. Currently employed at the Damon high school, he'd just finished his first year as an ag teacher, and was already considered a phenomenon by the school officials. Most important, his devotion to his bride was manifest in everything he did; she was a jewel in his eyes during the ceremony.

As for the untimely pregnancy, her father, once he'd cooled off, had mustered enough wisdom to take it in stride. "These things happen," he said, adding magnanimously, "who will know the difference in twenty or thirty years?" When pinned down by Nancy, Sean hadn't been able to back away from having mouthed off to her, for years, that a marriage ceremony was merely a validation, not an absolute requirement for lifetime cohabitation, having claimed that there were, historically, many isolated, primitive peoples whose only option had been a mere agreement of minds. Then too, though never married, some of his G-I buddies had common-law arrangements that were conventional and monogamous, indistinguishable- on the surface at least- from any others. And successful, as well- as long as legal rights of all offspring were firmly established.

Nancy, on the other hand, had kept quiet about some personal premonitions that the marriage might not work out very well. Brian unwittingly picked up on it as he faced his stunning bride-to-be as she was proceeding up the aisle holding the arm of her father. Nancy's eyes, not surprisingly, were brimming with the usual feminine wedding tears- more appropriate to a funeral- but far worse, she was studying Brian's face as though pondering for the first time whether he might be some unknown, wild beast in disguise that would, some day, perpetrate a monstrous tragedy on her daughter. Seemingly easy and comfortable with each other in the past, thus perplexed, he gave her a restive smile. To no avail. All she did was glower all the more. Brian had to assume she was more upset by Penny's pregnancy than he realized. He breathed a sigh of relief when, at last, he could face front with Penny- free from Nancy's strange gaze- to share their vows.

Amazingly, Nancy had been the one that originally seemed most understanding and realistic, having said from the very first that since the girl *was* in child there was no choice, and that it would be no trifling matter for her to have a baby and no husband. So, if she had misgivings at the time, she let them lie. Certainly, she'd insisted, Brian had many virtues and would be a good, loyal provider for Penny.

Of course, there was a skeleton in her own closet. Despite her mature, placid nature, Nancy had once traveled the same road as Penny. She had been spurned by an older man that had infatuated her for three years, marrying someone else. In fact, so torrid was her infatuation that she'd tried to get him to leave his wife and run away with her. Subsequently, on the rebound, she'd conceived by Sean, married him out of dire necessity, delivered her hydrocephalic infant early- stillborn- and never conceived again. So, like many women, she had married out of pragmatism rather than passion. Yet she knew full well that she'd had rivals who would have crawled on the bottom of the ocean floor over a bed of broken glass to catch Sean- but it was not to be- because *he* wanted her. Some day, she thought, the world should grow up. Why should it be considered so indecorous for a woman to fling artifice and passivity aside and initiate such things *herself*?

In the not so distant past, when horses and buggies ruled the roads, proximity and practical concerns had been the driving force behind most marriages. Despite that, they seemed to have worked out well. And Nancy suspected that most wives today would- at least secretly- confess to something of the kind, having married a "second choice" for similar reasons, hoping that some deeper affection might unfold between them as time went on. Which usually occurred, once her spouse's less obvious virtues manifested themselves.

Furthermore, she had observed that wedlock born of little more than physical passion had a very poor track record and was much too often damaging to the offspring. This seemed to her especially evident among numerous celebrities who, presuming liberty licensed *libertines*, had crawled and clambered into some self-adulating, phony paradise of upside-downville. In the process of time, Nancy had grown up.

After all, as Nancy's mother had often said to her during her early wedded days, it is more tiring to keep stoking a blazing fire with kindling, trying to keep it under firm, steady control, than it is to relax near the comfortable and uniform glow of a log's embers. How many women would end up with the bounder of her choice rather than an adoring prince, had she married her first serious crush? Compared to Sean, the more dashing man that Nancy, as a girl, had fancied, turned out to be no catch at all. Not exactly a bounder- but chronically unable to weather any inconvenience or steady work, a moocher and gambler with an enormous potbelly, ugly teeth and foul breath. Somehow, when his wife left him, it didn't even occur to Nancy to leave Sean and snatch up her golden opportunity.

In her musings over Penny, Nancy had recognized enough other parallels to her own life that she wondered what percentage of women had actually kidded themselves about their spotless virtue. When Penny was about fifteen, she had found Penny's little diary in plain view next to a chair in her bedroom. Somehow stumbling over it, it fell off a table to the floor and flopped open. While fumbling desperately to close the little booklet again without looking at its contents, she just couldn't help noticing it was written in English rather than early Sanskrit. Thus she simply couldn't resist the urge to check her daughter's syntax- as any mother would naturally do when her daughter is so plainly destined to be a novelist. To her great surprise, she could see that a great novel was on the way- a *purely* fictionalized account of some young heroine's torrid imagination. Evidently uninformed as to the legal aspects of literature, each of her fictional characters happened, unfortunately, to have the same name as one of Penny's acquaintances. There were numerous salacious remarks such as "She who is chaste is unchased," a direct quote from the lips of the fictional heroine- some girl by the name of Erna. At first, Nancy laughed. She had just discovered the daughter beneath the gentle, ladylike facade. She parked the little diary back where she'd found it but then- as she trod slowly back downstairs- she sobered, realizing her daughter's her poor choice of friends but, especially, her troubling conflicts.

It was not that Penny didn't know she was flirting with devils. On numerous occasions she had fled to her church's altar seeking some sort of personal exorcism through silent prayer. But, as she grew older, there seemed no way she could hide from the mischievous burlesques that popped into her head from nowhere, settling into the backroom parlors of her mind and making themselves quite comfortably at home. Gradually coming to think she was foreordained to fall prey to her nagging libido, she hid it from the world as best she could as a Lady Lovely personified. But her darkest suspicions about herself, her genetics, as it were, were confirmed by her infamous mother- Frances- who, except for her business acumen, was very much like Erna Vries' parents. Spawned from a woman with no conscience, Penny had little doubt that she, too, would eventually prove to be the same, despite her horror of such a thing. Sometimes she hated herself for her wild impulses, wondering if, some day, she would break down, sneak off, do some wicked thing and be found out, shamed and humiliated. If so, she would rather die. Was that to be her fate?

Then, speaking of fate, there was the matter of the events that had changed her life. To start with, why had Frances been able to bribe the courthouse employee as to her whereabouts, enabling her to be located? By what fate had she gone to Washington at precisely the wrong time? Who would have thought that such an uninitiated person could walk into a police raid in her first stay with her own birth mother, find herself helplessly thrown into the company of seedy characters and mistakenly put into a cell overnight? What did that do to her confidence, her sense of worth, when she was already in a state of self-reproach? And why did that man with the camera show up precisely as she was leaving the police station, and later give it to a second-rate scandal rag not always available in her home town, showing her with Mother Frances, the madam of the Washington jet-set, and fresh out of the can with all her bawds?

So it was that, even on her daughter's wedding day, it was abundantly clear to Nancy that she, though ostensibly cured of her mental problems, was not completely out of the woods. It had been a long, painful haul from the day she had hidden herself away at home, hiding in her room most of the time, reluctant to talk with anyone but her family, or, maybe, with Brian. Torn in one direction by her upbringing, and in another by her heredity, her "bad seed," as she called it, she seemed, indeed, too fragile to be married. It was as though Penny, feeling doomed- condemned as bad seed from the time of her birth by some heartless, unknown and uncaring sovereign power- had decided God was either unjust or asleep. He was to blame because He made her that way. Nancy had heard her saying that to her friends. That was not a healthy beginning for a new bride; And that was why Nancy was worried about her.

Milk Strike

A few years later, in the midst of the big AFO milk strike, Drew Auchinachie suddenly passed away. Maybe it was too much for him. He didn't believe in such things. There was a large turnout at the funeral- mostly farmers- held at the same church where he and his wife had been married, attending Sunday services faithfully almost every week thereafter. There in the quaint churchyard cemetery dotted with the graves of the earliest settlers from Connecticut and Vermont, Drew was buried among his ancestors.

Truly a Christian, there was little reason for tears among those attending. Instead, there was rejoicing- even among some dubious believers- for having shared in the life of such a warm and notable man, one of them saying that, having known Drew, he had escaped becoming born again only by the skin of his teeth. Among his family's old friends at the reception- held at the farmhouse- was B.J., Sean's controversial comrade, who was now an agent for the Farmers Home Administration after losing his own farm by foreclosure. Slipping over unseen behind him while he was talking to someone else, he grabbed Sean's arm. Sean instantly knew who it was. Turning to him, they shook hands and chatted for awhile without really saying a lot. As often happens, that led to a weightier discussion. "I have a question for you, Doc. What do you think of our milk strike?" said B.J.

"What strike?" replied Sean, kidding, of course. "I haven't followed it much, B.J., why don't you tell me about it? All the paper says is there's a sudden shortage of milk- don't seem to say much about the farm side of it, except they're unhappy, claim they're on the short end of things and all that."

"I know," said B.J. "The paper seems to focus a whole lot more on what it will cost the public to buy a quart of milk, than whether farmers will ever be paid what they honestly deserve."

"How much are you looking for? I haven't heard anything yet that I can really believe is the truth. Seems to depend on who I'm talking to."

"That's just it, Sean. All we're asking for right now is recognition of our right to negotiate contracts- *legal* recognition- just like the labor unions do when they start up," said B.J. "They won't even agree to that. We hadn't even *planned* to discuss the terms of any contract yet. There are other things besides price that we're concerned about, like the fact we have no due process at all. None. If they say we're remiss or guilty about something, anti-biotics, bacteria, low butterfat, and so on, we're guilty, and we pay the penalty- that's all there is to it. We even had a couple of guys that had to pay for a whole tanker-truck's load of milk because they decided, of all the farmers' milk that went in that tank, they were the ones who must have contaminated it with antibiotics. They claimed they had found an antibiotic that, it turned out, neither farmer ever could have had on his farm. Didn't even know what it was. Never heard of it. Another guy was getting gypped on his butterfat test because the trucker didn't bother to refrigerate the sample he took at the farm and it was hot enough, that summer- and what with the truck vibrating- that a lot of the cream churned into chunks of butter, lowering the test, of course."

"As well as the price," said Sean. "That's like that deal you had, when I sent you, like a blamed fool, to Judge Clancy. No recourse. By the way, what are you guys getting right now? I haven't paid much attention of late."

"Well, you know how it is. Kind of depends on the milk plant. But right now, our blend price for milk is running around $5.70-$6.30 a hundredweight. We aren't complaining about that. For once, we're getting a fair share of the retail price of bottled milk. It's just that we think the time has come when we farmers have a real *voice* in what we get paid, and change the way we're being treated- like we're a bunch of second class citizens. Don't you?"

"Well," said Sean, "for one thing, I certainly don't let somebody else tell me what they'll pay *me* for my effort, like you guys do. So you want to negotiate, then. Is that all?"

"For now, that would be enough. We think there should be a contract of sorts, where we farmers work together, guarantee so much milk of a certain grade for a definite period of time, at a predetermined price."

"Seems fair enough. And if there's a shortfall of milk?" said Sean.

"Then we have to find some somewhere and buy it… ship it in, until we get back up where we belong."

"How ya' doin' with the idea?" asked Sean.

"We were doing pretty well, but we're having a battle now with some of the older cooperatives. Got them pretty well teamed up against us. If we lose, maybe it will at least shake them up enough so they'll quit feuding with each other and pull together for a change. But we'll just have to wait and see how it works out. Say, how is Eric making out with your dad's old farm? I tried to get him to join, but he didn't do it."

"He's doing real well at the moment, except he's got three or four neighbors that moved in here, close-by, a couple of years ago right after he got married to Jill. They're giving him a real rough time about his spreading manure and stinking up the air."

"How long that farm been here, anyway?" inquired B.J.

"Try a hundred and fifty years, more or less."

"And they've been here… what did you say…, two or three years? Case closed, I'd say."

"So would I, B.J., but they're making a big stir about it being a public nuisance. Taking him to court if the town won't do anything about it."

"The town won't, will they?" said B.J.

"You wouldn't want to know who's on that board. Not a farmer on it. All suburbanites- recently moved in the area. They got us outnumbered now. Guess they don't want native hicks like us to stick around anymore. Just go away and evaporate somehow."

B.J. scowled. "That's the way it is over in three or four more townships where our farms are being crowded in by the swimming pool set. Buy the land cheap…, then build a fancy house and bitch about the operation next door that'd been there for years without a single complaint- long before they were born."

"Say, B.J.," said Sean, "look out for that cat!" He tried to head off his mother's cat, but, already leaping from his perch, he landed on B.J.'s shoulder. B.J. winced as the cat dug in, trying to hang on, rubbing his cheek on B.J.'s cheek.

"Yow!" said B.J., as Sean reached over and removed him. "Boy he sure purrs, doesn't he? Nice cat, reminds me of Alex, that cat I had in my barn for so long. Remember him?"

"Yeah. How could I forget him? He landed on my head right off your water heater in the milkhouse one winter when I was there. Didn't even see him coming. Let's see, what was that cat's name?" said Sean. "It was kind of a funny name, great mouser you said."

"Oh, sure. But that wasn't Alex. That was that old gray cat- a tom cat- his cheeks all puffed out from battle scars, you said. We called him "Pounce de Leon" because he was always jumping on people like that- real friendly, but it's a wonder somebody didn't hit him with a shovel after he landed on them. I thought old man Rogers was going to do that, you know."

"Rogers? I haven't thought of him in years. He's the guy, you know, that called me up one time saying his cow had crapped a snake. Did I tell you about that?"

"Nope," said B.J.

"Yeah. It was wiggling in the drop behind the cow when I got there. Of course, like always, he called me during his evening milking. I don't know what he thought I was going to do about it. But I went, anyway."

"Snake? Right in the manure?"

"Right in the manure. It was a baby snake, little bit of a garter snake the cow passed in her manure- must've hatched in her gut after she swallowed a snake egg out in the grass. I felt kind of sorry for the little rascal, even though I don't like snakes a whole lot better than I do lawyers and other vermin. Wonder he didn't smother inside the cow when he hatched."

"I'll be darned! What did you do then?"

"Fished him out of the drop and put him in the grass outside the barn. He tried to bite me, of course. Wasn't much bigger than a night-walker."

"I mean..., about the cow...."

"Oh... the cow! Nothing at all. She was all right, of course." Sean rubbed his nose, a sure sign something else was occurring to him. "Say, B.J., what's this I hear about you trying to get Penny to help out the AFO?"

"That's right. Nobody could seem to get your son-in-law- Brian, there- interested in joining, once he heard there was a strike in the wind. But then I happened to think your daughter had been getting around in the county Farm Bureau. Secretary, no less. And like it or not, she's become something of a celebrity after that newspaper thing. I hear they still talk about her down in Washington, even when they don't remember her name. I figured she might have some pull getting some of those backsliders out in the hills interested in joining. Of course my job with the F.H.A. doesn't let me recruit members anymore. Not openly, at least. Conflict of interest, they tell me."

Sean was amused. "I knew you'd been there talking to her. Has she said anything yet? She told me she was going to think about it for awhile."

"She's going to do it. They gave her some material to hand out just last week."

"Wow! That's great!" Sean almost hollered hallelujah, relieved to think Penny's confidence might finally have been restored. Had he heard the news in church, he might even have jumped over a pew, clicking his heels. Then he sobered. "But what did Brian say?"

B.J. winked. "Penny's spunky, just like you. I guess Brian doesn't tell her what she can or can't do. She was all for the AFO. In fact, she told him he never should have signed up with his regular co-op, because they were not well capitalized. If they get called on the debt they're carrying, it'll come out of every one of their patron's milk checks. And I hear they're in real deep."

"Yeah, I hear that too," said Sean. "But I don't know..., they've been around quite a long time now. Brian told me they've paid their patrons more than the other co-ops for years."

"I know they have. But, you ought to see the debt they've accrued since they added that other plant up north. It's pretty scary, I'd say. I understand their backer is not very happy with them."

"They're behind on their payments?"

"I'll say. Big time. And I work with their backer some. I've got it straight from him. He says they might have to sell some of their other old assets off to get out of trouble, but that's bound to shake up their membership pretty good. They're already sweating it out, and they might just jump ship before it gets too hot."

"Well, I suppose there is some kind of insurance to cover the farmers if they default," said Sean.

"Don't bet on it..., don't bet on it," said B.J. "But I didn't say anything, if you know what I mean. Don't even tell Brian, or I'm in a hot spot."

"Don't even tell Penny?"

"Mmmm," said B.J., puckering his lips as he mulled it over. "Don't tell her why, or who told you. But if she can get him out, okay. But don't do it yourself. He's right over there in the far corner of the room looking at us right now."

"Okay. I'll play it cool. Hate to see him get in trouble- he's doing so well."

"Say, that makes me think. How's he doing..., I mean *really* doing? I see he's milking his heifers now in my old barn. I guess he's still teaching?"

"Yeah, he's milking them real early, so he can get to his class on time..., over at the school. Got twenty first calf heifers now, all fresh in the last month or so. Seems to be real sharp. And did you see Penny's three boys?"

"Yeah, she must have had them bing, bing, bing right after she got married. How long has it been now?"

Sean stroked his chin, cogitating. "Let's see.... Five or six years now, I'd say. The first one, just between us, came a little quick, if you know what I mean."

"I know," said B.J. "Too bad about the second one."

"You mean one with the hare lip?"

"Yeah. And he seems like a real good little fellow. Looks like the docs fixed it up pretty well, though."

"We thought so, too. It was more than a hare-lip. He had a cleft palate, too. But he's real bright. I think he'll get along pretty good, though they had a pretty hard time nursing him without drowning him, when he was first born. Penny was about to crack up when she saw the little fellow, so afraid she couldn't handle it, and just sure as she could be that it was her bad genes that did it."

"Can't blame her for that. My brother had a kid like that, you know. Twenty years ago."

"How'd he come out?"

"Real good. No problems at all," said B.J. looking at his watch, "say..., old buddy, I've really got to take off. I've got to be at a meeting in another half hour."

"You aren't staying for the dinner? We'd like you to stay, you know. My mother would like to..., I'm sure. She asks me about you a lot."

"No, Sean. I've really got to go. By the way, what gives with the bridge down below, where your road comes out on the highway?"

"Oh, that. Well, I think you can get through now. They've had to take out the old bridge. Too narrow for the traffic. Since that new mall went in, up the road from there, they've really had to widen the road."

"I suppose so. Sure has changed, though, in the last ten years. I never would've believed they would put so many houses and roads up there on those four farms that used to be there.... They're all over the place. Much less raising a big mall like that. Never saw so many cars as they got parked there. And they tore down the old grade school that used to be there."

"Things are changing, aren't they, B.J.?"

"Sure are. And fast! Won't be a farm for miles the way its going now, since that big defense plant moved in."

Serfs on a Fief

Having overheard some of the high school boys discussing the subject during his morning ag class, Brian had decided to open up a debate that afternoon at their meeting of the Future Farmers of America. It was his habit to teach by first stimulating controversy, thus challenging their minds to think for themselves or, at the very least, if they must parrot something, let it be something else besides what they had learned in the classroom. Accordingly- shifting his eyes back and forth between the most voluble pair- he asked them what they thought of the "diggings."

Now there wasn't a boy in the room that didn't immediately know what he was talking about. Early in his sessions he had explained some of the prehistoric geology that had formed the region. The Susquehanna in that area currently flows through a deep and long gravel bed, a relic of the last ice age, when a mountainous column of ice pressing south from Canada, thousands of feet deep, melted into oblivion when it spread to its southernmost extent, depositing there a deep accumulation of stones scraped from bedrock along the way and then shaped into imperfect globes. Sitting on top of these gravel deposits, called terminal moraines, were miles of well-drained, fertile flats- silted over by ancient, post-glacial floodwaters and lakes into a silt-loam- not lacking much, after organic deposits were acquired, of being a most productive sort of farmland. Farmers almost drool when they see soil like that.

However, the demand for concrete was steadily expanding to build major new highways and other construction projects planned in that general area. That settled it. There was money to be made, and the soil- fertile or not- would take years as mere farmland to earn what could be made in a few short years by juicy diggings of gravel. Crops could be grown elsewhere and the organic soil on top of the precious gravel moraine would have to go. What happened to it was almost immaterial to the diggers- perhaps it could be profitably sold for topsoil for the new residential lawns, suburban parks and golf courses that would eventually be overlooking the valley beautiful left naked and sterile below. Or as an alternative, just so he could get underway without too much opposition, the gravel miner could convey the initial impression (ho, ho) that he would, *of course*, eventually replace the topsoil into the barren depths that were created and make a nice cozy whatever out of it, once digging was over. Unless you were one of those ubiquitous, cantankerous old fogies or some sort of preservationist Neanderthal, this process of ripping up miles of farms and transforming them into uninhabitable, barren pits was sanctimoniously called *progress.* Another case of provender for one being poison for another.

Of course, Brian and his FFA boys had no idea at the time of their discussion how much farther the devastation might go. So far, though only a small cluster of prime valley farms along the river had been sold for this hallowed hollowing of the gravel beds, the fathers of two boys in the FFA had recently been approached and were also seriously considering selling their farms. Even though one of these was the fourth generation of his family to farm the land, just the prospect of the jingle that might soon be in his pockets was already like music to his ears. No more work, either. Just sit on the porch and count the money accumulating as truckload after truckload passed his house. The other dad's main concern was that his upland fields were of no interest to the gravel industry, thus he would be left with some land that would neither support a farm nor be of much interest to a residential developer, being mostly scrubland and wooded hillside.

Brian was surprised by the number of the older boys wondering how many prime farms would eventually be swallowed up before the demand for gravel would ease off. Normally, only older men concern themselves with such matters. Were their own plans for the future blowing away in the wind as farm after farm disappeared? If so, some of them thought there should be a law against it. Certainly it would be ruined as cropland for a century or more, since some of the abandoned gravel pits were already flooded by the nearby river. Some of the young fellows from the outlying hills had overheard their elders saying there might ultimately be so many major farms depleted that the agricultural infrastructure would fade away- such as feed stores, equipment dealers, various service outfits such as vets, and milk plants. That could be the death knell for the remaining farms.

Brian, his curiosity piqued, asked the FFA kids how they thought such a law should be written. After dithering around, the majority finally concluded that the best land- not just here, but across the country- should be legally preserved for agricultural purposes, with no development of any kind allowed unless related to farming. Otherwise, they thought, the day might come when there was insufficient land to feed the populace, say nothing of exporting food to a hungry world. One young buck commented that the day might come when urbanites might try to tear up city concrete in an effort to find some soil where they could grow their own food. Brian, of course, gently dismissed that as so much hyperbole. After all, the day might be saved by advances in hydroponics. Even at that, the young fellow insisted, wasn't there something amiss when people were starving around the world, and American agriculture was dismissed as though that should be of no great concern? To that, another boy responded that a nation of the starving would be unlikely to pay anything for the food. Yet another added that if we did that, even if they paid us, those countries probably wouldn't thank us, but have their pride so offended they would come to hate us. Besides that, their populations would grow even faster than they already were, and eventually exhaust the food supply.

No, something else needed to be done to control the possibility of famine in the future. It still seemed that there was something immoral about letting people around the world starve while we were paying farmers to take land out of production to maintain prices. So, when the boys were putting their heads together, summarizing their opinions, they still thought there should be legislation to preserve agricultural land.

At that, Jan Vederdt spoke up. An exceptional student, he was the only son of a highly successful poultryman in the area by the name of Herm Vederdt- an immigrant from Germany during the thirties- who had a fairly large chicken farm with 12,000 Leghorn hens, crating and selling his eggs to local stores and, much to his advantage, without involving any middlemen. He had made a lot of money, even during the depression. His son, whom the other boys in the class had good-naturedly nicknamed "Feathers," had been sitting in the class for some time, taking in the exchanges of opinion among his peers without comment because dairy farms were not his bailiwick. But at the mention of legislative control he rose to the occasion. This country, he said, is supposed to be a land of liberty and opportunity, and what the other boys were suggesting would mean his dad could never sell his place for anything near his investment. That, he said, was because his only choice to recover his investment was to sell his place as something other than a farm.

Speaking with surprising insight and eloquence for a kid of seventeen, he recounted what almost everyone in the room knew, that the day of the traditional independent poultryman had been practically phased out in a matter of just a few years, due to a handful of large mid-western feed corporations having bought out countless independent chicken farms, seemingly so they would have a captive market for their chicken feed. In the process, they had replaced many of the older poultry houses on the properties they'd bought, having more than enough capital to install the most modern and labor-efficient facilities and methods. Oftentimes, they hired back the former owner to run the place, with somewhat better compensation than he'd ever made on his own. The market price of eggs, even if it went down, was of less importance to the feed companies than the amount of feed they could move, since they were already forcing out of business a multitude of competing independent feed stores. As a spin-off, later on, when they'd squeezed out enough middlemen, they expected their corporate size would avail them of a larger share of the nation's grain production in the mid-west, enhancing their ability to reduce their cost of grain from the farm elevators. Though quick to deny it, monopoly was their ultimate goal and everybody knew it, though, if unimpeded by political processes, it could eventually come down to a contest between the last few mammoths- winner take all.

"Feathers," of course, had been well drilled by his disgruntled father, who had been caught napping and now had a farm that was nigh unto useless either as an operation or as prime residential real estate. Lacking the advantages of their huge new corporate competitors (cheap, wholesale chicken feed, as well as the capital to modernize facilities for more efficient production) they would need to revamp their whole operation. But that would require more capital than it would be worth, since the wholesale price of eggs at the farm was not keeping pace with the times, squeezing Vederdt even more between rising prices for their purchases and lower prices for their produce- much as was occurring to farms in general. After all, unlike the corporate chicken farms, the price of *their* chicken feed, bought retail, was at least as high as ever. It was a hopeless situation that resulted in the disintegration of countless independent poultry farms across the country, almost overnight.

In summary, the primary object of the grain corporations was plain: to monopolize a captive market for their poultry feed and capture the broiler industry where the real money was, rather than the egg market. Rumors of the same process seemed to be in the wind for the national hog industry, where the independent farmer was also in jeopardy. Agriculture was undergoing a broad, national takeover by huge capital interests, against which no small-time farmer could compete and greatly devaluing his own capital assets. "Legislation prohibiting sale of our land outside agriculture would be the worst thing in the world for our family," protested Feather heatedly, "because there would be hardly any market for it, nowadays."

Brian broke in at this point. "But this is the natural price of *progress,*" he told the young fellow. "It's like what the automobile did to all the horsemen and farriers. What progress does, and what has made America great is that people have the *liberty* to replace outmoded ways of doing things with better ones. Some people are hurt, but the overall effect is well worth it. That is why America has outstripped the rest of the world."

Jan Vederdt frowned, suddenly realizing that in his earnestness he might have overstepped his privileges in Brian's class. Toning down his voice, he continued, "Mr. Miller," he said, "I think my dad would pretty much agree with you, but he sure is leery of 'big' interests. He saw that happening in Germany. I've heard him say time after time it doesn't even have to be a monopoly..., whenever a single industry gets into the hands of just a few, it's almost as bad as a monopoly- and whether it's a few corporations or the government, it will *eventually* result in higher prices and poorer quality for the consumer, and some sort of slavery for all the grunts- peons like us! My dad hates the thought.... He came to America because a man could start fresh and make something of himself over here, and he could see which way Germany was going. He says that the way we're headed, right now, we'll probably be just a bunch of serfs on a fief- all over again.

"I don't agree with you guys. Nobody should even think of telling a landowner what he could do with his own land, even if he wants to park a junkyard on it. At least," he said, "he should be able to sell it to the highest bidder. If my dad wants to sell his farm, I think he should be able to sell it to whoever wants it for the best price he can get, without having some fool bureaucrat or politician telling him he has to sell it for peanuts in order to keep it agricultural. Otherwise, we've lost our liberty. I think we might as well admit- right here and now- that a *farm*..., is already little more than a four letter word, at least here in this country."

Brian, addressing the whole class, quickly admitted that "Feathers" had a good point. Mr. Vederdt, most likely, could best reclaim what he had in his farm by selling it to an escapee from urban chaos, one who had sold his former property to acquire a quiet and picturesque haven for a third or half that price out here in the sticks.

"It ought to be the same for every single landholder," said young Vederdt, then adding, "after all, that might be the only way a farmer could really cash out big." He turned to his buddies and muttered, "and you all want to put a stop to that?" They had nothing to say.

Brian then asked the class if they had ever heard of an agricultural district, such as was currently being bandied about in various state governments as one way to preserve agricultural land, the current thought being to limit such projects to collections of farms in specified areas. "Agricultural Districts" would then be classified as such on the tax rolls and given corresponding property tax relief for a few years till renewal time, when the voluntary terms might be renegotiated.

The flip side of the proposal would be that, should a housing developer buy such a farm, no public funds would be provided him for pavements, sidewalks, street lights, water or other public utilities. Hopefully, that would greatly reduce the likelihood of the farm being sold to such a developer. At the same time, it would reduce the potential sale price of the farm. The odds were that it would then remain agricultural for the full term of the agreement- but with lower property taxes as the pay-off for the farmer.

Various plans of this type, Brian went on to say, were being considered in several different statehouses- due to particularly strong pressure from the farm organizations regarding onerous property taxes- sometimes amounting to 40% of annual net farm income. Though opposed by urban interests, they had successfully argued that residential assessments and tax rates should not be applied to agricultural operations. Once a modest interest for his many capital investments was subtracted from a farmer's annual income over operational costs, his remaining income (per hour of labor) usually turned out to be buzzing around at half that of the *average* industrial laborer, sometimes less. Brian ended up his monologue by saying, "But then, nobody ever said that this life would be *fair*, did they?"

This thought was echoed by another boy, who had previously kept his trap shut, though listening avidly. "My uncle and aunt from the city came out to see our farm about three weeks ago. They don't know *nothin'* about farming. They look around and they think we're rich. Dad says they don't have any idea that we still owe money on a whole lot of the stuff, and the rest of it- most, anyway- ought to have been junked 'cause it don't work too hot, no more. Anyway, he says it's the insurance company and the FHA that owns most of the stuff we got. And as far as the lawyer is concerned, he doesn't seem to know the only reason we got anythin' at all is 'cause we live like paupers. Besides that, Ma..., she drives the school-bus..., and Pa- he does some custom work for other farmers- they have to work their heads off to do it. It's like that with a lot of our neighbors. I know one what fixes cars and trucks in his spare time..., welding..., things like that."

"What's wrong with that?" said another boy. "So you don't make enough on your farm to get along. That's your own fault."

"That ain't so, Herbie, and you know it. We never had to do that till recently- last ten years or so. We got along for years on what we had- didn't have to look for other work to fill in the gaps. But thirty cows ain't enough no more. Why should we always have to get bigger?"

"Because everybody else is, dummy!" came a voice from the back of the room. "You got to keep up with the times!"

"Now boys," said Brian, "let's not get carried away. I won't have any name-calling here. One thing we want to get across when we're discussing things like this is how to act like adults."

"Like adults...? Huh!" said another kid. "You should have heard my dad bawl out those guys a while ago about his social security. That's the kind of adult I want to be!"

The class exploded with laughter. Brian scratched his head, wrinkling his brows. "Social security? What do you mean?"

"Oh..., probably I shouldn't have brought it up. But..., well, anyway, here goes. Dad bought a new Farmall tractor once and when the dealer started making out the credit agreement, Dad just sort of snorted and made out a check and handed it across the kitchen table to him and asked him if that wasn't that good enough for him?"

"The whole thing?" asked Brian.

"The whole thing. Paid in full," said the boy.

Brian laughed. "Not many farmers can do that. Wish *I* could. That's pretty good."

"Not near good enough," said the boy. "Dad about flipped his wig when the check bounced. According to his records, he had way more than enough in the bank to back it up. So he called up the bank. They gave him a big run-around, and then they put the bank president on the phone. Boy, did Dad give him an earful! The revenue agents had raided our bank account and emptied it out. Nobody even told my dad!"

"Nobody? Nobody at all?"

"Nobody!"

You sure? Not even the bank?"

"Sure as can be."

"Raided his bank account? Why? What was it…, back taxes?"

"Not exactly. He always pays his tax on time. It was when Congress decided farmers had to pay social security just like everybody else. Dad said when they started social security back in the thirties, they told farmers they'd never have to pay on it. Said farmers were exempt. Then, just a while ago, they changed it and said they did have to. Dad said if they couldn't keep their word, he was damned if he was going to pay it. He'd been fighting them off…, ignoring them for a long time."

"You don't mean they just walked in and took his money and never told him about it? No court, or anything?"

"I dunno, but I guess so. At least, that's what Dad said. When the bank didn't tell him either, that was the last straw. So the durned check bounced and Dad had to send the tractor back. Man, he was ticked off. You ought to have heard him go after those guys when he got them on the phone. The bank and the agency…. Both. I never seen him so mad!"

Normally, Brian would have been highly skeptical. Though seemingly incredible that this kind of thing could occur in the U.S.A., he'd recently read articles in some of the most reliable farm magazines about similar high-handed outrages committed by various federal agencies. But, having heard this story before from Sean, he knew they were consistent with each other. Furthermore, he personally knew that the boy's father was hardly the type to blow his top without cause.

"Before we break up," said Brian, "what do you fellows think about the milk strike we just went through?"

"It was a flop," said Feathers.

"O.K.", said Brian, "it was a flop. Did you all hear that? Hey, Jay..., will you quit jabbering in the back of the room there and pay attention! This is important."

"Yassuh, massa." There were titters and a few guffaws. Brian let it pass.

"Did you all hear me...?" Brian paused a few seconds till all eyes were front and center. "What I want to know, is how many boys here think the milk strike was a flop? Raise your hands if you think it was." All hands but one went up. All except Tim. "Ah, I see we have one voice of dissent. The rest of you think it was a flop. Ray, would you tell me why you think it flopped?"

"Not enough guys were in on the strike. Besides that, they all paid the scabs more to run through the lines and deliver the milk."

"Who do you mean by 'they?'"

"The milk plants. I heard that one guy- one of those scabs- said that, by golly, nobody was a big enough man to get in his way.... Said he'd run over any s.o.b. if he didn't move, and that the other damfools could dump their milk if they want to, but they were paying him a *premium* to haul in his milk while the strike is on!"

"I see. Well, I heard things like that, too," said Brian. "What do you think of having a picket line..., if you were in the line, would you hurt somebody that tried to go through?"

"I couldn't do that," said one boy. "How can you hurt somebody that you've known for a long time? We all know each other."

"Well, we just heard that one fellow said he'd run over somebody that got in his way. What do you think of that?"

There were a succession of murmurs from the boys, all talking at once. The consensus was that there weren't many farmers that would really be capable of that. And if they did, they'd be in jail for a long time. "How then," asked one, "do unions find people to fight the scabs, beating them up- even killing some people?" Nobody wanted to answer. Plainly, country boys were a different sort- said another one of them- partly because they considered themselves more like capitalists than labor. Several, agreeing, went beyond that to say "most of us were raised different. We were taught to respect property and other people so we couldn't hurt them. Church has something to do with it."

But in the final analysis, the boys couldn't agree about either the need for a farm union, nor how it should be operated. Brian used that discord to illustrate that farmers were too independent to organize. And if there was any doubt, Brian pointed out the numerous co-ops formed by farmers, most of them standing off by itself. The co-ops would not cooperate with each other. That was because American farmers were, in Brian's words, the most independent people in the world. And they paid for it dearly.

At this point, Brian asked the boys, "How many of you think the farmer is underpaid?" Every hand went up. "How many think farmers will never be paid more unless they cooperate closely?" Every hand went up. Then he asked them if farmers would ever actually do that. There was not one hand on that one.

"Tim," said Brian. "I'll give you the last opportunity to speak before we close up the meeting. Would you like to tell us why you don't think the strike was a flop?"

"Well…," drawled Tim, "I think the AFO got across a point that no co-op ever seemed to address. At least, not that I heard about."

"What's that?" said Brian.

"They were only asking for the right of a farm group to make a contract just like lots of businesses do, like construction corporations. It seems to me now, that small groups of farmers might eventually pick up on that one basic idea, refine it a little and agree to provide so much milk- whatever the creamery expects of them- no more, no less-month by month, with a set price, with a real penalty for more or less produce.

"Farmers would have to share the burden, somehow, if they had to buy milk somewhere else to fill the bill, and if a farmer goes over his quota, he would be personally penalized. Sort of like the futures contracts they do for grain at the Chicago Board of Trade. Then, if everybody did things like that, farmers would not be constantly producing more than the market wants, and would assume some responsibility that way that they never seem to do otherwise. I think if they did that, then they'd get a fair price. But you can't expect a processor to just say to somebody, send me all the milk you can make and I'll pay you the same even if its over what I need."

An Abiding Obsession

Had he heeded only the advice he received from Drew- or Sean, or Eric- it might have worked out a little better for Brian. Particularly when there was a financial issue, his in-laws preferred to err, if at all, on the side of caution. Over the years, they had experienced sudden shifts in some aspect of the economy that could catch even an astute farmer flat-footed, leading to his ruin. When considering enlarging an operation- which, of course, could have its merits down the line- any farmer's current profit margin is especially critical, and even if that margin was better than average, Brian's in-laws never believed in risking everything you had as a short cut into instant prosperity. Who can predict the fate that lies just around the corner?

Brian would never be known as a believer in the usual sense, though he was surely a believer in himself. Unfortunately, never having suffered a real set-back, he was rapidly acquiring an overweening confidence that could easily become the cause of much difficulty for him and his family. First off, his marked success as an ag teacher had boosted his reputation among the local yokels, and when he had left that position to concentrate on his farming operation at B.J. Pierce's old place- where he now lived with his family- he had, aided by his wife's position, inveigled his numerous college connections to hold the first state-wide "Field Day" for farmers, right at his own place. Overnight, his name became a widespread subject of conversation, his farm having been converted into a demonstration site for thousands of farmers, eager to see his farm transformed- in a single day- into a modernized farm with the help of the college extension, numerous machinery dealers, barn-builders, pond-diggers, workers laying field tile and contouring hillside fields in the interest of drainage problems, erosion, and the like. Being a dry summer, the place was literally turned into a dust bowl. So fierce was the activity that, at day's end, the cars, which were stretched along both sides of the road for well over a mile, were covered with so much dust that the windshields had to be swept clean before people could see well enough to drive back home. Not a single participant escaped having eyebrows, hair and clothes covered with it. And it was interesting to hear comments of the men leaving at the end of the day, every one looking like they'd just crawled, sneezing and coughing, out of a Sahara sandstorm: "Man…, there ain't goin' to be nothin' left of that place when the dust blows away…" and "…Can't believe how they built that whole new pole-barn in one day, with a new milkhouse pret' near finished, to boot…!" or "Do you suppose that big hole they dug out for a pond will ever actually fill up with water…?" It was the first Field Day, and there was humor, there was mockery, and there was wonderment. And it wasn't all that bad. And the next day, after the dust was all settled, there was light.

With his fame- or notoriety, as the case may be- now widespread throughout several farm journals with pictures of Brian, Penny and his boys, he was thereafter pursued for talks, pictures, equipment dealers looking for a good ad, and just plain opinions by various farm interests. In short, he and Penny had become celebrities overnight. He was Mr. Big. The fame, as it happened, did not fail to reach the eyes of Washington politicians, and the local Representative to Congress, a member of the agriculture committee, was suddenly on a first name basis with him. B.J. Pierce, more active than ever in the AFO, despite their failed strike, was calling Penny in the hopes she would participate as a farm representative in a Congressional hearing sometime in the future, along with several big league movie stars who had suddenly become experts on farming by doing a film on the subject. And Mother Frances, too, back out of jail, was patiently trying to work out some intrigue, some scheme to regain her daughter's confidence. Surely, she thought, there must be some way she could exploit this windfall.

This was heady stuff indeed for the Miller family. But now, believing he should live the part of a Mr. Big, Brian wasted no time planning to enlarge his operation, confident he could do so if anyone could. For one thing, his fame was such that he no longer had to plead for farm loans. He could just walk in, and the bankers would grin and say "sure enough, Mister Miller." And with his oldest boy having reached fourteen- he now had more help on the farm and would be able to increase the size of his herd. Like most dairymen, basically the only way his farm income could be significantly augmented, whether in fair times or foul, was increasing total milk production. With the promise of two more sons not far behind the oldest one, and with Penny having recently moved up from Farm Bureau secretary to a steady secretarial job with the county extension service, things were really looking up for them. The future was, indeed, most promising.

Though he kept it pretty well disguised, Brian's good fortune was beginning to go to his head. Penny noticed that whenever he talked with his now numerous visitors, who treated him like an authority, spellbound, leaning on every word that spilleth from the mouth of the great seer, he did it with a new flair befitting Moses himself. Like many another successful entrepreneur, having acquired a sudden case of ego, he seemed to attribute his success solely to his own proficiency and good judgment. Actually, he had started out farming at an auspicious time, financially speaking, carrying the maximum debt load his operation could possibly sustain with no difficulty. But now there was a temptation to make the big leap into the future. All he needed was the money to expand, and the improvements in efficiency he had in mind should double his farm's net income in three or four years. He knew other farms that had done it. So could he. Basically, he planned to streamline his facilities even more, making it feasible to increase the number of milk cows, currently fifty, to eighty, that being from about 25 per man to 35 or even 40. Then, as the younger boys came on, even more cattle could be added, so that they could perhaps dream of two hundred cattle, if they hired a man or two. After that, he might even be milking a thousand- if he could hire a few Mexicans or other immigrants. That would also mean that their barn and field machinery would be used more efficiently, instead of sitting idle much of the time off-season. Oh yes, he thought, rubbing his hands in glee as he thought of it, my boys could have a great future here. The thought of spawning and expanding a grand and famous Miller family enterprise was becoming his abiding obsession.

Miller's Fall

The first step for Brian Miller was to get some bucks somewhere so he could buy the neighboring farm that was up for sale. The old man who owned it, having retired after his wife died, was eager to leave the place, which never held more than twenty or thirty milk cows in its day- far too few for the times. The buildings there were run down, but the acreage itself- though no longer enough to support a full-time, present-day dairy operation- lay on some of that good river valley soil that everyone envied. Then, having just enough extra land to grow the crops that his expanded herd would require, Brian could add on more cows at the main farm. Although he was already mortgaged to the hilt, he figured his reputation was now firmly enough established that the local bank would surely lend him the money to buy the land he needed. He planned to buy additional cows through a cattle dealer, financing them the usual way, through a chattel mortgage. They were more than willing to finance their sales. In fact, that was why most cattle were purchased through a dealer instead of at an auction- which usually required cold cash- even though they might cost somewhat more.

Meanwhile, the old man wanted to sell the place and get it over with right away. Like *NOW*. And there were other vultures in the wings sniffing at his door to buy the farm- bigger outfits than Brian's and with more equity. At the same time the old man wasn't about to hold even a second mortgage. So Brian went to his regular Farmer's Bank, the one he'd always done business with- where his checking account was- and where he was known on sight from teller to president. There he was told there would surely be no problem getting the loan to buy the other farm, but a loan of that size would have to go through the usual clearing process at main headquarters- that bank having recently been amalgamated into a much larger urban-based bank. It could take a few weeks, but the president of the bank personally assured him of the loan.

Brian was in a dilemma. There was no time to waste, or he'd lose the opportunity of a lifetime. But he was a schemer. He figured he had enough money on hand to buy the old boy out if he added to it a hefty short-term loan from a cut-throat loan agency, figuring to pay it all off later when the big bank loan went through, before the agency's exorbitant interest could eat him up. That would also require his stalling on some of his already overdue payments for feed, vet bills, and equipment dealers- borrowing from them, in effect. The risk was that all his liquidity would be shot till his regular bank came through. Having taken the risk, he paid the old man $60,000 for his run-down old farm- somewhat more than it was actually worth- and got the title. The price of milk was high, his cows were milking well, and so he had no doubt the temporary shortage of cash would be covered by the long-term, low interest mortgage money- the same sort of a juggling act that he and many other farmers had made a custom of doing.

The problem was that the mailbox price of milk- the farmer's share- took a sudden, precipitous plunge. (Not the store price) Nobody seemed to know quite why. But it was a terrific drop, and there were no expectations that it would be coming back in the near future. As a result, the bank reneged on their promise. After all, they said, Brian's business was already financed up to the ears- even granted a *good* milk market. They couldn't even consider a farm loan to *any* dairy farmer at the present time. It would be too risky. Nothing personal, of course. So here was Brian, with his head stuck in a financial guillotine, with his many, many short-term farm creditors hounding him for their money. Their businesses were hurt by the price fall, too, having extended too much credit to other dairymen.

What to do? That was the question. Tentatively talking with Penny about his dilemma- wondering if he ought to approach her father or brother about some help- didn't work. Instead, it backfired. Penny was most unhappy that he even suggested it. She would be embarrassed to death if he said a word to them. And Brian didn't need to be told what would happen if he did. He and Penny had only recently found their way back together after a shaky marriage: finally in the groove, pulling together. The last thing he was going to do was to go back to the old days when they were first married, when they fought continually, mostly over money matters. Penny, like her whole family, thought that Brian was a "spender" of one degree or another and took far too many risks. He figured he'd better find some other way to get out of his present situation, since she wouldn't cooperate under any circumstance.

It didn't take him long to head to a different bank- secretly. Like the next day. Then, that failing, he went to several more. Nope, no more farm loans for now. Sorry. No farmers wanted- not if they milked cows, anyway. Farms for some dadblamed race track or pleasure horses, well that would be another thing. So, okay, what else could he do? Could he sell some cows to get money? Scotch that. His cows were not salable, at least not the ones that would bring anything, because they were mortgaged cows- chattel mortgages. Sure, he could sell them, but probably at a loss, and whatever he took in would have to go to the dealer he'd bought them from. Desperate, hounded by his creditors, he ended up at a loan shark's establishment, a seedy looking place with seedy looking people, probably affiliated with some mob. Even they were a little cautious, but they let him have some money, but not all. So he went to three more outfits of similar ilk, finally getting short-term loans at high interest rates by misrepresenting the full extent of his debts. Could be called fraud. It was a last ditch measure, but to all appearances, he was still the same authoritative farm expert should anyone ask him for advice. The new loans were due in a few months, and the interest was staggering. So with the milk prices dropping still more, he began kiting checks, then skipping around from one shark to another borrowing more short-term, high interest loans to pay off the first ones, rapidly getting deeper and deeper into debt. It was a life of conniving and it kept him on constant edge.

Penny was totally unaware of these goings on, but she could see that Brian was not himself. Even Eric, his best friend, noticed something different about him. In the first place, he avoided any discussion of finances with vague, imprecise answers. In fact, he was practically non-communicative. Then she realized there had to be a problem when phone calls and nasty letters regarding delinquent payments started building up. When bill collectors began knocking on the door, and court appearances were demanded as well as notices of impending liens, she knew they were in really deep trouble. Finally she confronted him about it. At first he just walked out on her and drove off somewhere. That was not at all like Brian. When Brian's mail was no longer forthcoming at the house, she discovered he had opened a post office box, to which she had no access. Needless to say, their marriage was rapidly falling apart again. Shakier than ever.

On her own, Penny finally decided to ask her dad and mother for some money, telling them how serious their problems seemed to be but, at the same time, asking them to say nothing to Brian about where the money came from. Her father, faced at that time with a bunch of farmers that were falling behind on their vet bills, could only give her ten thousand dollars, which she distributed herself to various complainants, not realizing at first that it wasn't nearly enough to cover all the bills. Then, when a glowering, sputtering tractor dealer arrived unannounced one day and loaded up the tractor he'd sold Brian a year before, she knew they were in for it.

Once again she confronted Brian. After a slow start as a wife, not sure she'd married the right man, she had eventually warmed to him because of his unfailing dedication to her and their three boys. He certainly was a family man. But on this day, when he finally admitted how bad off he really was, she was shattered, her respect for him vaporizing overnight when she accidentally learned he had done some crooked things to get the money. She lit into him, and many deep wounds were inflicted as the argument became more and more bitter, till finally she stalked off, going into a chilly pout and barely speaking to him- other than a terse yes or no- for days without end.

That only made it worse for Brian, now at his wit's end. Sometimes he wished he could hide. Bad enough to fail, but to fall so quickly from the pinnacle of his fame within less than a year's time- while he was still being handed accolades and kudos- would be far worse than having failed inconspicuously. A mood of doom and gloom, depression, was not long in coming- deepening as he imagined he was already a laughing stock, the subject of sneering remarks like, "This was the man that thought he was such a hot shot."

Still, there was no let-up in the hiatus of fallen milk prices. Like many other dairymen, he wasn't making a thing. Those not seriously in debt, like he was, were only holding even- in effect, "living off their depreciation."

Farm equipment always costs something. First you have to pay off the installments to own it. Call that "stage 1." There is no escaping that if you want to keep your equipment. After that, you have only the upkeep, which can be expected to be, initially at least, not bad. When times are really tough, many farmers with equipment in this second stage simply stop spending money on less than immediately necessary repairs and, instead, live off the money they might ordinarily have spent on forestalled, minor repairs. That's called "living off your depreciation." Unfortunately, since most of Brian's equipment was still in stage 1, he was stuck. And most of his older materiel that might have been stage 2, was, instead, clearly stage 3- that is, not worth fixing. Practically junk. For him, there was no such thing as living off your depreciation.

To those more complacent and fortunate dairymen who, for the most part, had been exceedingly well established for years and years, the drop in prices was cheerfully viewed as another "rustic cleansing" of the farmlands- something that would eventually profit them. Having been through it before, they took it all rather blandly, simply waiting it out. They could afford to. Meanwhile, the tired old fellows and the younger, more venturesome dairymen were being caught flat-footed: suffering foreclosures or simply closing down operations- droves of them quietly selling off their farms at a loss, directly- or indirectly through realtors- to "downstate" shekelmaniacs of various citizenship, the bulk of them fat cat speculators with development in mind. It was, once again, the blessed American way.

Meanwhile, regardless of station in life, the rank and file of consumers and workers- at least those who regard every Hickville as a peculiarity, a sort of gawking zoo far removed from present-day reality- blithely continued their usual squandering in pursuit of the Good Life, mentally fondling their annual raises, portfolios, perquisites and vacation days, attending the musicals, the theaters, movies, and some such amusements. Some were happily caught up in vice- it need not be all that expensive, you know.

Farmers know very well that they are also caught up, not in vice, but in a different kind of vise, and it *is* expensive- the two jaws of a financial vise- the lower jaw being the *rising* costs of their business requirements, so-called inputs such as tractors and harvestors, costs steadily inflated by the non-stop escalating wages of unionized industrial workers- and through them trickling down to non-union workers. The upper jaw of the same vise- is the producer's *falling* share in the retail prices of their own commodities, driven by larger and larger conglomerates of competing food giants whose every thrust has been to undercut their competitors' prices so as to hog more business. Naturally, they don't plan to take any licking in their own profits. Someone else has to wear the squashed hat. And who would that be? It's a wonder of sorts that the primary producers- farmers- are still hanging in there.

It is axiomatic that as long as there is enough of something, it will taken for granted. Yet, when compared to the general economy, the fact that wholesale prices for all sorts of food commodities- not just milk- have rarely been commensurate with the investment and labor and skill involved in their production certainly doesn't require much of a scientist. While consumers in residential areas (hopefully) know you can't *eat* a coin or a hundred dollar bill, there are a few farmers around that would like to trade something they produce- that you *can* eat- for just a little better share of that jingle. And in the long run, a little more jingle might be a good investment for those fat-cat first-world consumers who would like to be assured of *never* becoming third world themselves and always having something for their kids to eat.

Once again, Brian and producers like him were, he knew, at least in part, the hapless victims of the Darwinistic "Good Old American Way," the ruthless self-interest that supposedly "benefits all," which, in its way, is not completely unlike the various, equally odious Marxist dictums that decide certain, more deserving classes of people are benefited at the expense of others of no account.

Yet, Brian thought the ordinary consumer was not to blame so much as unaware. With so many mouths dependent on so few, it had largely been the producers' own fault, not having faced the simple fact that it's a day of collectivism- like it or not. The power had been sitting right there, were they to recognize it and use it collectively as has been used- perhaps unwittingly- against *them.* So few providing such essentials for so many? Wow…! what a *potential*, thought Brian. But, either in their independent pride and stubborn arrogance or a holy zeal of some sort, he knew farmers have consistently shied away from the massive power that real collective action could provide to equalize matters and to ensure whole nations that a day of famine would never occur- short of natural disaster.

The Casino

Brian had hoped to keep Penny in the dark about the pickle he was in ever since the bank- after promising much- had later refused to lend him the money to buy the neighboring land after the price of milk fell. Currently most farmers were *paying* fifty cents more to produce a hundred pounds of milk than they were being paid for it. Admittedly translating to only about a penny a quart of milk each farmer was, in effect, paying the consumer to use his milk, it nevertheless meant that he was losing money every single day. In a year, an average farm would be losing around $75 per cow, at that rate- instead of making perhaps $400. For once, however, there were few farmers that figured the answer was to produce more- as it had been at other times of distress when there were actually a few pennies margin over the cost of production.

Penny had stumbled across a dun letter Brian had carelessly left where she could find it- from a loan shark outfit, no less! Not only had she no knowledge of his devious shenanigans, but when she decided to prowl around a bit, she found even more letters of the type carefully hidden in his desk. All in all, there were five such outfits demanding their money. She was staggered by the size of the debt. And that same day, before she even had a chance to clear up the matter with her husband, she received a phone call- followed in short order by a knock on the door- from two creditors demanding immediate settlement. She had never even heard of the outfits, yet they claimed she and her husband had both signed the notes. She told them, of course, that she'd done no such thing. When Brian appeared in the kitchen for supper, he already knew- from the cold glance his wife gave him- that he was in big trouble.

She took the letters off the top of the refrigerator and, nostrils flaring, eyes blazing, tossed them contemptuously on the kitchen table beside his plate. "Well, Mr. Miller, pray tell me what this is all about!"

Mentally kicking himself for leaving such incriminating evidence where Penny could find it, he mumbled, "Uh…, I'll have those taken care of in a few days. Don't worry about them. It'll be all right." His voice betrayed his nervousness, as he pushed even deeper into his lie,

"I'd mislaid those- found them yesterday. I'll take care of them this week."

Her voice sarcastic, Penny retorted, "Oh yes? You just found them? Maybe that's because you hid most of them so I wouldn't find them."

"Well, I didn't want you to worry about them. It's bad enough for me, you know, without getting you all upset, too."

"Well, one thing about it *does* upset me just a little," she continued. "I don't remember signing any loans with you. You didn't want me to know, did you? So you forged my name!"

Brian was not one to stay on the defense very long. "Well now, just tell me what else I could do? I asked you about talking to your folks for help. Nope, couldn't do that! So I asked you if you could sign a couple of notes with me. Nope! You couldn't do that, either. What in the blinking blue blazes could I do? I just figured you didn't give a hang about me when I was having trouble, so why should I worry about you! And you know perfectly well, the only reason I got in trouble was because the old man wanted to sell his place right off- or not at all- and then the bank let me down."

"Is that so! I told you at the time I didn't want you to buy that place. We were getting along just fine. But you..., you! You had to be Mr. Big, didn't you? Just like everybody in town says!"

"Now wait a minute, here, woman!" roared Brian. "Just whose idea is it to send our boys off to college?"

"We both agreed to that!" she snapped back.

"Sure. But they can do it on their own, like I did. That is, if they really give a flying gong. Where can I get the money to pay their way through, Miss know-it-all?"

"I don't know. That's your problem. Everybody else manages somehow. Look at my uncle, Eric. He's got lots of money!"

"Sure, sure. Eric has lots of money. And he didn't have to start up like I did, either. The farm was handed to him. Who handed this one to me?"

"That's a lot of hooey. He worked on that farm all those years before he went to school. Besides that, Gramps had no problems, either. He had the money to send Eric to school."

Brian was totally exasperated. "Sure, sure. Your family. Always better than mine. I didn't even have one. Who paid my way through school?"

"You were smart enough to get some scholarships. Our boys aren't smart like that. Besides, college costs a lot more now than it did when you went to school."

"You're forgetting that I made most of my money then working my way through college. Why can't our boys do that? I had four part-time jobs- all at the same time. Those scholarships weren't very big."

"We argued about that before, Brian. You just don't get it, do you? They aren't smart enough to work and get the grades they need, and you know it!"

"Well, then," muttered Brian, "Maybe they hadn't ought to go to school at all! Why do they have to go? What's wrong with sticking with the farm, like I'm trying to do? I'm just trying to make the farm big enough for them to stay on, if they want to..., that's all."

Penny was pretty hot under the collar. "Maybe they don't want to stay on the farm! Did you ever even ask them? Why should you tell them what to do with their lives?"

"There you go again. Mama and her babies," snarled Brian. "I get so disgusted with you. You're always standing up for them against me! Would you kindly explain to me what's wrong with me trying to provide a good place for them on our farm..., where they can be proud to say they...."

"Oh! Here we go again! Pride, pride. You're so stuck on yourself ever since you got to be a big shot..., in the papers, and...."

Flushed with anger, Brian turned on his heels and stalked off for the door, unbending, his voice low and hard as he growled, "All right, dammit! I've had enough! Nothing I ever do is good enough for you..., I can see that!" He slammed the door behind him, yelling over his shoulder as he made for his truck, "If that's the way you want it, so be it!" Then he drove off, headed for nowhere in particular, just to get away before he lost complete control of himself.

An hour later, having cooled off, he found himself at Eric's farm. Perhaps he thought he needed a friend just then. But Eric wasn't there. According to Hank Breslau, the hired hand, he'd probably be gone till late afternoon, having gone some sixty miles north to get a part for his tractor.

"That's a long way to go to get a thirty dollar part," said Brian. "Nobody around here carry it?"

"Guess not," said Hank. "It wasn't the new tractor, it's the old Massey Harris. Nobody around here carries Massey, ever since Middaugh lost his dealership."

"Boy, it sure is getting tough anymore. First we lost one feed mill, and then a couple of machinery dealers. And when Middaugh folded- guess he wasn't doing enough business for Allis-Chalmers- we lost the best outfit around here for getting odd parts."

Breslau nodded as he added, "I know. Eric said it used to be anytime you couldn't find a part for something, you could go to Middaugh's, and he almost always had it or knew just where you could get it."

"That's right," said Brian. "He had the best shop in the area. Been here for years and years. But, let's face it, now that the farms are disappearing, he couldn't sell enough Allis equipment to keep their dealership."

"Uh huh. Know what ya mean, Brian. Same thing happened to us down where I was in the Shenandoah. I guess the only dealership left here will be the big ones like John Deere and International- and they aren't exactly next door. Ya sure can lose a lot of time running around looking for parts, can't you?"

"Boy, I'll say," said Brian. "It's getting harder and harder to keep your head above water. I don't know when it's going to turn around."

"I figger it'll come back after awhile, but if there's money to be lost, it won't be the milk dealers or the guys that work for them, either."

"You said it, Hank. No. They'll get their cut anyway. There'd sure be a strike if they didn't pay their labor. But I better shut up. Somebody'll think I'm all in favor of us farmers forming a union, too. And also the bureaucrats- yes, I nearly forgot them. The guys that tell us how much our milk will bring us..., a month after it leaves the farm. They'll get their cut, too, you can be sure."

"The way I sees it, Brian," said Hank, "it's a little like my friend down in Virginia that had a feed store there. One of his farm customers filed bankruptcy. So he files for the feed bill the guy owed him for a long time. About fifteen thousand, it was- as I remember. So, when it was all settled up, who got first divs?"

"I don't know. Who?" said Brian.

"The lawyers that handled the case. The *last* ones involved. Now ain't that a piece of work?"

"How much did he get, when they got done?" asked Brian.

"Oh, I dunno. About four or five thousand, I think."

"Well, the grunts always are the last, you know. It's like the good old American Way. It's our holy of holies as long as it's some insignificant grunt down below you that gets the shaft. Like some poor dumb farmer."

"By god," said Hank, grinning, "you all sound like one of them there commies, to me."

"Believe me, I'm not," said Brian. But I sure don't think the cutthroat competition is going to work, in the long run. I used to think that was good. But lately, I'm beginning to see the other side of it. I'm afraid that someday, not too far off, unless something comes along to stop it, everything will be in the hands of a few big moguls."

More Trouble

If Brian thought he was in trouble with his wife, that February, he really hadn't seen anything yet. Penny was doing the dishes in the kitchen one day while he was sitting at the table working on his income tax. Hearing a vehicle slowing down out front, he looked up and saw the mail carrier stuffing his mailbox. No surprise there- it was ten o'clock. So he put on his denim coat and barn boots and, trudging outside through the well-packed snow, brought back the mail, breathing a sigh of relief at the sight of an envelope from his co-op that would contain the check for the previous month's milk. He was anticipating it would be the big one for the year. Already counting his chickens before they hatched, he wondered what price he would get this time. He had heard the butterfat price might come back up. It would help too if his cows were doing 3.6% butterfat instead the lousy 3.2% he was getting a few months back- due to churning, he figured, of the sample taken by the hauler in the heat of a summer day and not being refrigerated. If so, that would be a help. He needed every penny he could get.

The trouble, however, was that the amount written out on the check was but a pittance, a fraction of what he'd expected. Surely there was some mistake. But then, he perceived a brief notation, addressed to all the members committed to the cooperative. There had been some losses in the co-op's finances that the membership, which was legally liable, would have to cover- since the co-op was poorly capitalized and carrying no insurance. Therefore, a "small" sum had been deducted from each patron's milk check amounting, in his case, to a small loss: sixty percent of his expected receipt. There was an additional statement- that unforeseen circumstances involving their management's recent purchase of a cheese plant- stressing the words "which had been approved by the board of directors," composed of representative farmers- had been the cause of the problem, and that not until the next month would they know whether even more cash would be needed from the membership to cover these most unfortunate, unpreventable losses. Brian, back in the house, sat down and read it over and over, feeling a chill run up and down his back. Never had he needed the money more, and now it was gone.

Having finished her work in the kitchen, Penny was busily drying her hands when she saw the darkening frown on her husband's face. He was sitting there at the table, motionless, open-mouthed, his jaw dropped, staring blankly into space as though he had just been informed of a death in the family. Momentarily she forgot to maintain her chilly and childish sulk. Perhaps he was having a heart attack or a stroke. "Are you all right?" she blurted, staring at him. Then, seeing no response, rushing to his side, she touched his face with her hand, expecting some reaction. Still seemingly unconscious, he simply sat there in a daze, like a big bull that had been hit on the head by a blow from a post maul.

Seeing the letter still in his hand, she reached for it. He handed it to her, passively, his eyes still fixed straight ahead into empty space. She read it. She covered her mouth as she read it again, moaning, and then she dropped it on the floor and fled upstairs, throwing herself down on the bed, wailing uncontrollably, tears streaming down her face.

By now, stirred by the moans and sobs from over his head, Brian was beginning to recover, rubbing his brow and shaking his head in abject dismay as a thousand deliberations raced through his fevered brain. Could this be a mistake? Was it a joke? How could this be? He'd never heard of such a thing. Of course, he didn't know much about co-ops, how they functioned, how they reached their decisions and things like that. He just joined and then left that stuff up to his board of directors- most of them farmers he knew personally and respected, certainly not fools- so he could get on with running his farm. He trusted them. Could there have been something crooked going on? An accident, perhaps? How come he was responsible for the recovery costs? Were all the other members, too? Could he quit the co-op and get out of it? If so, when? He tried to remember what they'd told him when he joined. It seemed there had been some sort of escape clause after a certain interval of time.

Eighty percent of his herd was milking that month, including all of his best cows, the herd averaging seventy two pounds per cow per day. Never before had they milked that well. In fact, the DHIA lab reports for the last month had put his herd on top for the whole county. This should have been his biggest milk check for the year- even, so far, for his lifetime- and he'd been breathlessly waiting for it to arrive, hoping to stave off his creditors just a little longer. He might as well have dumped the milk down the milkhouse drain, for all the good it would do him, like many farmers had done during that last milk strike.

And then, as he heard Penny upstairs, still sobbing uncontrollably, his own eyes watered and tears streamed down his face. It had all been for naught- all his dreams, all his studies, plans, and efforts. He was going to lose everything. He was glad his boys were not home. Nevertheless, the school bus wouldn't be long in coming. He reached in his back pocket and pulled out his big blue farmer's handkerchief to wipe his eyes, and then wiped his face again and again- till it looked like a wet rag. Finally, he rose from the table and washed his face with cold water in front of the kitchen sink, dried himself, and then picked up the letter off the dining room floor and read it again, hoping this was just a bad dream. Then he picked up a different letter and read the return address on the envelope. That, too was startling. Addressed to "Brian Miller," it was from the welfare office in the county where he'd been a foster child years before. He tore it open, muttering to himself while wondering what in the world this would be about, finding a brief note from a woman he scarcely remembered- Miss Pratt. Good heavens, he thought, she should have retired long ago- maybe gone on to her reward. How come she's writing me?

Miss Pratt- upon her retirement about a year before- had found an old photograph, still in rather good shape, wedged in a crack of a file drawer while she was cleaning out her office. She assumed it must have slipped out of a file concerning Roger and Lillian Barnes' foster home where Brian had lived till he was thirteen, after being floated from one place to another before the age of six. Having finally located where he currently was and thinking he might like to have it, she was sending it to him in the belief it might be the only picture of the parents he'd never known.

Had he not just received such bad news, Brian would have smiled as he remembered those kindly country folks that had raised him as a foster child. But he could never forget, either, that rainy day when Mr. Barnes had been killed- in a common sort of farm accident- his tractor skidding sideways on a muddy slope, catching the big left wheel on a rock, pitching him off the seat and then rolling over on him. He had been the only real father Brian ever had, and Lillian his only mother. She too had died some long time ago. He shook his head sadly just remembering her funeral, when all the boys she and her husband had raised for the county had assembled from all over the country- some fourteen in all- to honor the lady who had treated each of them as the son she and her husband always wanted but could never have. And he remembered Miss Pratt, the county welfare commissioner, the kindly spinster, who came around every so often to check on the all the county charges, boys and girls, to see if they were doing all right. Not one of them, she said in her letter, had ever disappointed her. Hard-working, respectable. Brian looked at the photo, taken at a lake somewhere in the thirties or late twenties, judging from the clothing they were wearing. Flipping the photo over, he saw that someone had scrawled there, in an awkward penciled script, "Brian Miller's father and mother." That was all.

Almost unconsciously, he replaced the photo in the envelope and slipped it into a pocket of his denim jacket. There were much bigger things afoot. First he had to talk with poor Penny- if she'd let him. Usually her pouts cleared up whenever they had to face a serious problem together, even if she'd gone on like that for quite some period of time. Quiet upstairs, he went up to see if he could be the strong man once again, comforting and charming her, convincing her that he'd save her home or die in the process.

Brian knew he had to eat crow to win her back. This time, he couldn't blame their circumstances on anyone else, as he'd been tempted to do. He'd been too brash, he took too many chances, and he should have listened to the advice given to him over the years by her grandfather Drew, now dead; her dad, Sean; Eric- his best friend and college room-mate- and Penny herself. But he'd resisted their admonitions to be a little more conservative about new ideas. Like the ladino clover issue at the Grange Hall, such ideas were not always that great, and they thought it wise, for the most part, to let someone else try the novelties before joining the crowd.

Over and over he'd heard an entirely different litany from his bookish professors at school, and he'd swallowed it whole, having been told that skillful manipulation of credit would be one key to a modern farmer's business- bigness being the other key- and that there was nothing to be afraid of if you knew what you were doing. "The sky's the limit, boys!" He well remembered the words of the most optimistic- and *respected*- of his dairy science professors, when he'd lectured the class, "You have no idea how much money there can be in the dairy business," showing them chart after chart he'd taken from his studies of millionaire farmers that were popping up now, for the first time in history, in the dairy business. And that was no baloney. There were dairymen who'd made it big. But they said little or nothing about the relative numbers of those trying the same methods who had fallen into oblivion. That could have been because their contacts were not likely to be losers, but rather, publicity-seeking success stories.

Making millions as a dairyman had always been considered impossible, short of a great stroke of luck. The same prof recounted how these new technocrat dairymen spent most of their time on the office phone, maybe wearing a white shirt and tie as an executive manager making deal after deal- for hay, for feed, creating your own co-ops, bargaining with processors (which you could do if you're big enough), hiring workers and providing them the hours and wages that attract good labor. No longer were these bosses part of the dungaree set, merely a foreman among the hired grunts milking and feeding cows or cleaning the barn. The professor's graphs showed, based on careful research, that the profits to be made as a wheeler-dealer were truly astounding. And it was true. You just had to be a sharpie, that's all. Or, maybe, as Brian was finding out, a riverboat gambler. It was certainly no place for a novice. He wondered how many had tried that routine, and failed, and why it no longer sufficed that you could earn a living without going that route, as in the past. Would conscientious, persistent *hard work* no longer suffice- for success in this casino society now emerging?

An hour later, Penny came back downstairs. Brian knew she was all right again when he heard her playing the piano. That was something she never did if she was unhappy. And when the boys baled out of the school bus a little later, they went about their chores as though nothing unusual had developed. But their relationship was on tenterhooks.

There had been a reason that Penny was so upset- a very good reason. She had wanted Brian to join the AFO, actually a farm union for which she was procuring membership, and certainly not the risky co-op he chose. If not the AFO, she wanted him to join one of the older, well-established marketing co-ops- like her uncle Eric had done- which guaranteed its members a market. She would have accepted his not belonging to a co-op at all, though that would have meant no guaranteed market, the farmer being on his own and dealing directly with the processor- usually getting a premium on milk checks instead of a deduction, as co-ops do. For a number of reasons, mostly the shortage of cash while he was expanding his operation, Brian had chosen a co-op that required the least money up front, provided there were no cash failures. Were that to occur, the membership would have to bail out the co-op through deductions from their monthly milk checks. The risk of ruination was built into the contract he'd signed with the latter cooperative since, unlike the others, it was only marginally capitalized. The safest co-ops were so-called "closed" cooperatives, where a group of patrons actually put up the front money for the co-op, like a stock-holder. Thus they were rather well-capitalized, rarely running on a shoe-string.

Imagine the scenario a month later, when, once again, the co-op trashed Brian's milk check, announcing imminent bankruptcy of the co-op. This time, there was virtually nothing left of Brian's expected pay for the month. Penny was taking it even harder this time, close to hysteria, since that meant, between the two successive defaults by their co-op, they'd lost just about all the profit margin the farm could expect for the year- the money they could expect to live on. Even her personal check from the extension office where she worked was now in jeopardy.

At that point, a savior appeared from out of nowhere. Another co-op from a different state moved in to swallow up the membership that had been able to flee the one going bankrupt. They seemed to be on the level. A bunch of mutineers, including Brian, jumped ship and joined that one. Not that it was as easily done as it sounds.

Two months later, that co-op too, went bankrupt. When the news arrived at the Miller household, there was a great disturbance, harsh accusations and reprimands were exchanged, and with such venom and fury that Penny refused to sleep with her husband. Such a row had never been seen before in the family of Auchinachie. The three boys, not having been spared the miserable scene, were badly shaken, fearful that their parents were about to split. And even though some money was redeemed from one of the two bankruptcies somewhat later on, the damage was done. There would be no way for Brian to save the farm. He would be forced to sell out. The next day he went down to the sale barn to talk to old man Cicero and Glib, unaware that Penny was packing her bags.

Penny's Flight

Unable to reach anybody at the sale barn from his barn phone early the next morning, Brian finished up his milking, went back to the house and was glumly eating his breakfast with Penny and the boys. Hardly a word was spoken. Today was the day he would be contacting Glib and that old shyster, Cicero, at the sale barn- the auctioneer and his bankrolling partner- to arrange sale of the herd and farm equipment. Unless sold at the auction, the titles to the two farms would be held by the mortgagees. Then, if nothing was left over for remaining creditors, Brian might be prosecuted and incarcerated for fraud- wherever he had falsified his debt load to acquire more credit. He was in desperate, deep water that might extend above the neck.

The phone rang, with the family still chowing away. Penny, as was her habit, answered the phone. "It's for you," she said, holding the phone till Brian rose form the table and took it from her. It was another lawyer threatening to sue them if he didn't pay off his client that very day. Brian was not in the mood to argue so, after briefly trying to explain the situation- to no avail- he hung up on the guy. Then he took it off the hook.

"No use of talking, that's all there is to it," he mumbled. He was getting accustomed to the harassment, even if Penny wasn't. Of course, she was taking the brunt of it. In the last week, she had received at least twenty calls from their creditors. Having been raised in a vet's home- solvent, if not affluent- the affronts she was daily receiving were almost as bad as her episode in the D.C. jailhouse. Her emotions were spinning up and down like a yo-yo.

Brian finished up his breakfast as the boys raced out the door to catch the school bus. Her expression obviously melancholic, Penny watched them as they ran off, quietly grieving that this tableau was about to end. Angry, she turned to Brian, still seated at the table, prepared to give him another piece of her mind. But the instant she saw that terrible heart-rending pain so indelibly written on his face, she reversed herself. Her suffering was no worse than his. "Please forgive me, honey.... I'm so..., so..., sorry for the way I've been acting." Impulsively, she went over to him and, without another word, placed her hand on him, trying to comfort him as she gently patted his shoulder. Unable to speak for fear of choking, Brian lifted his chin until his weary, blood-shot eyes met hers. Then he rose from the table, drawing her close in his powerful arms as though it might be for the last time. They clung to each other, eyes moistening, for each other's sake struggling against glistening tears- refusing them permission to fall- kissing and embracing with a fervor Penny would long remember.

Brian still had to finish up his chores and when he left the house, headed for the barn, Penny wondered why in the world she'd packed her bags on the night before, prepared to leave him as soon as the boys went off to school that morning. How could she leave Brian, when he was hurting like that? She'd even written out a long note begging his forgiveness, telling him what to do with the boys, convinced that he shouldn't blame himself because she'd known from their wedding day that she wasn't right for him. Last, but by no means least, she'd asked that neither he- nor anyone else- try to find her- that she just wanted to be alone to "find herself," getting away from her job and all her family including Sean and Nancy. Eventually, she'd said- she might return.

But now, with the situation changing, she decided that when she went upstairs to make the beds she would unpack her things and quietly destroy that note. Her family would need her, hard as it might be. She would not be labeled a *coward*, come what may.

Somewhat later, Brian came back in the house and made a phone call to the sale barn, while Penny vacated the room- finding it too painful to listen as the plans for the cattle sale were discussed. Having been carefully built up from the best stock, many of their cows had been show cows for their boys at regional fairs and the annual state fair- having also been outstanding milkers and a source of great pride to the family. Each cow in the herd was an officially identified and pedigreed Holstein descended from carefully chosen lines, among the best in the nation. To dedicated farmers like them, while not exactly akin to pets, losing cows like those would be much like losing a valuable part of the family. Some of their best cows would be memorable for years, each a celebrity of sorts among the better breeders throughout the region wherever her progeny were.

Glib, the auctioneer, was not only pleased, he was absolutely ecstatic- enough so that Brian, very sensitive about the sale, began to wish he'd called someone else to manage the dispersal. Later, during the sale, he would quietly tell his friends that "the greedy s.o.b.," as he called Glib, "was practically drooling at the mouth when he came up and looked at the herd- counting his blankety-blank commission. Doesn't he know how much it hurts a guy when he has to sell out a herd like this one- after it took years to develop?"

Glib was indeed waxing eloquent, even on the telephone. Brian wanted to tell him to cut the bull, but thought better of it. True- that there would probably be scads of farmers from all over the state attending the auction and perhaps many from outside- those being the ones most apt to bid high provided the cows were tested and ready to move at sale time. Brian, having worked with Sean, didn't need to be told that. After discussing it a bit with Glib, he decided to hold the dispersal at his farm rather than the sale barn, since there would also be considerable equipment to sell: no use of trucking all that machinery around. It would be held on a Thursday afternoon three weeks off. Meanwhile, Sean would have to do the interstate tests and other vet work that were necessary and there would be all kinds of advertisements to be placed in the farm papers and newspapers, plus some radio blurbs. That settled, Brian left the house and slouched down to the barn to finish up some more work, almost sick to his stomach. It is a terrible thing to throw away years of planning, expectation and success- virtually overnight.

Deciding to do a wash, Penny reached in the kitchen closet where Brian kept his barn clothes to find any that needed washing. In years past, Brian had never seemed to empty the pockets of things he was putting in the wash basket. Having eventually given up reforming him, she had decided it would work out better if he just left all his work on hooks in the closet, where she could more easily check the pockets for paraphernalia before chucking them in the wash.

She had just thrown a pair of dungarees and two coveralls into the washing machine when she spotted his denim jacket. It smelled of cow. Rancid. Plainly, it needed washing. She rifled its pockets, coming out with the letter that Brian had recently left there and had, in the midst of turmoil, totally forgotten- the one from Miss Pratt, the woman that had recently retired from another county's welfare office.

Neither Brian nor Penny had ever been particularly secretive about who opened whose mail. Innocent, rather than curious, she opened it and read Miss Pratt's letter, then removed the photograph. She studied it carefully, initially unbelieving, becoming more and more wide-eyed as she read the back side till at last she let out a cry of dismay that would have raised the hackles on a timber wolf. Suddenly coming to life, she dropped everything where she found it, including the photo, raced upstairs to her room and, puffing, moaning and baying as though totally mad, carried all of her baggage downstairs to her car. Then she tore off down the road, narrowly missing a thoroughly frightened dog while her husband- still in the barn, oblivious to her frenzied hysteria- was talking on the phone to her father about the best time for the herd checks.

It was not till he went to the house and found his wife missing that he found the disarray of his work clothes, the photo on the floor, and moments later, her letter to him- left conspicuously on the dining room table where he would see it. There was no explanation for her sudden change of mind. She had seemed to be all right that morning. The boys would be coming home before long. What was he to tell them?

He called Nancy. Penny was not there. She called Eric. Not there either. Nor was Penny at her desk in the extension office, where she worked. "Leave of Absence," they said- acquired the day before. She had seemed disturbed, even then- so they said. Nancy and Sean came out to the farm immediately. There were no recriminations, only anxiety. They could only conclude, from what they saw, that under some delusion- obviously being very unstable based on her recent vacillations and mood changes that Brian told them about- she had finally exploded into utter insanity. Perhaps she was a manic-depressive. She needed help, and urgently. But where had she gone?

From Behind the Veil

Sean and Jim arrived to test Brian's herd for the sale three days after Penny had disappeared. Brian, beside himself with all kinds of worry- Penny, their kids, his farm, and his own future- was not much help. Having expected such might be the case, Sean- also upset, wondering what was going on between Brian and Penny- had carefully orchestrated his timing to coincide with Glib and his boys from the sale barn. They were more than willing to help him in any way that they could, such as rounding up heifers and restraining them while they were tested and vaccinated and also to do some of the necessary book-work, such as writing down tag numbers as they were called out, animal by animal. Meanwhile, Glib was going over the registration papers for the cattle, recording data as to milk production and confirmed pregnancy dates. Meanwhile, one of Glib's more experienced men was making a list of the farm equipment, also checking out and estimating what each piece of machinery should bring on the current market. That would be helpful to the auctioneer when he opened the bidding with figures of his own.

Sean's work was done in about two hours, and he took his blood samples and charts with him as he and Jim drove away. The auctioneer's crew still had another hour or two of preparatory work to do for that day. They would come back and fit the cattle the day before the sale, clipping them, washing them and brushing them down so well that even a scrub cow, if there'd been one, would look like a prize. Meanwhile, though he was technically no longer their owner, Brian agreed to help the crew feed and milk the cows until the conclusion of the sale. They all noticed, despite his stress, how calm he seemed to be. More and more so as time went on.

Jim and Sean said little as they drove away, each lost in his own thoughts. Sean of course, knew that the state police were already regarding Penny as a missing person, and would be keeping their eyes open for her, though a full scale search could not be legally justified until a few more days had elapsed. Consequently, the publicity that would have helped locate her was not forthcoming. Some of the police, fearing the worst, were quietly considering a body search.

After all, who knew but what Brian had murdered her, or that she'd gone off and committed suicide.

"Nancy and I just don't understand what happened," said Sean, as he and Jim were cogitating about the whole mess. "Of course, I'm no psychiatrist, but I can't believe what Brian said. First he says they'd had a bad day, quarreling with each other, that she wouldn't sleep with him that night, then the next morning they made up, and she seemed completely under control. Supposedly O.K., again. Then he goes to the barn and, while he's out of sight, she just disappears, leaving a mess of clothes on the floor in the kitchen, and clothes in the washing machine like she was interrupted before she could start washing.

"I know," said Jim. "And I just can't believe Brian would ever hurt anybody."

Sean nodded. "That's what I think, too. Besides that, her car was missing. Who else could have driven off in it but her? And the police haven't seen the car anywhere. But what I can't figure out is what in the world made her just change her mind like that after she and Brian had just made up."

"Maybe they didn't make up," replied Jim.

Sean sighed. "That's true. Who knows? Maybe they didn't make up, and she got to thinking about it and just took off while she was in the middle of her work. Besides that, she took a lot of baggage with her. Almost like she'd packed it ahead of time. She was never known for doing things that quickly."

"Maybe she had it packed for some time. I'll bet they were not on the best of terms, with all the trouble they were in."

"I don't know," said Sean. "It's like there is a missing piece in all of this, that nobody knows."

Jim was about to say something but, pursing his lips judiciously, he thought better of it and kept his mouth shut. He was not about to stir up a hornet's nest. Late one afternoon he had been driving by an old cabin-type motel, built in the thirties and no longer popular though kept up well. It was not long after Penny had started working at the Extension office, where work days were sometimes foreshortened when there was little to do. Two cars were parked side-by side at one of the cabins, with the only other car clear out front where the office was located, belonging to the owner of the place as everyone knew. And as he drove by, the door to the cabin opened, and a man and woman walked out, arm-in arm, stopped and embraced. He knew one of the cars, and he knew the woman that owned the car. It was Penny. Neither of them saw him, however. But there are some things you never divulge to anyone.

Not long after Sean and Jim left his place, the sale barn crew also left, and as it was getting toward late afternoon, Brian started his chores. The first thing on his agenda was to get the silage down, so he turned on the silo unloader and was loading up a cart so he could feed the heifers, figuring to feed the cows a little later when he was ready to milk. Turning his head just slightly, he caught a glimpse of a small figure standing behind him, startling him. At first he didn't recognize the woman. The intervening years had not been kind to her and she was now a dumpy-looking little broad. It was Erna, Penny's best friend until their altercation at the lake years before. Neither one had spoken to the other since.

Brian shut off the unloader so he could hear.

"Haven't seen you in a long time, Erna," he said, "what brings you here?" While she was not entirely unwelcome, he knew she wouldn't be there unless she wanted something.

Whatever the issue, she was never one to beat around the bush. "Is Penny here?"

Brian's face fell. It was an awkward moment. Why should he open up a pandora's box and tell a friend of Penny's- that was no friend- anything about their private business? His hesitation was all it took.

"She isn't here, is she?" she said, in that demanding voice of hers.

What else could he say? He hedged, "No, not right now."

She gritted her teeth. "I *knew* it! I just knew it! How long has she been gone?"

"Couple of days. Why?"

"She left you didn't she? You don't have to answer. I know where she is. And I know where my husband is. They've run off together, that's what they've done. And where do you suppose they are?"

Brian was taken aback. "I..., I.... You're nuts, Erna!"

"You poor dumb cluck. You didn't even know about it, I can tell." Her eyes glaring at nothing in particular, she continued, "I don't know either, but I'm going to find out. And when I catch her, I'm going to scratch her eyeballs out of her head, the little whore!"

With that, she flounced off, and as she sped off down the road in her pick-up truck, leaving Brian scratching his head, he watched her, wondering, and wondering.... It couldn't be true. Or could it?

When Sean and Jim got back from calls that night, Nancy met them at the door. First off, she told Sean that his old buddy from vet school, Buck Braddock, had called and wanted him to return his call when he came in. Urgent. Then she told him about Erna's bopping in on Brian unannounced earlier that day, adding that Brian, when he called her, was quite upset, and didn't know what to think: Seemed to be blowing his cork, almost believing Erna's suspicions the more he thought back over the years.

Sean made the call to Braddock. Buck was abrupt. "Did you know your daughter is down here?"

"Hell no. We're looking for her. Where is she?"

"You aren't gonna like this, Sean, but I'm not gonna mince any words. At the Frellesen trailer park. Got some guy there with her. Don't know who it is, but I know who it isn't."

After a few more words and very little ceremony, since Sean had earlier contacted Buck, asking him to keep his eyes open for Penny in case she headed down his way, they broke off the conversation. Sean hung up. The first words out of his mouth were not the sort you would say in church. Nor in a schoolhouse. Nor in public, unless you were in the service or cooped up in a jail or house of ill repute, where such words become a relished ritual. At any rate, he really let loose.

Settling down, at last, Sean looked at Jim. "I can't believe it! We didn't raise our daughter to be like..., like...." He stopped, seeing a funny look on Jim's face. "What in hell's the matter?" he said, wrinkling his brows.

Figuring the cat was already out of the bag, Jim told Sean and Nancy what he'd seen at the roadside cabin. Then he added that he'd seen her late one afternoon riding with some other guy as they drove past his house. He thought it had been going on discreetly ever since Penny had returned from Washington.

"Do you know who the guy was?" asked Sean.

"Sure," said Jim. "As long as you know all about it now.... It looked like Cashidy."

"Erna's husband!" exclaimed Nancy. "Oh, dear God in Heaven! What's the matter with her head?"

Sibs

It was only a few days before the sale when Brian got a call from Nancy. Penny is here with us. She came up yesterday and stayed overnight. Would you be agreeable to a meeting with her if she and Sean came along? Okay, he said.

"Where? When?" asked Nancy.

"How about right here at the farm?" said Brian. "Around one o'clock. You did say Sean would be coming along, didn't you?" If anyone would be in his corner, it would be Sean. Since the split, Brian had sensed a definite partiality in Nancy toward her daughter that surprised him a little, considering that she had run off with another man, though she'd never intimated that he was to blame. Yet, as he recalled the cold stare she'd given him at their wedding he suspected he'd never quite suited her, even as well as they'd known each other. Maybe that was the trouble. Having lived in their house before he'd married Penny, he'd sensed a certain displeasure in her having to cook for him and wash his clothes while he was working for Sean that summer. Probably she felt like a servant girl instead of mistress of the house.

Sean and Nancy sometimes seemed to be at odds about the split, particularly when Sean, plainly irked with Penny, repeatedly referred to her as "just another damfool shackee." Though he said little about the moral issue, he was certainly outspoken about the disgrace to him and his family, saying he'd expected her to have more brains than to run off with "a lecherous pretty boy" from a "family of good-for-nothings."

Penny had been very close to Gramma Rache who- bewildered by Penny's sudden fall from grace- had stayed with Sean and Nancy for most of a week until the previous day, hoping she could be some help. Having been convinced of Penny's conversion to the faith, based not only on her words but her subsequent actions, Rachel was in a state of shock and grief precisely *because* of the morality issue- unlike her son Sean.

Rachel truly *loved* life, even into her old age, just as her husband Drew had. Perhaps that has been an easier thing for country folk to do, surrounded as they've been by countless, splendid works of nature and much less of what is artificial. While so many people crawl out of bed expecting nothing of a new day but more dreariness, Rachel and Drew had seemed to possess an unfailing sense of thankfulness for the opportunity to live a *full* life, from which sprang that sense of peace that seldom failed them, right from the start of each day. Every *new* life, then, was to them a source of delight whether it was a new-born calf wobbling over to suckle its dam for the first time, or a funny little fellow creature as ugly looking as a baby opossum- peering timorously at them out of a hole in a tree.

Being farm folk, they understood better than most anyone else that death is a necessary component of the cycle that provides the means for new life. But precisely because life was so precious and beautiful to each of them- hating to see it senselessly diminished or destroyed- they lived out their own lives nobly but unpretentiously in the fervid hope of an eternity together in an even better life. And so it was that Rachel's sorrow for Penny led her to retreat to her room, where she closed the door and wept, praying devoutly alone, on her knees, that Penny would be rescued from the self-destruction she foresaw so clearly, as few do.

At her parents' house that morning- while Nancy had been calling Brian- still weary from the late night's drive back home, Penny had been lying abed, probably on purpose. She was by no means looking forward to a meeting with Brian, though she had been persuaded to do so by her family, especially Nancy. But by one o'clock- thanks to Nancy's persistent prodding- she arrived at the farm exactly as expected, escorted, almost dragged there, by both her parents. While the women stayed in the car, Sean looked around for Brian, who was neither in the immediate vicinity, nor was he in the house. Figuring he might be out in the barn, after spotting the auctioneer's truck on the far side of the corn-crib, almost out of sight, Sean suggested that Nancy and Penny continue to stay in the car. Then he walked over and disappeared around the corner of the barn.

"Brian is going to be shocked with what you have to tell him," said Nancy. "I didn't dare tell Sean about all of it quite yet. Just some of it. I'm not too sure Brian will even believe you."

Penny wasn't exactly comfortable about it either. "Are you sure I ought to tell him myself? Maybe I ought to stay out of it and let the lawyer talk to him. There's so much I found out...."

"No, I think you owe it to him to tell him yourself. I think…, eventually at least, he'll understand."

"I always knew there was something wrong with our marriage. I felt, right from the first day, like I was living with some stranger, and it lasted for weeks and weeks, especially when we went to bed. And, the other morning, after I stumbled over the photograph, I was so sick to my stomach when I thought about it that night, that I vomited- over and over. My doctor had to give me some pills to get over it."

"I'm not surprised," said Nancy, "I'd have felt the same way if I discovered I'd married a cousin, say nothing of a *brother*! What a dreadful thing it must have been for you to find that out! I think I'd have died! It's a wonder you didn't, especially after you'd had…."

"Go ahead and say it! *His kid*s! Well, actually, only Garth is really his kid. The first and third one are Chet's, but Brian doesn't have a clue- not yet, anyway. Chet knows, of course. I don't think I'll tell him today…. Not about that, anyway. And I have to tell you, Mother, I don't feel guilty about that anymore, like I used to. I may go to hell for it, but I don't!"

"It's hard for me to say anything," said Nancy. "I was no saint, either, I might as well admit, although your father never knew about it and I never want him to. So I'm certainly not anybody else's judge. Not even my own, probably. I have to leave all that to the Almighty."

Pausing briefly, she continued, "It's too bad some so-called Christians don't leave it to the Lord, instead of judging others the way a lot of them do. Seems to me, they'd better look in their own eye and pull out the sliver. Then when they have found their first flaw, keep on looking for more."

"Maybe you *do* think I ought to tell Brian about the kids?" said Penny.

"I sure wouldn't. That'll be too much for him. I think, after it sinks in that you are his sister, he'll do a big reverse gear on that, don't you? He'll be glad they weren't!" said Nancy. "That is, unless he's like the Pharoahs and patriarchs of Israel. They married their own sisters. Probably isn't as bad as we think it is, nowadays."

"I hope he forgives me…, I really do," said Penny.

"Of course, as far as getting married is concerned," added Nancy, "I think we all go through a let-down, don't you? I felt almost the same as you did after I was married. I think that's pretty normal. For awhile after I married your dad- he was like a stranger, all of that-though I don't think it took quite so long for me to get over it." She hesitated- while reaching in her purse for her comb- and then continued, "I told you I didn't think he was right for you when Brian was trying to go on dates with you. He was a nice guy and everything, but I guess it was just intuition. There were lots of good solid reasons. The rest was intuition, like I said. You were too young, in the first place. Not that he wasn't a good man.... But that's water over the dam. We've got to get this awful thing over with, first."

"I remember, when Garth was born..., with the hare lip," said Penny, "I just knew there must be something wrong with our genes. I've heard Dad say you get defects like that more often when closely related animals mate. I should have done something about it right then and there. But I was afraid the doctor would think I was nuts... even to ask."

Nancy started combing her hair. "Well, honey, you and I both know it. Let's face it. If you hadn't gotten yourself pregnant, you never would have needed to get married when you did. Brian wasn't to blame for that."

"I know. But I let him *think* he was. And I had to marry somebody.... And there was nobody else, either," said Penny. "I thought Chet would leave Erna and marry me, when I told him he'd gotten me pregnant. Now that we're together, he's admitted he should have. And my doctor wouldn't help me out when I went to him. Had to put on that big act like he'd never done an abortion before and that it was illegal, anyway."

"I thought he'd help you out, too. I know he did Nelly's daughter when she needed an abortion, years ago. Nelly told me so, herself. But something must have scared him off after they put Dr. Klein's nurse in jail for doing one. Everybody knew Klein had done lots of abortions, himself, before that. Some folks figured he paid her to take the rap for him. I don't know if it was true or not, though."

"Well," said Penny, "it's going to be hard for me to tell Brian the truth, after pretending I loved him all these years. And it isn't that I don't love him, in another way. I still do. But now I know why it's never been the same as it's been with Chet. I guess I can be thankful it's never been that way, as it turned out! I respected Brian but, until now, I didn't realize why I never really felt like his wife. I never wanted to hurt him, and I figured it was my duty to stay with him- especially after all the sneaking off with Chet that I'd done to him-

and to Erna over the years, even though I don't like her. I still feel so guilty.... It's been terrible..., especially when I got back home after being with Chet. I had so much to hide, and I was afraid he'd figure it out every time we were together.... Just waiting for the bomb to drop. Maybe you know now why I was acting so crazy sometimes. I just hope he won't hate me."

"Well, I think he'll get over it pretty well when he finds out you and he should never have gotten married in the first place. How else could it be? This was bound to happen, sooner or later, when you found out the truth. According to your lawyer..., what's his name..., Clancy..., Judge Clancy. He's good. Surely you can't hate your own *sister*. In fact, how can *you* ever hate *him*, when he's your brother? You're both just caught in a mess you didn't make, and you couldn't help, knowing so little about yourselves- that is, until dear *Frances* showed up..., after bribing somebody to release your adoption papers illegally, so she could find you. And of course, I don't think it helped you when you found out what *she* was like."

"Well, at least finding out what she was like, made me aware of why my own feelings weren't much like Gramma's. I wondered about that for a long time, though I never talked to Gramma about it. I wasn't designed to be like the Virgin Mary, though I tried to be. But I still don't know how I'm going to explain all those things to him," said Penny, "when neither of us were to blame for any of that. We just didn't know we were siblings! By the way, did you tell Dad about *all* of this yet?"

"Yes. I told him last night, after you told me on the phone yesterday. I had him sit down. Even then, for a minute, I thought he was going to have a stroke when he found out. But now he agrees that the marriage never should have happened.... He goes along with it- the annulment, if Clancy can get one at this late date. If not..., then a divorce. Of course, your dad doesn't know how we're *ever* going to tell the boys! After all, we don't want this to get around in the community. Can you imagine how they would be treated if this whole thing got out?"

"Especially if it got out to the press," said Penny, thinking of her travails after the Washington fiasco.

"And we better be sure, after Brian learns about it," said Nancy, "that *he* doesn't say anything about it to the boys, either. If *they* find out- being so young- one of them might let it leak out and they'd be getting a lot of wise cracks and things like that. People have such dirty minds! By the way, is Chet getting a divorce?"

"He's going to work on it when we get back from our honeymoon."

"After? Did you say after?"

"Sure. What are you getting at?"

"Penny, dear..., most people go on a honeymoon *after* they get married. Or hadn't you heard about that?"

"Oh. Well, I'm on leave of absence and he can get away, too. We both need to get away, and I think, after all of us explain things to Brian today, I'll really need to get away until he gets used to all this stuff."

"Okay. Say..., I see Sean coming out of the barn. And Brian is walking up here walking right behind him. But, by the way, before they get here..., what do we want to do with the kids?"

"Well, I don't know. I think they'd be happier staying with Brian until this is all straightened out. Don't you?" said Penny.

"Seems okay to me. Well, get ready, and keep your cool. He's almost here. This is really a screwed up mess isn't it?"

Distress Sale

The farm sale should have been a great success. Brian had many cows that could have sold for three or four times the going price for a purebred. At any other time that might have been, but even though the sale was well-run, the bidding active and the crowd large, only a few of the cows- the very best of them- sold for what they would have been worth only a few months before. With the price of milk having dropped and with no prospect of improvement in sight, a dairy cow just wasn't in great demand. On the other hand, Brian's farm machinery went somewhat better. Good secondhand machinery was in higher demand among the rank and file than new machinery at a time like this. Certainly, with current income-over-cost so low or, depending on the farm, non-existent- only those farmers with a stack of cash would even think of going any deeper into debt.

And who were the guys with the cash? Predominantly distant cattle dealers. Some were Amish, though they were noted for "thrift" when it came to expenditures; some others were from Canada, where the milk prices were buttressed by a governmental system of farm quotas, effectively restricting production; some more who had come to bid on one or two specific cows were successful farmers, but careful buyers; a few were local cattle dealers like Cicero- who was said to have such a pile stuffed in a certain Helvetian bank vault that some greenbacks might even be spilling out of it onto the street; and then there were many local dealers just watching, who would have the cash someday if they could just squeeze out enough from of a few of their debtors at the sale to register a bid.

Sean- seated at a desk in the auctioneer's trailer- could tell the sale was over when he heard the roar of engines outside- trucks, cars, even a Harley motorcycle, all leaving. He had already started to make out interstate health papers and Canadian export papers for those cattle leaving the state. Some of the cattle were going as far west as Ohio, Michigan, Washington and Idaho, others north to Quebec and the Tobacco country near Guelph, but most of them were not going more than a hundred miles away- especially the young stock, their potential production yet to be proven. It was a task that required considerable expertise: a vet could get in a whole peck of trouble from a single defective paper he'd made out. Each state had its own rules and requirements, its own specifications as to what tests were required, how they were to be interpreted, when they were done, and identification standards. Canada, of course, was even more difficult, except that the cattle would have to remain in the home state until the papers were countersigned by a federal vet in the state capital, which gave Sean some breathing room and a shared responsibility.

Most of the truckers, about twenty in total, were waiting rather patiently in a line in front of Sean's desk, holding sales slips identifying the animals they would be carrying. Now and then Sean rose from his desk and went over to the accountant to verify something that seemed questionable. Back at his seat, glancing down the line now and then as he sweated his way through his work, the trailer getting stuffier and stuffier, he noticed a number of familiar faces, and acknowledged them with a wink or a nod. Near the end of the line he saw Big S, whose face was, as always, fixed into a sort of sneer, but returned his wink. After selling out his farm to the gravel baron, he'd become a cattle dealer- still in possession of his house and the barn where he kept the stock.

Knowing these men couldn't wait all night for their papers, with a long ways to go in many cases, added to the pressure. But there was one stranger in the line, pretty well to the back, that began to grumble. Then he grumbled and complained more and more, steadily raising his voice till he had become a first class nuisance. It seemed he shouldn't have to wait in line like everyone else because he "had to be back" in New Jersey at a certain time with his cattle. As he became more and more vociferous, Sean, who pretended not to notice him as he was making out the papers, could see that a number of the other men were getting pretty disgusted. Finally one asked a compatriot in the line, just as loudly as possible, who that blankety-blank pain in the butt was that was complaining all the time.

Finally, with another seven men standing in line behind him, the protester wound up in front of Sean. As he handed his paperwork to Sean, still complaining like a spoiled brat about the ill-treatment he felt he'd received in having to wait, Sean lifted his face and coldly handed him back his papers.

Pain in the Butt, with a puzzled look on his face, said, "What's the matter? Something wrong with the papers?"

"Probably not," said Sean. "But we've all been putting up with your whining while I've been working as fast as I can to help you guys get out of here." His voice now rising, glowering at his gadfly, he went on, "You seemed to think you were more important than anybody else, so now I'll tell you what you can do. Go to the back of the line now, and I'll do you last! And that's that…, bub!"

Accustomed to getting his way by making a ruckus and now about to bawl like a baby- Pain in the Butt's next words were stifled before he could open his mouth, as the office exploded with riotous laughter from the rest of the men, thoroughly delighted with Sean's repartee. With that, the protester slunk off to the back of the line like a whipped dog licking his wounds, so overwhelmed that thereafter, whenever he encountered Sean, he was almost sickly sweet, bowing and scraping as the new King Solomon passed by, graciously smiling but wordless, nodding down to him from on high.

His work practically finished for the day, Sean left the trailer and, just outside, ran into Big S, his old client Strickland. "Gonna rain…, I think," said Strickland. "Just felt a few drops hitting my face."

"Been afraid of that. What did you think of the sale?"

"Damned nice cows. I bought one. But I thought they went pretty cheap. Didn't you?"

"Well, I thought so," said Sean. "But then, I'm biased. A lot of this herd descended from my dad's stock."

"If I didn't already know that, I'd have guessed it. Your dad always bred for the udders and legs. And because of that, they lasted a long time."

"Yeah, I know. Nowadays, it seems nobody goes for longevity anymore. Dad had ten or twelve cows…, I remember when I was just starting up practice- that gave over a hundred thousand pounds lifetime. That was a lot in those days. Nothing, now though."

"Doesn't surprise me in the least, Doc." said Big S. "Say…, did you notice how Brian was taking it? I thought he'd be all frazzled today. I sure would have been. Instead… Seemed as cool as a cucumber."

"Well, I guess I hadn't really noticed- been too busy to notice," came the reply. "But, come to think of it, a number of fellows that know him told me the same thing today. My brother Eric was here, you know. They were old school-mates… Good friends, and all… I was just talking to him a while ago- he said the same thing you just did. Real calm, collected…, and all that."

"Real outgoing. Never saw a fellow so relaxed when he was in so much trouble. He must be a real strong fellow. Of course…, I'm so sorry to hear about him and your daughter breaking up. What's going to happen to the kids?"

"They don't know yet," replied Sean. "The boys are going to stay at Eric's till they decide. In fact, they're there right now. Didn't want to come to the sale. Couldn't stand to see the cows go. I know one of them was hiding, so nobody would see him cry. Some of the cattle were their own 4-H projects, you know- ones they'd raised from calfhood."

"Sure. I can understand. Didn't one of their animals win at the National Dairy Show?"

"You remember that?" said Sean. "I guess that was two…, three years ago. Junior Champion. Yeah, we were all pretty proud of that. Somebody in Ohio bought her today. She isn't quite as good as a show cow as we'd hoped when she was a yearling, but she milked 28,000 as a three year old."

"Well, good to see you again Doc. Tell Brian I hope he makes out. He's a good fellow. Hate to see things like this happen when you get such a promising young farmer."

With that, Sean headed on over to the barn, where he saw Brian talking to B.J., standing near one of the few cows left in the barn, just as a trucker came to halter her and lead her out to his truck. Sean hollered to the trucker, "Where's this one going?"

"Down to Virginia, some place near Winchester," came the reply. "Got to pick up another one tomorrow over west of here, too. Going to the same place."

"Somebody else selling out?" asked Sean.

"Are you kidding? I never been so damned busy. Farms can't keep running on hot air, you know."

"No, they usually need to make at least a buck or two a week," said B.J. with a sardonic grin, "less than that, a farmer sometimes decides to quit."

Sean paused, looking Brian over. "So… Brian…, you look like you're holding up pretty well. How're you taking it?"

"I'm just fine, Pop," said Brian.

"You sure?"

"Couldn't be any better. I'm just glad it's over so I can get on with things."

"So what you figuring you might do, now?"

"I don't worry about a thing. I might even work for the A.F.O. here, if B.J. wins me over."

"Yeah, Sean," said B.J. "...Just talking about it right now. Maybe..."

"Excuse me, fellows, I see somebody needs some help." said Brian.

When he was gone, B.J. said, "...Can't believe how calm he is."

Sean agreed. "I'm relieved. Was worried about him. I want the boy to win."

"Don't worry, he will," said B.J. "You can count on it."

The Twisted Heritage

It was raining hard early in the morning after the sale when Judge Clancy dialed Penelope on the telephone. Chet, sounding half asleep, handed the phone to Penny- sounding equally frazzled. "Yes?" she said. "Who is it?"

"Clancy..., Hubert Clancy. Judge Clancy. This Penelope?"

"Yes. Yes, this is Penny."

"How soon can you get over to my office, Penelope? I have something to talk to you about. I just got a call from down in Washington from the private detective. It's very important that we get together as quick as we can."

"Okay," said Penny, pushing off her paramour's advances, whispering to him to wait a minute. "Okay. But what's it all about?"

"I can't talk about it right now. It's pretty involved. But it's urgent that you come in as soon as possible. Something has come up that is going to change a lot of our plans."

"Well, Okay..., I guess. What time is it?"

"It's six o'clock right now.... Just a little bit after six, according to my clock."

"Oh. When do you want me to come in?"

"As soon as you can. Can you make it by eight this morning?"

Penny gulped, thinking a minute. She would have to get some gas in her car besides taking her usual shower and fixing herself up. "I think so. I'll try. It's urgent, you say?"

"Yes. Some of the things I told you about your case are going to a court hearing this afternoon, and I've got to figure out what to do with these new developments. Things aren't quite like we thought they were."

"Okay, I'll be there. Eight o'clock..., right?"

"Right. I'll be expecting you, Penelope. Don't let me down."

"I won't," said Penny, as she pushed Chet away again, whispering to him. "Not now, Chet. It's the judge."

"What did you say?" said Clancy.

"Oh..., nothing..., nothing, Mr. Clancy."

"Okay. I'll see you then." With that he hung up.

Sometimes it can be awkward trying to hang up a telephone when you're flat on your back in bed. Penny couldn't quite hit the mark, nearly dropping it on the floor at one point. Chet sat up a little as he rolled over, reaching across the bed to help, taking the phone from her hand and hanging it up. He didn't roll back to where he'd been.

"No," said Penny, "not now. I've got to hurry or I'll be late." He murmured something in her ear, and she replied, a little wearily, "Okay, I guess..., But hurry. I've got to get ready. The judge is a stickler for time."

- - - - - - - - - - - - - - - -

"Judge Clancy," said his stenographer, "Mrs. Miller is here to see you."

Clancy looked up at the clock. Penny was three minutes late. "Send her in," he replied, "and bring me her file if you would, please."

The judge swiveled his chair around and faced himself out the window behind his desk, twiddling his thumbs as he slouched back and watched some pigeons strutting around on the roof of the next building, meanwhile mulling over in his mind how he was going to handle this case.

"Mrs. Miller is here, Judge," said the stenographer. "And here is her file."

"Thank you Mrs. Jamesson..., and would you have a seat and take notes, please?" said Clancy, as he spun back around and unslouched himself into an upright position. "Have a seat Mrs. Miller..., have a seat," he said with a toothy grin. "You made it in good time. Sorry for the inconvenience..., I don't like to make people jump around like that, but if I'd needed to cancel this court date, we'd be set back another three or four weeks before we could get another appearance. Now let me ask you a question. Has your husband filed any papers at all?"

"What papers?" asked Penny.

"Divorce, annulment..., whatever. Does he have a lawyer that you know of?"

"I saw him a couple of days ago, and he hadn't. And I don't think he plans to."

"Okay. That may simplify things a little. But you and I have got to clarify a few things this morning."

Clarify what, Mr. Clancy?"

"Well, okay. Let's look at something here…umm…," as he was reaching for her file and slowly opening it, "…Ummm, here it is," he said, as he pulled out a photograph and handed it to her. "Now, where did you get this…, once again."

"That's the picture that my natural mother gave me. It's a picture of herself and my father sitting in a boat with one of her friends."

"When was it taken?"

"I don't know exactly."

"About when, then?"

"I guess a year or two before I was born. At least she didn't look pregnant yet."

"Like you said, she doesn't look it in the picture. Now what was your mother's maiden name?"

"Frances Durst." said Penny.

"And the man in the picture?"

"Well, I was never sure. She was pretty vague about it. She didn't get along very well with him and then when he was killed in a motorcycle accident, she went back to her old name. So I guess I don't know his name…, not for sure, anyway. She lies all the time, you know."

"Okay…," said Clancy, "as you know, I hired a private investigator to find out some things about your father and mother…, so we could go for an annulment. And that man was, indeed Frances'- your mother's- husband- for about three years, and his name was James Fallon. The picture was taken not far from here, when they were at a state park, sitting in the boat."

"James Fallon? Well, okay. Then that's my dad."

"Not so fast, Penelope. He was *not* your dad, though he was your mother's husband."

"I don't understand," said Penny.

"Can't blame you for that, my dear. But while Frances was married to James Fallon, she got pregnant by another man…, a man named Jerry Zeller. And shortly before you were born, Fallon, who was wanted by the police at the time, died in an accident down in Alabama, probably thinking he was your father. Actually you are the daughter of Frances Durst and Jerry Zeller, who were never married. Now bear with me…, I'll answer your questions- and I can tell you have some already- but wait till I tell you the whole story about you and your husband Brian. First I'm dealing with your own parentage."

He looked over some of his papers, before he proceeded. "Now you know what your mother is like, I'm sure, since you were in a lot of trouble in D.C. because of her. She was always like that, from the time she was a girl, as far as we can make out. As for Jerry Zeller, he was a powerful member of the House of Representatives, from Alabama, from a very prominent family, and he was frequently seeing your mother while she was living in Maryland and Washington, and continued the relationship after she married Fallon, who she met in New York. Not long after her marriage, Fallon fled further south trying to escape the law- wanted for fraud and embezzlement and then, later on, it seems- for a confidence racket.

"Eventually it got so hot for Fallon that he and Frances moved to a friend's hide-out in Alabama, where he stayed while she worked as a hostess or madam in a brothel across the river from Fort Benning. She was pregnant at the time, of course. After Fallon died, knowing it was Zeller's child she was carrying, and desperate for money, she tried to extort paternity money from Zeller when he was home in Alabama, right during the Congressional campaign. But when he wouldn't marry her, she ditched you at the Catholic church and ran off so nobody would find out who the mother was. In short, she didn't want you- thought you'd be a burden…, till years later, when she found out where you were. Now, Penelope, do you have any questions so far? I know this must be very upsetting to you…, it gets pretty squalid."

"Just one, Judge." said Penny. "How did the Congressman get out of marrying my mother?"

"Well…, okay. I told you the end of the story. Now I'll start in a little before that. In the first place Zeller was already married. And he had enough pull that he could blackmail anybody who crossed him- he was good at set-ups- or do something even worse. There was a rumor at the time that he had another man murdered who tried to blackmail *him*. You have to understand that he was a Klansman with a lot of power, and he could get away with about anything down there."

"You mean, she was still seeing Zeller while she was down there?"

"Well, not exactly. Not till after you were born, and then only briefly, when she tried to blackmail him, threatening him with a paternity suit after Fallon had his accident. And, of course, Zeller didn't know about the pregnancy until then. Up till then, it appears they hadn't had any contact with each other, though Zeller knew she and Fallon were in the area. It was really a tangled web, you see. Before he died, Fallon had tried to blackmail Zeller over his previous relationship with Frances, quite apart from the pregnancy issue, since he didn't know he wasn't the father. The detective we hired said he even had a name he'd picked out expecting it would be a boy."

"What was that?" queried Penny, curious.

"James, of course," replied the judge. "And that makes me think. Nobody was ever quite sure that Fallon's motorcycle accident wasn't staged. He might have been murdered. If so, guess who was behind it. Anyway, Frances was pregnant while she was down there.... That's where Dr. Auchinachie and Nancy came across you. You were, as you know, born down there, near Fort Benning, where the military base was.

"Now let's get to the photograph issue. This is crucial to your problem. The picture was taken a few years before that, while Frances and Jim Fallon were still living in New York. That was when the boat picture was taken- but Jim had to get out of town in a hurry because the law was after him, so they traveled south, bit by bit. They were in Atlantic City, and then Maryland- near Annapolis- for awhile..., kept moving south so the police couldn't keep up with them, finally ending up down in Alabama. Your mother worked as a classy call girl in Washington for awhile, even while living with Fallon. Later on, when Fallon was hiding out near Fort Benning, Georgia, with the feds hot on his trail, she- her delivery being due soon- was a madam in a cheap brothel in Phenix City across the river..., that catered to the military, so she and Fallon could survive."

"Why was Fallon wanted by the police?" asked Penny.

"A little of everything. Petty theft, car theft, hold-ups, but mainly, he was a confidence man.... like the racket your mother got into later- probably learned from him. Skinning old folks out of their money. That was his specialty." Clancy stopped for a moment, studying Penny's face. She looked as though her head was swimming. She was thinking of how lucky she'd been to escape all that, having been adopted into a good, respectable family. And she was feeling more and more queasy as the story went on, realizing she had been falling into the sort of seamy life that she'd escaped years before, fortunately, as a foundling.

"Now," said the judge, "shall I go on?"

"Okay."

"You're all right, aren't you? You look a little pale to me. You looked so nice and rosy when you arrived."

"I think so. I guess it's even more sordid than I expected. I keep thinking, my God, what have I thrown away! God spared me that stuff, and…, But never mind me, keep going. I've still got to get out of this marriage to my brother. And we've just got to keep it awfully quiet for the sake of my kids."

"Your brother? Now here's where the rub comes, Penelope. I hope you're ready for this."

Penny screwed up her face for a second, puzzled. "What's that?"

"We can't possibly get an annulment. At least on the grounds of incest- I mean *sibling* marriage. Excuse my using that word…, since you couldn't have planned such a thing- it was sheer accident. In fact, I'm surprised, when I think about it, the way things are going today, that we don't have a lot *more* things like that going on- all by accident. I'm not using it in a derogatory sense, you understand."

"What are you getting at?" said Penny.

"Well, let's cut to the chase. You and Brian are no more brother and sister than you and I are. You are a Zeller, and he is really a Fallon, each with a different mother."

Penny sat bolt upright. "But…, but…, I saw that photograph that…."

"Never mind. Let me go on. Yes, we checked that photo- went to Brian and got his copy, and we compared it to the one that your mother gave you, and they were, in fact, identical copies. And James Fallon was the man, and Frances Durst was, of course, in the picture as well. We've confirmed that. But Frances never had a son…, and so…."

"Wait a minute, Judge, that's what she told me, too…. But I think she was lying. The pictures - both his and mine- said that my parents were in the picture, and so were Brian's. How do you explain that?"

"We checked into that picture real well. Brian's father and mother *were* in the picture, but as I just explained, your father was not, though your mother was."

"I can see that. Well, then- we're half-siblings. That's almost as bad."

"No, no, my dear. There was another woman in the picture if you remember. That other lady was Polly *Miller-* as in Brian *Miller…*, don't you see. We found that out the other day, and it's for sure. That woman was *his* mother, not Frances."

"But, Judge, the note on the back of…"

"I know, I know. You thought his father and mother were shown there. And that is true. The man was James Fallon- and while he was not *your* father, *and should've been*, he was *Brian's*, and he had been living with Polly Miller as common law man and wife for several years, until they met Frances. The man who took the picture was Frances' boy friend at the time, who had nothing to do with any of this. The man and wife in the photo, so to speak, were James Fallon and Polly Miller, and he was their son- but since he wasn't responsible for Frances Durst's pregnancy, because the Congressman was, you are not related to Brian Miller in any way. He is not even your half brother.

"It's so confusing, Judge. Could you explain it again? Maybe I'll get it then."

"Okay, let me put the history in another perspective, though this is partly theory, based on various police reports and public records, like the census. I'm telling you, Penelope, this sleuth I hired for you is sharp! An expert!"

"Okay, shoot," said Penny.

"Frances Durst and her nameless boyfriend at the time…, were on a double date with Polly Miller and her boyfriend James Fallon- soon to be her- that is, Polly's- common-law husband- when the picture was taken. They might have been living together at the time, we just don't know. Frances was a good friend of Polly, but later she stole away Polly's man- James Fallon- probably about the time Polly got pregnant by him. When he left her, she ran away and lived with her widowed sister in upstate new York till her baby boy, Brian, was born. The reason we couldn't find out much about her was because both she and her sister were killed in a train wreck shortly after his birth, leaving no relatives that could be found other than Brian, who had survived the train accident. He was, according to the hospital record, scarred on the top of his head. Did you ever notice a scar?"

Penny was shocked. "Why yes, there's a scar…, on top of his head. Not very obvious, though. He didn't know how he got that." She sat there in a daze. "So then, you're saying that Brian was the illegitimate son of James Fallon, whereas, while he was supposedly my father, he actually wasn't, though he was married to my mother at the time."

"Yes. That's it."

"How do you know that, for sure? If you're wrong, I could still be Brian's half- sister, through James Fallon."

"Well, we have a signed statement from a court in Alabama stating that a certain divorce between Jerry Zeller and Kathleen Zeller was on the grounds of adultery of the husband- which he admitted- with a certain Frances Durst and a subsequent child born of that adultery, named Penelope, whereabouts unknown. Frances then traced you down through that same court, by bribing a file clerk to give her the adoption record.

"Why didn't my mother keep the name of her husband- Fallon?"

"After talking to her, we found out he was her pimp. She hated him, and was thinking of leaving him because he was such a scoundrel. After he died on the motorcycle, and she failed to corner Zeller afterwards, she figured she would take every man for all she could get as long as she could. That's why she started up that bordello a few years later in Washington, where you got trapped. In my opinion, she became- and still is- a man-hater."

"Guess I can't exactly blame her for that. So, anyway, those pictures…, those pictures…. I was completely fooled by them! They meant almost nothing, after all, and Brian and I are married, and, and…." The realization hit her like a brick. With that she buried her face in her hands as she sat in the chair, sobbing softly. "I've got to go tell him! I've got to go tell…." She looked up at the judge, tears streaming down her face, blubbering, "I don't know what to do! What am I going to do? I just don't know! I've done him so much wrong…, oh my God…, have mercy on me. May he forgive me. He's such a good man…, he was always so kind to me."

Touched by the scene, Mrs. Jamesson, the stenographer, came over and consoled her as the judge- uncomfortable with anything that could lead to histrionics- left the room. "Do you want to hold off on the divorce proceedings?" asked Mrs. Jamesson, "at least till you think about it? I know the judge thinks that would be best."

"Oh, my God yes. And first I've got to go and see him…. Oh, I don't know how to…. What a mess!" With that, she buried her face in her hands, sobbing miserably. "What a fool! What a fool I am."

A Hymn for Brian

The temperature outside had hovered around forty degrees for three or four days, as unwavering and unrelenting as the drizzling mist descending from the murky, thick overcast hanging above. This was another of those dreary, cold and wet, early spring days common to the east, when even the birds and squirrels take cover from such a miserable seasonal dampness that it penetrates, as though through mere chiffon, layer upon layer of winter clothing- shirts, sweaters and coats- chilling the loins of the hardiest men more than a much colder but drier day might in the dead of winter.

Splashing through endless puddles and rippling rillets as she drove her car as fast as she dared through patches of heavy mist, Penny, having just left Judge Clancy, wondered if she would ever get back to the farm in time. Would Brian even be there? Sensing a strange urgency- nervously checking the time as though he would forever disappear from the earth if she didn't hurry back to him and make amends- she kept looking at her expensive wrist watch, the one she'd received from Brian's hands on their very first Christmas together as man and wife- when he hardly had a nickel to spare.

The gift had been awkwardly wrapped, as Brian was forever wont to do- and she had brazenly shrugged her shoulders and ignored it. As she drove along, revisiting now in her mind's eyes the sadness she'd seen on his face as though it were yesterday, tears once again misted her eyes for shame of having been totally indifferent to such an extravagant gift from his loving heart. But this was only the first of a poignant succession of her slights that were suddenly redounding on her head until- like the centurion sorrowing at the foot of the cross witnessing the murder of innocence- her self-reproach was more than she could bear.

Finally, she was there. And she saw Brian's truck sitting there near the house, right where he usually parked it. What would she say? How would she say it? There was no way she could make light of what she had done- but what did he know? Had he heard she'd run off with another man? What if he had? She realized, as she mulled over what might transpire, he might well reject her. How could she bear such humiliation? She prayed earnestly that she could return and be restored, once again, to his favor- needing forgiveness from both heaven and earth. He certainly had reason to be enraged. So be it. But she couldn't believe he'd be violent, even if he knew the very worst about her. He was too much a gentleman.

She parked her car and splashed on a dead run through the drizzle and puddles to the house, soaking her shoes and socks as she did so. Nobody there, nobody anywhere- upstairs, downstairs, in the attic or down cellar. She called out for him, and there was no reply. She went to the barn, looked in the milkhouse, the stable- now empty- in the feed room, the silo room, and then out back. Brian was nowhere to be seen, and when she called his name, there was no reply. She went up to the haymow, rolled open the big door on the front of the barn a couple of feet and looked inside. Being dark there, she called out Brian's name. Again, there was no reply. She rolled the door shut again and walked back to the house. Where in the world could he be?

She tried the phone, but though a lamp on the telephone stand was lit, the phone line had been disconnected. So she got back in her car and drove to her uncle Eric's farm. Eric was sure she'd find him at the farm, since he'd been there last night when he'd stopped to check out some things with him. He'd said nothing at that time about leaving. If his truck was there, he must be there somewhere. There were no more tractors there, and anyway, with the weather what it was, he just had to be around somewhere. Eric said he'd follow her car with his truck and see if they could find Brian together: Just couldn't be anywhere else unless somebody, maybe from the sale barn, had stopped and picked him up. Or maybe somebody wanting to drive around and look at the land, like a realtor with a prospective buyer.

Back at Brian's farm, they looked around the barn again. Still nobody. They looked in the house. No replies. Eric said he'd drive around the roads out back and see if Brian was there on the fields somewhere, and then he'd be right back. He had scarcely left when Penny started back out to the barn, purely on intuition. It was about a hundred yards from the house.

Suddenly, half-way there, she heard someone calling her. Or did she? It seemed to be Brian's voice, but she couldn't be sure of the words or if she'd really heard anything. She walked on a little closer to the barn, calling out Brian's name. This time there was a clear response. "Penny!" Just that, no more.

She called again. "Brian!"

"Penny!" Now she knew. It seemed to come from the haymow. He must be hurt. Maybe he'd fallen from one of the mows and, badly injured, couldn't reply when she was there before.

"Penny, help me!" Now she wondered again. Had she really heard something, or was she imagining it?

She rushed to the door to the mow, rolled it wide open and looked in. She walked in, looking around at the floor, covered, as it was, with hay chaff and broken bales. She yelled out his name, once again, fairly yelling, "Brian! Where are you, honey?"

There was no reply, but pigeons high over her head, evidently startled, took off, startling her as well, as they flew over her head and out the open window high in the peak of the main loft. She looked up, and her eye caught something there that she hadn't noticed before, off to the front side of the barn, in the darkest part of the mow. She hesitated. Was it…? Was it what she thought it was? She climbed over some bales, moving a little closer.

There, at least twenty feet over her head, about half way across the width of the mow, was an object of some kind, something there… hanging on a long rope from a cross beam, still, unmoving, like a sack of feed or something of that kind. She crawled over a floor beam into the mow and crept up close in the dim light, peering overhead. Then it hit her. It was a man's body, his head tilted grotesquely, with a slender rope around his neck, lifeless and still. She screamed and ran hysterically out of the barn, tripping, falling down, rising and falling again till she was outside, rolling in the mud, screeching uncontrollably, trying to tear her hair out of her head.

A few minutes later Eric returned, having heard clear on the back of the farm the most awful moaning and shrieking he'd ever heard in his life, and then, having hurried from his truck to Penny's side, where she lay fallen in a puddle of muddy water, weeping, sobbing, writhing and pounding the ground hysterically, begging God to forgive her at the top of her lungs, almost mindless of Eric's presence, and finally managed to scream, practically out of breath, wild-eyed, as she beat him with her fists. "He's there! He's there!"

"Who's there, Penny?"

"It's Brian!" she moaned. Then, like a voice of a lost soul howling in the abyss, she cried out, "My God! My God Eric! Brian's hanged himself!" Catching another breath, she screamed at the top of her lungs, a prolonged screech followed by a pathetic drawn-out wail, causing Eric to shudder and back away as she repeated it over and over- Oh, dear God! Forgive…me… Please… Please, forgive me…!"

- - - - - - - - - - - - - - - -

The state police came and cut Brian down. The coroner decided that Brian had ended his life right after the cattle sale, at least eight hours before, maybe twelve. The hearse took his body to the morgue for an exam, and established the fact there had been no foul play. And poor Penny was confined to a mental hospital, having gone mad. The psychiatrist was not at all sure how long she would remain deranged, promising nothing.

- - - - - - - - - - - - - - - -

Penny's three sons were living on the Auchinachie farm, with Eric and his wife, frequently going with them to see their mother at the asylum, though it was a great trauma for them, not only because, unkempt and inactive, she looked almost twice her age, but rarely showed any interest in the world and barely seemed to know them. Gramma Rachel, often accompanied by Pastor Lewis- who had led her to the altar some years before- and sometimes her Christian friend Beth- when she was back in town- went to see her two or three times a month, praying for her before they left. But there was almost no communication anymore. There was little encouragement from the doctors.

And of course, either Sean or Nancy were there to see her almost every day. But it was difficult to understand her gibberish, seemingly living in a far-off dream world, her hands trembling incessantly as she sat there huddled, bent over in her chair, expressionless, humming and absently whispering nonsense to herself that only she could understand, her bloodshot eyes staring into empty space at an invisible Brian- seeming to have a conversation with each other- with words all hers. When asked a question by a visitor, her answer- if there even was one, was apt to be a feeble- "I don't connect," or sometimes she would ignore the questioner and simply start humming the same tune over and over to herself. But when asked to play the piano, her hands steadied, a glow would come across her face and she would rise, go to the piano and sing and play beautifully, as though there was nothing wrong, her whole life evidently wound up in one hymn she played repeatedly: "My sin, O the bliss of this glorious tho't- My sin- not in part but the whole- Is nailed to His cross, and I bear it no more! Praise the Lord, Praise the Lord, O my soul!" It was Gramma Rachel's favorite hymn, its composer having resided in the Susquehanna region a few miles away- "It Is Well With My Soul."

About The Author

Born in central New York early in the depression and, with three siblings, soon orphaned, Gene Thomas Kemp was adopted and joined a family including newspaper reporters, teachers, shopkeepers and doctors. Receiving a degree as Doctor of Veterinary Medicine at Cornell University, he settled into veterinary practice in the Southern Tier of New York State, near the Pennsylvania line. For forty-three years he worked with the farmers of that region, specializing in the reproductive problems of dairy cattle. Serving on school boards as well as the local board of health, Gene was able to observe a broad spectrum of triumphs and failures of policies and people. The impetus for writing sprang from a desire to share these observations with others when retired.

Printed in the United States
872500001B